A
SWEET
STING
OF
SALT

A
SWEET
STING
OF
SALT

a novel

Rose Sutherland

DELL
New York

A Dell Trade Paperback Original

Published in the United States by Dell, an imprint of Random House, a division of Penguin Random House LLC, New York.

DELL and the D colophon are registered trademarks of Penguin Random House LLC.
RANDOM HOUSE BOOK CLUB and colophon are trademarks of Penguin Random House LLC.

Library of Congress Cataloging-in-Publication Data
Names: Sutherland, Rose, author.
Title: A sweet sting of salt: a novel / Rose Sutherland.
Description: New York: Dell Books [2024]
Identifiers: LCCN 2023007143 (print) | LCCN 2023007144 (ebook) |
ISBN 9780593594599 (trade paperback; acid-free paper) |
ISBN 9780593594605 (ebook)
Subjects: LCGFT: Mythological fiction. | Lesbian fiction. | Novels.
Classification: LCC PR9199.4.S88 S94 2024 (print) |
LCC PR9199.4.S88 (ebook) | DDC 813/.6—dc23/eng/20230421
LC record available at https://lccn.loc.gov/2023007143
LC ebook record available at https://lccn.loc.gov/2023007144

Printed in the United States of America on acid-free paper

randomhousebooks.com
randomhousebookclub.com

2 4 6 8 9 7 5 3 1

Book design by Jo Anne Metsch

To anyone who has ever been lonely.
Keep searching, your people are out there.

A
SWEET
STING
OF
SALT

PROLOGUE

June 1813

The ship was burning.

The men at the shipyard stopped their work to point and shout. People came out from the little wooden buildings along the shore of Barquer's Bay, lining up at the water's edge to stare, chattering with ever-wilder theories as a thin white line of smoke stretched up and up, vanishing into the pale sky. The schooner had only just appeared in the water out past the point; at that size it was a privateer, and therefore American, and therefore of interest, although everyone agreed the war was very nearly over and might have been months ago, for all the more it had touched them in the village.

Four-year-old Jean, unlike the others on the shore, spied something nearer to hand and of much greater interest to her than a speck of a ship and a wavering line. She tugged at her father's sleeve. Normally he was quick to respond, seldom brushing her aside as most adults did a child her age, but caught up in the drama on the water, he waved her off.

Mr. Schnare, the shipbuilder, was speaking with her da in a

hushed voice—*Not one of mine, I'd know it by sight. But I hear they been out chasing that* Young Teazer *a week past, clear down Lunenburg way and back*—so Jean returned her gaze to the pair of harbor seals that'd surfaced not twenty feet from shore and caught her eye.

They were sleek and plump, silver-gray and speckled, and paler underneath when the little one rolled, showing its belly. They bobbed where the river current bumped up against the bay, making an eddy and a deep pool, where a stick thrown in might start floating out to sea but slowly loop back to you again, the water circling back toward the shore. Jean's father had showed her the trick of it, a thing that only worked when the tide was up.

Climbing onto one of the sturdy blue rocks of the breakwater, Jean threw a quick glance back over her shoulder to be certain she was not about to earn herself a tongue-lashing. A British warship had rounded the point, closing in on the schooner. It was drifting now. Her father was still talking to Mr. Schnare, and no one else had any attention to spare for her.

Jean had no attention to spare for anything that was not seal shaped. The little seal was looking—really *looking*—at her with big dark eyes. It was coming closer, drifting, letting the circle current pull it along.

Jean crawled out farther on her rock.

The seal's damp black nose sniffed at the salty air, a spark of light glittering in a drop of water on one of its whiskers. The whisker twitched, and the droplet flew off. Jean giggled. The seal blinked slowly, like a cat, then made a soft huff and pointed its nose toward her, drawing closer still.

It had to be a girl; it was so soft and pretty. Jean leaned forward, stretching a hand out over the water and wiggling her fingers, coaxing, willing it to come right to her. The seal's spotted coat was velvet-rich looking, and Jean had never wanted anything so badly as she wanted to stroke it, even just once. It had the most marvelous eyes, too, fringed with long, curling lashes, dark and gleaming as a mystery, or the water in the deep bottom of a well.

It was so close. Another foot and the seal would be near enough to touch, and Jean leaned out even more, stretching as far as she could, small fingers reaching—

The burning ship exploded, a flash of light and sound.

The larger seal gave a sharp yelp, as if someone had made a cruel throw and hit it with a rock. The little seal started, and dove.

Jean overbalanced, the shivering reflection of her face and rusty hair rushing up at her.

A yell, and a hand closed hard on the back of her dress, yanking her upright with a jerk, taking her breath away. In half an instant, Jean was up in her father's arms, carried as if she were still a little baby. *A great girl your age and still you can't mind! Can I not trust you even one moment while I talk? How many times must I tell you to keep away from the water on your own?* But she was not minding him even now, though her father did not realize it, his voice coming to her as if from a great distance, or in a dream— *Schnare, wait on me; I'll drop Jean up the mill to play with the Keddys' girls, and we'll put out together.*

As he strode away from the shore, men scrambled into their boats to go do whatever there was to be done, to see if any soul was left to save in the deep water off the point. A thing that once was a ship settled there, black and burning against a thin pink evening sky.

Jean stared back over her father's shoulder until they passed over the river bridge and the buildings blocked her view, but no sleek, cunning heads reappeared in the bay.

The seals were gone.

1

November 1832

The ship was burning.

"Sorry . . . ?" Jean looked up from drying her hands on a worn tea towel, frowning at the non sequitur.

"Last night, the ship was burning." Ida Mae Eisenor waved toward the window over the table in her kitchen as she sat herself up on the sofa. "The moon was full. Everyone says the ghost ship burns in the bay on full-moon nights. Did you see it, out where you are?"

"Oh, sure." Jean closed the lid of her basket, solid and real. "Had the captain in for tea, too, don't you know?" She rolled her eyes as she spoke, teasing.

"Jean Langille!" Ida leveled her pinky and pointer fingers at Jean, warning off the evil eye. "You oughtn't say such things! You'll have the devil at your door." With that, she stood, shook her skirts back into place, and went to poke a finger into her dough, testing to see if it had risen enough to go in the oven. When it was done baking, Ida would run a knife 'round the finished loaf and lift it out, rather than turning over the pan and risk turning a ship over with it. That was the superstition, among the German families.

The British had brought the Germans to the South Shore, fresh out of people of their own to settle the colony with, or at least any willing to pay for the dubious privilege of a perilous trip in exchange for hard work and an uncertain reward. England had gone recruiting and come up with a few boatloads of Germans, some French like Jean's father's people, and even a handful of reluctant Swiss.

Farmers all, they were set down on a land so full of trees and rocks that they were forced into working the seas and the forests instead. Only their mingled superstitions took root, and those had twined around one another until it was hard to say where one story left off and the next began, which were fanciful and which were true. If something followed you through the wood to the stream, you didn't know whose boat it had got off of, nor did you care, and you didn't slow your steps to ask if it was something older still, one of the things the Natives talked more around than about.

The *Young Teazer* might not have made port on its final voyage, but it had found firm anchor among all the other tales in the twenty years since its demise, said to round the point tipped in silver flame on clear, full-moon nights, only to vanish as sirens and selkies and mermaids did. It was a pretty and romantic notion, the ghost ship, and harmless—as so many pretty, romantic notions were not.

As the village midwife, Jean had seen where romantic notions got you and considered the newly minted Mrs. Eisenor fairly solid evidence of it. A handsome enough lass of seventeen, Ida Mae Mosher had first found herself caught in the family way— and then found herself married within days of the thing being known. The young man involved, Richie, was a pig farmer's son with a good head of hair and a ready laugh, who'd kissed her breathless after a dance at the hall. The pair of them had certainly had a romantic time, stolen away in a hayloft during a summer thunderstorm, but now it was November, and the three-weeks' bride was starting to be swollen and sore-footed and not entirely happy with her pig farmer's son, who hadn't brought much more to their union than good sausage.

No, Jean wasn't much for romantic notions herself, not like Ida Mae. Not anymore, for all that some might expect it of a young woman, living all to herself out along a wild stretch of the Nova Scotian coast. Certainly no one had made any effort at trying to court Jean, not since she was nineteen. Not unless she considered the fellow who'd cornered her once and said he'd show her "what was what and set her right" as courting her. She'd caught him in the soft parts with her knee, and she was fairly sure Laurie had had some words with him, too, later, when he was in off the ships; well, words by way of knocking several of the man's teeth loose, and him off the end of the wharf.

Laurie Ernst was the younger of her mentor Anneke's two children, and six years Jean's elder. He was properly named Laurence, though no one ever called him that, and as a child Jean idolized him, following him everywhere she could get away with as though he were truly her older brother. He'd always been astonishingly patient about it. These days, he crewed on a schooner that was back and forth a dozen times a year to the Caribbean, returning with cargos of rum and sugar and fruits that tasted of sunshine. At any rate, between her bony kneecap and Laurie's fists, Jean hadn't had similar trouble again.

"Jean?" Ida's voice interrupted her rambling thoughts. "What do you think you should do, if your marriage is . . . dull? Richie . . ." The girl paused, choosing her next words diplomatically. "It ain't quite what I expected, being married. I thought there'd be a bit more romance to it somehow. He's not hardly touched me since the wedding."

Jean shrugged. She couldn't say she knew much about marriages, except that she was unlikely to ever make one herself. The village girls had been leaving her out of their gossip for long enough now that her home visits were about as much a look in on the institution as she got. Jean did know about babies, though, and they all knew she did. They respected her as a midwife, at the very least, even if they did still keep her at arm's length otherwise.

Ida's babe would be a good while yet in making an appearance—not until well into the new year, God willing. The mother-to-be was healthy and strong, if not in the highest of spirits, but Jean had an answer for that. "Ida, the best thing for you would be to get out of this house for a while, even if it is a bit brisk, on these late fall days. Richie could go along with you."

It would do the girl good. To take a bit of air, walk a little every day, see people besides her husband. A body needed friends.

Ida hummed and turned toward the cupboard. "Cup of tea before you go?"

"No, thanks." Jean knew better than to try to become one of those friends herself. It might have been a genuine overture, but she couldn't bring herself to accept it. She'd learned it was better to keep her distance. She swallowed. "I ought to get back home before the light goes. You're doing fine, Ida. I'll be in town to check on you again around the holidays when Evie Hiltz is due, but you can always send Richie out for me before, if you need anything."

"Too bad. I'm dead curious 'bout that new Mrs. Silber, and I thought maybe you'd have . . ."

Jean let the rest of Ida's chatter drift by without absorbing another word, bundling herself into her yellow woolen shawl.

She supposed it was a blessing the latest gossip wasn't about her, but that didn't make pursuing it as a pastime any more attractive.

As she went out, Jean spotted the young Mr. Eisenor at work in the pigpen and paused, considering. A dull marriage. *Maybe Ida isn't the only one who needs advice,* Jean thought wryly, then snorted and went to lean on the top rail of the pigpen.

"Richie?"

He paused in his work, shovel half lifted, dripping muck. "Yes, miss? Everything all right with Ida?"

He was so young, his answer the same one he'd have given the teacher at the village school a scant few years before. There were only about six years between the two of them, but it might as well have been sixty. Richie, newly married at eighteen and soon enough a father for the first time. Jean, already settled. A spinster midwife at just four and twenty.

"Ida's well; there's nothing for you to fret over. I told her she ought to get out a bit, though, fresh air's good for more than just sheets. She did say her feet are sore by the time the day's done . . ." Jean let the line trail, to see if he might take it up on his own.

He did not. "Oh, aye. She's on them all day, sure enough."

Jean's fingers itched to pinch the bridge of her nose, but she kept her tone kind.

"Perhaps you might give them a rub for her, of an evening? Ida'd appreciate it, I'm sure, and I think it would help." Even if it didn't, the gesture might go some little way toward improving domestic relations.

Richie Eisenor seemed to be thinking along similar lines, and maybe some besides, for he went pink and hemmed, mumbling something vaguely like an agreement down into his collar before declaring he'd best get back to it. He stabbed his shovel back into the muck of the pigpen, and Jean went out at the gate.

As she set off along the shore road toward home, she rather wished she might find someone waiting to rub her own feet when she arrived there. She also wished—not for the first time—that instead of every family in town gifting her live chickens or smoked hams after a birthing, they might pool resources and buy her a sturdy pony.

She might wish it, but it wouldn't do to ask. It was only an hour's walk along the shore road anyhow. Jean straightened her back and lifted her chin as she passed over the bridge and went by the last of the brightly painted houses of the town, and tried not to imagine anyone's eyes following her, or their whispers. For much of the last four years she'd had nothing but slander from one half of the town and cool indifference from the other. She'd worked long and hard to gain the respect she had now, and she'd not have anyone looking down on her again after all that effort, saying she was asking special favors, or that she wasn't capable of managing just fine on her own.

The wind started blowing into her teeth as dark clouds began to pile up in the sky, biting at her cheeks and whistling down her ears. Coming around the cove, Jean spotted a sleek, dark head in the choppy water and stopped, shielding her eyes from the wind with her hand.

She'd never lost her love of seals after the first time she remembered seeing one up close, the day the *Teazer* had blown up out in the bay. They had a hint of mystery about them, the curious way they watched you as you watched them before disappearing back under the waves. This one vanished beneath the whitecaps almost as soon as it had appeared.

It was edging on toward evening and Jean struck out on her way again, faster than before. She didn't fancy finishing her walk home in the dark, with the woods looming on one side of her and the open sea on the other.

The road curled back on itself in a stand of windswept pines as she came over the last rise, then dropped down toward a stretch of pebble beach, a wide view of water and sky. Far out in the bay, Jean could make out the lonely tower of the harbor light atop the red cliff on the Scotsman's island. Soon, old Mr. Buchanan would light the oil in the lamp there and set his great curved mirror to spinning, a steady, flashing star to guide lost souls home.

Just before the weathered bridge over the marsh stream, Jean turned up the dirt path to her little wooden house.

Her father, William, had built the cottage tucked up against the edge of the forest as if to hide it from the salt, wind, and sun that had long since bleached its shingles a soft silvery gray. The house had no call to hide from sunset tonight, for it had been swallowed by the gathering clouds, but the wind was picking up as Jean came to her door, tugging at her shawl, her skirts, and stray wisps of her hair. She wanted nothing so much as to go inside and get the fire and the lamp lit before the last of the light went and the threatened rain began to fall. This time of year, if the wind turned the wrong way, it might even sleet before morning.

Jean sighed, heaviness in every bit of her body, and set her basket down on the slate step, turning away toward the goat pen.

She had chores yet to do.

"We ought to be careful."

Jean sat in the stern of her father's little wooden dory, exactly where she always used to when she and her father went out in the boat, and she absently hoped he wouldn't be too angry that they had taken it without asking his permission. They'd already lost both the oars; it was good they had stayed in the marsh pond and not gone farther.

Jo Keddy looked up from the prow and grinned, rosy pink with laughter and exertion under the shade of her bonnet. Her hair hung in long gold waves down her back, spilling over her shoulders as she tried to paddle with her hands over the side.

The pond was smooth as glass, a shining mirror. Jean wondered if they ought to worry about getting back to the shore. There was something important she was meant to be doing, but she couldn't remember what it was. She put her hands in the water, too. The two of them, together, would be able to steer the little boat straight.

Jo looked over at Jean and pushed down on the side of the boat to make it rock, laughing. Jean laughed, too, and did the same on her side. Anything to make Jo smile at her like that.

The boat rocked. They went in a circle.

They were making great waves in the still pond, the boat pitching with a force that made Jean's stomach drop. She stopped laughing.

"Jo," she said. "Be careful."

Jo looked at Jean from under the wide brim of her bonnet, her eyes as blue as the forget-me-nots by the stream. "Shh." She pushed her side of the boat down once more, making it dip low.

Jean's side tipped up even higher than before and fell back again, unchecked.

Before Jean could do anything, Jo toppled into the water with a shriek and disappeared without even a ripple.

"Jo!" Jean cried. "Jo—!"

The echo of her own cry followed Jean back up out of dreaming, and for a moment she lay there panting, her heart hammering. She was sure it had been real, someone calling out from the yard, in fear or pain.

It was ridiculous. No one would be out, not at such an hour, nor in such torrential weather. Maybe in the direst emergency, like the night Jean's father had gone out looking for her mother, with Jean only a month old and left alone in a basket by the hearth. Anneke, who had been the midwife then, had told Jean about it when she was old enough to hear, and bold enough to ask someone besides her father about what happened to her mother. But this night, Jean was safe in her own bed, no one had gone missing, and neither of the women she was tending now were anywhere near their time. If they were, she'd be staying in the village with Anneke, and one of the town lads would've come out to mind the animals for her.

She sat up and tried to still her racing heart.

Jean was glad she could sleep beside the warm embers. If it hadn't just been her, the house would have been too small—a single room with a loft, a solid table and a few cupboards, a pair of comfortable old armchairs by the fire, brought new from town when her parents had first married, and the bed tucked into one corner. It was where her father used to sleep—Jean had slept up in the loft as a child, adrift in the big bedstead that had been meant for her parents. After Jean's mother passed, William hadn't wanted to sleep in the big bed without her, and he switched to the bed downstairs that had been meant for his daughter. The upstairs bedstead had stayed empty until Jean was big enough to leave her own little cot.

When her father passed, just over a year before, Jean had moved downstairs, too. It was warmer by the fire in the winter, and curling into her father's old bed made her feel safer somehow, less alone. Perhaps it was the smallness of it. It was comfort, in a way. A small bed, a small house, a small world—but one that was entirely her own, where Jean was safe and free to live her own life, just as she pleased.

There'd been arguments, after her father had died. Anneke had wanted her to move to town, said it wasn't safe for her to be on her own so far out, and Laurie hadn't been completely sold on the notion of Jean keeping the place alone, either.

Once upon a time, she wouldn't have minded living in town. Once upon a time, she'd liked it there, and she missed how safe and welcoming the town had seemed to her back then. But Jean couldn't imagine ever being truly comfortable there now, no matter how much she did to cement her good reputation again. So she'd dug in her heels. She was fully capable of keeping the place on her own; she didn't need anyone to help her, and she wasn't scared.

Jean perched on the edge of the bed and studied her toes, debating whether she should take off her socks. It had gotten every bit as chilly as she'd feared, the wind howling down from out of the Northeast.

When Jo Keddy had still lived in town and they'd still been friends, Jean had stayed over with her family sometimes. They'd shared Jo's bed and Jean would leave her socks off on purpose, to press her icy toes to Jo's in the dark and hear her squeal and giggle, and then Jo would catch Jean's feet between her own to warm them up. The memory opened up a hollow between Jean's shoulders, where her spine ought to be, as empty and cold as the hours after midnight.

Josephine Keddy was married to Victor Gaudry these four years past and had moved clear across the colony, closer to his people in French Acadia. Jo didn't even speak French. Still, she'd not gone against her family, not fought the marriage, not fought for Jean.

Not that Jean had fought any of it, either, though God knew what she could have done to stop it. That was the biggest shame of it all—that she'd not even tried when Jo had needed her. Jean's throat tightened painfully, and she shoved her feet down under the covers and the memory away, curling on her side in a tight little ball. There was no one outside the house, no one calling for help, and she should stop letting her mind run away with her or next she'd be imagining ghosts drawn by her own loose

tongue, just as Ida Mae had warned her; the drowned captain of
the *Teazer* come ashore from off his flaming ship.

Flame.

She'd left the lantern burning on the table. She cursed. Oil
was expensive, and even turned low she couldn't afford to leave
it to sit and burn the whole night away. Jean sighed and slid her
feet back out from the covers, dropping them onto the plank
floor.

A cry from outside caught her halfway between sitting and
standing. It was unmistakable, sharp, and *real,* not a dream at all.

There *was* someone out there, and something was wrong to
have brought them here now, in the night, in a storm. Jean
grabbed up the lantern, raising the flame she was now thankful
for, and went to open the door, a blast of wind and icy rain stealing her breath away and whipping her hair across her face. She
squinted into the dark, straining her eyes to make out anything
in the darkness beyond the circle of lamplight as she stepped out
into the yard.

Blackness. Slowly she turned, her eyes adjusting, the chill
wind flattening her shift against her body. A darker black behind
the house, the trees. The woodshed's bulk at the corner of the
wall, the chicken coop, the goat shed . . . *there.* A pale spot, blue-
white and rippling at the edge of the marsh, its presence spec-
tral, unearthly.

Jean's scalp prickled, and she froze; the breath turned solid in
her lungs. An icy trickle of water ran down the back of her
neck. She was going to be murdered by ghostly privateers. She
was mad to have come out of the house at all at this hour, by
herself. Laurie was right; the last time he'd visited Anneke he
said that Jean ought to have a rifle, out here all alone. Although,
if it *was* a ghost—

The white thing in the darkness contracted in on itself, and
carried on the back of the wind came a moan. A moan that was

altogether human, full of pain and despair. Jean's heart started beating again, and she pressed forward into the teeth of the wind and rain, suddenly sure—at least in part—of what she would find.

It was a woman, shaking and sodden, clad in nothing but a wet nightgown. No shoes on her bare feet, which were sunk ankle-deep into the thick mud at the edge of the marsh pond. Another step and she'd have been in the water. The woman was hunched over so that Jean could make out nothing more of her, save that she had long dark hair. She was in danger of catching her death out in a storm like this.

"What on earth—?" said Jean, breathless. She caught at the woman's arm to pull her toward the house.

The woman straightened with a yelp, jerking her arm back and nearly toppling over.

"No, come, get inside—" Jean reached out to steady her, and the stranger's eyes widened and sparked, a short breath puffing out of her mouth, still ajar. The woman grabbed at Jean's wrist, tugging her toward the marsh pond, dark eyes pleading in her pale face. She was much taller than Jean, and heavier, too, strong and solid. Jean's heels dug into the soft earth as she resisted, trying to keep her footing in the wet grass. Tugging Jean's wrist again, the woman pointed off into the night, first to the pond and then away over the road toward the sea, as she began to speak in hushed tones, rapid and urgent.

Jean couldn't understand a thing. The woman's words were strange, liquid, rolling things that growled in her throat before being whipped away by the wind that flapped her thin nightdress around her like a bit of loose sail. They cut off abruptly as she doubled over again, moaning and hugging her round, taut belly. Her legs nearly buckled beneath her, but Jean had her now, one arm tight around the woman's waist to keep her on her feet.

Jean drew her away from the marsh, across the yard, and into the house, not allowing for any refusal. She held firm even as the stranger cried bitter tears, pleading brokenly for God only knew what in her strange language. Jean still didn't know what the woman was trying to tell her, but this . . . *this* she knew. She had to act quickly. Understanding could wait; the baby would not.

2

Jean rethought the importance of understanding the moment she guided the stranger across her threshold. When she shut the door, the woman balked, whining in the back of her throat. It was the sound of an animal who had been closed in a cage. She pulled back toward the door, head swiveling to take in the small room, looking for some other escape.

Jean wasn't having it. She needed to get the woman warm and dry and figure out just how deep into things they were. She'd have to examine her right away, learn how far apart her pains were, and how long they'd been coming. Jean kept her voice firm and steady but low, pitched to be reassuring.

"No, you *must* stay here. Your baby is coming now, do you understand? Baby." She let go of the stranger's arm, as she seemed steadier, and mimed rocking an infant in her arms. The pangs that had nearly dropped the woman out in the yard had passed, and Jean urged her toward the bed she'd only just vacated herself, making a mental checklist of the things they were going to need, and soon.

First, before anything else: "You need out of these wet things." Jean caught at the woman's sopping nightdress, giving it a little tug upward, hoping she would get the point. Turning away, Jean didn't waste a moment—she went immediately to the hearth, poking up the embers and adding a new log, swinging the copper kettle into place over the fire.

A strange sort of calm came over Jean at times like these, like being at the eye of one of the great hurricanes that sometimes blew up the coast at the end of summer. She moved quickly, but her feet and hands were steady as a ship at anchor, while her mind whirled through everything yet to be done. Past the hearth, she went fishing into a basket of linens with one hand, opening a drawer with the other at the same time. From the drawer, fresh tallow candles—they would need more light. She set them on the table without looking, sure of her aim, then dug both hands into the basket.

An armful of clean rags joined the candles, and Jean emerged with one of her own spare shifts. "I'm afraid I'm a bit smaller than you are, but these things will fit nearly anyone, and you won't care if it's short, I don't think . . . ?"

She looked up. The woman was still standing by the bed, staring at Jean with big round eyes, her black hair dripping water onto the floor. Her mouth opened once, then closed again. Her eyes darted toward the door.

"No." Jean shook her head, putting herself between the woman and the exit, just in case she foolishly tried to flee. "You aren't going back out there. Now, here—" No-nonsense, Jean set the clean shift down on the bed, and in one motion made to haul the woman's sodden one up and over her head. At the last second, she understood what Jean was trying to do and pulled away, wrestling the garment back down with a sharp yelp.

Jean breathed in through her nose. Reaching down, she grabbed the dry shift, and shoved it toward the woman. "This."

She pointed at it. "On *you*." She pointed at the woman, who winced at the jabbing motion. Jean gave it a second. The woman just stared at her, breathing quick and shallow. "Now!" Jean thrust the garment into her hands and went back to her own preparations. *Take the hint,* she thought. *Please.*

This was not going to be an easy night.

Fortunately, all of her kit was neatly together in the basket next to the chair where she'd been working earlier. Jean moved that to the table as well, then put the candles into holders. She'd light them later when it became needful. As she began laying out her scissors and spoons, a quiet huffing breath came from behind her, followed by the awkward slurp of wet fabric being peeled away from skin.

Maybe the poor woman was only shy. After all, they were perfect strangers, and here Jean was, trying to strip her naked within five minutes of laying eyes on her . . . although Jean would become acquainted with a great deal more of the woman, and rather more intimately, before their task was done. Jean could only hope she wasn't balking because of any rumors she'd heard, as some of the town girls had done.

Jean went back to laying her tools out on the table: needles, thread, gauze. Her father's old silver pocket watch, that he'd insisted she keep—she'd start counting the next time a pain took the woman, hopefully not for a while yet, with any luck. Maybe she'd even won enough time to put on something a bit less damp herself.

When she glanced back up again the woman was clad, although Jean's shift was comically short on her and barely covered her thighs, her muscular legs impossibly long. On Jean, the same garment came down past the knee—the stranger was no small thing. Jean took a moment to really look at her and breathed a sigh of relief. She was strong and healthy looking, and generously proportioned, with good, solid hips. Nothing like

Jean's own scrawny ones, and barring any unforeseen problems, they boded well for the birth. A handsome woman, really, quite striking if you ignored her current resemblance to a half-drowned rat.

She had long lashes and black eyes in a grave oval face, and as color crept back into her cheeks, it revealed a warm complexion ill-fitting the ghost Jean had taken her for outside. An irregular spray of freckles flecked across the bridge of her nose, which had a slight Roman curve to it, and below it she had a soft, pretty mouth.

Jean was sure if she'd seen a face like that in the village before, she'd not have forgotten it. But then again, before tonight Jean would have thought that if any neighbor near enough to find her on foot was with child, she'd have known about *that,* too. The woman trembled—she was still shivering. Jean lifted her woolen shawl from where she'd left it folded over the back of a chair and offered it to her guest with a welcoming smile, hoping to put her a bit more at ease.

"You're cold."

The woman looked at her for a moment, holding herself stiff and straight. Slowly, she reached out and took the shawl from Jean's hand, winding it around her own shoulders with a nod of thanks. She ran a careful hand over the soft yellow wool, then went on to rub the tip of her nose with her fingers to warm it, giving a delicate sniff. Keeping her dark, wary eyes on Jean, the woman made no move to sit.

Jean motioned toward the bed: *Lie down.*

The woman shook her head: *I shan't.*

Inhaling through her nose again, Jean rubbed at the space between her eyebrows with a fingertip. Funny, how a person could give you a headache without saying a word. Jean wasn't exactly renowned for her patience; in fact, she was more known for being no little bit demanding, and doubly so when it came to her work. She knew well enough the only reason people put up with her was because she was damn good at what she did. You listened to the midwife, because the last thing you wanted was to ignore her demands and have it end in sending for the doctor. Everyone knew, when it came to mothers and babies, that once you sent for the doctor, one or both were surely doomed.

Jean blew the breath back out and shook the grim thought away. Her unexpected guest seemed calmer now, anyhow, less likely to bolt back out into the—

The woman gave a mewling cry and grabbed at the bedpost, curling over herself, knees bowing. Jean was at her side instantly, one arm around her, a hand supporting her elbow, leaning to try to meet her eyes. "It's all right. You're all right. I have you." Jean's pulse quickened, but her voice stayed calm and steady. "I have you."

The woman shook her head, grimacing, her long damp hair falling forward around her face again. "Ah-ah-ah!" No strange words now, but a clear expression of pain. She groped for something with a long-fingered hand, and Jean let go of the woman's elbow to catch it in her own, letting the woman squeeze her fingers, bearing down a little, her forehead creasing. Jean responded with a comforting *shhhh-hhh,* her other hand low on the woman's back as her muscles tensed and released.

She panted slightly as the pain ebbed and faded away again, and at last Jean managed to ease her down to sit on the bed. As she reached for her father's pocket watch on the table, Jean's mind ticked back through the minutes since the stranger had arrived outside her door. Had it been ten minutes yet? Perhaps. Maybe more? Maybe less. It was hard to say. The woman clutched at Jean's wrist, more than a little wild-eyed, not wanting Jean to leave her side.

Jean sighed, but relented, kneeling to study the woman's face in the flickering lamplight. If it was ten minutes, they still had a good while yet. Even if the stranger didn't speak a word of English, Jean was sure she could manage to get at least one thing across. Touching her own chest lightly with her fingertips, she met the woman's gaze. "Jean. That's me. Understand?" She pointed at herself again, less subtly. "Jean."

The woman blinked, then gave a small, tight nod. "Jean." Her accent softened the name, rounding the vowels, her voice rich and deep.

Jean gave the woman a long moment, and when nothing further was forthcoming, lifted an eyebrow, pointing at her guest with a questioning shrug. Realizing what Jean wanted, she laid a trembling hand on her own chest, pressing down as if to steady it. "Is . . . is I Muirin."

The order of the words was wrong, the grammar gone completely awry, but they were something that passed near enough for English. Jean's spirits lifted at the victory, even if it was only a small one. "Muirin?"

Muirin nodded. "Is I, Muirin." She stopped, made a face, and corrected. Slightly. "Am. *Am* I, Muirin."

Jean felt her lips twitch. Such a sincere effort, though the fragment of a sentence was still an utter mash, more question than statement. Still, she nodded, repeating it once more, with a smile of encouragement. "Muirin." It was a strange name, not one Jean knew, and yet there was something familiar about it, if she could just figure out what— "Wait. Muirin?" A woman she had glimpsed only once—and at a distance—sitting stiff-backed in a wagon, looking off to sea. A pair of wide, dark eyes set in a grave face, under a lace-trimmed bonnet, and a bit of gossip about a new bride and a very sudden marriage. "You're Mr. Silber's wife! Tobias Silber!"

Muirin gave a slow, reluctant nod, placing an unconscious and protective hand over her round belly. "Tobias. Am I, wife . . ." She paused, contemplating her own words. "Yes?"

"Yes," Jean replied, not caring about the broken explanation. Now she knew where the woman had come from, at least. Tobias Silber was a fisherman who'd gone out on a seven-day voyage the spring past, early for the season and in spite of warnings and uncertain weather. He'd come back without a single fish but with a plump pretty girl in his boat, and the pair of them went straight from the wharf to the church to post the banns, or so went the romantic story she'd overheard outside the mercantile. A girl he'd met at some Scottish settlement up the coast the autumn before—her strange growling language must be Gaelic, then. Jean's own mother had supposedly spoken it in her youth, and Jean wished, not for the first time in her life, that she might have gotten to know Janet, while she'd lived.

One of the girls in the mercantile had been the minister's daughter, telling the others how the mysterious new bride was standoffish, a snob—*thinks she's better than us, that one, not a single word when I said how lovely her dress was after the service*. But Muirin wasn't a snob at all, only unable to understand a word that had been said to her. How could they not have seen the difference?

God alone knew how Tobias had won Muirin with that sort of a barrier between them—though as with Richie and Ida Mae, perhaps it hadn't been with words at all.

How was it that Jean hadn't heard the woman was with child? But then, Tobias had his house even farther out along the coast than she did. Hadn't Ida been asking if Jean had ever seen Tobias's wife earlier? She'd never noticed Muirin with her husband in his wagon when he made trips into town over the pitted dirt road that passed by her gate. Perhaps no one knew. Muirin would have been dreadfully isolated out there, and most likely lonely, away from her family and friends, other people who spoke her tongue. Jean was their closest neighbor, and she'd not spared a thought about the stranger she'd only glimpsed the once. And now it had been—well, around nine months she supposed. Jean's skin shrunk, prickling with guilt.

But—why hadn't Tobias come to ask her for advice, once he'd known his wife was pregnant? It didn't make sense. Jean was the midwife, for God's sake.

Unless *Jean* was the problem.

Her heart sank, but she swiftly gave it a firm, logical whack back into place. That couldn't be it, not still. Once she'd turned her first breech baby, and word went 'round that she had a knack for midwifery, *good hands,* people in the village had left off whispering about her, mostly. Another prick of guilt—she'd been glad that day in the mercantile, when Muirin first appeared, that the girls whispering behind the rack of ribbon and thread hadn't been talking about her anymore.

Jean always acted respectably with her mothers, kept a polite distance, and didn't make waves outside of the birthing room. She'd made herself indispensable in the village, and a solid five miles up the coast as well. That was what mattered. Besides, she couldn't imagine a stolid, private man like Silber was privy to much of the town gossip anyhow.

Jean gave her mind a sharp kick back to the matter at hand. Muirin must have come all the way down from her and Tobias's house up on the point, through the woodlot, and across the marsh stream, a good fifteen- or twenty-minute march at the best of times. By herself, in the dark. In the driving rain. In nothing but a nightgown, without her husband, without even shoes on her feet. In *labor.*

Where on earth was Tobias Silber? Why had Muirin—?

Her thoughts were cut short as Muirin grabbed at her wrist with a sharply drawn breath. Jean looked up into her pretty face as it contorted in pain, mouth open, brows drawn together, eyes squeezing shut. Tears leaking. A low, keening whine rose from deep in Muirin's throat.

There was no way it had been another ten minutes, nor even five.

Three, at the absolute outside, since the last contraction—which meant things were progressing faster than Jean might have hoped or had even expected. Alarm stirred within Jean's gut, and she clamped down on it, hard. Even if it was to be a fast birth, she was right here, not a frantic wagon ride away. They still had time. They had everything they needed. She spoke to Muirin softly but with authority. "Don't hold your breath. You should breathe—"

Muirin shot her an uncomprehending glance, eyes feverish bright, her fingers digging into Jean's arm. Jean forced out a heavy, shuddering breath herself.

"Muirin." She caught the woman firmly by her upper arms, her voice taking on an edge of command as she fought to regain Muirin's focus. "Like this—" Jean began taking deep, exaggerated breaths, holding Muirin's gaze. After a moment, Muirin began to do the same. Her face relaxed a little, the panicked light in her eyes fading, and then the pain let her go again.

Jean's heart was beating too quickly. She wasn't going to be able to be diplomatic about this; she needed to know where they stood, right now. What if she needed to turn the baby? Much as she hated to admit it, Jean was terrified of another birth like Evie Hiltz's last, a stubborn lad she almost hadn't been able to shift in time, for all her trying. There had been so much blood. She shuddered, once, and quickly got herself back under control.

Muirin hadn't yet caught her breath before Jean was trying to explain. "Muirin, I need to look at you."

Muirin blinked at her, blank-faced.

It was as bad as that one German girl Jean had helped to deliver two winters back, without a lick of English to speak of. Worse—at least then she'd had the girl's husband there to translate for her.

Jean swallowed and gestured at her eyes. "See. Look." She pointed, without a hint of delicacy, at exactly which parts of Muirin she was talking about. "At you. The baby is coming. The baby."

Muirin stared at her and shook her head in horror. Struggling to rise from the bed, she batted Jean's hands away as she tried to stop her. "No! Not! Go, I—waterrrr—unnh!" Pain circled around to grip Muirin once again, pulling her back down like an undertow, a twig caught in an unstoppable current. What little English she had fled, and she cried out in her own language, her voice rough with fear.

Jean bit back a curse, trying not to let even a single crack show in her composure. If she panicked, they were lost. She had to get control somehow, make Muirin understand. After that, Jean could get her some water, but not now, with everything already happening so fast. Pushing too soon might slow the labor in the wrong way, if Muirin wasn't truly ready, draw it out and exhaust her. Jean had seen it happen before and was keenly aware of how badly it could end. The woman had already exerted herself far too much tonight.

Muirin let out a long, low moan that was half a sob, suddenly rolling over on the bed and pushing herself up onto her hands, her arms ramrod straight and shaking. Arching her back, she pressed her heavy belly down into the mattress, rocking firmly from side to side, her legs straining, thrust out long and stiff behind her. Jean had never seen a woman do a thing like it, not once in the years she'd been attending births. Hands and knees was common, but not this—

"Wait! No!" Jean was certain of what would follow, her own futile words echoing in her ears. "Not yet, stop! Don't! I don't know if you're ready, *Muirin*—!"

Muirin bared her teeth, feral, her eyes glinting like a wild thing's.

It would be now, right now, and there was nothing left for Jean to do except pray.

And catch.

3

Jean barely caught the little lad he came so quick. Muirin rolled over unexpectedly, right at the end, almost striking Jean in the mouth with a foot. The new mother sat up, getting in the way of everything and pushing for a look at her child, mewling some odd wordless concern. The baby was inside of a thick caul, tossed out into the world like a kitten in a sack—Jean had heard of such a thing, but she'd never seen it before. Snatching the child out from under Muirin's nose, she cursed and went scrambling for her knife to cut him free.

Muirin bared her teeth like she might attempt to rip the membrane open with them when Jean grabbed up the child, and she growled as if she would bite the midwife instead before realizing she was only trying to help. As Jean pierced the caul to free the baby, her breath caught in her chest. Muirin retreated to the head of the bed and huddled there, still and silent. The second the cool air hit the babe, he let out a lusty wail. Jean very nearly let out a sob of her own, leaning upon the table for a moment to let her heart resume its normal pace before carefully wiping the baby clean with a soft scrap of linen. She'd never attended a birth like it, and she hoped never to again.

When Jean made to pass the babe to his mother, Muirin turned her face away, refused to meet Jean's eye. It was unthinkable that Muirin might refuse to accept him, and for a brief, awful moment Jean stood stunned, unsure of what to do. The child made a pathetic snuffling sound in her arms, rooting helplessly at the wrong set of breasts. Somehow, his needy whimper changed everything: Muirin twitched, as if back into wakefulness, and pressed her lips together, thrusting out her arms to take her son.

The moment Muirin held him, her entire face softened, her lips parting around a tiny *oh*. She put the babe to her breast as natural as anything, without a single word needed to encourage her along. Jean perched on the very edge of the bed, keeping quiet as Muirin bowed her head low, the tip of her nose brushing the dark, damp cap of the baby's fine hair, breathing in his fresh new scent, her lips curving in a wondering smile. It was like magic, how swiftly peace fell over the room, like a soft, warm blanket onto a bed. All was calm and quiet, except for the small, content gruntings of the baby. A tiny hand waved.

"Oh." Jean reached out to still it, letting the little one catch her finger.

Muirin looked up with a questioning expression. Jean nodded, directing her gaze toward the baby. As Muirin watched, she gently spread out the child's wrinkled wee fingers.

They were webbed. A thin bit of skin stretched between each small digit, clear down to the first knuckle. Carefully, Jean reached for his other hand and found it to be the same. Muirin looked at her again and shifted the babe against her chest, guessing Jean's intent. Stroking a cautious fingertip along the bottom of each tiny pink foot, Jean watched as the little toes spread, then curled. Webbed. Not as obviously as the hands; and, in shoes, who would ever know? But the hands—

Jean knew what the doctor in the village would say. He'd say to cut them. Worse, that she should do it *now*, that a fresh baby didn't have the nerves to feel such cuts yet. She didn't believe that, not a bit, and the very thought of it made Jean sick. A thin blue tracery of veins ran beneath the child's translucent new skin. It would bleed. Who knew how much? And there was always the chance of any cut going bad—who would take such an unnecessary risk with a healthy baby, and for what? Vanity? No. She wouldn't do it. Looking up into Muirin's face again, Jean smiled.

"He's perfect."

Muirin smiled back, tired and happy and beautiful, then reached out and took hold of Jean's hand, as if inviting her in to share in the new mother's simple joy. As if Muirin knew what the word *perfect* meant.

❧

In the chair before the fire, Jean tried to still her hands. They'd obeyed as long as she needed them to, but once everything was over, the very second she'd managed to extract the clammy hand Muirin had been clutching with such tender gratitude, both had started shaking, and it was only now they were beginning to show any sign of stopping.

Not that anything had gone wrong. It was just that the midwife had been taken by surprise, and that the birth had happened with such dizzying speed, by far the fastest Jean had ever witnessed. She'd have expected Muirin to be torn from stem to stern, but no. Jean had put one stitch in her. One, after all that, and barely any bleeding to speak of. Though she'd had to explain when Muirin had seen her take up the needle and thread—

Stitch. Tie. Knot, to hold together, so it stays. To help, I promise—Muirin had repeated the new words back to her, testing them in her mouth, considering, before she nodded her permission to proceed. How a woman so close to birth could have made it *anywhere*—let alone down through an overgrown woodlot, over a fast stream, and into a salt marsh, at the tail end of *November,* no less—and still been on her feet for Jean to find was a mystery, and only the very tip of the strangeness of it all.

The baby was fast asleep, swaddled in a nest of soft, clean rags in Jean's hastily emptied basket on the floor beside the bed. Muirin breathed as deep and easy as the babe, the rosy glow of firelight flickering over her smooth cheeks as she slept. Nothing in her appearance betrayed the ordeal she had been through, her sleeping face lovely and serene.

Jean pulled her gaze away and considered curling up in her chair to catch a moment's rest for herself, but when she glanced toward the window, it was brightening with the dim gray light of early morning. Spreading her fingers wide, she gave them a hard shake and squeezed them into fists, then released them. They were steady.

No rest for the wicked, then. It was nearing dawn, and there was still Tobias Silber to be found. He needed to know his wife was safe, and that he had a new son waiting to meet him. By now he *had* to realize Muirin was missing, even if she'd managed to slip out of the house without him knowing as he slept. The man would surely be half frantic.

It was likely Muirin would sleep for as long as the baby didn't fuss, after the night she'd had. Jean might as well go now. She might be tired, but she wasn't falling on her face quite yet, and hopefully she'd be back again before the goats could start their morning racketing.

After pushing herself up from the chair and stretching limbs adamant that they were not meant to be moving again already,

Jean made short work of getting herself properly dressed and out the door. She set the latch before pulling her woolen mittens from under her armpit and jamming her hands into them. It had gotten even colder last night once the rain had stopped, leaving the grass silver tipped and furred with frost. Turning, she caught a flash of red out of the corner of her eye.

It was the birch hill fox, sitting on the path to Jean's door, peering at her with its head cocked to one side, probably wondering why she was out at this hour. The little creature must have felt the morning chill as well, for its bushy tail curled tight around its dainty paws, with only the white tip turning up at the end. It seemed as if the fox was waiting for something.

Jean huffed out a misty breath. The fox likely only came 'round the pond to beg for treats and eye her chicken coop because she had fed it all last winter after it showed up limping, having escaped from a trap and leaving a trail of blood speckled on the snow to show where it had hidden, away under her woodshed. Whatever the reason, the two of them had reached a sort of understanding. Jean could be outside hanging laundry to dry, and the fox would be rolling around in the dust of the road not ten feet away, neither minding the other at all. It felt companionable.

It felt like having a friend.

If more than a few days passed where Jean didn't catch the fox's odd, bouncing gait from the corner of her eye as it went padding through her yard, or spot the red tail flying like a banner along the far side of the marsh as it made its way home to the den under the tall stand of birch trees on the hill, she worried for it. She wondered if the little vixen felt the same about her, or if it just liked to sit outside her door and follow along at a distance as Jean went about her daily chores because it knew eventually she'd stop and say a few words to it, and probably feed it something.

Maybe she ought to give it a name, even if it was a wild thing and not a pet.

"Yes?" Jean asked it.

The fox's sharp yellow-green eyes flashed. It uncurled its tail and dashed off, disappearing into the dry reeds along the edge of the marsh. "Friendly, you are." *Nothing like a nice one-sided conversation.* Jean snorted at herself. "Keep warm, then."

She set out to round the inland end of the pond and cross the stream there, where it ran fast and narrow out of the woods and into the marsh. It was the quicker way to get up to the Silber place, more direct than the road that twisted along the coast, adding miles between destinations that would have been set cheek by jowl, were it possible to get to them in a straight line.

Although the pond was tidal, the ocean did not push its salt far enough to shift the water in the stream, except at the spring tide. A narrow path wound through the tall marsh grasses, from Jean crossing this way in warmer months to hunt for herbs and pick berries in the wood across the pond. The land wasn't hers; technically everything on the far side of the stream was Tobias Silber's property. They were neighbors, the nearest had by either, though his house was a solid mile's trudge up the hill. Most likely this was the way Muirin had come, through last night's storm. This morning, the sky was tinged with pink in the east, glowing red over the water as the last wisps of the night's dark clouds fled out to sea on a stiff, cold breeze.

Jean kilted up her skirts to hop the swift stream—one step onto the dark wedge of rock that sat midstream, with its rough seam of quartz and flecks of fool's gold, and a true jump from there to span the rest, just a few inches too wide to cross with a normal stride. Her heel slid in the frosty grass on the far bank, and Jean caught her balance with a jerk before she could fall backward into the water. It wasn't so very deep, but she could do without an ice-cold dunking this morning, thank you very much.

Jeanie, you be careful playing around that stream! Split your head on that rock, and you'll be gone without a ripple to tell the tale!

Her father's voice echoed out of her memory, clear as if he stood there beside her. He'd always spooked her with warnings around rivers and shores, but Jean couldn't truly blame him. Not when her mother had met her end floating in this very brook, back deep in the woods, and no one ever knowing quite how the thing had happened. Jean's father had found her body after a two-day search, and he'd never quite gotten over her loss.

Jean vaguely recalled dreaming the night before of her and Jo Keddy, in her father's boat. They had taken it out in the pond when they were about sixteen and managed to turn the dory over in all of about three feet of water. She remembered the pair of them laughing and splashing about, squealing as they wrestled together in the brackish muck, and how Jo had caught hold of her muddy fingers, squeezing them, while Jean's father roared at her after he saw what they'd done. Jean had felt lower than a snake's belly, because she knew it wasn't anger that raised his voice.

Muirin had gotten over the stream somehow. She had not fallen, nor slipped on the rock and split her head. If she hadn't cried out, though, or Jean hadn't heard her, and she'd dropped her babe out in the storm somewhere, in the marsh or on the beach—Jean shook her head, swallowing against the lump that had risen in her throat. She needed to put such notions out of mind. It hadn't happened. She had found Muirin, and both mother and child were safe. She had good news to bring this husband. Tobias Silber's missing wife would come home to him again, and his child would know its mother. All would be well.

Blowing out a deep breath, Jean continued on from the

stream and headed up into the trees just as the sun peeked over the horizon, tipping the frosted branches with icy fire. It wasn't an easy place, this harsh coast, but at times it struck you with wild beauty, openhanded, stopping you short. Jean wasn't immune, but she soon shielded her eyes, dazzled and blinking away spots, to turn her gaze downward. It wouldn't do to trip over a root making her way up the slope, and go ass over teakettle in the dead leaves. She had places to be.

Perhaps she was more tired than she thought. Jean was concentrating so hard on the ground beneath her feet that she made it well up the path through the woodlot before she realized there was a voice calling down through the trees, accompanied by the crashing of someone pushing their way through the tangled undergrowth in haste.

"Muirin! Muirin, are you there?" It had to be Tobias Silber, and he was coming straight for her, judging from the noise. He'd probably been following the traces of his wife's passing through the wood like a hunter, heard Jean squelching through the soggy, half-frozen leaves, and assumed her to be the person he was searching for.

She called back into the trees. "It's Jean! Jean Langille! Muirin is in my house, she's fine!"

"How the hell did she get all the way— Ahh!" The sound of a large man crashing his way through the brush toward her became the sound of a large man falling on his face with an almighty thud.

Jean strained not to laugh, her mouth twitching. These were serious doings, after all, and the man had every reason to be haring about. He had more urgent matters on his mind than his footing, and he was unaware she came bearing glad tidings. Jean schooled her voice carefully before speaking.

"Are . . . you all right?"

A grunt. "I'm *fine*. Just—stay put, won't you? I'll come to you, it's a tangle of sticker bushes in here!"

He'd found the blackberry patch, then.

"All right." Leaning on a bare trunk, Jean waited as Tobias fought his way clear of the thorny bramble with no small amount of grumbling and thrashing, and much snapping of branches. Finally he came stumbling out of a thick cluster of young pine trees several feet up the path. The man was a sight—hastily thrown together, and red-faced and breathless with exertion, covered in leaf bits and burrs and thin scratches. He wasn't remotely dressed for the chill morning, with his coat hanging open over an untucked shirt. His hat was missing entirely, his thick blond hair pushed straight up on one side as if he'd only just risen from having slept upon it. Which was probably the case.

"You've had a morning, I see."

Tobias ignored the comment. "She's in your house? And well? God, I didn't think she could just take off like that, especially not now, and she never seemed like to up and run—"

Jean cut him off, lest he start babbling. "Muirin is well, yes. And the babe—you have a fine, healthy son."

He gaped at her, his blue eyes going wide. "What, already? I didn't think—"

"You certainly *didn't* think!" Jean was being waspish, impertinent, but really, it was *ridiculous*. The man hadn't been bothered to seek any sort of advice for his wife, and the poor woman could hardly speak up for herself. It made Jean's ears burn. "Didn't you realize how close she was to her time? If you'd brought her to see me back when you first found she was with child, you would have known what to—" Then the reason he hadn't come finally occurred to her. "You sent word to *her* people. Because of her English, of course, she'd have wanted her family to help her." Jean tsked. "Bad luck, the baby showing up sooner than they did, in that case. You must be expecting them in the next while, then?"

Tobias was staring at her, his mouth hung slightly open. Jean sometimes had that effect on husbands.

After a moment, he simply nodded. "It—yes. As you say. But—Muirin, I should go to her. You ought not to have left her on her own." He made as if to push past her.

"Mr. Silber—" Jean stopped him with a hand on his arm, quickly removed. "Yes, you should go to her, but perhaps first we might fetch her some clothing? Muirin arrived at my door in nothing but her nightdress, soaked to the skin. She was sleeping when I set out, and it should be a good while yet before she wakes, or the babe, if I'm any judge."

He glanced back down the path toward Jean's house before meeting her eyes and nodding once, crisp and decisive. "I suppose you'd know, then. Come along, you can ride back 'round with me in the wagon."

Turning on his heel, Tobias set off up the hill with long, purposeful strides, not waiting on her answer. Jean kilted up her skirts again and hurried after him.

4

Jean waited outside the house as Tobias set himself to rights and gathered a few of Muirin's things. Then he headed around back to the barn, to hitch his horse to the wagon. They had exchanged barely six more words between them, Tobias anxious to get under way.

His house was only slightly bigger than Jean's, but it commanded the Lord's own view, set on the very top of the rise and surrounded by fields gone fallow for the winter, now that his hay was in. The woodlot sat at the back of his property, at the bottom of the field behind the barn, and in the other direction you could see down a long drive to the road, and the shore, where his boat bobbed at its mooring. Beyond it lay the whole open sea, glittering and studded with islands. The bay had one for every day of the year, people said. Jean squinted into the dazzle of morning sun on the waves, raising a hand to shield her eyes.

They probably never wanted for a breeze out here on the point. She imagined there must be days when the wind could lay a man out flat, and she pictured Muirin standing here as she was, looking out at the view, with her long dark hair whipping out behind her. Jean moved her hand to her own rusty hair, trying to smooth it where it was escaping from hastily placed pins.

The wagon rattled around the corner of the house behind her, and she turned as it came to a halt. Tobias was still on foot, leading the big horse by the reins.

Jean hitched her skirts in one hand to clamber up and got as far as setting her foot on a spoke of the wheel before Tobias cleared his throat. "Nah, miss, let me——"

Catching her about the waist, he heaved her up to the spring seat like she was nothing more than a particularly ungainly sack of potatoes. Jean bit the inside of her lip, fighting the urge to bristle at his taking such a liberty without even *asking* first, when she might just as easily have climbed up on her own. She reminded herself that Tobias was worried about his wife and set on making haste. It wasn't fair of her to be irritated about such a thing, all considered.

Climbing up himself, Tobias settled onto the bench beside her, leaving a respectful space between them and placing one casual foot on the running board. He twitched the reins, clucking his tongue at the horse, and the huge animal gave its head a ponderous shake before stepping out with its great feathery feet, heading down the dirt lane.

Dull with tiredness, Jean stared vacantly at the horse's broad muscled rump as it moved along the track. Once all this was settled, and the goats milked, she was going back to bed. It wouldn't do to fall asleep as they drove, though—she'd wake up having tipped to one side, leaning on her companion, possibly drooling onto his sleeve, or else she'd loll the other way and fall right out onto her head, which seemed only marginally worse. Instead, she cleared her throat.

"He's a big horse." Not the greatest opener, but a conversation might stop her nodding off as the wagon swayed along.

"Mm?" She got the impression Tobias was not much more awake than herself, now that he wasn't in a panic. "Aye. He's a good, strong lad—pulls trees out from the woodlot for me when it's too rough for seagoing, and I can sell them down to the shipyards."

Jean nodded. It was a smart notion. Fishing wasn't practical year-round, and the wood probably made Tobias a decent extra income to help support his family through the lean season.

"It must be nice, not being out here by yourself anymore."

She caught him smiling a little, from the corner of her eye. "Oh, aye." Tobias coughed once, as if embarrassed to admit he might have been lonely before, or that he enjoyed the company of his wife, but his tone when he spoke was one of affectionate amusement. "Muirin's a good little housekeeper. Nice, having a lady's touch 'round the place. Keeps me looking smart, too. My darning was making me a laughingstock before."

"Must be hard, though, her not having much English." Jean was aware her question was a bold one even before she asked it, but she was curious. "I couldn't hardly have a conversation with her. How did you manage to court a girl you couldn't talk to?"

Tobias swallowed, making a quiet harrumph. "We got ways of talking without too many words. She's a fine dancer; that's how I noticed her." Shifting on the seat beside her, he put the reins into his right hand and scratched at his forehead with his left thumb, lifting the brim of his hat, uncomfortable. Then he went on, saying simply: "We get by. We understand each other."

Making a soft hum of comprehension, Jean slid her eyes to the side under her lashes, studying him. The morning sun was behind him as he drove, and it gave the hair falling into his eyes a golden glow. Tobias was tall and well built, with a good jaw and a straight nose, and she supposed that he was quite hand-some, objectively speaking. She could see how Muirin might have been attracted to him, even without a language in common. She would be very striking on his arm at a dance, with her dark good looks—like his softer shadow. Jean tried to picture the two of them together, walking arm in arm along the shore. It made her feel a bit queer for some reason.

She already suspected Muirin could speak volumes without ever opening her mouth. The way she'd clung to Jean's hand . . . but really, it was her eyes. Huge and expressive and deep, shining dark as the scrying mirrors that witches used for looking into the future. Jean wasn't sure when she'd last seen lashes so long as Muirin's, either—

"You say Muirin's well, though? She and the babe?"

Jean jumped, her heart skittering. She'd been staring off into nothing, her left thumb massaging the tingling palm of her right hand as if she'd had a cramp, without her noticing. She curled her mittened hands together, dropping them to her lap. They were almost clear around the point, already coming past the birch grove. She turned her attention back to Tobias.

"Oh, yes. Quite. It was just a shock, her turning up in the night like that, so close to her time. And I've never seen the like—" She stopped. It was unusual that Jean would have an in-volved conversation with the father about the actual process of a birth, and she wasn't quite sure how much she ought to say. There were things she'd normally explain to the new mother afterward that she might end up having to put to Tobias instead, if she couldn't make Muirin understand.

Likely it was better not to get into how odd some of it had been, though, especially with him a fisherman. In Jean's experi-ence, the men off the boats were ten times worse for superstition than any old granny she'd ever met. Maybe because they saw things, out on the water. If he somehow got the idea in his head that his boy was a changeling, Jean didn't want to have to try to convince him otherwise. Those webbed hands—

Tobias broke into her thoughts again. "I can't figure what possessed her. To go running off in the night like that. She could have woke me, I would have got her help; I ain't— Pardon." Jean didn't mind fishermen's grammar, but it seemed Tobias was mindful of it, trying to make a better impression on her. He went on, voice gone tender. "I would have got her whatever she needed. It's a husband's job, to take care of his wife, and instead, her run off in the night, like—" Words failed him.

Jean was capable of something besides sharpness when it was needful, and she spoke gently. "Sometimes a woman can get a bit—desperate, around a birthing. And Muirin can't communicate very well, what with the language. Perhaps she panicked, when she realized what was happening, especially if she didn't really understand." A hint of disapproval crept into her voice. "Some folk let their daughters go frightfully ignorant of—how such things work."

When she was not much more than seventeen herself, Jean had attended such a girl, who'd not thought anything except that she was "getting fat" until she'd dropped a babe, and a poor skinny wee thing it had been, too. Although she and the young mother were almost of an age, Jean had never seen a child less fit to be holding a child of her own, her white face a perfect mask of shock. Back then, Jean had only been assisting Anneke, and she was still grateful she hadn't had to explain it all to the girl herself.

She pulled her mind back to the present situation. "Muirin wasn't making much sense last night, truth be told. I only found her by purest chance, out in the marsh by my place. And I got the strangest impression that she was aiming for . . . I'm not sure. Maybe the beach? I thought for a minute I was going to have to drag her into the house. It's a shame she hasn't more English, so

I could have understood what on earth she was thinking of." Tobias turned his head, looking at her with sharp eyes, and Jean couldn't tell what he was thinking of, either. "I'm just glad she fetched up where she did. She happened to cry out, and if she hadn't, I shudder to think—" She stopped, taking in the look on his face.

Tobias said nothing, and Jean wished she'd halted her tongue a bit sooner. After a long moment, he found words again. "I am—very glad that she made her way to you, Miss Langille. It was good luck for her, and for me, that she didn't get any farther. I am so grateful."

Jean gave a one-shouldered shrug at the gratitude, with a little smile. "It's all right. It's just—what I do." She sniffed and added dryly, "Though generally it's less dramatic? If you really want to thank me, come see me ahead of time when Muirin's next with child, so we might have everything ready for that one." The comment made Tobias easier than anything else Jean had said from the first moment she'd met him crashing through the woodlot. He laughed, sheepishly, and his tense shoulders dropped as they came around the last curve of the road.

Jean seldom came upon her home from this direction, and she was struck by how pretty it was—the sea rolling up the pebble beach on one side of the road, the salt marsh and still pond on the other, surrounded by long, waving grasses, and past that, nestled at the edge of the trees, her little gray house. You could see her entire world from here. A thin line of smoke wafted up from Jean's chimney, from the coals she'd left banked, and as they crossed the rickety bridge over the marsh stream, the breeze mingled the scent of smoke with the freshness of the woods and the sharp tang of the sea.

"A lovely spot," Tobias said. "I see why your father picked it when they parceled up the lots out this way. If you folks hadn't already been here first, I might have spoken for that patch myself. Though I like to be up a bit farther from the shore. You're lucky you've not got swamped by a big blow yet."

Turning her head, Jean looked at him. "I've never seen storm surge up farther than the bottom of my yard, Mr. Silber. But the village *has* to get a crew out to replace the bridge every second spring so *you* can keep coming over the shore road."

He laughed again, his blue eyes crinkling. "A fair point. Though I ain't judging where you want your house— Oop! Whoa now—!" He caught a tighter hold on the reins as the horse shied to the left, wresting its head back down with strong arms. A flash of red shot out of the tall dry beachgrass, right beneath the horse's nervous hooves. The fox slowed her lopsided gait halfway up the path to the house and turned back to glare at them, unimpressed. Tobias narrowed his eyes at the little animal.

"That thieving beast will be after your chickens, miss. Once Muirin's settled back to home, I'll come by and set a few snares for you." He said it like it was a decided thing.

Jean shook her head. "No, don't. It's—she's not a pet exactly, but we have an understanding. She's never once gone for my chickens. Really, it's fine. I like seeing her around."

Tobias darted a glance at Jean, as if he thought she were a bit daft. "Suit yourself. But you can't let a beast like that have free run of the place. Mark my words, that little vixen will steal your whole flock out from under your nose if you don't get rid of it." His eyes followed the fox as she lifted her tail in disdain, marking her path as the animal trotted off around the corner of Jean's house, vanishing into her favorite hidey-hole under the woodshed. "You ought to let me, if you're too softhearted for it yourself." When he looked back at Jean again, she got the uncomfortable sense that he was measuring her somehow, her spine creeping. It reminded her a little of the look her father used to get when he thought she was being stubborn. "That's a fine pelt. You could make up a nice muff with it, to match your hair."

"No." Jean was firm. She was sure he was only trying to be helpful, knowing that she hadn't anyone to take care of such things for her, and feeling he owed her something for aiding his wife. The man couldn't possibly understand her attachment to the little fox. Still, the idea of Tobias setting snares at her gate made Jean distinctly uncomfortable, and she didn't much like him making note of her hair, either. She shook herself and scrambled down from the wagon before he could offer to help her with anything else.

5

As Tobias tied up his horse and wagon at the gate, Jean slipped into the house to make certain Muirin was ready for visitors. She found her guest awake and sitting up in the bed with her back propped against the pillows and the baby in her arms. The new mother made peculiar little noises at it—somewhere between cooing and purring, like a cat. Jean couldn't help smiling.

Looking up, Muirin smiled back. She seemed content and, amazingly, well rested—a far cry from what Jean would have expected, and even further from the specter the woman had appeared when she first arrived in the night.

"Good morning," Jean said. "Did you sleep well?" She spoke slowly and clearly, but other than that she didn't bother to change her speech for Muirin's sake. She'd spent too much time these past few years wondering how Jo Keddy was faring among her husband's French relations to do otherwise, imagining how miserable it would be to have people talk to you like a child for not knowing their language, as if you had no sense. How would one ever learn that way? Jean was rather gratified when Muirin spoke up in response.

"Is good morning." She fought with the words, rolling the *r* like a growl, then gave the baby in her arms a gentle jog. "Is good boy, mine."

Jean nodded. "Yes. He's a fine lad. Healthy and strong."

With a pleased hum, Muirin turned her full attention back to the babe, caught up in the fascination unique to a new parent beholding their own creation. The soft delight in her face as she watched the infant yawn and shift made Jean wish she didn't have to interrupt it.

"Muirin, Tobias is here. He was very worried when he woke and found you gone."

Muirin's head shot up at Tobias's name, as if she'd forgotten the rest of the world still existed outside of Jean's little house, even her own husband. Muirin's round eyes gave Jean the impression of a deer, caught in the frozen moment when you came upon it in an open meadow, just before its white tail went up and it bolted.

She took a step toward the bed. "Muirin?"

"Muirin?" The door swung open, just enough for Tobias to put his head in. He grinned widely on seeing his wife, relief written clear on his face as he pushed the rest of the way through. Remembering himself, he paused and looked to Jean, hovering awkwardly just inside her door.

"It's all right, I think we're past standing on ceremony. Come in."

Needing no further invitation, Tobias stepped straight over to the bed, sitting down on its edge with a look of wonder on his face.

Muirin lowered her head, her face hidden behind a long waving lock of black hair. Her husband reached out, brushing it away with the back of his hand, and tipped her chin up with his fingers, speaking soft and gentle, as if she were a shy, skittish animal he was trying to tame. "It's all right. I'm not angry, I promise. Only worried. Were you very scared, love?"

She did not meet his eye but gave a small nod.

He stroked her cheek with the pad of his thumb, and Muirin looked up at him. Raising his eyebrows, Tobias tilted his head at her with a questioning shrug.

She raised her own shoulders with an answering shake of her head. There was a still, weighty moment where the two simply looked at each other, a wordless communication. Heaving a deep sigh with the air of one who felt he spent a great deal of his time being very patient, Tobias moved to smooth her hair.

Muirin bowed her head under his touch, silent.

Looking down at the baby, a smile ghosted around Tobias's lips, and he reached out, one finger extended, to touch a tiny hand. Muirin made a murmur, shifting the child tighter against her chest, possessive. She cut her eyes toward Jean, who swallowed with the acute impression that she was intruding on a private and all-too-intimate conversation, in spite of the fact that this was her own house, and in spite of the fact that neither of them had actually *said* anything.

Jean cleared her throat. "I'll give you two a moment . . . ?" Her voice echoed in the pressing silence, and she was quick to grab up the milking pail from behind the door and get out of the house. She sucked in a deep lungful of cold air. Tobias and Muirin had taken up all the air in the room, crackling like sparks between them, and it was rather a relief not to have to hold her breath to keep from interrupting any longer.

Tramping over to the henhouse, Jean opened its little door to a chorus of subdued and sleepy clucking. One of the hens poked out its head, blinking at the light and the furring of frost that still tipped the grass. Hopefully it would burn off as the sun crept higher. Jean wasn't ready for winter to set in completely just yet, and she didn't particularly fancy the idea of sending off an hours-old baby to catch death of a chill on the way home, either. The day would warm, that was how it went this time of year. The hens weren't put off, mincing out into the yard as Jean continued on.

Irritable bleating greeted her several paces before her arrival at the goat shed. It wasn't even that late, despite everything, but try telling that to a goat who was swollen up with milk. Honey wouldn't complain; she was a sweet-tempered thing. No, the racket had to be the red-eared one, Kicker. Who *did* kick, the beast, nearly knocking Jean flat the first time she'd gone to milk her. It was good that her aim hadn't been quite true, or Jean would have been laid out on the ground by the milking stand for a week or more before anyone happened by to pick her up.

As she lifted the latch, there was a sharp crack against one of the walls, followed by an even higher-pitched bleat as Kicker emphasized her displeasure. Jean snorted. It was a wonder the beast didn't give milk as sour as her disposition.

That bleat, though, reverberating through the door of the shed, put her in mind of Muirin's arrival again. Her anguished cry, which Jean was lucky to have heard at all in the stormy night. It made no sense for Muirin to have struck out on her own, and in spite of Jean's earlier words of reassurance to Tobias, she began turning the whole thing over again in her head as she wrestled Kicker into the milking stand, narrowly avoiding another errant hoof. The milk steamed as it streamed into the tin bucket.

Tobias obviously cared a great deal about Muirin. Surely he would have done whatever he could have for her, had he known what was happening. It was more than likely they'd still have turned up at Jean's door in the middle of the night, but at least it would have been together in the wagon, traveling at full speed and bundled against the weather. Why would Muirin have left behind the only person she could even somewhat communicate with? There was something not quite right about it all, but God alone knew what.

Snorting, Kicker shifted her weight menacingly. Jean was cautious about letting her loose from the stand. "I ought to give you a boot one time. See how *you* like it."

The goat craned her neck, unleashing a dreadful scream of a bleat in response. Calling Kicker a word she wouldn't have dared to utter in polite company, Jean set her free in the pen, then went to repeat the process with Honey.

This was a fair bit easier, and Jean found herself resting her cheek against Honey's flank, warming her cold hands on the goat's soft udder, and once more losing herself in thought as the milk hissed into the pail.

Nothing about Muirin's behavior made a lick of sense. No sane person would even have thought to go down to the shore in her state. She seemed steady enough now, of course, but— Anneke had said as much about Jean's mother.

Anneke Ernst still considered the death of Jean's mother her greatest failure as a midwife, even all these years later. Jean suspected her mentor's guilt was part of why she'd been so set on taking Jean as an apprentice, back when she'd first shown an interest in learning midwifery herself. If Jean was honest, what happened to her mother might have been part of what had drawn her to the profession to begin with. Janet's death was certainly why Anneke had been so ever-present in Jean and her father's life when she was small, why she was the closest thing to a mother Jean had ever known.

It was also why Anneke was so honest about what had happened, when Jean had asked her. "It happens, sometimes. Always, always, check back in with your mothers after. Not just once, but several times. To see that they're coping, that everything is as it ought to be. And don't just talk to *them,* mind, you need to check with everyone. With the husbands, the mothers-in-law, the people who know a woman best. She might be sad after, that's known. But sometimes it's more. I don't know why it is. But it can be like that."

People in town didn't often speak of her mother's death, but ever since she'd been young Jean had caught folks whispering when they thought she wouldn't hear. About how her mother had "run quite mad" after her birth.

You discussed a suicide only behind your hand, and never with the people it affected most.

Her father had worried at some of the little things Janet had said and done for years after, like a bear with a thorn in its paw, trying to figure out what he might have missed, some point where he could have stopped her, somehow, if he'd only known. Instead, he'd found her floating facedown in a stream.

If Muirin had gotten into that pond . . .

Swallowing around a great lump that had appeared in her throat, Jean shook her head, clearing it of such dark thoughts. She was too tired now, and her exhaustion was making her dramatic, overwrought.

Honey craned her head around, lipping at the back of Jean's hair. Shoving herself up from the stool, she let the goat out of the milking stand. Honey gave a polite bleat, and Kicker responded from their pen with another of her forsaken shrieks, eager to have her companion back. Jean opened the gate and shooed Honey inside, wishing people were as easily understood as goats.

Returning to the house with her pail of milk, she found Tobias standing in the light of the front window, holding the baby in the stupid way of large men who seemed to realize the size of their hands for the first time only when they held a new life.

The awkwardness of it always made Jean nervous, but as she stood watching, the new father relaxed, tucking the babe into his elbow, closer to his body. Looking up at her, he smiled.

"He's a fine lad. Tobias, like me, and my father. Toby, for now. I think he'll be dark, like his mama." Nodding in acknowledgment, Jean glanced over at Muirin. She looked as if she wished to leap up and grab the babe back from her husband's arms. Meeting Jean's eyes, Muirin gave her a pleading look, eyebrows drawing together. The woman who had first seemed as if she might not take her own child to nurse had grown attached quickly.

"Mr. Silber—" Jean began, setting her pail down on the table.

"Tobias, please, Jean. After all of this—there's no need."

Jean hesitated. His removing the layer of formality from between them put her instantly on edge. It would have been rude to rebuff him, though, without a real reason. She forced a smile in response, her cheeks stiff. "If you wish. Tobias, I'd like a moment alone with Muirin before you're off, to examine her and Toby properly, now the light is better. There are a few things I ought to try and explain to her as well. If you would . . . ?" Jean held out her hands.

Now it was Tobias who hesitated, his brow furrowing, before carefully placing his son in her arms.

"Oh, pish. If I could catch him last night, surely I won't drop him now!" she said lightly.

He responded with a tight smile. "I'll go fetch Muirin's things, then. I left the bag in the wagon." Glancing over at his wife, he observed her pensively for a moment, then let himself out the door.

Baby Toby shifted in Jean's arms with a fussy grumble. She gently bounced him, and he stilled again. When she looked up, Muirin's eyes were on her, imploring. She stretched her arms out toward Jean in silence, her brows drawing together.

Some things, at least, were easy to understand. Jean brought the baby back to his mother, placing him in Muirin's waiting arms, and sat down on the side of the bed.

"Muirin."

She met Jean's gaze again, with a short lift of her chin that said *Go ahead* almost as clearly as words. Jean spoke slowly, and carefully. "Tobias is going to take you and the baby back home. I'll come by to see you tomorrow, or the day aft—"

Before she could finish, Muirin's hand shot out, grabbing her own so suddenly that Jean flinched. Muirin shook her head quickly, furtive, her eyes gone wide and pleading. Arguing with those eyes would be a very difficult thing, indeed. Jean had to clear her throat before she could speak again.

"What is it? Can you tell me?" If Jean had any idea what the problem was, where Muirin's fear lay, maybe she could somehow set her mind at ease. Every mother was scared with their first, afraid to err. It was a hard thing to have to learn by doing, caring for a child.

Muirin looked away, as if hoping her eyes might light upon something that would help her explain, passing over the things from Jean's kit, still spread out on the table from the night before. The spoons they hadn't needed. The scissors. The needle, the thread. Muirin's eyes sparked, and she bowed her head again, thinking, then peeked up at Jean through her long eyelashes. Opening her mouth, she hesitated.

Jean put on her best listening face.

"Tie," Muirin said. "Tie, is. Him—" She glanced toward the door, where her husband had gone out. "Tie, hold together. Tie—knot, good knot, is." Muirin's face was painfully earnest, like her words explained everything. Her eyes searched Jean's for a hint of understanding, and her grip increased, knitting their hands together even more tightly.

Baffled, Jean shook her head, her fingers aching. Muirin and Tobias, tied by marriage, that had to be part of what she was getting at. But none of it made sense, told Jean what was distressing her. "Knot is right. I wish I could untangle what you're trying to tell me." Her hand had gone damp and clammy in Muirin's grip. Jean wished she could pull it away.

Muirin growled, her nose twitching. "I, *here.*" Her voice dropped, taking on a stubborn edge like she meant it, might dig in her heels and refuse to leave. Jean found herself reminded of Kicker. Clutching her hand harder than ever, compressing Jean's knuckles almost as much as she had in the middle of laboring, Muirin leaned forward over the baby, as if in the hope of simple closeness making her meaning clear. All at once she released Jean's hand, catching at the end of Jean's braid instead, the scrap of ribbon that bound it, and shaking it in her face. "Tie, to stay. Good knot. I——" Muirin's voice cracked, on the knife's edge of tears, frustrated at her inability to explain herself. "I here. I, water go——" Dropping Jean's braid, Muirin gestured toward the window. Toward the window, and the sea, and she spoke a few rolling words in her own tongue before breaking off, frustrated, her last syllable a mournful, defeated *woo.*

A cold chill ran down Jean's spine.

Muirin stared at her, dark eyes begging for an understanding that Jean didn't possess. What was Muirin thinking? Had she been trying to get to the marsh pond, the sea, on purpose? The pointing and pulling, her desperation, the attempts to leave again even after Jean had gotten her inside . . . God. She had to have been, to still be thinking of it now. *Water——*

What Muirin thought she'd do when she achieved her goal, Jean didn't want to even consider. Her stomach knotted. What might happen if she sent Muirin off home with her husband, didn't see her for a day or two? Maybe it would prove to be nothing, but if it wasn't? If Jean guessed wrong it could end up her own mother's tale, all over again. Her fault. Jean's throat tightened. Her duty to Muirin hadn't ended just because she'd placed a healthy baby in her arms.

There was a tap on the door, and Jean started.

Muirin sniffled. Jean studied her for a long moment, then nodded, giving the woman's fingers an awkward squeeze before pulling away. When she reached the door, she stopped and smoothed her skirts with trembling hands, her right one red and sweaty. She glanced back over her shoulder. Muirin was still tracking her, eyes wary. Jean opened the door just enough to slip out, pulling it shut behind her.

Tobias was obliged to take a step back from the threshold to make space for her and stood clutching the bag with Muirin's things in it, confused. "Jean?"

She realized she had no idea what to say to him. *I think your wife might be a danger to herself or the child, but I'm not quite sure, since all I have to go on is stories about my dead mother; try not to worry too much?* It would be far too easy for him to dismiss her concerns as paranoia, Jean too sensitive about her own long-buried past. Something was *wrong,* though; she could tell. It was there in Muirin's pleading eyes as she begged to stay, and Jean had to do something. She couldn't let this sad-eyed, beautiful woman end up like her mother, a tragedy whispered behind hands. Not if she could do anything to help her. Jean was sure she could, if she could figure out what was wrong. If Muirin could only *talk* to her—

Tobias was still waiting, a worried furrow deepening between his eyebrows.

"She doesn't understand me," Jean blurted. Tobias did not look any less puzzled by this statement, and she pressed on. "I mean . . . there are things she needs to know, about caring for a newborn. I can't tell if she understands what I say, and it worries me. I'm going to have to show her how to do everything." She paused. "It's going to take time."

Tobias narrowed his eyes. "You want me to leave them here." The very notion seemed to displease him, his voice growing deeply dubious. "You said I could take them home. Why change your mind now?"

"It's not just the language. I know what I said, but I keep thinking it over and . . . well, it's so cold outside. I wouldn't feel right sending little Toby off so soon. Babies are delicate; it wouldn't do for him to take a chill." Jean feared she was talking too fast, certain her burning ears were turning red. Her heart struck up a fluttery, rapid pattering, insistent upon her saying whatever she needed to convince Tobias it was best Muirin stayed with her. Of course Jean wanted to help Muirin, she would have done the same for any woman in her place, and Tobias wanted the best for his family; surely he would go along if Jean could make it clear that she wanted the same.

"We could bundle the baby up warm," he put in with an air of desperation. "I have to take Muirin home—" He must have been lonely indeed before he'd married. Jean couldn't find the room to pity Tobias; he'd have to cope.

"*Muirin* was up all night—she came all this way in a storm, soaked herself to the skin, and then had the baby on top of it! It's a miracle nothing else went wrong, and you've still *got* a healthy wife and son. She ought not set a single foot out of that bed for the better part of a week, and if I'd not been up all night with her myself, I'd have realized it sooner!" Catching herself, Jean flattened her lips tight together to stop anything else escaping them, breathing hard through her nose.

Tobias appeared to be contemplating an act of mutiny. Abruptly turning away from her, he stalked a half-dozen paces down the yard, yanking off his hat to gaze straight up into the clear sky, silent.

"I just want to help," Jean said to his back.

He turned and squinted at her, considering. His jaw twitched. "Not more than a week?"

"Not more." Jean wondered how much English a body could learn in a week. If she was going to help Muirin, she needed to know for certain what was going on inside her head.

"Fine," Tobias said. "I'll be here every day, until I can take them home again."

6

Muirin watched Jean at her daily chores as if she'd no idea how to do such things herself. Jean wasn't used to such scrutiny within her own house; Muirin's eyes resting on her made her prone to small fits of clumsiness.

There was a soft touch on her arm, and Jean nearly knocked a greased loaf tin off the table with her elbow. Muirin removed her hand, nodding at the mass of dough Jean had turned out onto the table, and raised an eyebrow in one of the questioning looks she was so good at. Jean slowed her movements to show Muirin the way of punching down the dough and folding it over itself, all the while wondering how any woman could have gotten past the age of ten without knowing such a thing. Maybe Muirin's family had been well enough off that someone else did kitchen work for them, but it wasn't the sort of thing you asked a person.

Jean split the dough between them, and they each kneaded a loaf side by side. Muirin took to the task handily. She had proven to be curious about everything over the past five days, her eagerness to learn turning joyful as she first cautiously—and then with growing confidence—pressed Jean for the English name of nearly every object in the house. It was clear she had a keen mind, for she was picking up the language with remarkable speed, even if she occasionally mixed things up. The two of them simply laughed over the resulting confusion. It was a shame she wasn't so easy about making mistakes talking to her husband. She could still barely be convinced to say more than a handful of words to Tobias when he came to call.

Muirin's long fingers sank into the soft dough, and she laughed, showing her very white teeth, when it stuck to her hands. Jean's throat tickled, and she coughed into her elbow to avoid her own floury hands, tearing her eyes away.

"It's sticky still," Jean said when Muirin gave her a quizzical look. "*Sticky*. It sticks to you. Here, try a bit of flour on your hands."

"Stick-y. Yes." Muirin wrinkled her nose, delicately picking the wet dough from between her fingers before pinching some flour from the jar Jean slid toward her. "In mine, is—" The sibilant word Muirin spoke even *sounded* sticky to Jean's ears, made her think of the sucking mud around the marsh pond at low tide. Jean could barely recall when she'd last spent so much time with another person. She'd not made friends easily as a child, and after Jo had gone, the girls they'd both known from the village school were standoffish. Of course they were, with what people were saying. But Muirin wasn't from here, she was from away, outside of the village gossip.

Muirin looked at her expectantly. Jean attempted to say the word, very nearly spitting on the table between them. She would swear the words that came out of Muirin's throat weren't meant to fit in a human mouth, but if making a fool of herself in Gaelic would set the woman more at ease about using English in front of others, Jean was happy to do it. Muirin stared at her for a moment, then began laughing all over again.

Her cheerful mood slipped as the bread baked and the morning faded into afternoon. By teatime, when Tobias came knocking, Muirin was just as she'd been on the first day they'd met: still and silent as a clam.

As good as his word, Tobias Silber had come calling like clockwork every afternoon for the past three days, and Jean's already limited ability to sit and make pleasant small talk was growing increasingly strained. It was only a matter of time until it became obvious to the man just how tiresome she found their conversations, especially with Muirin still so reluctant to join them with her broken English, despite Jean's best attempts at drawing her out.

"I went out for a couple hours this morning, since it was so fine, and caught you girls something for dinner tonight." Tobias grinned at Jean, holding up a string of fish. "They're bony fellows, but tasty ones. You're going to want to be careful about getting all those bones out, and scrape them well, or you'll have a mouthful of scales, but Muirin—"

Did he seriously think Jean didn't know how to clean a fish? Her father had been a fisherman, for God's sake. Muirin looking over Jean's shoulder as she worked was a pleasure, but she'd be damned if she put up with the woman's husband doing the same, giving her helpful tips on deboning his undersized cod the entire time.

"Actually," Jean said, stopping the flow of his words midstream, "I need to go out while you're here. I have to . . . gather some moss. For Toby's diapers. I'll deal with the fish when I get back. But thank you. Muirin, the tea is ready, you can pour." Muirin gave Jean a confused look, then swiveled her head toward her husband. Her expression suggested she didn't know what to do about this particular turn of events but had absolutely grasped that Tobias was the cause of it, even if *he* hadn't.

Throwing her yellow shawl around her shoulders, Jean snatched an old cloth sack from one of the hooks behind the door, certain Tobias and Muirin were having another of their strange wordless conversations behind her back. She couldn't get out the door fast enough.

Let him keep an eye on his wife for a while if he's so eager, Jean thought peevishly as she headed up the path to the spring. *Give me some time to think.* Even if it meant the pair of them sat and stared at each other like owls the whole time without her there to ease the conversation along.

Maybe some time spent alone together was exactly what they needed. After all, Muirin had been talking to Jean all morning when it was just the two of them. Perhaps her ease with Jean stemmed from how they'd been thrown together, strangers forced into such intimacy the minute they'd met. Muirin seemed a different person altogether when her husband came around, and Jean had no idea why—not beyond creeping suspicions, ones that didn't square with what she was seeing, for all her watchfulness.

She wished she dared leave Muirin alone to go into the village and talk to Anneke. Jean's mentor might have been able to see through Muirin's baffling behavior as Jean could not. She'd have understood why the way Tobias kept pressing Jean to send his wife home with him made her want to shove him out her door, pleased to see the back of him when he left, too. At least Anneke had provided Jean's excuse to leave: The shallow, rocky earth in the stand of pines behind the house was a perfect spot to gather absorbent moss to fold inside of little Toby's diapers.

Anneke swore by moss to keep babies dry and prevent rash. She'd learned it from her own mother, a Native woman from over at Indian Point, where the Natives still returned to camp and fish and dig clams in the summers, though there were fewer and fewer of them who came now, every year. People kept stealing the point right out from under them. Even when one of them did hold a deed, someone would contest it, and such cases always came out the same way—the trees came down, a new farm went up, and the Natives had to move on. Jean had always thought it didn't seem fair, not when the Natives had been there first.

Jean was so caught up in her thoughts and using her knife to pry up a thick wedge of green moss in a single piece that she didn't realize at first she had company. When she looked up from tucking the moss into the old flour sack she carried, the birch hill fox was settled on its haunches on top of a rotting stump several feet away, regarding her with curious green-gold eyes.

"Hello," Jean said, soft and even. "I didn't see you there. You haven't been around since the other day. Have the visitors made you nervous?"

The little vixen cocked her head to the side without making a sound.

"You'd get on well with Muirin. She's as quiet as you are." Sitting back on her heels, Jean thought a moment. "At least when her husband is around. Do you make noises when I'm not around? I doubt it; I think it's not your nature. I can't figure what Muirin's nature is . . ." *If she were always the way she is with me,* Jean thought, *I wouldn't be so worried.* The way Muirin sat huddled with the baby during her husband's visits made her look like an invalid, and it was worrying him almost as much as it was Jean. Tobias was questioning nearly everything the midwife told him at this point.

"I can't even blame him. It's like she's two different people. I just don't know which one is really her." Had Jean's mother been like that? That was how Anneke had missed seeing something had gone wrong, after all: Janet had tried to hide what she was thinking and feeling, acting as if all were well right up until the day she disappeared. The day she died. Jean wished she could know what her mother had been like when she hadn't been pretending. Although if Muirin was only pretending with Jean, why would she drop the pretense in front of her husband, with Jean still right there?

What if the way Muirin behaved with Tobias was the real pretense? There was more than one reason for a woman to be quiet and melancholy, so Jean had been watching the man out of the corner of her eye all week. Watching, and seeing nothing there. Although it would have explained the way Muirin withdrew in his presence. Even physically—she kept startling Jean when it was just the two of them by calling her attention with a silent hand on her arm, or a brush of fingers at the back of her shoulder. Jean shifted her shoulders just thinking of it.

The fox yawned, showing its sharp teeth and long curling tongue, then stretched its back and hopped down from its perch, disappearing into the underbrush.

Jean huffed out a scoff. "Sorry to have bored you."

Probably the fox was heading for home; the days were drawing in shorter than ever as true winter got closer. Jean went on filling her sack with moss as evening crept on and her fingers grew cold and numb, knowing full well she was stalling her return until Tobias had gone. The shadows were long and blue by the time she came back down the path from the spring, the ocean a dark emptiness off across the beach, though she could hear the rolling of the waves on the shore. Lamplight glowed golden through the windows of her little house. A welcoming thing, having Muirin waiting for her, knowing it would already be warm when she stepped inside.

Someone had shut up the chickens and goats already. Tobias

must have done it, at the end of his visit. He'd not been comfortable going back out with his boat for more than a few hours
at a time while things with Muirin were so unsettled, which had
left him with time on his hands. Jean had gotten a full account
of how he'd been occupying himself at home, with the replacing
of shingles and stopping of drafts, the building of a new cradle
for little Toby, which made Jean wonder why he'd waited until
after the birth to build it. The babe's arrival seemed to have
caught his father entirely flat-footed. Tobias clearly didn't want
anything else catching him unprepared—he'd meticulously de-
tailed his securing of the family's henhouse to her as well, "seeing as there's a fox about."

Jean wasn't about to budge on the fox, nor allow Tobias to set
a snare at her gate, but she did feel a moment's guilt for allowing
herself to entertain suspicious theories about the man while he'd
been checking in on Muirin and his son, and doing Jean's own
chores as well. Tobias was a touch overfamiliar perhaps, a bit too
sure of himself, but then, Jean thought there might not be a man
alive who didn't overstep that way, now and then. She really
ought to cut the fellow a bit of slack. After all, Jean couldn't
point to any single thing he had said or done to make her question him. It was only that Muirin was so unlike herself whenever he appeared. Jean snorted. Funny, that she was so certain
she knew what Muirin was like, after less than a week.

Once Muirin finally got out and met people in the village,
they would be just as charmed by her as Jean was. She rather
childishly hoped Muirin would still want to see her now and
then, even once she'd talked with the other girls. That Muirin
might want to remain friends after she had gone home with her
husband again, and no longer needed Jean. Her throat tightened. Maybe she could empathize with Tobias, just a little. It
was wrong of him not to help Muirin with her English, of

course, but it meant that she stayed close, needed him. He didn't have to share her with anyone. Jean could see the appeal of that for someone like him, even if she didn't agree with it.

A slapping sound like a leaping fish or a seal's flipper echoed over the black water, and Jean started. Why was she still standing out in the gathering dark? Foolish. A spark of light flashed, off to sea, then spun away: Buchanan's lighthouse. Jean took a deep breath of the cold, salty air and turned herself, pushing open her door before the beacon came around again.

A wave of warmth hit her, her cheeks tingling at the change from the temperature outdoors. The fire was crackling in the hearth, and the scent of fried fish wafted in the air; her mouth began to water. Muirin looked up from poking at the pan, smiled, and in three steps was right before her, closer than propriety. She cocked her head to one side, looking at Jean. Her nose twitched. Jean wondered if Muirin could smell moss and pine on her.

Jean's mouth had gone very dry. Muirin had the darkest eyes Jean had ever seen—nearly black. She could hardly tell where the pupil ended, even standing this close, and they glowed in the lamplight like dark pearls. Jean swallowed hard as Muirin leaned toward her, closer than ever. *What*—

Closing the last inch between them, Muirin nuzzled the soft tip of her nose into Jean's chilly cheek. Jean couldn't move. Wasn't sure if she should. Was sure she didn't want to, not in the slightest.

Muirin pulled away again, just an inch, her eyes level with Jean's.

"Hello."

She regarded Jean a moment longer, then laughed, pulling away and going back to the fire, to flip the fish in the pan as though Jean were not still stood next to the door like a stick, in all her outdoor clothes, trying to remember how breathing worked.

At last she settled on a full-body shiver, one that was as much a reaction to whatever the hell *that* had been as an adjustment to the warm room. She began to pull off her mitts and unwind her scarf. "You didn't have to make dinner for me—" Jean had been doing all the cooking for them both, and the change was unexpected.

Muirin's head jerked back up. "No? Is . . ." Her eyes shuttered for a moment, looking inward for words that might explain her thoughts. "Is your house. You go out. Made, I, for . . . the coming-in?" She raised her eyebrows, as if to ask, *Is that right?*

Jean made an attempt at setting it all in order. "Since I was out, you wanted to make dinner for when I came back?"

Muirin nodded. "Wife does, yes?"

Jean choked. "I suppose so. But you aren't *my* wife, so I wasn't expecting it. It's very nice of you, though. I'm used to coming home and doing things for myself."

The corner of Muirin's mouth started to quirk upward like she found something amusing, but then it dropped, and she let out one of the slow considering hums that Jean was already becoming familiar with. They put her in mind of a cat's purr. Muirin's head tilted again, her eyebrows drawing together as she examined Jean's face. "Is house cold?"

"Sometimes. In the winter." Jean wasn't sure she liked the thoughtful look Muirin was giving her now. Jean was fine on her own, could take care of herself. Casting around, her gaze landed on the baby, who was tucked up into a bundle on the bed, quiet but alert as he watched them both with his round black eyes. She went over and scooped him up, giving him a bounce, careful of his head. "Hullo, Toby! Have you been good for your mama while I was gone?"

He hooted at her and fought one of his hands out of the blanket he was swaddled in, catching at a curl of her hair that had sprung loose.

"No."

Jean turned, surprised at the sharpness in Muirin's voice. She was standing beside the table, about to slide the fish from the pan she held onto the plates laid there, but had stopped mid-motion, fixing Jean with a colder look than she'd have thought the woman capable of. Jean carefully removed the baby's hand from her hair. "I . . . pardon?"

"He, Toby is not. Not Tobias." Muirin held herself very upright.

"Oh." Jean blinked. "Then what—?"

"*My* boy, *Kiel* is name." She said it proudly, as if she had somehow won something with this pronouncement, then deflated, wary of Jean's reaction.

She simply nodded acceptance. Muirin took a deep breath and nodded back.

Jean hadn't been expecting it, but it wasn't such a strange thing. Men always wanted to name their sons after themselves, and more than one of her mothers had their own name for a babe—usually it became a middle name, or the mother's pet name, at least until the child grew too old to stand for such things.

"It's a good name. Is it from your family?" It certainly wasn't one Jean had ever heard before. She thought of the keel of a ship pushing forward through waves and wondered how it was meant to be spelled.

Muirin hesitated before answering, studying Jean. Her demeanor softened again as she spoke. "Father is." She paused. "Was."

Jean understood that clearly enough. "It was your father's name. He died? I'm sorry."

Muirin gave a shrug. "Long time. I small. Him, up on boat with men was, it—" She stopped, thinking. This was more complex than most things she said, and Jean was reminded once again that, while Muirin seemed to understand a great deal, putting together words for herself was going to take a while yet to come easily, no matter how much progress she was making, or how quickly. Muirin pulled a face, knowing her words weren't remotely right. "Boat fall, down, in sea. Much fire?" She waved a hand back over her shoulder. "Was long."

Jean nodded. "Boat sank," she said, then caught herself. "*The* boat sank. And burned. A long time ago? A boat did that in the bay here once, when I was little. The *Young Teazer.* It caught fire and exploded. I'm sorry that happened to your father."

Muirin shrugged again, as if to say it was in the past and didn't matter, then made a small, eloquent gesture, inviting Jean to sit. Jean crossed to her, placing the baby—*Kiel,* she reminded herself—in Muirin's arms, and pulling out the chair for her to sit first before circling around to take her own place. The first mouthful of fish brought Jean up short, and she blinked at Muirin in amazement.

"This is wonderful." It was an understatement. Although Jean couldn't put a finger on exactly what was so special about it, the taste was incredibly clean and just slightly salty. Maybe it was only that she hadn't made it herself. "My fried fish never comes out like this. What did you do to it?"

Muirin gave one of her mysterious, curling smiles, one that held a playful edge. "Is my fish . . ." She groped for a word, then gave up and put a finger to her lips, making a *shh* gesture, and laughed.

Jean laughed, too. "Secret. It's a secret recipe. Something you don't tell people, that no one else knows."

"Secret." Muirin nodded, looking thoughtful as she considered this new word. It was a while before she spoke again, taking time to slowly chew a mouthful of fish, set down her fork, and adjust the baby in the crook of her left arm before looking at Jean. "I, much secret."

Jean nodded. "You *do* have many secrets. Maybe, when you have more words, you can tell me." She smiled, gently teasing. "For now, you get to be mysterious. A mystery." She thought her tone was suitably light, but Muirin's face became serious and grave.

"Mystery." She considered that, too. "Much mystery, yes."

Jean waited, but Muirin didn't say anything further. She gave up. No mystery was going to be solved before their dinner went cold, and it was too tasty to let that happen.

Jean sat in one of the armchairs by the fire, half working on wrapping a ball of yarn, and half watching Muirin, who was seated on the rug before the hearth with the baby balanced on her legs. She was bouncing him, holding on to his little fists, and Kiel was chuckling. He had a funny barking laugh. Jean had never heard a baby make a sound that so reminded her of a puppy. Suddenly, his little eyes widened, and he let out a mighty burp, followed by a shocked silence. Muirin laughed at his surprise, saying something to him in her rolling tongue, leaning in to press his wee button nose with her own.

She made a pretty picture there, glowing with firelight, playing with the baby, happy. She seemed so, anyway, content to sit on Jean's hearth as if it were just the spot for her. Their entire evening had been cozy and comfortable and warm; even the quiet during dinner was companionable. With Muirin in her house, the whole week had passed that way, and Jean thought, with a pang, that it was a shame it would have to end. Muirin had her own hearth and home to tend, and she couldn't stay with Jean forever. Nor would she want to. Jean focused her attention on her yarn again, pulling the woolen strand hard enough that it dug into her fingers, striping them white and bloodless. She wound the yarn up tight around itself, so it wouldn't be in danger of unraveling.

Muirin was ready to go home again. She was happy, adored her child, and knew perfectly well how to care for him. She'd not made another mention of water, or the sea, since that first morning. She was clearly in her right mind.

Jean knew she ought to be pleased. With no more baby to wake her with his crying in the night she could go back to her own routine. Besides, she and Muirin were friends now, and more than that, neighbors. Neighbors needed one another out here. They could go back and forth visiting each other all the time; she could go on trying to help. Continue with Muirin's English lessons. Maybe not as much through the winter, but once spring came, surely.

It would be nice, having a friend so close to hand.

Jean supposed that she and Muirin were too old to go running off to build little houses in the woods as she and Jo had done, well past the age when the other girls had set aside such silly things. They'd said they'd have a real house together one day, and Jean had thought they really might somehow. Maybe they'd been foolish to even think of it. They'd only been girls, and maybe they'd have wanted different things if they'd had more time. Jean wasn't the same person anymore, had grown solitary and focused on her work, tied to her home. Jo had always been so social—she'd have been happier in town, surrounded by people.

It was the not knowing that tore at Jean. Less the thought of what could have been, more wondering how Jo had fared in her new life. Jean would have given nearly anything to know for certain that she was all right. Happy, somehow, in spite of everything, though it seemed impossible. Jo had been stolen so far away, to a place where she barely spoke six words of the language. Jean had always assumed Jo's husband would have helped her, having both tongues in his mouth, but perhaps Jo had found herself as isolated as Muirin, silent and still and locked up in herself, not as fortunate in her neighbors, no one to help her along. Jean hunched over her ball of wool as her eyes prickled hot and dry, her throat tightening—

There was a light touch at her knee, and she raised her eyes. Muirin had inched closer to Jean's chair and was peering up at her with a strange expression on her face. "Is all right, Jean?" she asked. She made a slight frown, as if from worry, then dropped it again. "Is . . . wrong, a thing?" Jean realized it was her own face Muirin was trying to imitate, and shook her head, trying to school the furrow out from between her eyebrows.

"Nothing is wrong. I was just thinking."

"Mmm." Muirin studied Jean for a long moment before turning her face back toward the fire, but she didn't press further. Jean appreciated it all the more because of the sense that Muirin had seen right through her but was choosing to let Jean pretend everything was fine, if that was what she wanted. Muirin shifted Kiel in her arms and rolled her neck, yawning and shaking her long hair back from her face. Then she leaned herself comfortably against Jean's leg, settling again. Tilting her head, Muirin rested her cheek on Jean's knee. Her eyes closed, and her lips curled in a soft, contented smile.

Jean was instantly unsure if she should move or not. Even to breathe.

Now she was stiff.

Surely Muirin could tell how stiff she was. Her knee was knobby; Muirin couldn't be comfortable, not when Jean was nothing but angles. When was the last time someone had been so easy with her? No one, since Jo—

She ought to relax. Muirin would wonder what was wrong with her.

Muirin was just an affectionate person, that was all. Still, when Jean looked down at the head of dark, glossy hair at her knee, she wanted very badly to stroke it. Maybe that would be all right? She lifted a hand from the ball of yarn in her lap.

A blast of wind shook the little house, followed by the sudden roaring rush of rain pounding on the roof. The fire hissed as a few drops made it down the chimney. Kiel startled and let out a wail. Muirin straightened up, holding him more securely, making hushed reassuring sounds, cooing and cajoling.

Jean took a shaking breath and gripped her ball of wool. Her ears were drumming almost as loud as the rain. She went back to winding her yarn, her fingers stinging, and kept her eyes trained on her work.

It was a good thing it was time for Muirin to leave.

7

It was still raining come morning, the sort of cold, drooling, early-winter rain that went on all day and never quite managed to turn to snow, though it clearly wanted to. Jean made exactly two trips out of the house—once to tend to the animals and bring back water from the spring, and after that, to fetch more wood for the fire. By the time she was done with those chores, she was soaked through, water dripping from the chill tip of her nose. Muirin met her at the door, throwing a dry cloth over her head and rubbing it vigorously. Jean laughed breathlessly and batted Muirin's hands away to do it herself, rusty hair frizzing out in all directions.

Once she was dry again and had pinned her hair up more respectably, Jean made a bit of fresh cheese from some of the goats' milk. Muirin watched, fascinated, as Jean first scalded the milk, then curdled it with white vinegar, stirring and salting the curds before hanging them in a bit of cheesecloth to drip the last of their whey into a bowl. It was yet another task that Jean would have assumed Muirin knew how to do, but she reacted as though she had never seen such a thing in her life, gasping when the milk separated into curds and whey after Jean added the vinegar.

"How?" she demanded. "Magic, is!"

Jean tried to explain, but she wasn't sure how much sense she made. She'd never thought about the *how* of it before. It was just the way things worked—you added something acid, gave it a stir, and everything else thickened and curdled.

As the cheese was draining, they made biscuits. Muirin had rather taken to baking, and she cut rounds from the biscuit dough with an upturned glass and childlike pleasure, while Jean held Kiel on her lap as he dozed. He was a remarkably unfussy babe and seemed not to mind which of them held him, never becoming tetchy unless he needed changing, or if he was hungry, when only his mother would do.

Once the biscuits were baked golden Jean sat them on a chipped plate in the middle of the table, next to a bit of the cheese and a jar of last summer's blueberry jam. She was reaching for the kettle when a knocking came at the door. Muirin fell silent as Jean went to let Tobias in, slipping into her seat at the table with the baby in her arms.

It would have taken more than rain to keep Tobias from his now-customary visit. He was wrapped up in his fisherman's long yellow oilcloth coat, which he hung behind the door as he said his hellos. Water dripped soft and steady off the coat and onto the floor as Jean poured them all cups of steaming-hot tea.

"So," Tobias began as he settled himself at the table across from his wife, accepting a cup from Jean with a nod, "did you enjoy your fish yesterday? I thought maybe Muirin might do them up for the two of you, since she's up and about again."

Jean sat, taking up her own cup. "She did. Thank you—it was a treat."

Tobias blew across the top of his tea, helping himself to a

biscuit. "Muirin's good with fish. Can't cook anything else to save her life, though."

Muirin didn't say anything.

Jean looked at her.

Tobias set down his tea, realizing his words might have sounded harsh. "Ah, now. I don't mean anything by it. It doesn't matter to me if she can cook or not."

"Muirin made that biscuit you've got." Jean was not letting it go by.

"Really?" He blinked at the biscuit in his hand, then looked at Jean. "She didn't know how, I thought. Guess she's learning a fair bit from you, then." He shifted his gaze to his wife, considering, before taking a bite.

Muirin avoided his eye, glancing at Jean.

Playing go-between for the two of them was exhausting. Jean took a sip of tea that just about burned the skin off her tongue, then made herself set the cup back down on its saucer with a clink. There was no sense putting it off any longer, especially if no one else was willing to help Jean carry the weight of the conversation. Her sip of tea curdled in her stomach. Jean took a deep breath, linking her fingers together on the table before her. "So. I think Muirin is ready to go home again."

Muirin's and Tobias's heads both snapped up at her words. Neither said anything, so Jean went on.

"Not today, perhaps, what with the rain? But if it's stopped tomorrow, I can't see a reason to keep you here longer." She gave Muirin a smile that felt oddly stiff. "I'll be sorry to see you go, of course, but you and the baby are both doing well, and keeping you longer will only stop you settling into your own routine at home, as a family." Jean glanced at Tobias, then looked to Muirin again, trying to gauge her reaction to this news. "I think I've kept you from your husband long enough."

Tobias turned a wide grin on his wife. "Good. That's— It'll

be good, having Muirin back where she belongs. And Toby, too. He ought to get to know his own home!"

Alarmed by the sound of his name, or his father's hearty tone, the baby chose that moment to start fussing. Muirin bounced him, in an absent, off-rhythm way. She had turned pale, gazing down into the wood of the table with a far-off look in her eyes.

"Muirin?" Jean asked, dropping her voice.

Muirin lifted her head, blinking, as if she'd been lost in thought. She looked from Jean to Tobias, then back again. "I . . . I . . ."

Tobias leaned forward, regarding his wife with concern. "Muirin . . . ?"

Muirin shook her head slightly, then looked at Jean again. "Tired. Up, I . . . ?" She gestured toward the narrow stairs to the loft room, where Jean had been sleeping since Muirin and the baby had arrived, and tucked the baby closer to her shoulder. He quieted somewhat, subsiding into a bit of snuffling. Muirin slid her gaze toward Tobias, as if it were him she was asking. "Please."

Jean pushed out her chair and stood, guilt prickling under her collar. "Of course. Muirin, you should have said something if you were feeling tired; I'm sorry I didn't realize."

Tobias stood as well, a moment after Jean, and stepped around to pull out Muirin's seat for her as she rose. "Yes, you go rest. It will be a big day tomorrow, love." He caught Muirin's elbow, and turned her to look at him, leaning close to murmur something into her ear, too low for Jean to catch. His large hand cupped the baby's small head for a moment; gently, as if he worried he could crush the infant. Then he smiled at the baby and stepped back to let Muirin pass.

Jean followed Muirin to the foot of the stairs and put a hand on the railing to stay her before she could start to climb. "Muirin." Jean kept her voice low. "Just tired? Are you sure? Nothing is wrong?"

Muirin was dark-eyed and solemn. Jean had the feeling that she ought to be able to read something in the depths of those eyes, but Muirin shook her head, looking away from Jean and down, mindful of the narrow step. She set her hand on top of Jean's, pressed it, soft and insubstantial. "Is all right," she said in a subdued voice, and went up the stairs.

Jean breathed out, then turned back to face Tobias. He still stood by the table, worry etched into his face.

"She's fine. Really. She's just recovered so quickly that I forget she might still tire easily. Having a baby is hard work. And then it wakes you up every night, after." Jean felt like it was herself she was trying to reassure. The back of her hand tingled, as though Muirin's touch had left behind a ghostly echo of itself, and Jean rubbed it as if it were a smear of ash that could be erased, wiped away with a wet thumb.

Tobias's face relaxed, and he sat back down. He picked up another biscuit from the plate and inspected both sides of it, looking thoughtful. Jean came back to take her place across from him again and watched him turning the biscuit over in his hand. She slid the butter dish toward him before venturing to speak.

"Tobias, I wonder if I might . . . make a suggestion to you? About Muirin."

He looked up at her. For a moment she thought his eyes narrowed, but then he simply waved a hand at her before taking up the butter knife. "Go on," he said. "Can't hurt, I don't think."

Jean nodded. "It's only . . . I want to be sure Muirin's all right up there, after the two of you go home, and I can't keep an eye on her as much. I think she may be feeling isolated, all the way out here with only you for company, and you out on your boat half the time."

Tobias spread butter onto the bottom of his biscuit with a gravelly hum. "I suppose? Though there's hardly need. I'll be home with her now, until the fleet heads out again in the spring.

Weather's got too dicey since last week." He nodded in the direction of the window, where raindrops trickled down the pane.
"Only luck and a south wind kept that from being snow. So
she'll have company."

"Mm." Jean wondered if the man truly thought his wife could
be content with him as her whole world. "That's something.
But I was more thinking you ought to get her out of the house
a bit. She's been there since you were wed; it must get lonely.
Maybe take her into town with you one day? She ought to make
some friends."

Tobias glanced up from the jar of jam. "Well, you're her
friend now, aren't you? You're out here alone most of the time,
too. You can visit." He seemed genuinely baffled. Jean was
struck, not for the first time, by the notion that, while men
might not be terribly different from women in theory, they
seemed to have some rather peculiar blind spots when it came to
socialization.

"And I will. But that's not the point. A person needs to not
be in the same four walls all the time. To see people. To talk.
Tobias, I know the two of you seem to get on well enough
without saying much, but you must start speaking with her,
properly. She's—" Jean hesitated. She wasn't even entirely sure
why. She might have told Tobias how much progress Muirin had
already made, just from the two of them talking all week, how
he could build on that foundation. And yet. Muirin was always
so reluctant to speak when he was there, as if she wished to keep
how far she'd come to herself. Her secrets weren't Jean's to share,
however little sense they made. "She needs to be able to communicate. Being around other people would help with that, too.
I think she'd pick up the language quick enough, if she had
more people to use it with."

He set down the jam; his knife still stood upright in the jar.
"I noticed she's already got a couple new words, just being here

with you. She understands, and that's enough for now, I'd say. Besides, I ain't sure I should be taking her and a fresh new baby off to town, everyone gawking and gabbing at them. Muirin ought to be at home, after all this business. Less excitement."

Jean restrained herself from rolling her eyes. She needed to keep on Tobias's good side if she was going to make him see reason, and she wouldn't feel right sending Muirin back to his house if the man was only going to keep her shut up there with no one to see or speak with all the long winter, wife or no. Jean knew how that could make a body feel like a prisoner. "I'm not saying you ought to be off to town with her *tomorrow*. Just that Muirin might be more content if she saw some different faces once in a while. She was so strange when she first got here, and I worried—well. Maybe in a few weeks, if there were a fine day, you might go then. Visit one of your brothers, maybe, or go to church on Christmas? Stop in at the mercantile, whatever you think might be interesting for her. I mean, I could mind the baby for you, if that's your worry."

Tobias gave her a long, measuring sort of a look. "About the baby," he began, then paused.

"Yes?"

"His hands." Tobias frowned. "They aren't . . . right."

Jean had been wondering when it would come up. She'd been pleasantly surprised that first day, when Tobias had spread the baby's tiny fingers and seen the webbing between them, and hadn't said a word about it. His mouth had tightened, and he'd glanced at Muirin over his shoulder with a look of concern, but then he'd seemingly brushed the small strangeness aside. Jean had hoped he'd decided to accept it as a given. Tobias had seemed the sort to give a stoic shrug and not worry about it, especially after all that had already happened with Muirin and Kiel, but it only made sense he'd bring it up eventually. Perhaps he'd not wanted to say anything in front of his wife and risk upsetting her.

"There isn't really anything wrong with them," Jean said, trying to sound as though this was something she'd dealt with many times, and not anything out of the ordinary. "His fingers look a bit different, perhaps. But they won't give him any trouble. It's just a bit of extra skin."

Tobias was blunt. "We ought to cut them. It's uncanny, is what it is. Not natural."

Superstition and folktales and nonsense. Chances were Tobias wouldn't have minded if he'd known about Kiel being born in a caul, not when everyone knew that it was proof against drowning. His son's webbed fingers, though, had spooked the grown man as much as the extra finger people said told a witch. No wonder he'd not said anything in front of Muirin. Jean imagined she'd have been furious, no matter how closemouthed she usually was with her husband. It was one thing to put a coin in a baby's cot to keep the fairies away—whether they existed or no, it wouldn't harm the babe. Jean had slipped a sixpence into the bottom of Kiel's basket herself. But this . . .

She didn't quite manage to keep all the scorn out of her voice. "Don't be foolish, man. He's not going to turn into a—a *duck,* for pity's sake! And I won't do it." Jean was firm; she intended this to be the only time such a thing was even discussed. Tobias looked taken aback at being spoken to in such a tone, and not terribly pleased by it.

"He's my son—"

"And you have his best interest at heart, I'm sure," Jean placated, trying to make herself sound as if she understood completely. Sometimes that was the best way to convince a person you were right—to let them think you weren't necessarily saying they were wrong. She made her tone as conciliatory and reasonable as she could. "Toby is a perfect child in every other way, strong and healthy, a fine son. Would you truly want to risk him for such a small thing? Muirin would be crushed if anything were to happen to him, and you know as well as I do how any little cut can go bad. He could take septic. Or worse—"

Jean paused to draw a breath, putting on her most serious face. "I can't see what lies under the surface of his skin. What if we were to cut him, only for him to bleed to death? Tobias, I won't do such a thing to him. It's too great a risk." She didn't have to feign how much the idea bothered her, her stomach roiling.

Fortunately her words seemed to have impressed Tobias, who looked shaken by the scenario she'd presented. "I . . . no, no, of course. I didn't realize." He took a fast gulp of tea and coughed. Jean would swear he had gone almost as pasty pale as Muirin had earlier. Several long moments passed in silence, with Tobias squinting down into his teacup like he was fixing to tell Jean her fortune. Either that, or tell her off.

Leaning forward, he lifted his gaze, staring directly into her eyes. "You swear it's nothing but a bit of skin? Nothing else odd about the boy?"

Jean did not look away, leery of being the first to blink. "I promise. He's a perfectly normal child." She tossed out a laugh that rang hollow in her own ears, and forced a smile. "You know boys. He'll be the awe of his classmates when he starts at school. I bet he'll swim like a fish."

Tobias gave a slight twitch. Then he swallowed and shook his head, laughing. He smeared a bit of jam onto his biscuit, then leaned back in his chair and began to tell her about a boy he'd once known, who could touch the tip of his tongue to his nose.

"Muirin," said Jean. "Where are we going?"

Jean sat in the stern of her father's little wooden dory, exactly where she always used to when she and her father went out in the boat, and she absently hoped he wouldn't be too angry that they had taken it without asking his permission. He'd been angry when she'd taken it out with Jo.

Jo had gone away in a wagon, under a bonnet, with a stiff back.

Muirin looked up. Her face was plain and calm, silvered by the moonlight. "Is secret," she said. Her hair was loose, and it hung in thick, glossy waves down her back, spilling forward over her shoulder as she bent to pull the oar. She had only one.

They went in a circle.

Jean looked around them. The sea was smooth as glass, a dark mirror. She could not see the land. She wondered if she ought to worry. There was something important she was meant to be doing, but she couldn't remember what it was. "Muirin," she said again, "I don't understand. Where are we going?"

Muirin pulled the oar. She had only one.

They went in a circle.

A chill went through Jean, although there was no hint of a breeze. The little boat rocked. She wanted something solid under her feet. "Let's turn back. It's time to go home."

This time Muirin did not look up. "Good knot," she said. "Good knot."

The baby laughed.

Jean looked around the boat. The baby wasn't there. Something curled in the pit of her stomach. "Muirin. Where is Kiel?" Jean began craning her neck. "Kiel? Kiel!"

There was a splash behind her. The baby was in the water.

"Muirin! For the love of God, stop! Kiel!" Jean turned, leaning on the back of the boat, looking behind them. A seal popped its head out of the water. She leaned out as far as she could, fingers reaching.

Muirin pulled the oar. She had only one. They went in a circle.
Jean overbalanced and fell forward.
The baby laughed.

Jean sat bolt upright with a gasp.

The house was dark and silent, the only light a dim grayness at the loft's single peaked window. The rain had stopped sometime in the night, and the absence of water pounding on the roof made the quiet beneath it feel heavy and thick.

She flopped down onto her back again, trying to slow the pounding of her heart. The dream was already dissolving into an unsettling mist, and there wasn't a sound from downstairs. Muirin and the baby were both sleeping, and the laughter that rang in Jean's head couldn't have come from Kiel. He was barely a week old, after all, and babies didn't laugh for the first few months—

Jean froze in the middle of turning over her pillow.

Because he *had* laughed.

Last night, as they sat before the fire, the baby had laughed. Jean was sure of it. It had seemed so utterly natural in that warm, glowing evening that she hadn't considered it strange, beyond how much Kiel had sounded like a puppy trying to bark. She'd been distracted, tired after a long day, a proper dinner. Too many thoughts rattling in her head. Muirin, leaning against her knee. Long dark hair, soft and shining in the firelight.

Jean's fingers twitched. Holding herself very still, she stared up into the inky darkness between the rafters and kept her thoughts on Kiel. A babe might be more advanced in some way or other; it wasn't so unusual. This one rolled over sooner, that one spoke before their brother. There was a silver coin in Kiel's basket, and even if there hadn't been, fairy changelings weren't real.

But . . . *laughing.* Already.

Nothing else odd about the boy?

I promise. He's a perfectly normal child.

Jean yanked the covers up over her head, squeezing her eyes shut. He hadn't laughed. She was being ridiculous. Kiel . . . *Toby* . . . was a perfectly normal child, just as she'd claimed to his father. He made a lot of strange puppy sounds, and she had taken one of them for laughter. That was all.

She tried very hard not to think of anything else but going back to sleep.

8

Every morning of the past week, Muirin had woken as Jean tried to creep past the bed where she slept. Jean would let herself out to tend to the animals, and Muirin would be up and dressed by the time she returned, the kettle hung over the fire. Not today. Today when Jean came down the narrow stairs, tired as if she hadn't slept at all, she found Muirin already up and ready to face the day, dressed and just finished feeding the baby. Kiel was at her shoulder, and she swayed rhythmically from side to side, turning in a sort of dance as she patted his back, waiting on a burp. Muirin was a lovely dancer, just as Tobias had claimed: graceful and smooth, as if she were moving through water. Jean could have stood and watched her all day. Muirin looked up at Jean's step on the stair, giving a soft and slightly wistful smile.

Jean set a foot wrong at that smile, and slid on her heel down the last step, landing with a thump. She grabbed at the rail to keep from going down in a heap, laughing weakly. "Clumsy. No wonder I always wake you! You're up early." It wasn't quite a question, but it was close.

Muirin was soft voiced. "Morning, is last here. I go out, with you."

Jean felt her eyebrows creep up. "I'm not doing anything special, Muirin. You really want to watch me feed goats?" It seemed a bit silly, but Muirin nodded, all eagerness, and a flush of warmth rolled over Jean. It was hard not to be flattered that Muirin wanted to snatch a few extra moments with her before she left. Still, she was going. By this afternoon, Jean would have the place to herself again. The warm swell ebbed, and Jean shrugged. "If you want to, then. But bundle the baby up, it's cold."

Muirin rolled her eyes, making a face. "I know is cold, Jean."

"I know you know." Muirin blinked at the repetition, then laughed, and Jean smiled. "I'm sorry. Just because it's your first time taking him out doesn't mean you can't figure out how to dress him. Some people just have no common sense, and I'm a bit too used to that sort, I'm afraid."

Muirin didn't seem offended. She simply nodded. "Think I, not much common is."

"What, common sense?" Jean snickered. Muirin had a wit on her, and it was coming out more and more by the day. "You're not wrong."

Muirin had already set the kettle over the fire to heat for a cup of tea on their return, so they both wrapped up in shawls and scarves, making ready to go out. Muirin's shawl was the color of the bluish-gray rocks along the harbor shore, and instead of mitts like Jean's, she had a pair of fine felted gloves to match. Tobias Silber might not have been a rich man, but he had taken pains to see his handsome wife well outfitted, whether or not she ever went anywhere that she would be seen.

As Muirin wound a thick blanket around Kiel, making sure his little webbed fingers were well tucked in and his head covered, Jean stole a glance over her shoulder at him and was met with a gurgle and the blinking of round black eyes. It threw off the last of the odd, unsettling mist that had trailed Jean out of her dreams—she really was imagining things. Laughing, indeed. It was a shame, though, that she'd not be there for his real first laugh, now they were going. She fetched the milking pail from behind the door as Muirin picked Kiel up and settled him into her arms, and out they went.

Jean held the door, letting Muirin go ahead, and then nearly ran right into the back of her when she stopped abruptly just outside the door, breathing deep in the fresh salty air and taking in the view: the dry, yellowed grasses waving along the road, and beyond them, the green-blue sweep of the sea. The breeze was brisk, and the sky low and gray, although Jean thought it didn't seem like rain anymore, but only a dark sort of a day.

She slipped around Muirin, squeezing herself past the door-frame, and set off toward the henhouse. After a moment, Muirin followed along behind her. Jean opened the door for the chickens, though it was unlikely they would venture out right away on such a bleak morning, and lifted the lid to peek into their nest box. It really was coming on winter, for there wasn't a single egg. She hoped there might be at least a few more before the hens left off laying until spring.

"Jean!" Muirin's fingers plucked at Jean's arm like a harp string, her voice quiet but excited. "Jean!"

The vixen was padding down along the path from the spring, her white-tipped tail high and bouncing, coming straight toward them. Muirin stared at it, round-eyed. Realizing it had become the center of attention, the little red fox stopped midstride, one dark forepaw held above the ground, staring back at them both with golden eyes.

All was still, aside from their breath, coming out in white puffs in the cold air. Then Kicker let out an ungodly, wheezing bleat from inside the goat shed, impatiently waiting for them to move on from the chickens. They leapt together, Jean clutching Muirin's arm, and the fox flattened itself low to the ground, bracing all four of her paws wide before racing straight past them into the tall marsh grass, vanishing in an instant.

"Damn that goat," Jean said in a shaking voice. Muirin looked at her, and they both laughed. Jean realized both her hands were still wrapped around Muirin's arm. Releasing it, she stepped back.

"What is call, she?" Muirin asked.

"That's a fox," Jean told her, breathing evenly as she tried to slow her heartbeat. "A vixen."

"Ah." Muirin glanced off toward where the animal had vanished, then turned her gaze back to Jean. "Red, she. Like—" She reached out, stepping close once more, and Jean froze again, her heart skipping a beat. *It doesn't mean anything,* she told herself. Catching the curling end of Jean's rust-colored braid, Muirin drew it from the folds of Jean's scarf, pulling it forward over her shoulder with gentle, deliberate fingers. "Is same." Muirin's voice was low, musical. She looked right at Jean. "Eyes, too."

Don't be foolish—she's just touchy-feely, is all. You know she is. Don't be so stiff, she'll think there's something wrong . . .

Muirin wet her lips with the tip of her tongue.

Christ. Jean was going to fall over if she went much longer without breathing.

Kicker made another anguished bleat, and a loud bang came from inside the shed. "For Christ's sake!" Jean blurted, jumping again. The end of her braid slipped out of Muirin's hand, thumping against Jean's chest in time with her heart as she turned and tromped away toward the rough clapboard building, wondering when, exactly, in the past week she'd become so skittish. It had to be too much time spent dealing with other people. "Shut up, I'm coming!"

Muirin's lips were twitching as she caught up, but she didn't say anything else, leaning quiet and thoughtful with her back against the fence and observing Jean as she dealt with the goats. They'd be completely dry in another week, or two at most, if Jean had to make a guess. She'd have to see about getting a billy goat brought 'round for a visit, and soon, if she wanted kids to sell and milk again come spring. She'd already left it awfully late in the year.

They were halfway back to the house after milking the goats when Muirin stopped.

"Jean," she said, "have you boat?" Changing course, Muirin headed toward the shore of the marsh pond. Jean's father's old dory was there, turned upside down to keep the rain out as it had been since the final time he'd gone out in it, nearly two years before. Its pretty teal paint had come off in great curling peels, leaving the little boat as bleached and silvery as the shingles of the house. Jean set her half-full pail of milk down in the frosty grass of the yard and followed her.

"It was my father's," she said. "I don't take it out myself. He showed me how, of course, but I'm not sure I'd be able to row it back alone if I got into trouble."

Muirin pulled the oar. She had only one. They went in a circle.

Jean shook herself. Bad enough dreaming by night, let alone with her eyes wide open. She considered the boat again, and a notion occurred to her. "I wonder if Tobias might buy it. He'd have a use for it, at least."

Muirin put out her hand to stroke the soft gray wood of one of the old oars leaned up against the side of the dory. "No," she said, calmly certain. "You keep. Might need."

Jean laughed. "I doubt it. I'm not likely to take to fishing. But maybe I will keep it, just for . . . hmm. Sentimental reasons? Da used to take me out in it." Muirin nodded, understanding, then looked out over the marsh pond. There was the tiniest wrinkle in the middle of her high, smooth forehead.

Jean swallowed. "Muirin?"

Muirin turned to look at her again. "Hmm?"

Jean took a careful step closer. "What were you doing, the night Kiel was born? Why were you out here?" She hadn't asked yet, and seeing Muirin in almost the same spot where Jean had first found her, knowing she was about to go back to the place she'd started out from, Jean was struck with a need to be certain. Certain Muirin was truly safe to send home, not beset with hidden melancholy, as Jean's mother had been. Surely by now Muirin would be able to tell her, would trust her with such a thing. Would have the words she needed, even if they weren't exactly right.

Muirin's lips pressed together. Her eyes slid from Jean to the baby in her arms, and then off across the pond, up the hill toward her home. When her voice finally came, it was dull, flat, the rich rolling burr gone right out of it. "I . . . fool. Think—" Muirin stopped and shook her head. After a moment, she went on. "Glad, of you. Was good. Is." She smiled at Jean. "Friends now."

Jean felt a pleasant, unfamiliar warmth in her chest as she smiled back, though it did cramp slightly as well. They'd best get on with breakfast. Tobias wasn't likely to arrive before noon, but it was better she had Muirin and the babe ready. "Come on," she said. "The kettle must be hot by now." They started back toward the house together. Jean was bending to pick up the pail from where she'd left it in the middle of the yard when Muirin spoke once more.

"Jean? What *thief* is?"

Jean stopped mid-motion and looked up at her. "Thief? Why? Where did you hear that word?"

Muirin shifted the baby in her arms without meeting Jean's eye. "Tobias. Say fox, red one? She thief. Want to catch."

Jean sighed and lifted the half-full pail. "I already told him to leave it be. Thief . . . A thief takes things that don't belong to them. They steal things. Sometimes foxes get into a coop, and eat eggs, or even the chickens, so people say they steal them. That their hens were stolen."

Muirin considered this with a small frown. "Steal is—take away." She paused before the door of the house, turning to gaze out across the road again, toward the sea.

Jean paused, too, contemplating the hungry, longing look on Muirin's face, and set the pail back down on the stone step.

"Muirin," she said, straightening, "would you like to go down to see the beach before you leave?"

Muirin's head swiveled, and she stared at Jean as if she couldn't believe what she'd heard, before breaking into a broad smile. She caught Jean's hand and squeezed it, nodding enthusiastically.

If Jean had harbored any lingering doubts about Muirin going down near the water, the look she was giving Jean now was enough to make her forget them. Anything that lit Muirin's eyes like that could only be good for her. Jean managed an awkward smile in return, and patted Muirin's hand once before she released it again.

They followed the path out through the gate, crossing over the road and the bridge, then picked their way down through the dry grass and rocks to the pebble beach. Little stones rolled under their shoes as they walked toward the water. Muirin watched the sea and its slow heaving out beyond the waves that broke along the shore and rolled in, foaming, toward them.

Jean mostly watched Muirin. The wind was stronger along the shore, and it blew her black hair out behind her like a banner as she turned her face into it, her eyes welling up with tears from the stiff, cold breeze. Jean looked down quickly, before her own stinging eyes could do the same, and caught a glimpse of something gleaming dully among the pebbles. She bent to look closer. It was a bit of pale blue glass, slightly bigger than a halfpenny piece, worn smooth by the sea.

Funny how the sea could do that, wear off all of a thing's too-sharp edges. Jean wondered how long she would have to be rolled about in the waves to smooth out her own.

Pulling off her mitten to pick up her find, she dug her fingers into the loose pebbles. A small, sharp pain caught her by surprise, and she winced, letting the bit of glass drop with a hiss. Jean couldn't even see a cut at first, until the barest hint of blood welled up to the surface, a thin red line in the pad of her index finger. The part of the glass that had been hidden under the stones must still have held an edge.

She hadn't realized Muirin was watching, but suddenly she was there, crouching down next to Jean as she tucked the baby into the crook of one arm. Picking up the piece of blue glass between careful fingers, Muirin turned it, inspecting its edges—there was the broken place that had caught Jean unaware, shining sharp and bright compared to the milky-soft smoothness of the rest. Muirin regarded the offender with a sigh.

"Ready not," she said, then stood and threw the bit of glass out into the waves before looking at Jean again. "In sea." She touched Jean's hand, a light brush of slate-blue felt, then pointed toward the water, her firm tone reminding Jean of the way she herself often spoke to her new mothers. "Is good for hurts." Muirin kept her eyes fixed on Jean, her lips pursed.

She had a point. Salt water was good for sore throats and the like, drawing out pain and swelling. Jean swallowed and turned away to follow a wave out as it receded. She dunked her hand under the water for an instant, then darted backward with quick steps before the next wave could break and wet her skirts. At first, the only sensation was numbing cold, followed by a keen, sweet stinging in the little cut. Jean flapped her hand about for a moment, feeling foolish, then shoved her mitten back on.

A seal popped its head out of the water, barely fifteen feet offshore.

"Oh!" Jean breathed. "Muirin, Muirin, look!"

Muirin gave a sharp gasp beside her.

The seal let out a high-pitched bark, and a second sleek head popped up, and then a third and a fourth, smaller than the first two. All were silver-gray and speckled, some lighter, and some darker, all with long twitching whiskers and great dark shining eyes. Jean had never seen so many at once, nor so close. One of the bigger seals pushed in closer to the shore and made a rolling, curious inquiry that could have been either a purr or a growl. Jean took a quick step back, in case it was the latter. She wasn't sure what one did in the event of being attacked by a herd of seals. It seemed wise to keep a distance.

Muirin began speaking in a rapid and excited babble. She had lapsed back into her own language, and at first Jean was bemused by her having forgotten herself, unsure how to respond. But then Muirin plucked Kiel from her shoulder and turned him to face the water, pointing and waving, bouncing him, and Jean realized that no, Muirin was talking to the baby, showing the seals to him. She let out a loud, free, barking laugh that surprised Jean, but not half so much as it seemed to surprise the seals, who responded with a raucous chorus of barking of their own, huffing and growling, and a great deal of splashing about.

Jean had never seen anything like it, had never realized how *big* they'd be up close. The nearest seal made another lunge forward, as if it might come right up onto the shore. Jean gasped and grabbed Muirin's arm, trying to tug her away from the water. Muirin set her feet and bark-laughed again, thrilled.

"Muirin!"

Tobias's voice split the air like the crack of a whip.

Jean jumped, releasing Muirin's arm, and Muirin whirled about so quickly that Jean feared she might drop the baby and reached out to steady her. Kiel set up a wail. Tobias jumped from his wagon, striding over the road and down across the beach toward them, pebbles crunching under his boots. Muirin stood statue-stiff next to Jean, eyes glued on her husband as he came, all the laughter and excitement gone out of her. He stopped a few paces short of them, and Jean was glad of it. He had a storm cloud look on his face like none she'd seen on him before, and she was half certain he was going to grab hold of the pair of them, shake them both soundly, and then march them back up to the road by the ears like children he'd caught doing something foolishly dangerous.

"Muirin," he said in a low, tightly controlled voice, "fetch your things. It's time to go." Muirin gave a bobbing nod. Turning to Jean, she pushed the still-blubbering baby into her arms before scuttling off up the beach and toward the house, leaving Jean standing there staring at Tobias, trying to work up some saliva in her dry mouth to say something to him.

Finally, she found her voice again. "Tobias, I—"

"Wild animals." He cut Jean off. "Those are *wild* animals! Have you never seen the teeth on a seal? Never, *never* let them get that close to you." His voice shook, his breath uneven. He barely blinked, glaring at her as if she'd somehow purposely summoned the animals herself to spite him, or perhaps because he simply couldn't believe her colossal lack of judgment. Then he squinted at her sharply. "Why are you out here?"

Jean wasn't quite sure how to respond. He was accusing her of something, but she had no idea what. Her shoulders went tense and tight, as she made her voice even and calm, placating. "We were just taking a bit of fresh air. It's good for the baby, and Muirin, too. Tobias, why don't you come in for a cup of tea?" The man could stand some calming down; he was positively twitching with nerves. "I wasn't thinking you'd be here so early."

"Neither was I," he said. "I was planning on driving into town for a few things first, but I saw you down the shore when I came 'round the point. I . . ." Tobias peered over Jean's head, out to sea, his blue eyes scanning for some threat on the cloudy horizon. He cleared his throat. "I ain't sure about this weather holding. I'd rather we got home now, as I'm here."

"If you really think so . . ." Everything was moving too quickly. They were supposed to linger at her table over a last cup of tea, discuss what to expect from the baby, set a time for Jean to come by to check in on Muirin . . .

"I do," Tobias said. "We'll have snow later, mark my words." He turned and tramped back up the beach toward the road. Jean followed along in his wake, trying to soothe the crying baby as she went. It was hard to keep up with such a long-legged man, especially over such uneven footing. They arrived at his wagon just as Muirin came out of the house, carrying her small bag of belongings.

Jean glanced up at Tobias as he watched Muirin's approach. He had a hugely relieved expression on his face, and she wondered if he'd worried for his wife this much the whole time she'd been away. It was one thing to be protective, but this seemed overmuch. There couldn't have been a safer place for the young mother and her newborn child than a midwife's cabin. It made Jean wonder, and she had already done a great deal of wondering.

"I'll come up to visit in a day or two. Check in, see how you're getting along on your own. Tobias . . ." Jean paused, adjusting the baby in her arms as his wails subsided into snuffling, then she went on, cautious, "You'll remember what I said, won't you? Muirin can't stay in the house all day, every day. It's not good for her."

He nodded without taking his eyes off Muirin as she joined them, then took her bag and put it up into the back of the wagon without a word. Muirin stopped before Jean, giving her a long look, with her lips pursed as if she had a great many things she wanted to say but wasn't sure where to start. Jean discovered that a lump had lodged itself in her throat, and she coughed.

"Muirin," she said, "it was . . . so nice having you to stay. I promise, I'll come up to visit you— Oof." The air left her lungs as Muirin threw her arms around Jean, the baby held tight between them.

"Soon come, Jean." Muirin's warm breath stirred the hair by Jean's ear. "Please. You are friend, mine." She took a deep breath, then gripped Jean's arms as she spoke again in a sudden rush, her voice so low Jean could barely make out her words. "Good knot, is. Good knot."

Jean's stomach lurched, flopping over like a landed fish, like waking from a nightmare. Muirin drew away to give her a deep, searching look before darting forward and brushing a kiss on her right cheek. Then she released Jean's arms and stepped back. Tobias caught his wife about the waist and lifted her up into the wagon.

"Thank you, Jean," he said as he took the baby from her unresisting arms. He smiled. "I won't forget how good you've been to Muirin. To all of us."

Jean nodded dumbly. Her feet were nailed to the ground.

Tobias passed little Kiel up to Muirin, then climbed up to sit beside her, taking the reins in hand. He gave them a flick, clucking his tongue at the big horse. As they drove off up the rise, Muirin turned, looking back.

Jean had done this before, had watched another girl drive away, in another wagon, with another man. She hadn't been able to say a word then, either. She wasn't sure if Muirin was looking back at her or at the sea, but somehow Jean managed to raise her hand before the wagon disappeared behind the trees.

Then she stood alone in the road, the cold wind stinging against her right cheek, and turned woodenly to look back out at the water herself. The seals were gone.

Good knot. Muirin's voice echoed in her hollow, ringing ears, and Jean swallowed. How could she have missed it, have not understood her from the very start? Muirin's silence in Tobias's presence. Her reaction, when Jean had pronounced her fit to go home. All that time, watching Tobias for a reason for Muirin's behavior, a reason for her own uneasiness and distrust of the man, and never finding a single solid thing to set her finger on. Under it all, nagging at Jean even in her dreams, was the tangled answer Muirin had given the very first time she was asked. Not trying to speak of how she was tied to her husband in marriage, but of the union itself. *Good knot.*

Good, not.

Not good.

9

No matter what herbs were hanging from the beams in Anneke's kitchen, the woman's tidy house always smelled faintly of sage. That, and milky tea. Jean had never known Anneke not to have a pot of tea on the stove in all the years she'd been her mentor, or even before that, all the way back to Jean's earliest memories. Her father used to joke that Anneke wasn't happy with her "cup of brew" unless she'd boiled the pot until it was strong enough to stand a spoon in. In Anneke's opinion there was only one good way to drink tea, and that way was "thick."

Opinions were something Anneke Ernst had always had in abundance, and that hadn't changed a bit as she'd gotten older. She'd been midwife back when the town had got its first real, permanent doctor, and she'd butted heads with the man constantly, trying to convince him she knew what she was about. Anneke hadn't been much more than a girl herself then, and the fact that her mother was Native hadn't helped. There were people like Anneke scattered across the colony, where there had been intermarriages between the newcome settlers and the

Natives—men and women with thick, dark hair and wide-cheeked faces that were looked on with suspicion, more often than not. That their names were German or French or Scottish or English didn't make much difference. It had taken her years to earn even the doctor's most grudging respect. Anneke knew what it was to have a man not really believe what you said, even when you clearly knew better than he did.

Anneke's husband had been lost along with a whole fishing crew in an August gale when their children were still young, and without him there to gainsay her in any of her whims, she'd gotten used to never being contradicted. Her heavy black hair had long since gone to silver, her hands twisted up with arthritis until she'd had to leave off catching babies. Her grown daughter, Mary Beth, came by nearly daily to keep the house and fill the kettle for her now, but Anneke was still more than happy to tell you exactly what was what with only the smallest excuse, grinning out of her broad, brown face the entire time.

Jean was generally glad of this. It was why she'd made the long walk to Anneke's house in the village straightaway, as soon as she'd gathered her wits back together. There was no one whose advice Jean valued more.

But right now, Anneke was not grinning at all, and Jean was starting to think that in spite of how she'd longed for the woman's advice all week, she'd set herself up for a good bit more opinioning than she'd really wanted when she'd told Anneke about Muirin. Although Jean supposed it could have been worse; Anneke's son, Laurie, might have been there, too, in off the boats with a mouth full of sass.

"That *is* a fine tangle." Anneke's forehead wrinkled. It was already furrowed so deeply on its own that this wasn't necessarily a sign of her thoughts on the matter. That was the other side of Anneke's opinions: how cagey and closemouthed she became while she was working up to arriving at them. The elderly woman's mouth had drawn up tighter and tighter at every word as Jean explained the situation with Muirin and Tobias, until her mentor had resembled nothing so much as a dried-apple doll. "But you're not worried anymore that this Muirin of yours is likely to do anything rash, then, at least?"

"I don't think so. I kept thinking of Mama at first, when Muirin was acting so strangely, so I couldn't *not* get involved, but maybe I should have realized—"

"No, no, I would have wondered the same." Anneke ran a gnarled thumb along the rim of her teacup, then squinted at it thoughtfully before fixing her gaze on Jean again. "You were right to keep a weather eye on her until you were sure." Jean had known Anneke would see the similarities between Muirin and her own mother. Both of them young and pretty, both Scots, even. Neither a local girl, each newly come from away to a remote place where they knew not a soul, far from their family and friends. Each freshly married, and with a baby soon after. Though Janet had at least been able to speak the language, had made friends in the village. Not that it mattered in the end.

Muirin had no one at all, except for her husband. And now Jean, who was at least certain at this point that the woman did not, in fact, intend to fling herself into the sea, however strange her behavior was. Now Jean had other suspicions.

"You never saw a man with a longer face than Silber's was when I first said I wanted Muirin and the babe to stay put. He looked half ready to try to steal them away in spite of me." She forced out a humorless laugh. "I thought he was just lonely out there, with only the horse to keep him company."

"Hmm. Well, there *is* always the chance he was just over-reacting this morning, I suppose. No doubt he'll rest easier with his wife and the babe safe to home again," Anneke mused. It was entirely reasonable, as was her tone as she went on, a thing that made Jean wonder what else the woman was thinking and not saying. "And so will you, Jeanie. You look exhausted; you've got bags. If the woman recovered well and hasn't said anything else to make you uneasy, there wasn't any good reason for you to have delayed her going home."

Wrapping her hands more securely around the blue-and-white teacup, Jean inhaled the fragrant steam that rose from it and pointedly ignored the comment about her appearance. "I told you, she's not said a thing to put me in mind of Mama since that first morning. She's a bit of an odd duck, maybe, but she's not a danger to herself. It's what she said as they were leaving, after he blew up like that."

Exactly *what* Muirin had meant wasn't clear, except that something was wrong, and not at all what Jean had originally thought. Not something wrong with Muirin herself, but something at home. Something to do with her husband, Jean feared. Something that was enough to set Muirin to whispering low and secret, her breath warm against—

Jean twitched and rubbed at her ear with the heel of her hand. "I don't know. I just wish you could have seen her, Anneke. There's something about her that makes me wonder how she even . . ." She trailed off, mistrusting the look Anneke was now giving her, as if she suddenly found Jean's judgment suspect. "What?"

Anneke spoke exactly two words, giving Jean a too-knowing look. "Josephine Keddy?"

Jean flinched. It wasn't fair of her mentor to bring up Jo, and it wasn't like that. Not at all, and it never could be. She and Jo had been the closest of friends, joined at the hip, telling each other all their secrets. Friends first, and then more than friends, right up until the awful Sunday at church when Jean found she couldn't get close enough to exchange a single word with Jo anymore without some member of her family appearing to hurry her away, a solid living barrier sprung up between them.

Mrs. Keddy had slandered nineteen-year-old Jean to anyone who'd listen, that she wasn't to be trusted around their daughters, a filthy sinner and a bad influence . . . and in what seemed like no time at all, Jo had been married. She hadn't tried to see Jean again once she was Mrs. Gaudry, not even to explain what had happened, how they'd been found out. Jean was so angry that Jo could have just gone along and done what they told her, married some man and gone away—Jo'd liked the boys, too, but Jean had been so sure Jo had wanted her more than anyone else. And she'd been young enough to think that it would matter.

Anneke was the only person who had really understood, except for Laurie. Anneke had been the one to sit Jean down after and put cup after cup of sweet, strong tea in front of her and say that Mrs. Keddy was a stupid, spiteful old cow, that Jo probably hadn't been given a choice. The one who'd linked her arm in Jean's and insisted she keep coming along to births and pretend nothing was wrong when people went on whispering in the village, even after Jo had gone. Who insisted Jean act proud and strong, like she had nothing to hide, however she felt. Anneke had started refusing to set foot in a birthing room unless Jean was welcomed there, too, and pushed her to work harder than ever, until no one could argue with her skills, would respect her whether they wanted to or not. Besides, with how quickly her arthritis had been progressing, Anneke had needed Jean to be ready to take over as midwife by the end of that year. People needed to trust her again.

Jean had found life was easier if she didn't involve herself with anyone too much outside her work. For four years now she'd kept her distance from everyone unless she was needed; that way no one could ask any awkward questions. There was no reason for any more talk. Jean kept no close friends save Laurie, who was never home anymore anyway, and she never lingered for tea with anyone, either, except with her old mentor.

No, Anneke didn't need to worry. Jean wasn't letting anyone get that close again. If being alone cut, well. She'd learned to deal with that hollow sting. But loss was a filleting knife, and Jean didn't think she could take another of those slashes under her ribs.

She drew a deep breath before responding and kept her voice steady and firm. "It isn't anything like Jo. Not at all. I mean, Muirin's lovely; you'd have to be blind not to think so. But it's nothing like that, why she's so on my mind. The whole thing is just so strange, and I want to help her. She needs help."

Anneke raised an eyebrow and pursed her lips but said nothing.

Grateful for small blessings, Jean pushed on with the original topic. "Something isn't right with them. I wondered at first if he might be cruel to her, when she was always so quiet and strange around him. But it didn't seem to fit before, with how he acted. Now, I'm not so sure."

Anneke gave a considering hum. "Well . . . there's things as don't show on the outside, that go on in a home."

"Exactly." Jean leaned forward on her elbows, relieved that Anneke saw the possibility, too. "They're so isolated out there. There's no one for her to talk with. And there's another thing! She and Tobias hardly talk at all, or at least, they never did in front of me. I honestly think he *doesn't* talk to her! When she was with *me,* she spent every minute pointing to things asking, 'Is what, is what?' and as far as I can tell, she never forgets any of it. Muirin's bright as a new pin, and her English has gotten better these past few days, more than some people's would in weeks! She'd be bright and cheery, babbling to the baby . . . and then *he'd* come in and she'd go silent all over again." Jean paused to take a breath and blew it out, irritable. "I wish Laurie was home. He knew Tobias, didn't he, at school?"

Anneke shrugged. "Wasn't one of Laurie's friends, but they're close enough in age they would have been in school together. Tobias might have been a class ahead of him? I remember I was out-to-there pregnant with Laurie when Tobias was born, waddling around looking like a snake that swallowed an egg." She paused, considering for a moment. "Big head on that baby. Like all the Silber boys. Stubborn hardheads, the lot of them, and the parents, too. Small wonder they don't any of them talk to each other. I recall him being a sweet little lad, though I think he mostly got lost in the shuffle, being the baby. Eleven children, that woman had, and not one girl, if you'd believe it."

Jean could believe that more easily than she could Tobias Silber—with his big fisherman's hands—having ever been anyone's sweet little lad. "Hardheaded or no, Tobias thinks Muirin hung the moon so far as I can tell, and I've watched him. Before today, he never once raised his voice, and he's always been so gentle. He seemed more scared than anything, and he comes on like he'd do anything for her—but then that's the other thing that makes me wonder; you'd think he'd have been trying to teach her English himself all along, and that she'd want to talk to him, now she's starting to figure it out. But if anything, I'd swear she was hiding it! And, unless he's doing something I can't see, it doesn't make any damned sense." Jean kept her mouth shut on the fact that she'd made herself complicit in Muirin's silent charade. She'd done the right thing, keeping Muirin's secret, she was sure of it.

Anneke didn't respond right away. She pulled the china sugar bowl toward herself and stirred another spoonful of sweetness into her now-cold tea, slow and thoughtful, before looking up at Jean again. "It's been a long week, for all of you. Perhaps it *is* nothing. But even if it isn't, you ought to keep well out of it. It's not your business. There ain't anything wrong with being a friend to the girl, though, and I can't see any harm in you talking to her yourself, helping her with her words. Not just for her sake, either, Jeanie. You keep too much to yourself still, after all this time. *You* need friends, too, whatever you want to think."

Jean drank down the last of her tea.

"Laurie's coming home at Christmas, by the by. To stay for the winter."

"What? Really?" Jean couldn't recall the last time Laurie had been home for more than a few days, let alone for a whole season. No, she could. At thirty, he was something of a perennial bachelor, in rather a similar fashion to Jean being a spinster at four and twenty. He swore he'd not be tied to anyone but the sea until Christmas three years past, when he'd spoken to Jean of a fellow who was teaching him to speak Spanish, who lived on some island in one of those warm places he went to. Dalian was his name. Laurie's tone had been full of affection, and the next fall he'd sent a letter to say he was overwintering down south, with Dal. He'd done the same again last year.

"Strange, I was sure he'd stay south again."

"Mmm," Anneke hummed. "I ain't got a mind to question it, if it means he's here more than a week for once. Children are born to leave you, fine, but they ought to pay a visit more than once a year!"

Jean snorted into her empty cup.

When she lowered it, Anneke was looking at her again with one eyebrow quirked, considering. "It took him a while, but Laurie found himself someone, and he's been happy. I ain't gonna begrudge it, even if I wish he'd found them closer to home. Now if only we could do the same for you, Jeanie!" Her face cracked with one of those smiles that said Jean was about to be given a hard time. "Remember what I told you, after that mess with the Keddy girl?"

Jean remembered the summer after Jo went away. Sometimes, Anneke's Native cousins would come by her house in the summer and visit, crowding into the kitchen—a great flood of women, young, old, and everything in between, carrying on a dozen conversations at once, in and out of at least three languages, while children ran everywhere underfoot. Jean always felt there were far too many of these women to all be Anneke's true cousins, and sometimes she found them a bit strange, but she liked them all the same. They were interesting, and they smiled more easily than most of the people she knew in the village, and laughed more readily, too. Anneke had gone so overboard that July trying to make a match for Jean with the daughter of one of her cousins that Jean had finally laughed for the first time in months, and told her to knock off flinging the poor girl at her.

She rolled her eyes, setting the teacup on the scarred wooden table with a dull click. "Anneke, for pity's sake—!"

Anneke squinted one of her bright black eyes and pointed a gnarled finger at her. "It's never the first wave that swamps you—the second one is always bigger!"

Jean couldn't help laughing. The woman looked positively gleeful. "You're ridiculous. Muirin is a married woman, with a child!"

Anneke sat bolt upright in her chair. "Who said anything about the fisherman's wife?" she demanded, her voice sharpening like a midwinter wind. "Don't go getting caught up in that kind of a net, missy!"

Jean's cheeks burned. "I'm not looking to get caught up in it! You think I haven't any sense?" she snapped, before she could stop herself. Taking a breath, she forced her shoulders back down. Anneke was infuriating, but Jean knew she shouldn't rise to the bait. "Muirin doesn't want me for anything but a friend, and that's plenty."

Anneke cleared her throat, tetchy. "If you say so." She did not look convinced. Worse, she clutched her teacup close below her nose with both of her crabbed hands, peering over the rim as if she knew something that Jean did not.

"What?"

"I'm glad she's out from under your roof. You need some breathing space, to get your head on straight again, and they need to settle." Anneke knit her eyebrows together, frowning again, stern. "You keep well clear of the pair of them for a week or two, at least."

"I told you, I just want to help!" Jean was not going one step further down this road. Besides, she already knew she ought to give Muirin and Tobias time, no matter what she thought Muirin had been trying to tell her. It would seem strange if she came knocking at their door too soon.

"*Any*way. I'm going to stop in on Evie Hiltz before I head home, seeing how I'm in town. I'm sure she's going to drop around New Year's, and I want to be close to hand, after her last one. I thought I might come stay right through Christmas? I can help out while I'm here, so long as it won't be too full a house for you with Laurie here, too—"

Nodding, Anneke sat back in her chair as Jean went on, her expression unreadable as she blew over the surface of her long-cold tea.

The mail coach passed through the village late in the afternoon, and Jean caught a ride perched on its backboard with her teeth rattling clear out to the cove, before the coach continued south along the overland route toward Lunenburg without her. She walked the last curves of the shore road quickly as night came on, with her breath puffing in the damp, chill air, wanting to be through the cluster of pines before full dark fell. It wouldn't do to turn an ankle on a stone she couldn't see and have to hobble the rest of the way home.

The slow, steady blinking of Mr. Buchanan's lighthouse had already begun for the evening by the time Jean broke clear of the trees, glowing ghostlike through the sea fog out over the bay. She turned up the path to her house; there was no light glowing in the windows to welcome her tonight, and when she lifted the latch and opened the door, she was greeted by nothing but cold, quiet darkness. She should have banked the fire before she'd gone.

Jean almost fumbled the matches onto the floor, taking them from the tin holder on the mantel in the gathering gloom. The tinder didn't want to catch at first, and she cursed it under her breath as it smoked. Once the fire was crackling, she straightened up, stretched, and shoved her fingers deep into her frizzling hair, unseating most of her hairpins in giving her scalp a moment's good, solid scratch.

She was so tempted to just sit down and not bother with dinner.

Jean stood there for a long moment, then sighed and put a pan over the fire to heat. It had been so much easier somehow, when she'd had someone else there to cook for.

Her house was stark and silent without Kiel's little homely sounds, and Muirin's laughter and questions. Jean packed all of her midwifery tools back into the basket she'd come to think of as the baby's, and sat it away under the table to await the next time she had need of them. She made up Muirin's bed again as well, and it stayed that way.

Jean went on sleeping in the big bed upstairs, unsure of why she didn't want to move back down into the smaller, warmer one, now it was empty. It seemed that in just those few short days with Muirin, she'd grown used to company, used to seeing another shawl hung on the hooks behind the door alongside her own when she went to put it on.

Used to setting out more than one cup for tea.

Used to talking.

Jean found herself talking to the chickens as she scattered corn for them the next morning, and to the goats as she let them out into their pen, and back into their shed at night. Kicker managed to connect a hoof with her shin, and she talked a good deal louder then, in language fit to strip the barnacles off a ship's hull.

Jean talked to the little vixen, too, when she met it again in the yard, telling it her worries, and the wild creature proved a better listener than the livestock, cocking her head in response before she slipped away into the dark space beneath the woodshed. Later, the fox reemerged with a limp mouse dangling in her jaws, and trotted off around the marsh, back toward the den she kept under the roots of the birch trees on the hill, leaving her dainty clawed tracks behind in the thick frost.

Inside Jean's own den, the fire still needed stoking, and the kettle to be heated, and she forced herself to make up the dough for bread and knead it on her own. The quiet echoed in the marrow of her bones.

10

The afternoon of the fourth day after Muirin and Kiel went home found Jean trudging up through the woodlot to the Silbers' house under a sky the color of slate. It was very still, the air tinged with the sharp, damp smell that said snow. She had a basket hung on her elbow, with a loaf of fresh bread, a small jar of green tomato chow, and a larger jar of good, thick soup tucked into it. The sorts of things one brought on a visit to a house with a new mother in it, one who might be having a hard time keeping up with child and cooking and doing a half a hundred other things all at once. Jean carried along her worries, too, tucked cozy into the back of her mind.

Most of them boiled down to that too-hasty departure, Tobias's strange and sudden show of—Jean still wasn't sure what. She couldn't decide if he'd seemed more angered that last morning, or afraid, and either way his behavior was terribly at odds with what she'd thought she knew of him. The cold, stern man she'd seen on the beach was not the soft-spoken fisherman she'd ridden around the point in a wagon with back when all this had begun, who'd blushed when speaking of his wife.

And then there was Muirin.

Muirin, looking back at Jean as Tobias drove her away, the young woman's dark eyes asking something of her that she wasn't sure how to deliver. Muirin's voice at her ear.

Good, not.

Muirin's lips, warm against her cheek.

That, Jean didn't think about at all. It came to her mind, but she most definitely didn't think about it, no. Not when there was so much else to turn over in her thoughts. Jean examined every moment she could recall of both Muirin's and her husband's behavior, every one of the scant few words they'd exchanged in her presence, setting each thing that made her wonder down together in her head, and rearranging them over and over like the pieces of a puzzle, hoping she might somehow make them fit into a clear whole.

Jean's foot scuffed through the dead leaves on the path, and a red squirrel set up a racket of scolding from the branches overhead. Looking up, Jean chirped at it through pursed lips, to no effect. It twitched its tail furiously and went on with its ratcheting, calling her out for an interloper as she continued up the trail.

For all that Muirin had said something was wrong, Jean didn't know for certain if it was truly Tobias, or just the entire lonely situation Muirin had found herself in. Jean wasn't quite sure yet what she could do to help either way, but until she had a better notion of what was going on, her hands were well and truly tied. When Jo had gone away with her husband, Jean had had no choice but to let them alone. Muirin she was free to go and see, at least, but Jean felt the need to be cautious, even so.

She was leery of seeming overeager, of pushing in. How soon would be too soon? Hopefully she had given it long enough.

Anneke wouldn't have thought so, but what Anneke didn't know wouldn't give her reason to peck at Jean, no matter how much she liked to stick her beak in.

Jean wished sticking her own beak in came more naturally. She wasn't even entirely sure what she ought to ask Muirin when she found the chance, although there was at least one possibility she wanted confirmed or denied as soon as she could get a moment alone with the woman. Assuming she even could, of course, with Tobias always hovering. And then what, once she knew for certain? Jean stumbled over a twisted root and caught herself up with a few hasty steps.

Well. She'd do whatever she could to help.

When she came out of the woods, she spotted Tobias almost immediately—he was up on the roof of the house, peering down into the fieldstone chimney. There was no smoke; the fire must have been put out for him to work on whatever he was doing. Jean hoped it wouldn't take him too long or the house would lose all its heat, and that wasn't good for the baby.

Tobias raised his head, spotting Jean as she came up the hill across the frost-feathered field. She couldn't make out the expression on his face with the sky behind him, in spite of how low and dark it was. Maybe that was why he'd chosen to work up on the roof today; the wind had died down as the skies had lowered, and he was less likely than usual to be blown clear off. He waved one arm in greeting. "Go on in," he called down as she approached, cheery and casual. "Tell Muirin it's all right to light the fire again, won't you? I'm about done."

"All right," Jean called back, and headed around the corner of the house to the door, breathing a sigh of relief. The strange mood of the last time she'd seen the man had passed like a storm blown off to sea. Perhaps he really had just been alarmed to see a huge seal so close to his wife and new baby, and Jean had been overreacting herself, out of surprise at the change in him.

As he'd said she could go ahead, Jean didn't bother to knock at the door. She lifted the latch, and put her head in. "Muirin?"

Muirin stood at the cupboard with her sleeves rolled back to her elbows, washing up some dishes. Or rather, she'd long since finished with her washing up, for the glasses were upturned and drying upon a tea towel, but Muirin still stood trailing her fingers through the cooling gray water in the enameled dishpan, gazing wistfully into the last swirls of soap as they rotated and dispersed in the lazy current she made. She started at Jean's voice, turning in a whirl of skirts, her hands dripping dishwater. "Jean!"

Shaking free the last drops of water clinging to her fingertips, Muirin came to Jean smiling, and pulled her into the room with damp hands, shutting the door against the cold outside air. This time, Jean was a bit more prepared when Muirin's warm nose was pressed softly to her cheek, although it was still a passing strange sort of a greeting, to her mind. Heat crept up under Jean's collar, her body caught out stiff and awkward without the knowledge of how to reciprocate. Muirin pulled away slowly, as if disappointed, but then she brightened again, waving Jean toward the chairs before the empty hearth.

"Sit," she said. "Sit, and talk me!"

Jean almost laughed. "Talk *to* you, you mean?"

Muirin nodded, and Jean snorted.

She sat her basket down on the table and began unwrapping herself from her outdoor things. "Muirin, one day you're going to learn enough words that you won't need me around at all anymore. Then what will I do?"

Her attempt at a joke felt flat. Muirin shook her head and reached out to touch Jean's arm, painfully earnest. "Not is true!"

Jean sidestepped, forcing a laugh as she unwound her scarf. "I swear, you will. Oh," she added, folding the scarf with her shawl over the back of a chair by the table, "you can light the fire again if you like, before it gets any colder in here. Tobias said he was about done on the roof." Muirin glanced up at the ceiling as if to check for herself, then nodded, and went to the hearth to see to the fire.

Jean looked around. The inside of the Silbers' house was neat as a pin, and bright with natural light, the walls the soft glowing gold of pine. It was bigger than she'd thought the day she'd been up here with Tobias, surveying it from the outside. Two windows over the table by the door looked off southeast toward the sea. There was a second, smaller room at the back of the house, the foot of a bedstead with a quilt folded over it visible through its half-open door, and another window, facing westward over the field to the forest beyond. A set of stairs went up to the left of the bedroom, into a loft: If it was anything like Jean's house, their attic was probably full of squashes and baskets of apples and potatoes at the moment, with braids of onions hanging from the rafters. She'd stubbed her toe against a pumpkin in her own loft yesterday morning while getting out of bed.

Which reminded her . . .

"I brought you a few things." Jean began unloading her basket onto the table as Muirin coaxed a spark to catch her kindling. "There's a jar of pumpkin soup here for the two of you, and some of those pickled green tomatoes you liked, the night you made the fish? And a loaf of fresh bread from this morning. Thought I'd save you cooking for one day at least, if I could."

Finished, Jean set her basket beneath the table and went to look into the baby's cradle where it sat between the two chairs placed before the hearth. Tobias had done good work on it, she had to admit—she'd never seen a more storybook-perfect cradle. He was skilled with wood carving, for not only did the cradle move smooth and soundless on its rockers, but a jaunty wooden boat sailed across the headboard, over curling wooden waves. Little Kiel was bonny and bright, fixing his sparkling black eyes on Jean and gurgling happily, kicking his feet beneath the blankets. She bent to pick him up, and her back gave an unexpected twinge. She ought to know better than to lean over so far without bending her knees by now. He really was a big baby—if she didn't know better, she'd swear he'd grown noticeably in the mere four days since she'd seen him last.

"Uff," she said, shifting him in her arms so she could hold him more easily. "Kiel, you're like a lead brick. He's still eating well, then?" She turned, and nearly collided with Muirin.

Muirin had straightened from the fresh kindled fire and was watching Jean and the baby with a funny crooked smile on her face. Jean realized this might be the moment she'd hoped for— Tobias was outside still, and they were alone, both of them slotted together into the small space between the chairs and the fire, their skirts bunched together, fabric pressing against Jean's legs.

She took a step back and sat down, fussing to rearrange Kiel's blanket around him in her arms as Muirin slid into the other chair.

"Eats much. Not much sleep, me." Muirin lifted both her hands in a querying shrug. "Big fast is good, yes?"

Jean nodded. "He will grow fast, yes. That's really all babies do to start out. Eat, and soil themselves, and get bigger. Muirin? I need to ask you something." Jean dropped her voice, and Muirin leaned in toward her.

"What is?"

"You said, as you were leaving the other morning with Tobias, that it was . . . not good. I thought that was what you meant, anyway, that you didn't want to come home, and I hadn't realized before. I . . ." Jean steeled herself and cut right to it. "Does he hurt you?"

Muirin blinked. "Hurt . . . ? No, not. Not . . . hurt, him."

Little Kiel suddenly seemed lighter in Jean's arms as an invisible weight tumbled off her shoulders. She didn't know what she would have done had Muirin's answer been yes, but she'd had to ask, to know, before she could do anything. "What *is* wrong, then, Muirin? Can you tell me why it's not good here? I want to help if I can."

Muirin gave her a long, measuring look, as if she was unsure she ought to say anything, or was trying to decide whether she still felt Jean was as worthy of her trust as she had when she'd whispered into her ear that day by the beach. Turning her gaze down to her hands in her lap, Muirin rubbed one of her thumbs over the nail of the other. "I . . . not want be wife. Not want. Have to, I." She looked up at Jean again.

"But why— Oh." Jean glanced down at the baby in her arms. Kiel looked up at her with his wise-old-man's face, the one all babies had, and began to whine. Muirin put out her arms, and Jean passed him to her in silence.

It hadn't even occurred to her, but it explained so much. To-bias's rush to marry a girl that he could barely speak to. His eagerness to please his unhappy wife, to make their life seem so idyllic, with Muirin's fine clothes, and the baby's marvelous cradle. Perhaps this was why he'd kept Muirin away from the prying eyes of the village for so long, even from Jean herself, the village midwife, who would have surely been able to guess—to prevent whispered suspicions about their hasty union. Muirin must have been pregnant *before* they'd wed. That was what had tied them together, the secret Muirin had tried, and failed, to tell.

No wonder her family still hadn't turned up. They probably weren't pleased about the whole situation, their daughter caught in the family way, gone off with a complete stranger . . .

No wonder Muirin was unhappy. It was an old story, and a common one. She'd not have chosen to marry a man like To-bias, to live out here in the middle of nowhere, a place where she didn't even speak the language of her neighbors, not if she didn't have to. Not a woman like Muirin, who was so clearly intelligent, and funny, charming, and lovely enough to have had her pick of suitors, educated men—people she could talk with— back where she'd come from. And now, here she was, stuck, a plain fisherman's wife.

"I'm sorry," Jean said. "That . . . I didn't realize. I wish I could make it easier for you. It's harder to adjust to a thing, I think, when it isn't what you'd wanted. Do you miss your family much, living here?"

For a second Jean was afraid she had said the exactly wrong thing, for she was sure Muirin was going to cry. But Muirin turned her eyes up to the ceiling and blinked hard, then looked at Jean again, bouncing Kiel gently in her arms. "Miss . . . yes, much. Mother, and," she paused, looking for a word, ". . . mother-sister?"

"Aunt? Your mother's sister would be your aunt."

Muirin gave a short nod. "Aunt. Live we with aunt, and . . . aunt-husband?"

Jean was still following. "Uncle. You and your mother lived with your aunt and uncle."

Muirin nodded yet again. "Two childs, they have. Is . . . light-man?"

"They have two children. That makes them your cousins. Your uncle is a—a light-man?" Jean frowned. "Muirin, I'm sorry, I don't know what—"

"Light-man!" Baring her teeth, Muirin gave a low growl, and for the first time Jean truly glimpsed the depth of the woman's frustration at her inability to say what she meant. Muirin muttered a few harsh-toned words in her own language, shaking her head, then drew a long breath and tried again to explain. "On the small land, he lives; high house, with big light. Help boats not to fall down in sea."

It took a second, but Jean arrived. "He keeps a light! He's a lighthouse keeper, on an island! So boats don't sink!"

Muirin bobbed her head up and down. "Yes, yes! Lighthouse! Boats not *sink*. You tell 'sink' before—" She made a face, waving her fingers next to her ear. "Flew, it."

Jean laughed. "It flew away? I like that. You *forgot*."

Tobias cleared his throat from the doorway, making them both jump. "Sounds like she ain't *forgot* much, has she?"

Jean couldn't help herself. "Didn't your mother ever tell you not to sneak in at doors, man?"

Tobias stared at Muirin, as if he had no idea who she was.

Muirin said nothing, but gazed at him steadily, defiant.

"You *are* learning," he said. "I'd no idea how much. Jean said I ought to talk with you more; guess she was right."

Jean's chest tightened. Perhaps she had wrong-footed, and badly, in keeping Muirin's improvement hidden from him, despite her good intentions—to let Muirin tell him in her own good time. Or perhaps her instinct to do so had been completely right. "Tobias," she began.

The man transferred his gaze from his wife to Jean, blue eyes boring into her as if he wished he could see straight into Jean's head. Then he shook himself like a dog come in from the cold, removing his hat and thumping it against his hand before catching it on one of the hooks near the door. "I think it might be best you head for home, Jean."

Jean was sure she didn't like that, not at all, not now. "I only just came," she said.

"Aye," he replied mildly. Shucking off his coat, Tobias gave it a good shakeout before hanging it up as well. "But snow's starting. You'll want to be to home before it gets too heavy, I figured. I was just coming in to tell you."

Jean turned to look out the window. The first fat flakes were drifting down, slow and silent, coming thicker and faster even as she watched. Tobias was right. She needed to go soon, or the little family might end up stuck with her for the night, and maybe even longer if it were to turn into a bad blow.

Excusing himself, Tobias went through into the bedroom, not bothering to shut the door behind him as he opened a drawer and began to rifle through it. Jean and Muirin looked at each other. Muirin pursed her lips and glanced toward the bedroom door, shifting Kiel in her arms, then shook her head at Jean: *Don't push him. I'll deal with it.*

Jean stood with a gusty sigh and reluctantly went to put her things back on.

Muirin set Kiel back down in the cradle, leaving him to fuss softly as she came to Jean by the door. Reaching out, Muirin finished settling Jean's scarf around her neck for her, catching the ends and tucking them securely under the edge of her yellow shawl. Then Muirin picked up Jean's empty basket from beneath the table and passed it to her, with eyes gone dark and serious. "Come soon back, Jean," she said, leaning close.

Catching up Jean's mittened hand, Muirin gave it a furtive squeeze, then let it drop as Tobias came back out of the other room, carrying a fresh shirt in his hands.

"Goodbye, Jean," he said, his tone pleasant. "I'm sure we'll see you again soon. Muirin and I will have to practice our English together until then. I can't wait to see how much she's learned." He put an arm around Muirin's shoulders, turning his head to smile at her. "We have a lot to talk about."

Muirin's mouth tightened.

Tobias raised his eyebrows at her. His head tipped toward Jean, the tiniest twitch.

Muirin glanced at Jean out of the corner of an eye, then looked to her husband again, head tilting as she studied his impassive face. Jean wondered what she saw there. Finally, Muirin gave a tight nod. Slipping out from under Tobias's arm, she pulled the door open to let Jean out.

"Goodbye," Muirin said. Her eyes had turned as deep and unreadable as a starless sky. Jean opened her mouth to reply, but Muirin's fingers brushed the small of her back, turning her, ushering her smoothly out over the threshold before she could decide on what to say.

This time, Muirin did not urge Jean to *come soon*.

The door shut behind her, with a quiet *tunk* as the lock turned.

Snow began falling more heavily as Jean headed back down over the field, catching on her hair, and scarf, and yellow shawl. At the edge of the wood, she paused, glancing back over her shoulder at the house on the hill. A perfect snowflake caught frozen in her palm, and Jean shivered as she watched it slowly melt away, wondering what, exactly, had just happened.

11

The flurry that afternoon didn't stick, but it heralded the true start of winter. When it began snowing again two days later, in the middle of the afternoon, Jean thought at first that it would melt away just as quickly. Instead, the snow kept up, creeping to cover the blades of dry grass, until Jean's entire yard was blanketed in white. The goats went into their shed early, and she piled their hay twice as deep as normal. She hauled in extra firewood for herself, panting as she pushed through the building drifts. Her eyes blurred and teared as the wind blew tiny, sharp flakes into them, and the cold bit at her cheeks.

Jean peered out the frost-edged window. The wind had turned, coming down out of the northwest, and the snow spiraled and whirled until everything past the near edge of the marsh was lost behind a shifting veil of white. Nothing about this snow was light and soft and fluffy. Her father used to say, "Little snow, *big* snow," and it was almost always true. The smaller the flakes, the more of them were likely to fall. There wasn't a thing Jean could do about it, either, except stay inside and keep the fire going as the temperature fell.

Bundled into bed that night as the snow hissed over the roof, she curled beneath the heavy blankets and hoped Muirin and Kiel were warm, and that Tobias had done a good job of his work on the chimney.

In the morning, Jean's front door wouldn't open.

Or rather, it opened, but there was nowhere for her to go outside of it. The entire doorway was blocked by a solid wall of snow that bore the impression of the door's planks, and a single hole from the doorknob, but didn't shift at all.

The window was nearly covered, too. Jean was obliged to climb up onto the table to look out of the upper pane. At least the snow had stopped falling, thank God, although the sky still looked darkly ominous. Jean sat, her legs dangling off the side of the table. The snow heaped around the little house muffled even the subtle sounds of the wind and the distant waves and the creaking trees, so that Jean's pulse echoed inside her ears in the thick silence. She couldn't remember this ever happening when her father had been alive.

The goats would be fine for a day. Maybe two, if their water held out. The chickens? She wasn't sure. Her? Well, she had food, that wasn't an issue. She'd been smart to bring in so much wood, and the snow would help keep the heat in, so she could maybe stretch her supply for a day or two.

Jean eyeballed the half-empty pail of water. She should have made a trip up to the spring yesterday, even if it had been getting dark. She swallowed, the spit drying in her mouth.

It was nearing the middle of December. Jean was supposed to go into town to spend the holidays with Anneke and wait on Evie Hiltz's baby to decide when it was ready to put in an appearance, but it would be another week and a half before John

Hiltz came out to get Jean in his wagon—his sleigh now, she imagined—and bring young Robbie McNair with him, who'd stay in her place and mind the animals while she was gone.

In a week and a half, the livestock would be dead in their shelters. And she'd not fare much better without any water. Jean's mouth soured. Maybe Tobias would think to check in on her? She doubted the man would leave Muirin and the baby alone for that long, though, and they'd not have reason to suspect she was in trouble. Jean pressed her face into her hands, clamping down hard on a rising bubble of panic. *Think. Think. What would Anneke do?*

Jean let out a sudden, sharp laugh. "Idiot," she said into the empty air. She wouldn't run out of water; she could melt snow dug out from the doorway. Taking a steadying breath, she slid off the table, then fetched her biggest stockpot. She opened the door again and began scraping snow into the metal pot with her bare hands. It was almost full, her hands stinging and pink, when a thin stream of snow started to fall of its own accord from the back of the hollow she'd made. With a great *floomph,* the entire wall of snow collapsed into her house, sending Jean scrambling backward from the avalanche, wet snow heaped cold around her ankles. Her stockpot was buried a foot deep.

When Jean put her head out the door, it was clear. The snow had drifted straight up against the house seven feet deep—but only two feet thick. On the opposite side of the drift, the wind had scoured the snow down to bare earth. Jean groaned, dragging a chilled, red hand over her face, and got her boots. The shovel was in the woodshed, and she had digging to do.

In the days that followed, the cold grew less damp and more biting. Jean wore an old pair of her father's long woolen drawers with the legs rolled up under her dress and petticoats when she went out to tend the animals each day, aching all over from shoveling out the drift before her house until she could see out the window again. Otherwise, she stayed indoors, carefully banking the fire each night before bed so she wouldn't wake in the morning to a house gone cold and the water frozen in the pail.

There was plenty with which to occupy herself, even alone in her echoing house, and Jean was glad. The weather, and preparing for her upcoming stay in town, kept her mind busy and away from her neighbors, although her thoughts stubbornly strayed up the hill in their direction several times a day. It was the worst in the evenings, when Jean sat before the fire to knit, or mend, or read, although it strained her eyes to do so by firelight.

Respooling the cotton thread for her kit, Jean caught herself over and over again with her hands stilled, staring into the flames and imagining Muirin once more sitting by her knee in the fire's glow, warm and soft. Muirin's funny, often backward way of talking, her easy sort of affection—Jean couldn't recall the last time someone had been so eager to take her hand and squeeze it, or kiss her cheek. Or worse, she could, and remembered exactly how well *that* had turned out. Swallowing down her bitterness, she went on with her work, filling up the hours until she could justify going to bed.

Jean was fine on her own, living her own life, and it was better to put anything else out of mind. She had a friend she might visit now, sometimes, and that was good enough; she didn't need anything more.

Maybe she should get a cat.

The morning before Jean was due to leave for town was fine and bright, if chill, the sun glittering so brightly on both snow and sea that she had to squint, or else little black dots began dancing before her eyes. Jean hadn't been back to the house on the hill for well over a week and had to push a path through knee-deep snow most of the way around the marsh and up through the woodlot to get there. The stream was crusted with ice, and she went carefully crossing it, water burbling black and cold beneath the thin surface.

Maybe she might get Muirin out for a walk, in the air. It would be good for her. Jean wanted to see Muirin again before she went to town, at any rate, to be certain all was well with her and the baby before she left, and to explain why she wouldn't be by again until the new year. It wouldn't do, Muirin thinking Jean had lost interest in her company now she wasn't staying in her house anymore.

Despite her better understanding of things, Jean had a lingering uneasiness about the whole situation with Muirin and Tobias that she couldn't shake. The way Tobias had hustled Jean out of the house on her last visit, the way he hadn't seemed pleased with Muirin's progressing English, still sat heavy in the back of her mind.

By the time Jean made it up to the house she was breathless, and she didn't have to see a mirror to know she was flushed the color of cranberry jelly. When she tapped on the door, it was Tobias who answered, and he looked her up and down and laughed. "Getting your exercise in this morning, then?" He glanced back over his shoulder and stepped outside in just his shirtsleeves in spite of the temperature, pulling the door closed behind him.

"Jean." He dropped his voice. "I'm not so sure we ought to keep pushing the language lessons. I think it's upsetting Muirin."

Jean frowned. "Upsetting her?"

"Aye." He nodded, all concern. "She's maybe not getting it so well as you think. Keeps getting her words mixed 'round and says things that don't make sense at all. She got into a right flap trying to tell me about her mother being in the sea—"

"On an island is in the sea, in a way," Jean put in.

"Still, I can't convince her it ain't the same, and she got all worked up. And I hate seeing her upset."

Jean wasn't buying it. It didn't fit; Muirin had been speaking better than ever the last time she'd seen her, and seldom repeated an error more than once after you explained it, so long as you ignored her grammatical strangeness. She certainly didn't get "worked up" over it, not unless you considered justifiable frustration at trying to find the word for *lighthouse* to be the same thing as an outburst. Although, given her usual meek manner around Tobias, he might well take it that way. Jean wondered if the man really knew his wife at all. She wasn't certain she'd be so sanguine were their roles reversed, but Muirin was a steady, unflappable sort, patient and eager to learn. Easygoing, or so she'd always seemed.

Tobias shifted, leaning his shoulder on the frame of the door. "She told you much about her folks, then?"

Jean shook her head. "Not a lot. It's hard, of course, with the language. I got that her uncle has a lighthouse, somewhere, and her mother lives with him and her aunt. That her father died when she was small. I thought you said they were coming to see her, by the by. Whatever happened with that?"

"Ah." He rubbed the back of his neck, awkward. "Don't know exactly. If I'm honest, I think maybe they still aren't best pleased with the two of us going off like we did. Or not with me, at any rate."

That, Jean could believe.

"Point is, maybe give her a little rest? From the family talk, and the English. I'm worried about her." His concern seemed genuine. Jean didn't trust it, but at the very least it gave her the opening she'd hoped for, and she stepped right into it.

"Actually, I'd thought I might take Muirin out for a walk today, as it's so fine? It would be better than sitting indoors and trying to talk, if it's been wearing on her. Fresh air and sunshine are good for more than just sheets."

Tobias gave Jean a long, considering look, then hummed. "I suppose. Maybe. If it isn't for too long? She could do with a bit of perking up. Come on in." He pushed the door open and led her inside. Jean caught a glimpse of Muirin's back past his shoulder; she sat on the bed in the far room, gazing out the window at the sea.

Jean couldn't have said why she was sure Muirin was looking over the woodlot to the distant bay, and not at the trees or the empty field behind the house, but she was certain of it, somehow. Muirin had grown up on an island, and she could be twenty miles inland and still have seagulls in her eyes, was the sort who'd pine if she were kept from the shore for long. Jean knew sea-longing too well not to have seen it in Muirin. Some people had salt water in their blood.

"Baby's just gone down to sleep again," Tobias said quietly, breaking Jean's reverie, then spoke up as he went to the bedroom door. "Muirin, love. Jean's come to take you out for a little walk, if you like?"

Muirin didn't reply, but steadfastly kept her eyes cast to the horizon. Tobias stepped into the room with her and set a hand on her shoulder. Now she looked up at him. He shook his head, disapproving. "Come, love. It wouldn't look right not to visit with your friend."

Jean had seen Muirin quiet before. Now she was subdued in a whole different way, and Jean wondered what had happened to the laughing woman who'd been a guest in her home. This Muirin put Jean in mind of the ghost she'd first taken her for in the marsh, as the new mother rose and came out to meet her, then stopped halfway across the room.

Muirin looked over at the baby in the cradle, and then back at Tobias, unsure.

"It's all right, Muirin," Jean spoke up into the smothering silence. She had to get her out of the house. It was as if Muirin had fallen right back into her old melancholy, only worse, for now she had words to express herself, but had abandoned them. "I know you haven't left the baby before. But Toby's sleeping, it'll be fine. If he wakes, Tobias will call us in." Jean looked at him. "Won't you." It wasn't a question so much as a command, and Tobias blinked.

"Oh. I— Of course."

Jean nodded, turning her attention back to Muirin. "See? All's well. Won't you come out with me? It's cold, but so lovely and bright. You need some air. Please?" Muirin opened her mouth, then seemed to think better of it. She shut her lips and nodded, with a swift sideways glance at her husband. Tobias gave a barely perceptible nod. Jean's own mouth tightened. Whatever was going on here, it was not the thing Tobias was trying to convince Jean of.

As Muirin began bundling into her outdoor things, Jean went to take a quick peep into the baby's cradle. Little Kiel was sleeping soundly, round-cheeked and in the pink of health. Whatever else was going on, Muirin was still taking good care of the babe. He seemed even bigger than he had been on her last visit.

"Toby looks well," Jean said, turning back around. "I want to take a closer look at him before I go today, after we're back. I won't be so close to hand the next while; I'm going into town until Evie Hiltz has her baby. Robbie McNair is going to be taking care of the animals, though, so if you need anything—"

Muirin's head jerked up, and one of her gloves dropped to the floor at her feet. Tobias bent and retrieved it. Instead of giving it back, he slipped it onto his wife's unresisting hand himself as he spoke. "Odd one, that boy. You know he talks to animals. Not like most people, but like they *understand* him? Nice enough lad, but strange."

Jean had heard less kind assessments of Robbie in her life. People said he'd maybe been touched by the fairies as a lad. He was about the only person Jean could imagine minding her place for her, fairy-touched or not. It was true he was an odd boy, but he was a good sort, and clever, and he had a deft hand for animals of any kind. He could also tell you the name and the year of launch of every single boat that had come from the many shipyards around the bay, and when he wasn't working his job at one of the lumber mills that supplied them, Robbie turned his hand to carving jointed dolls and finely wrought instruments— delicate violins and the like. He had taught himself to play as well. People often treated him as though he was a bit dim because of his strangeness, when it was clear to Jean he was anything but.

"I suppose, if you were going to trust anyone with your place, he'd be good." Tobias settled the cuff of Muirin's sleeve down over her glove, so there wouldn't be a gap for the cold to creep into. "Quiet, keeps to his own business. He doesn't mind it's Christmas?"

"Not at all. I think all the noise and excitement around the holidays set him on edge, coming from such a big family. But then, you'd understand how that is, with so many brothers yourself." Jean couldn't keep her eyes on Tobias as she responded. They kept drifting back to Muirin, who'd given over completely, allowing her husband to finish dressing her for the weather like a living, breathing doll. Muirin watched Tobias from under her lashes as he focused on her clothing in a way Jean found unsettling, while holding herself so stiff and still she might have been carved from a block of ice. It struck Jean as odd that *his* family hadn't come to help with the babe, either; had he even told them of Kiel's arrival?

Tobias grunted in a noncommittal way that might have been agreement, or not, knotting Muirin's scarf around her throat.

She closed her eyes as he secured it, tucking in the loose ends, and flinched when he spoke again suddenly. "Not down by the shore, mind. The rocks are icy. It wouldn't do for either of you to slip and fall down there." He locked his gaze on his wife's and gave his head a slow shake.

Muirin responded with the barest of sullen nods.

Jean forced a hearty, cheerful tone into the still space between them all. "I thought we might go for a walk in the woods. Not as hard on the eyes as it is out in the open." Pushing the door open before Tobias could lay down any further commandments for them, Jean added, pert: "Thanks for lending me your wife, Tobias. I promise, I'll have her back by lunch."

Catching Muirin's arm fast in her own, Jean pulled her out the door.

Muirin nearly tripped going over the threshold, blinking owlishly against the day's sharp brightness. Jean found herself wondering when Muirin had last been outside. Had she seen the sky since the day they'd walked on the beach together, except through a window?

Not a word passed between them as they went around the corner of the house and past the woodpile. Once they were behind the henhouse, out of view of the bedroom window, Jean stopped. "Muirin," she said, turning to face her. "What's wrong?"

Muirin stood looking at her for a long moment, pursing her lips as if she wasn't sure what she ought to say. She glanced over her shoulder, back the way they'd come, then shook her head. The little wrinkle Jean had seen on Muirin's forehead that day by the marsh was back.

"Muirin," Jean said again, firm, holding her gaze. "You can tell me. Truly. Whatever it is."

Muirin's eyes softened. Stepping in, she nudged her nose against Jean's cheek, her normal greeting come late. It was a routine shared between them now, but even in this, Muirin was subdued, less free than she'd been before. She didn't linger as she usually did, was already pulling away.

Jean turned her face, pressing the cold tip of her own nose into Muirin's cheek. It was warm and soft. Muirin stiffened, then exhaled a muted laugh, the first sound to come out of her since Jean had set eyes on her sitting in the bedroom. Muirin burrowed her nose into Jean's cheek again, lingering this time, and warmth bloomed in Jean's chest. She'd done the right thing, returning the gesture. A sudden urge struck Jean, to wrap her arms around Muirin and pull her closer, but she pushed it down, shut a lid over it. *Too much.*

Muirin drew a deep breath and stepped back. "We go?" Her body had relaxed, but her voice, when it came, remained tentative and uncertain.

"Yes." Jean examined Muirin's face again. What exactly could have gone on in the past week to bring about such a change in her demeanor? "We're going for a walk. In the woods."

"Fuck," said Muirin mildly, just as Jean took a first step down the hill. She nearly tripped over her own feet.

"What?" she choked out.

Muirin looked at her friend, her eyebrows drawing together. "Fuck?"

Jean's jaw worked, but it took her a moment to organize any words to come out of it. "Muirin," she said carefully, "I don't know what it is you're trying to say, but that doesn't mean whatever you think it does."

Muirin blinked at her. "No . . . ?" She shot a glance back up the hill behind them, frowning.

"No." Jean had a sudden suspicion, one she didn't much like. "It's not a good thing to say. A bad word. You shouldn't say it; it's not polite. Where did you hear it?"

At last, speech came tumbling out of Muirin again, in a mortified whisper. "Sorry! Sorry! Not know! Not want say bad,

want say good—good to walk! Means sounds good idea, says—"
She paused, pressing her lips tight together again, still not answering the question, but her eyes burned with slow simmering
anger, and her head swiveled toward the house once more.

Jean knew she was right.

"Tobias."

Muirin's face crumpled as if she were about to cry. "My talk
not good, says he! Says my words wrong way are, always, and
stupid sound, that—that—you not want talk if I *wrong* always.
Not be friends, we, if not can talk, and I should not—" Her
frustration and unwarranted shame couldn't have been more
clear, no matter what words she used or how she slotted them
together.

"Muirin, Muirin, shh, it's all right." It was *not* all right. Jean
wanted nothing so much as to march back up to the house and
choke the life out of Tobias Silber with her own two hands.

The thing was clear. Tobias did not want Muirin talking, and
he was actively trying to sabotage her, handing her a word like
fuck to drop where anyone sane would have said, "That's nice."
Likely it was for fear of something his wife might say about *him,*
of that Jean was absolutely certain. Never mind trying to con-
front him about his behavior, for if Tobias even *suspected* Jean
knew of it, she'd be banished from their home, and nothing else
to be said by anyone. She could hardly believe he'd let Muirin
come out alone with her at all, except he must have thought it
would look suspicious if he didn't. He clearly thought himself
that clever, and his wife that cowed by him. Although Muirin
wasn't nearly so cowed as she let her husband believe, not if that
unsettling, surreptitious way she'd been watching him earlier
was any indication.

The bastard. A thing like that, dropped into a conversation
with someone Muirin didn't already know, would have put
every woman in the village off before any of them exchanged

more than a dozen words with her. Muirin needed someone who cared about her, a friend, someone who wasn't interested in keeping her small, and silent, and hidden away. He was trying to make certain that Muirin would not make friends here, not have ties except to him, and Jean couldn't understand why.

Jean couldn't have said what the expression on her face was, but it must have been dark indeed from the way Muirin was looking at her, worrying at her own lower lip with her teeth. Jean tried very hard to make her voice reassuring when she spoke again, less murderous than she felt. "It's not your fault. I promise, Muirin, I don't mind how you talk, I like talking with you. I *want* to." She placed a hand on Muirin's arm. "I think perhaps your husband doesn't like that we talk as much as we do. So he's trying to make you feel bad, to make you make mistakes, and say things that might shock me, so I'll be put off. I'm not. We won't stop talking. I'll keep teaching you, I promise. But he can't know, or there'll be trouble. We'll have to keep it from him, so be careful. We don't want Tobias to think there's more to what we're doing than what he already knows." Just to be certain Muirin had taken her meaning, Jean pressed a finger to her lips. "Shh. You see?"

Muirin nodded. "Is secret. I remember." Her eyes were wide, concerned, and she set her hand over Jean's. "Jean," she said. "Angry, him, if he know. Sure you want?"

Jean's heart clenched. The poor woman. Her husband trying to tie her in knots, and yet she was trying to protect Jean, only concerned that their friendship might bring her trouble. Maybe Anneke was right, and Jean ought to keep out of it. But how could she? If anything, the look on Muirin's face only made Jean want to find a way to help her more, to fling caution entirely to the wind. At the very least, Jean could find ways to make Muirin happy, help take her mind off her fool of a husband when it was just the two of them.

"I am," she said. "Certain I have one other secret for you, too." She gave Muirin a sly grin.

Muirin blinked at her, confused. "Jean?"

Jean bent, scooped up a handful of loose snow, and threw it directly into Muirin's face.

Muirin let out a high-pitched yelp, followed by a shriek of laughter. "You!" she said, spluttering, pointing a finger at Jean. "Oh! You—!" Muirin scooped up her own handful of snow, and Jean ducked, making a run for it down the hill toward the wood-lot, giggling madly, her skirts hitched well up over her knees.

She paused just inside the wood, pulling back a snow-covered fir bough. She released it just as Muirin caught up behind, and it flew back, throwing even more snow into her friend's face. Muirin whooped, pausing to scrape snow from her eyes before narrowing them at Jean.

She turned to run again. At her second step, Muirin was already on her, by merit of her longer stride, although Jean was shocked to be tackled clear off her feet, Muirin's arms catching tight around her waist. They tumbled down into a deep drift, Jean letting out an undignified squawk, Muirin crowing triumphantly. For a moment, they rolled and thrashed about, floundering, Jean trying to fight her way up, Muirin growling and trying to scrub a handful of snow into her face. Finally, Muirin pinned Jean down, half sprawled on top of her, both of them red-faced and panting.

Jean's laughter caught in her throat, her heart pounding in her chest. Muirin stopped laughing. She had snow in her hair and sparkling on her eyelashes. Her lips parted as she looked down at Jean, curling into a cat's slow smile. The woods were utterly still. Jean couldn't tear her eyes away from Muirin as another breathless moment flashed in her mind. Her and Jo, nineteen, and making a right spectacle of themselves at the hall, dancing all the round waltzes together—Jo had led, she was the tall one—until they were both dizzy and laughing, and slipped out the back to catch a bit of air.

A fine mist had been falling, and they'd kept tight to the wall, trusting the overhang of the roof to keep them dry, pressed together in a crush of skirts and petticoats, giggling. Then everything between them had gone still, as still as it was now. And Jean had kissed her. Jo had kissed her back, hands catching in Jean's tangling hair until the door of the hall opened and they sprang apart, panting, eyes locked on each other. Two men staggered past down the lane, leaning on each other and weaving through the mist until it swallowed them, tunelessly singing as they went:

Now when I was a little boy, and so me mother told me
Hey haul away, hey haul away
That if I didn't kiss the girls, me lips would all grow moldy
Hey haul away—

The girls had dissolved back into laughter, until Jo said, "Well, we *mustn't* let our lips go moldy," and pulled Jean close, and kissed her again . . .

Muirin's nose twitched, and she sneezed directly into Jean's face.

"Augh!" Jean rolled to the side and out from under Muirin, her heart still trying to pound its way out of her rib cage. Muirin sprawled facedown in the snow, helplessly trying to apologize between fits of giggling. It was all Jean could do to pull Muirin back onto her feet, she was laughing that hard. Jean laughed, too; it helped her ignore the nervy fluttering in her belly, the tightness in her chest. One of her boot's buttons had slipped its buttonhole, and she pulled off her mitts and tried to force it back through with shaking fingers, keeping her head bent low until her ears stopped buzzing.

When Jean looked up again, Muirin was watching her, clutching her elbows with her lips drawn tight and twitching. As soon as their eyes met, they both started laughing all over again.

It was most of an hour before they staggered back up the hill to the house, rumpled and breathless, and still giggling. Tobias met them at the door. He stared for a moment at Muirin, now bright-eyed, rosy-cheeked, and smiling on Jean's arm, transformed. He turned his eyes to Jean, quite speechless.

Jean wasn't sure what the man was thinking. She was quite sure that she didn't care. Smiling at him blandly, she raised one shoulder in a careless shrug. "I think I managed to put some cheer back into her." Jean couldn't help the cheeky lift of her chin as she added: "You were right, Tobias. I didn't need so many words."

12

Jean wanted to tell Anneke everything right away the next day, as soon as she got to her house, but she'd barely made it through the front door before it clattered open again behind her and Laurie came in, whistling. He swooped in to embrace his mother without even knocking the snow from his boots, then turned, let out a loud whoop, and caught Jean up in his arms, whirling her around in a circle of flying skirts. "Red!" he cried, then set her back on her feet. "Come for Christmas with Ma, too, then?"

"Laur! When'd you get in?" Jean took a step back to get a proper look at him. Laurie hadn't changed much since she'd last seen him, but the thick black hair he'd inherited from his mother had grown far longer than was fashionable. If he released it from the low tail he had it in, it would brush his shoulders. Jean swore he grew more tanned with every winter he passed down south, though he would likely never be as dark as Anneke. Nevertheless, his complexion made his blue eyes, the legacy of his father, more startling than ever. He was a rather pretty man, although

Jean wasn't sure she'd dare to say so to his face. Laurie's features might be sharply delicate, but he was lean and sailor-strong, with the smooth, rolling stride of a man who worked on water, and he'd like as not hoist her under one arm, carry her out back, and pitch her into a snowdrift for it.

"Just this morning! Brought a skip up from Lunenburg with a few other lads; we only made port down there last night."

"I can't hardly believe you're here at all, it's been that long!" Jean said, as Laurie sat to pull off his boots. They were already making puddles on Anneke's floor, and she was quick to shake a finger at her son.

"All this time, and first thing you do is make a mess! Just like you never left." Anneke grinned. "You're a sight for sore eyes. I'm glad you decided to come up this year. Took you long enough to drag yourself away, though. You're lucky, I might have took you for a stranger and barred the door."

Laurie's fingers fumbled in the laces of his boot, and they went into a knot. He kept his head bent low as he worked it loose again. "Eh, Ma," he drawled, "you'd never. Home's where, when you have to go there, they got to let you in."

When you have to go there. Laurie finally got his boot off, and he and his mother went right on teasing each other, as if making up lost time in friendly insults. Jean shook her head at them, laughing, and wondered: Had Laurie truly just missed them as he'd said in his letter? Or was there something more to his return?

His spirits seemed high enough. Of course Laurie had missed them after so long, and she was reading too much into things; her constant puzzling over Tobias's behavior had her searching for some hidden meaning behind every word from everyone. Jean resolved to try to forget about Tobias and Muirin for the time being, at least until she found the chance for a private word with Anneke.

It was easy to keep distracted, especially once Anneke's daughter, Mary Beth, came crowding in hard on Laurie's heels with her husband, George, and their brood of three in tow. Jean was happy to let the family's warmth and chatter flow around her, lending her hand to chopping onions and carrots for an impromptu homecoming dinner, and taking it in good humor when Mary Beth included her in the teasing, flatly refusing to let Jean help with the dumplings, for fear they'd come out "tough as a boiled owl."

Laurie began winding the children up as they all got settled around the table, spinning increasingly tall tales of his time at sea and visits to far-off ports as dinner was served around. Jean very much doubted he'd met Captain Kidd in Barbados as he was insisting to Matthew and Little George, given that the outlaw pirate had died over a hundred years before.

Though his stories were fascinating, Jean got the creeping sense there was something missing from them as Laurie carried on goading the little ones into fits of shrieking laughter, never letting the conversation become more than ankle-deep. It was like there was some crumble-edged hole that he was talking around. Jean would much rather have heard tales about the men from his ship who he worked with for such long months each year. Or Dal, the man he'd spent so much time with away from them. She wanted to hear about his real life.

Nothing was obviously wrong, but Jean couldn't help finding his heartiness suspect, somewhat more than was necessary. The barest hint of a shadow lingered below his eyes. Was it just the long voyage home, and Laurie's early start from Lunenburg that morning, or a sign that he'd not been sleeping as well as he ought to be?

Perhaps Anneke was entertaining similar thoughts about his far-fetched stories, for she led the tale-telling in another direction, to the kind of old family yarns that got repeated over and over whenever people got together, and grew in the telling: The time Anneke's husband had tried to bake her a pie when they were fresh married, for a surprise. He'd used salt instead of sugar by mistake, and *that* particular surprise had been such that not even the pigs would eat it. Mary Beth told how she had knocked Big George off the back step the first time he kissed her, because he'd assumed she liked him and not asked first. George was quick to point out how he'd seen the error of his ways, and since she *had* liked him, it had come out all right in the end. Jean liked these stories better—they were a thread connecting the family to one another and their past in a sort of crazy quilt, and by including her in the telling they made Jean feel almost like she was part of the same fabric. Less like she'd been patched in. Though it sometimes pricked her with the awareness of how unlikely it was she'd ever build a family of her own.

She tried to ignore that thought, focusing on Laurie again as he chimed back in with the time one of his cousins had taken him out hunting on skis. Laurie'd gone straight down a hill unable to stop, and managed to cross an ice-rimmed open brook balanced right up on the tips of the skis like a pair of stilts before careening headlong into a sticker bush. Mary Beth's boys were near to falling out of their chairs in stitches as their uncle tried to demonstrate with his two pointer fingers exactly how he'd accomplished such a thing, tip-tapping them across the table beside his plate, but Sarah sighed, rolling her eyes with all the scorn a ten-year-old could muster. It made the girl strongly resemble her mother.

"No one cares about *you,* Uncle Laurie."

Anneke hooted with laughter, and Jean almost toppled off

her seat, while Mary Beth buried her mortified face in one hand. Laurie caught a hand to his heart, as if the girl had hit him with an arrow.

"Stung!" he cried. "I'm a boring old man now! Fine, what do *you* want to hear, then, missy?"

Sarah crossed her arms. "I want a fairy story, like the fish with the ring in it, or the one with the water horse! Something romantic."

Laurie scoffed at the very notion. "You can't want to hear *those* old things again? A great girl like you, you're old enough for a proper ghost story!"

"Laurie . . ." Mary Beth began. He ignored her, launching into the story they all knew, even the children: the wreck of the *Young Teazer,* and the ghost ship. That was well enough, but next he started in on the death knock, a tale that usually set even Jean's spine to tingling.

"Good God, Laurence," Mary Beth broke in, the second she realized what he was about. "I'll never get them to sleep tonight, if you keep on with *that*! You'd know better, if you'd children of your own. Aren't you ever going to find yourself a nice girl and settle down?"

It was not a new question. Mary Beth usually managed to drop it into conversation at least once every time her brother was home, and it never ceased to irritate the hell out of Laurie, to the point where he and Jean had long since made it into something of a joke, or had tried to, anyway.

"I dunno." Laurie turned to look at Jean, grinning. It struck Jean as more of a pained grimace, but she doubted Mary Beth would ever know the difference. "Red, you think *you'll* settle down ever? We could always try to make a go of it!" Jean made a gagging noise into her plate, and the two of them both started snorting and snickering as one.

"Mary Beth!" Anneke poked her spoon in her daughter's direction. "I taught you better than to ask things like that. Mind your own beeswax, missy, and pass down the butter!"

Jean noted from the corner of her eye that Laurie only pushed the food around his plate after, in spite of his continued cheer.

Dinner went long; it was almost nine before everything was cleared up and Mary Beth and her family departed to make their walk home through the snow. When Jean shut the door behind them, Anneke asked her to put the kettle back on. "We could use a good catch-up now it's just us three. Laurie, you write the worst letters I ever saw. You leave out everything good! I want to hear what you've been up to down south these past couple winters, you and that fellow of—"

There was a knock at the back door. Laurie leapt from his chair to open it, and Jean busied herself filling the kettle from the hand pump to cover her amusement over his bald relief at the interruption.

It was a couple of Laurie's old chums, the Burgoyne brothers.

"Hope it's not too late," Clary Burgoyne said with a nod to Anneke. "Ma'am. Noble saw Mary and them going off as we were passing, and we wondered if we might not be able to steal Laurie away for a bit?"

Clary and Noble ended up dragging Laurie off up to the big hill behind the cemetery, to test out the toboggan that Noble had made for his boy's Christmas gift and "make sure it would run all right." Laurie was quick to throw on his coat, absolutely thrilled at the prospect, and Jean and Anneke caught each other's eye and tried not to laugh as the three grown men set off in the darkness to go sledding like schoolboys.

Anneke choked, spluttering on hot tea and black rum, her eyes going wide. "She said *what*?"

Jean would have laughed at her mentor's expression, except for the seriousness of the topic. "You heard me."

"And she got this from . . . ?"

"Guess," Jean said darkly. "Tobias, of course. I'm telling you, I wish I was a man! I'd knock him flat."

It was edging toward midnight, and Jean and Anneke were still sitting together in the kitchen, slowly destroying several slices of fruitcake and a pot of heavily doctored tea. Jean had been catching Anneke up on all that had passed since she'd last seen her a few weeks before: Her certainty now that Muirin was perfectly sane, and that the reason why the woman was unhappy was her husband. How Tobias's strange behavior the morning he and Muirin left her house had only intensified when Jean had gone up to visit them afterward, and her new discovery that he was trying to isolate his wife on purpose. The fact that she was beginning to think Muirin would knock Tobias flat herself were she free to do so, Jean kept to herself.

"I'm not imagining it, Anneke. He was nervous the first time I was up there, when he realized how much we were talking together, and I didn't understand it! I could kick myself!"

"Ah, now, Jeanie—"

"No, truly. He spent the whole next week mocking her every time she opened her mouth, and trying to convince her the only friend she has wouldn't want to go on talking to her because she was so bad at it, after all the progress she's made. And then teaching her an awful thing like *that,* so anyone else who tried to talk to her would end up thinking she was—I don't even know what!"

"No, you're right there." Anneke sighed. "That's insidious, is what it is. I—" She hesitated, giving Jean a shrewd sideways look. Anneke rarely hesitated. Jean was sure it meant she wasn't going to like whatever her mentor said next.

"What?"

"I *want* to tell you to keep out of it. I said it already, once! A man like that . . . You say she told you he's not laid a hand on her, but I'm telling you right now, the woman's either lying to you, or it's only that he ain't done it *yet*."

"Anneke, I am not about to just—"

"Jean." Anneke's voice was firm. "I want to say it, but I won't. I know better than to think you'll listen. Lord knows I wouldn't have, when I was your age. But you've never stopped pushing to help them all, since that mess with the Keddy girl, more than you should, and you can't go trying to intervene in a thing like this. It doesn't work, and it might be dangerous. For you *and* your new friend."

Jean tightened her hands around her cup, her knuckles whitening, and ignored the comment about Jo, refusing to dignify it with a response. "I know. I don't want him thinking I'm a problem, poking into their business. I'm not sure he isn't thinking it already, some, and if he runs me off, then what? Muirin would be completely cut off all over again, trapped with a man who clearly doesn't have her best interests at heart. No, I'll be careful. We *both* will. Muirin's smart, she understands we have to be quiet about it if we want to keep on, me helping her with her English, and us seeing each other, so hopefully I can find out what Tobias is after. And she's good at making him think she's going along with him. I just—I want to keep close, to help, as much as I can. It's not right, what he's doing to her."

Anneke scoffed from the back of her throat. "You like her."

"Of course I *like* her, she's my friend."

Anneke fixed Jean with a look like she was about six years old and had been caught trying to tell the woman that, no, of *course* she wasn't eating cookies before dinner, with her hand still stuck up to the elbow in the jar.

"Anneke, don't start."

"If there's anyone who ought not to start—"

"I'm not about to—"

"Umm-hm. Sure you aren't." Anneke waved her crabbed hand, cutting Jean off. "I know, I know. Married woman, baby, husband, blah blah. You like her, Jeanie. I can see it when you talk about her."

"What would it matter if I did? She's married, just as you said, and to a man she must have liked well enough—at *some* point at least—to have ended up having to marry him like she did. Absolutely nothing is going to happen, and nothing would." Jean set down her drink and pinched the bridge of her nose. "Anneke, I'm trying to be a good friend to her. To help. That's *all*. The rest doesn't matter."

Anneke frowned at Jean for a long time before replying. "If you say so. I just worry. People make stupid mistakes when they think too much with their hearts."

Jean rolled her eyes up toward the ceiling. "Oh, lord."

Anneke snorted. "I've been around longer than you yet, missy. Look, just take some advice: You want to try and stay close, fine. You want to help, lovely; you have a good heart. But you don't want to go making things worse for the girl, even by accident. You play it nice and neighborly with them. Don't go up there to visit more than once a week, at the *most*. Keep your conversation with her boring and civil, especially if there's any chance he's in earshot. Never say a thing to anyone else about what you're thinking—if Tobias caught any whiff of a rumor about him and his wife in town, he'd go looking to see where it started."

"I know that; I wouldn't dare. Who you think I've got to tell besides you, anyway—"

"Good. And if you think things have got too badly out of hand, you ask for help."

Jean had a thought. "Do you suppose there's anything more I

might be able to do for her?" she asked, careful. "I mean, would they give her a divorcement, do you think? If I were to back up a claim for her, about her being unwilling, maybe?" It wasn't likely. A married woman was essentially her husband's property under the current law, at least so far as Jean understood it.

Anneke shook her head. "'Tain't right, but there it is. And a man's allowed to"—the word came out more a growl—"*discipline* his wife. No good even trying in that direction."

"I thought not." Jean turned her china cup in a circle on the table, pointing the handle away from herself. "Anneke, if it were to be bad enough that she said she needed to get away—it isn't, and I hope to God it doesn't ever get that way, but if it *did*—if I could get her here to town, do you think you could hide her and the baby away for a bit? Until we could get them on a boat back to wherever her family is?" Muirin, stepping onto a boat in the bay, never to return. Looking back, and then turning her face away into the wind, as she had in Tobias's wagon. Jean's stomach dipped as if she'd stepped into a shifting sloop herself, and she pressed her fingertips firmly into the tabletop to steady her nerves.

Anneke considered with her lips compressed, then nodded. "Aye. *If* it came to such a turn, I could mind the woman for you. Could even send her off with my cousins for a few days, if need be." Her lips twitched, and the creases around them pulled into a wide grin. "If only because I know you're so fond of her, mind."

Jean stared at her a second, and then started laughing. "I can't tell if you're trying to warn me off or fling her at me! You're impossible!"

The back door opened, letting in a curling, cold breeze, and Laurie, caked with snow from head to foot. "Impossible? Who? Not *my* mother!" Peeling off his scarf and coat, he hung them up behind the stove to dry. The fresh air seemed to have restored his earlier high spirits. "You two must be having a good jaw, it's past midnight."

"Oh," said Anneke airily, "just discussing all the local in-laws and outlaws."

"Laurie . . ." Jean had a notion. "You know all the fishermen and such down to Lunenburg. You ever hear anything about Tobias Silber?"

Anneke shot her a look, which she ignored. "Him and his wife are my neighbors, and I'm trying to suss him out."

Laurie fished another teacup down out of the cupboard and bypassed the teapot entirely, in favor of a splash directly out of the bottle of Jamaica rum. Anneke's mouth tightened, but Jean thought perhaps a drink might do him some good, given his earlier performance. She suspected he was putting up a show for some reason. Or a shield. Whichever it was, the man was clearly of a mind to be distracted, and she was happy to oblige him on that count.

Hooking the handle of his cup with the crook of his finger, Laurie leaned on the wall next to Jean, crossing his legs at the ankle. "Ooh, the mysterious Mrs. Silber? Have you got a glimpse of her yet? There's talk; I heard a fellow swear she was imaginary and Silber'd gone and married his right hand."

"Laurie!" Anneke tried to sound scandalized, but the effect was lost to laughter.

Jean snickered. "His left would get jealous, wouldn't it?"

"Jean!" This time, Anneke actually did sound shocked, but Laurie hooted.

"Wish I'd thought of that. Well done."

Jean grinned and lifted her teacup, clinking it against his. "Seriously, though, she's lovely. Muirin—she's a big handsome girl, dark. They just had their first, I delivered it. Barely speaks any

English, though, she's Scots. And I'll be darned if I can figure out how he ended up with her; it seems an odd match."

Laurie took a prim sip of rum from his teacup. "Aye, that's the talk. And you know sailors and fisherfolk, they're worse than any old church ladies when it comes to gossip. But Silber . . . hmm. I don't know him myself, not really, especially since I ain't been around as much. He was a class ahead of me at the village school when we were kids. Quiet, mostly. I remember he had his cap set for one of the Mosher girls back then, the oldest one, maybe? Ima? Ava? Ella?" He shrugged a shoulder. "Whichever, they all have near the same name, those girls. Anyway, it didn't work out, she went and married . . . I forget who. Dan Barry, maybe? God knows if she's still friendly with Silber or not, that she'd know anything." Laurie rubbed his nose thoughtfully, then shook his head. "Anyway, I ain't heard a word about the man since, except that story about his imaginary wife; that he went out on his own last spring, early, before the fleet. Came back with some pretty girl, got married, and been cagey as all hell since."

Jean raised her eyebrows at him. "*Cagey's* a word."

Laurie snorted. "Ain't it, though. You know what a superstitious lot we are, that go out in boats. Some of the lads think they hear sirens singing every time the wind whistles down their ear. But. Huh." His mouth quirked. "I heard Abe Rafuse went and made some joke to Tobias in the summer, that he couldn't believe Silber'd found a woman that'd have him, smelling like fish, you know, that stupid sort of thing, and how she must be some mermaid he plucked off a reef someplace? Anyway, Tobias about beat the snot out of him for it, 'knocked him near into a cocked hat,' was what Clary said."

Anneke and Jean looked at each other.

"What?" asked Laurie. The handle of his teacup slipped on

his finger, and he nearly lost the last of his rum onto the floor. "No." He gaped at Jean, wide-eyed, shaking his head like he didn't want to even consider the thing he was asking. "She—she ain't . . . ?"

Jean laughed at the sickly look on his face. "Don't be daft, Laurie. Holy God, you're just as bad as the rest of them! Mermaids! It's only—that's a heck of an overreaction from Silber, isn't it? Over a stupid thing like that. Anyway, you can set the fellows straight, Muirin's a flesh and blood woman. I'd know better than anyone, all considered." Jean had delivered the woman of a child, for God's sake, or that's what she meant to imply. But then, there was the morning before, Muirin's hands catching 'round Jean's waist before they went tumbling into the snow, her warm breath when she nosed at Jean's cheek in greeting . . .

"What?" Jean said, the tips of her ears tingling. Anneke and Laurie were both looking at her with their heads tilted on an identical angle, a pair of bright-eyed, nosy little birds.

"Nothing." Mother and son spoke in unison, exchanged glances, and then laughed.

"Eh, Jeanie." Laurie uncrossed his ankles and poked her leg with one wool-socked toe. "They tell some mighty tall tales about you 'round the shipyards, too, don't you know?"

Jean's chest tightened. "Dare I ask?" She wasn't sure she *wanted* to know. It was in the past now, and buried, the whispering that had followed her around the town after Jo. It was supposed to be . . .

Laurie took in the expression on her face and jumped on explaining. "Oh, it ain't nothing bad! Not like . . . well. Just, Jack Sarty's been telling anybody who'll listen clear down to Liverpool that the midwife up here's got magic hands, and anytime someone's wife's in the family way, he tries to convince them they need to come up and pay you a visit. To hear him tell it, you're some kind of fairy witch." He grinned. "Maybe it's the hair."

Jean pulled a face even as a wave of relief washed over her. "Where'd the fool get an idea like that?"

Laurie shrugged. "Who knows with them lads? But Jack said you saved his sister Evelyn a year and some gone, that you managed to turn her upside-down baby right-way-to, all at the last minute, and the whole family sure she was done for. I wasn't half proud!"

"Breech!" Anneke cut in. "You'd never know I raised you. Really! Whose son are you?"

He snorted and raised his teacup in her direction. "Breech, then, Ma. Anyway, Red, they say as if you ain't a witch, or fairy-touched, then you've been blessed right enough."

Jean sniffed. "They all love to talk about the ones that go *well*. That's Evie Hiltz he was talking about, the same woman I'm in town for now, and I hope to hell it goes better this time than last. I don't know what it is with these farmers' wives—come the end of summer, they all want to try and have their babies feetfirst. It's a nightmare. I'm hoping this one'll come out right, it being the dead of winter and all."

Anneke nodded sagely. "It was the same story back when I was making the rounds. Harvest is when you're most like to lose one. Then, and spring planting. God, I still think about that poor Annie Clark, back when you were, what, sixteen or so? Just coming along to watch, really. I wasn't sure you'd want to again after that."

Jean blanched, recalling, and pushed her empty cup away. "Right. Well, luck or fairies or redhead witchery, I got the last one out of Evie all right, so just keep your fingers crossed for me to do it again this time, won't you?" She made her good-nights and headed off toward the bed that had been made up for her in Mary Beth's old room. Jean was halfway up the stairs when Laurie stepped through from the kitchen and called softly after her.

"Hey, Red?"

He was only half lit by the glow from the lamp in the other room and wore an expression Jean couldn't quite place. "Hmm?"

He glanced back toward the kitchen, then took a breath. "John Keddy was on the skip up this morning with me and Clary. He mentioned some of the girls were maybe going to be home this year, too."

Jean's hand tightened on the smooth wooden rail. She tried to keep her face plain, even in the dark stairway, but her voice came out flat, even to her own ear. "Jo?"

Laurie twitched one shoulder up, with a slight shake of his head. "I asked, but John didn't know for sure. Just said that he'd got word a couple of his sisters might be visiting over the winter. I thought you ought to know, just . . . in case."

"It's all right, Laurie. It won't be her. The other two are closer; she's all the way over to the Digby shore. Besides, she hasn't been back once since . . . since." Jean swallowed, and the lump from her throat settled in her stomach. "Even if she did come, it's nothing to me now. Thanks, though."

Stepping right to the foot of the stairs, Laurie set a hand on the banister. Jean stiffened, glad of the darkness in the parlor, for it meant she didn't have to see whatever look he was giving her.

"You sure, Jeanie?"

"Sure as I am that you'll never get up the guts to bring that fellow of yours up to meet us." She regretted it instantly, the words souring the whole inside of her mouth. "Laurie—"

"It's fine," he said, then sighed into the dark. "You ain't wrong. I just . . . Look, it's complicated. Ma says she don't mind, and I'm sure she means it, especially after how she was with you, before. But. It still ain't easy, you know?"

Jean knew. She also knew there had to be more to it than

simple worry over what his mother would say. There was something else buried here, for she was certain Laurie knew better than to think his mother would ever disapprove at this point, and Jean pressed forward with caution. "Did something happen, that you decided to come up here for Christmas and not stay with Dal—?"

"Leave it."

Jean recoiled at his sharpness. It wasn't like him, not at all, and was more telling than his earlier cheer had been. "Something's bothering you. You don't fool me, Laurie. Come on, we could always talk, even if nobody else understood."

Laurie shook his head again. "You won't understand this. Just—let it be. I'll figure it out."

"If you say so." Jean smiled, her lips stiff and false. "I suppose a man ought to be allowed a few secrets."

Laurie turned and headed back through to the kitchen, dropping his words behind him as he went. "To hell with secrets. I'm sick to death of 'em."

13

Jean didn't press Laurie any further in the days before Christmas, but she watched him. He could almost have fooled her with his high spirits, but she could tell his secrets were nagging at him. He kept himself busy entertaining everyone around him and pitching into every little task that caught his attention, but more than once Jean caught him sunk into dispirited silence when left to his own devices, with a pained look on his face that he shook off the second he realized he had an audience. He dodged his mother's attempts to draw him into a real conversation, but Jean wasn't sure if Anneke realized just how off her son was. Laurie was good at making his mother laugh, and smoothing things over by being agreeable to her every whim otherwise. He didn't even complain on Christmas morning, when Anneke insisted they were all going to church for the holiday service.

Church was near the worst thing about being in town, as far as Jean was concerned, and normally Laurie was of a like mind. Living as far out as she did, no one expected her to make the walk in each Sunday, but when she was in town . . . well, attending was simply what one did, like it or not. Much of village social life revolved around church activities, and the hours were tolled by the bell in the tower, ringing out over the bay and dictating the pace of life even when it wasn't Sunday or a holiday. Jean didn't mind going to church so much in and of itself, for she rather liked singing the old hymns, the talk of loving your fellow man, and the colored light from the windows. The high wooden ceilings had been made by shipbuilders and bowed like the belly of an overturned boat above her head.

No, what Jean minded about going to church was the people. She was already beginning to chafe at being so closed in with neighbors and didn't want to be in town long enough to have to come again next Sunday. She wasn't used to having to see and talk with a dozen different people or more each day. Maybe in a bigger place it would be different? Where you'd see people but not know them all by name, and have them know you, too, and want to stop you to tell you all about their children, and their business, and their neighbors' business, too. Where you wouldn't have to wonder what they were all thinking about you, or guard yourself as close.

A young boy at the very back gave Jean a shocked look as she passed him on the way in, following behind Laurie as he helped Anneke to her place. Letting out a gasp, the boy leaned across his father to poke his sibling in the ribs, whispering and pointing. Their father said something low and growling through his neat, gray beard, shaking his head, and the boy sat back up, tugging at his collar like it was strangling him. Jean stole a glance back down the aisle as she slipped into her pew. Oh. It was Mr. Buchanan, from out at the light.

Buchanan and his wife had been keeping the lighthouse together since before Jean was born. Now and then, she'd spot him in town, when he came to get supplies in his boat—he had gimlet eyes, with deep lines in their corners as if he was the sort to smile . . . and he was a Scot. Maybe Jean could find a subtle way to ask him if he knew anything of Muirin's family after the service? Both of his children were still gaping at her, their eyes round and dark beneath the brims of their caps. She rather hoped they'd heard the rumor Laurie'd told her, about her being a witch, and were waiting to see if she'd explode at the first mention of Our Lord and Savior.

By the time Jean spent an hour ignoring other, less amusing attention, she rather wished she could oblige the Buchanan children, if only to be done with the whole thing.

The Keddy family took up an entire pew near the front of the church. Jean hated having to sit the whole time staring into the backs of their matching blond heads; it made her stomach knot and her shoulders twitch like there was a target painted between them. She couldn't tell which of the women was which under all their hats and bonnets, until Mrs. Keddy started craning her neck around and scowling back at Jean, where she sat with Anneke's family. One of the daughters made as if to turn and look as well, but Mrs. Keddy jammed her elbow into the younger woman's arm with a pointed glare. Her daughter's back went very stiff, and the young woman went back to staring straight forward. Jean wondered if it was sour Margie who'd been going to look back, or Bess, Jo's younger sister, who'd always seemed a bit more sympathetic. Shame Jean *wasn't* a witch. She'd have liked to hex Mrs. Keddy straight into the new year.

So much for loving thy neighbor.

Jean turned tail the minute the sermon ended and fled before she had to face any of the Keddys as they came down the aisle. She even beat Buchanan and his children out the door, and them in the very last pew. The little ones were still gawping at her, and Buchanan opened his mouth like he might apologize for them, but she brushed past them without waiting to find out. By the time Laurie and Anneke caught up to her, Jean had made it all the way back to the house and put the pot on for tea ahead of them.

Evie Hiltz still hadn't gone into labor, though she looked about fit to burst. The slight, mousy-haired woman had been up from her chair three times in the quarter hour since Jean had arrived, ignoring her tea in favor of pacing the room in her nightgown and robe, kneading at her lower back.

"This is miserable. I can't get comfortable any way!" Evie leaned on her chair instead of sitting back down again. "I swear, I'd ask if you had a way to speed things along, except . . ." She stopped, but Jean understood. If *she* was uneasy after Evie's last birth, it was nothing to the woman's own worries.

Jean pushed up from her chair. "I doubt you need it. You're restless as a cat about to kitten. I won't be half surprised if I'm back here again before the end of tomorrow. Come on, then, let me check you over before Frankie's up from his nap, or he'll be in the middle of everything. You won't be able to spoil him so, once this one arrives. But Evie, after this . . . maybe try to hold off on the next for a bit?"

Evie made a wry face as she swung her legs up onto the sofa. "You know, I said that with this one? But you know how it is. I couldn't stand to keep putting John off—"

"I *warned* John—"

"Peace, Jean. It wasn't all his doing. I missed him."

Jean blew out a breath. Evie was sweet, but neither she nor her husband was long on forethought. There was no putting the horse back in the barn now, certainly, and she might as well get down to business. There was a grounding comfort in doing her work, something familiar and normal for the first time in weeks. Solid ground beneath her feet. "Well, let's see if this babe is going to be more cooperative for us than Frankie was."

Jean began to feel her way around the mound of Evie's belly, her hands firm but gentle as she worked to get a sense of where the baby lay, and how. Evie was carrying lower with this one than she had with Frankie this close to the day, which boded well. "I can't imagine you'll be waiting much longer, Ev—Oop!" The baby gave a powerful kick against Jean's palms, just under Evie's ribs.

"Uff!" Evie grunted. "Good lord, child, not the lungs!"

Jean grinned. Baby's head was down. Just as it ought to be, and thank God.

It was a rare fine winter day, and Jean was cautiously optimistic as she headed back through the village toward Anneke's house. Everything seemed to be progressing as it should with Evie, and while there was no saying for sure, Jean was almost certain they'd end up sending for her overnight, or sometime the next day. Which would be the eve of the New Year, and wouldn't that be a thing? A new life and a new year, all at once.

She hoped that would actually be the case. The days since Christmas had been oddly stretched, as time always was between then and the New Year, with no one doing things on quite their usual schedule, eating meals of strange things at strange times, drinking too much, and paying social calls on their neighbors unannounced.

Laurie had grown quiet and sullen since the holiday. Jean knew better than to go on prodding him after their earlier talk, but Anneke had begun pushing. A few days after Christmas, he'd snapped at her, and gone stomping off to Noble Burgoyne's place for several hours. When he came back he was in a better mood, but it was clearly due to him and his friend having gotten a bit too deep into the Christmas cheer, Laurie no more willing to open up than he'd been before.

All in all, Jean looked forward to going home again. She sorely wished to check in on Muirin. Thinking of her out there, alone in that house with no one but Tobias for company, made Jean uneasy, especially after Laurie's tale about the man and his reaction to even the most foolish of tales about his wife.

She was pulled from her thoughts by a soft tapping on the inside of the window of the mercantile as she passed it by, a movement at the corner of her eye. Jean turned her head and stumbled to a halt, her mouth falling open.

It was Muirin. She was in her good gray dress, with her blue shawl and gloves and her lace-trimmed bonnet, the baby swaddled in a thick white blanket in her arms. For a moment, Jean wondered if she was imagining things, but then Muirin waved again, gesturing for her to come inside.

Jean went, the little bell above the door tinkling as she entered. Tobias was leaning in the doorway to the back room, talking to Mr. Zwicker, and the voices of two women filtered through from behind the rack of fabrics. They were discussing colors for a dress, but she couldn't care less about any of that.

"Muirin!" Jean said, embracing her. Muirin's nose brushed Jean's cheek, and Jean pressed her eyes shut to return the gesture, taking a deep breath. Salt spray and sun-warmed stone, fresh bread with rich butter. She pulled away quickly before their greeting might be noted, gathering herself to speak. "You came to town! I didn't think you would"—Jean glanced over toward Tobias, and then finished—"what with the weather."

Muirin leaned closer again, speaking softly. "Said he would go today, him. So I say want come. Thought would say no? But he say, you said was good."

Jean was stunned. The last thing she'd have expected was Tobias taking any of her advice, especially given the rest of his behavior. She couldn't imagine he'd had a change of mind and decided he wanted Muirin working on her English after all, not after what he'd done, nor that he'd suddenly become sold on the idea of his wife making more new friends. As if sensing Jean's confusion, Muirin seized Jean's arm and pulled her to one side of the front door, wedging her in between a barrel of salt cod and one of sauerkraut.

"He funny. Like angry, but not—is less? Different. He say want I smile for him, like when we go walk. Thinks if he bring me to see town, will be happy. I want to see *you*. Jean, not town." Now Muirin *did* smile, a sly, curling thing that crinkled her dark eyes. "Stupid man."

Jean half strangled trying not to laugh. "He's *jealous*? Because you don't smile for him? And you played him, for a trip to visit me—Muirin, you're too much!" She tried to press down the bubble of glee rising up in her before it carried her away. However it felt, Muirin wanting to see her badly enough to put one over on her husband didn't mean anything, except that Muirin was lonely.

Muirin seemed smugly pleased with herself, to be honest, but then her expression shifted, becoming more serious. "Is baby here? When are home again, you?"

"I'm not sure," Jean said, leaning in to take a peek at Kiel— Toby. She had to keep a watch on that. Tobias would no doubt be furious if she accidentally said the wrong one in front of him. The baby was asleep. Stunning how fast they grew; she'd have sworn he was bigger again already. "Soon, I hope; maybe in the next day or two? I'm a bit nervous about this one," she admitted.

"Ner-vuss?" Muirin's accent made the word strange—the *r* growled, the *s* hissed.

Jean nodded. "Nervous. It's a little like scared, but different. Less scared, and more . . . waiting. Worried."

Muirin frowned. "Why, is?" she asked. Jean sighed.

"This lady, her last birth was difficult. The baby was upside-down. I don't think it'll happen again this time, but it was very bad. Sometimes women die." Jean took a deep breath. "It's a problem in the fall for some reason, with the farmwives. But not so much in winter." She spread her hands, giving a shrug. "I wish I knew why."

Muirin made a small moue, considering. "Wife, on farm is? Work in field?"

Jean wondered where Muirin was headed. "Mmm. Yes. Fall is harvest, and everyone helps as much as they can, even mothers. But I don't see why that should matter—"

"Here, hold." Muirin cut Jean off, pressing Kiel into her arms. "Easy, is. Too much time this—" She bent over forward, from her waist, as if reaching to pull weeds, or pick potatoes from the dirt, then straightened again. "Is wrong. Baby goes wrong way if dive too much down, mother mine told aunt. Is better, this—" Muirin squatted, bending her knees deeply, but keeping her torso upright, without an ounce of self-consciousness, or even seeming to realize that what she was doing was utterly bizarre in the middle of a shop. "See, you?"

Jean was flabbergasted. "I . . . that's . . . my God." She offered Muirin one of her hands, helping her back up. "It . . . that . . . it's so obvious! I can't believe no one's ever, that *I* never thought— Muirin, you're incredible." Muirin flushed, pleased. The baby made a quiet gurgle, and Jean looked down at him. "Kiel, your mama is a genius!"

Muirin laughed softly, still holding on to Jean's fingers. She had gone a very pretty pink.

Jean stepped in, leaning closer to her ear. "When I come

home, we'll find time to talk more. Go out walking again, since it makes you smile. I probably shouldn't come too much, but I will come. All right?"

"Jean?" Muirin's voice went wary, the smile sliding off her face. "Who is, she? Think she not like you." Jean turned her head, following Muirin's gaze.

It was Mrs. Keddy. She was standing with Tobias, down at the far end of the counter, and Jean froze as both of their heads turned in her direction. Mrs. Keddy smiled right at her, a mean and brittle thing. Tobias's face was perfectly, carefully blank.

Muirin's fingers slipped from Jean's bloodless hand.

Jean's voice echoed oddly in her ears as she turned, pushing Kiel back into his mother's arms. "Muirin, here, take the baby. I think maybe—"

"Muirin." Tobias's voice came from directly behind Jean, making her jump; how did a man so big cross a room so quietly? He spoke low, and rather too calm. "Take Toby and go wait in the wagon. We're done here."

Muirin seemed to know better than to argue with that voice. She glanced once at Jean and then scuttled around her husband and out the door, the bell jangling over her head as she went. Jean couldn't have moved if she tried. She was mired, her boots sunk clear into the floor.

"Jean," Tobias said, like he'd only just spotted her now that he was standing directly in front of her. Mrs. Keddy had disappeared again, behind the bolts of fabric. There was no whispering behind the shelves now, only a heavy silence. "I should have known we might see you here. Always popping up. Still staying with Anneke Ernst?"

Jean's tongue had become too big for her mouth. She nodded.

"I hear her Laurie's back for the winter. He's a good talker, that one. Must seem a full house for you."

She found her voice again. "I don't mind company."

"Suppose not." Tobias's eyes narrowed. "You seemed to like having Muirin over to yours well enough."

Jean wasn't sure what to say to that.

"Must be lonely," he went on. "You, having no one else to home but yourself. Someone ought to check in on *you* now and then. Maybe I'll put my head in myself when I pass next, make sure all's in order."

"That's . . . kind of you." Jean's throat was dry. She wanted to swallow. "I'm fine, though, really."

"Oh," he said. "Ain't no bother. We're all awful isolated out our way, if anyone were to run into trouble somehow. I'd feel better if I had an eye on you. Besides, a body ought to be *neighborly*." His mouth stretched in a tight-lipped thing that did not quite pass as a smile; Jean got an impression of bared teeth, the fine hairs at the back of her neck prickling. "Well. I'm off. No doubt we'll see you again, once you're home."

"Tobias—" Jean began, but he'd already turned, going back to lean on the counter.

"Almost forgot. Zwicker, you got any snare wire?" Tobias scowled back over his shoulder at Jean, and his lip curled. "There's a little vixen been sniffing around my henhouse."

Jean still couldn't make her feet move. Couldn't speak, couldn't think, as Tobias got his coil of copper wire, and slipped it into his pocket. A low, angry hissing came from behind the fabrics—*But why? It's not like it's any of*—but everything was strangely muted, as though Jean's ears had been stuffed full of lambswool. Tobias went past her out the door without another backward glance, as if she had become invisible, faded away into the plank wall. Time only started moving again when the tinny little bell over the door jangled as it closed.

Jean stumbled outside after him. Muirin was already sitting in the wagon, and Tobias swung himself up next to her as Jean looked on. There had to be something she could say, something she could do, but she didn't know what, and her mouth was full of ash. They drove right past her, away up the road, and Muirin did not look at Jean but stared straight ahead, hidden beneath her bonnet. Her back was stiff and straight, and it was all happening again, was Jean's own fault, just like—

There was a muted tap on the inside of the glass window of the mercantile, a movement at the corner of her eye. Jean turned her head.

It was Josephine Keddy. She lifted a hand, pressing it to the window. Mrs. Keddy came up behind her, glaring at Jean through the glass. She caught Jo by the elbow and pulled her away.

There's a little vixen been sniffing around my henhouse.

Never come near my daughter again, you filthy little witch!

Jean and Jo had been so careful, all that last summer, as they kissed behind cowsheds and henhouses, even in the loft of Jo's own father's mill. Kept things quiet, so no one would realize anything between them had changed. It was nothing new, Jean staying over with the Keddys as she had that final night. She'd been a fixture there since she was a child, she and Jo playmates and fast friends. The two of them shared a bed, for they always did, but the secrets they whispered that night were their new ones, and their usual giggles gave way to more kisses, to murmurs and gasps and bold explorations, pressed close to each other in the dark. *Shh,* Jo had said to her once, near the end. *Shh.* The next morning they were bashful and a little awkward but couldn't stop smiling at each other over breakfast, their eyes dark with lack of sleep. Jo's oldest sister, though, Margie, who had the room next to Jo's, she'd glared silent daggers at Jean until her father arrived to take her home. It hadn't occurred to Jean at the time that it might have had something to do with the thin wall between the two bedrooms.

Within the month, Jo had been married.

Mrs. Keddy had been so smug that winter in town—*Oh, yes, doing so well! I'm sure we'll hear they're expecting their first any minute now!* She'd relished mentioning Jo's new life whenever Jean was passing by, and Jean couldn't tell if the heavy burning inside her chest was anger, or sorrow, or something like shame, but she put her chin up and marched past as if it were nothing to her, even as she was shaken by a fresh new horror: Jo pregnant, frightened, and in pain, with only strangers there to help her when it should have been Jean holding her hand.

Later, alone, Jean had wept, angry not at Mrs. Keddy but at herself, for blaming Jo when she knew full well there wasn't a single thing she could have done once her parents' minds were made up. For not having done anything to stop it all—and for having been so foolish to begin with. It wasn't as if Jean could have married Jo herself.

Jo's going away had been Jean's own fault, she was sure of it. And now Muirin was gone, too, and how was she ever supposed to help her now, when Tobias thought . . .

Jean should have been more careful.

14

Jean wasn't quite sure how she got back to Anneke's.

She was standing in front of the mercantile, and then, some-how, she was walking through the back door of the house into Anneke's kitchen, without a single thing between. Anneke glanced up from the scraps of fabric she was sorting for a quilt, took one good look at Jean, and made to get up.

"Laurie! Laurie!" Anneke's voice alone brought her son run-ning from the other room. He stopped dead in the doorway, staring at Jean. "For God's sake, Laurie!" Anneke snapped. In a matter of moments, he had Jean sat down in a chair before the stove, and was pressing a chipped cup with a splash of the left-over Christmas rum into her shaking hand.

"Drink that down," he commanded.

The burn of the pure alcohol down her throat brought Jean back to herself, at least enough to explain what had happened, about seeing Muirin at the mercantile, and Mrs. Keddy, and what Tobias had said. How Jo had been there and seen it all. Jean wasn't sure how much sense she made. It was like a thick bank of fog had rolled in around her, and she sat shivering and clutching the empty china cup in both hands, trying to collect the rest of her whirling thoughts while Anneke explained to Laurie all that had come before.

Jean's mentor rounded out her accounting of events with a sound cursing of Mrs. Anna Belle Keddy before turning back to Jean. The lines around Anneke's mouth had pulled tight, her forehead furrowed as deeply as a field planted with potatoes. "That was a threat he made, and no mistaking it. Keep a neighborly eye, my aunt Fanny. Jeanie, you'll stay out the winter here in town with us, let things blow over."

"What? No! I'll do no such thing! Anneke, it'd be as good as admitting I'd done something wrong, and I never did. And Muirin, she—"

"Made her own bed; let her lie in it. And you ought to not put another toe near it, or her, missy!" Anneke's blunt words and sharp tone stunned Jean completely speechless.

"Now, Ma," Laurie put in. "I know you're worried—"

"Worried?" Anneke snorted. "You heard what he said!"

"Aye." Laurie nodded, maddeningly calm and sensible. "I'll come out there and stay with you, Red, just for a bit. Make sure there's no trouble."

"That'd be almost as bad as me staying here!" Jean thrust herself up from her chair, nearly knocking it over. "Damn it, Laur, he'd think I was scared of him!"

Laurie frowned. "Jeanie, that ain't—" Whatever he intended to say was interrupted by a sudden pounding at the door. Laurie turned and jerked it open, and John Hiltz, red-faced and breathless, all but tumbled into the kitchen.

"Sorry," he puffed out, "but we needs you back to the house, miss."

Jean could almost have kissed him.

Her sense of relief faded as Evie labored long into the night and right through to the next morning, the pair of them taking long slow turns around the room together in the small hours when Evie felt she simply had to move, until at last Jean refused to allow it any further. Normally such movement helped, but Evie was exhausting herself, and still the child didn't come. For all that the babe had pointed itself in the right direction, the birth was by no means an easy one. Jean sent John for the doctor near the end, fearing for mother and child both.

No sooner had he gone running out than Evie dredged up a last scrap of resolve that Jean hadn't been sure she had left. By the time John came panting back through the door with the doctor, not more than ten minutes later, Evie had her new daughter safe in her arms.

Jean decreed that Evie not set a foot out of bed for the next week. Which meant staying several days in the house herself, cooking and cleaning, and feeding little Frankie and his older brother, trying to keep the pair of them quiet and entertained so their mother could rest. John helped, of course, but the man still had wood to chop and a barnful of cows to deal with, so Jean's being there was necessary to keep Evie abed. The only time Jean left was to pay a short call at the Eisenors' place, where she found all in order: Ida Mae was rosy, round, and in much higher spirits than she'd been on Jean's last visit.

All the work was a blessing, in a way, for it kept Jean's hands busy and her mind occupied, off her own problems. Still, her stomach refused to budge from the sharp, tight knot it had locked itself into. Once Evie was back up and about, Jean was obliged to return to Anneke's, and the argument over what she ought to do about Muirin and Tobias.

The week's respite had not soothed anyone's frazzled nerves. Anneke ambushed Jean the minute she was in the door.

"You aren't going back out there."

"The hell I'm not." Jean was having none of it. "It's my parents' house, *my* house! I'm not abandoning it just because Tobias Silber can't be civil—"

"*Civil?*" Anneke's voice cracked. "He thinks—"

"I know what he *thinks!*" Jean's face burned. She thought she might go up in flames if Anneke said it out loud. She set her chin, prepared to be as stubborn as Kicker, waiting for her back at home. "He's an idiot! I'm going home, Anneke."

"I should have insisted you come stay in town long before any of this mess! Anything could happen to you out there by yourself, and no one would have a clue for days, even without that man having a bee in his bonnet—"

Jean laughed. "A bee in his bonnet? You make him sound like a prissy milkmaid—" Laurie had been caught out in the doorway between the kitchen and the parlor, leery of drawing attention to himself by moving, but this made him snort.

Anneke's voice rose high and shrill. "Don't you dare laugh, missy! You aren't setting foot out of this house until things are settled down again, I won't have it—"

"You haven't any right to tell me what I will or won't do!"

Laurie finally dared to add his voice. "Jean, maybe . . ."

"Don't you *dare* take her side!" Jean rounded on him, furious. "Maybe *you* can go haring off to sea whenever you want a bit of room to think, or whenever anyone looks at you funny, but all I have is that house—"

Anneke ran right over top of her. "You should've *stayed* in your bloody house and kept out of the Silbers' business, like I told you at the start! But no, you've gone so foolish over this Muirin—"

Jean's whole body blazed hot, and then as cold as if Anneke had dropped her into the ice-edged bay. "*You* talk some sense into her," she hissed at Laurie. "She's your mother, not mine!"

Anneke clamped her mouth shut on whatever else she'd been about to say, her face shuttering as if she'd been slapped. Jean fled past Laurie, upstairs to her bed.

"There's no talking you out of this thing, is there?"

Jean caught her breath, pressing her back to the wall beside the kitchen door before she realized it was only Laurie. Anneke must have gone to bed, but her son was still up, sitting alone in the dark parlor, staring into the last orange embers that remained in the fireplace. Their shifting light deepened the lines in his face, turning him haunted and fey. "Can't sleep?"

Jean shook her head. "You either?" She pulled the blanket she had wrapped around her shoulders tighter. "I shouldn't have said that, before. About her not being my mother. She's always been as good as."

"She'll forgive you; you know she will." Laurie turned to look at her, throwing his face into shadow. "You can't push everybody away, Jean."

Laurie had only been refusing to talk to anyone about anything real for the best part of two weeks himself. Jean almost said *pot calling kettle,* but caught herself, thinking better of it. She'd already let her mouth run quite enough for one day. She squinted at the mantel clock, but it was too dark to make out the hands. "What time is it?"

"Late."

"Don't be an ass."

Laurie sniffed, and went back to staring sullenly into the fireplace. He didn't say anything else, so Jean went through to the kitchen and poured herself the glass of water she'd come down for from the jug beside the pump. She wasn't going to push Laurie if he didn't want to talk, and he'd have done the same for her.

"G'night, Laur," she said, starting back up the stairs.

"I'll take you out in the morning."

Jean stopped.

"I'll borrow the wagon from the Burgoynes. But I'm coming out there to visit you a couple times a week if you won't let me stay. At least until we know for sure nothing's going to come of this whole mess with Silber and his wife."

"Laurie—"

"That's my condition, Red. It was bad enough before, you all the way out there on your own where anything could happen and no one'd know for days, Ma's right about that. But as long as you let me check on things, I'll back you with her." Laurie shifted in his seat, reaching for the brass poker beside the hearth. "I can tell how important it is to you, being out there for your . . . for Muirin."

Jean supposed it might work, him coming out to visit. After all, he'd not been home in ages, and everyone knew they were as good as siblings. It would look a lot less suspect than him setting up permanent camp in her house, at any rate. Hopefully it would settle Anneke's nerves some, too. "All right," she said. "Thanks, Laurie. I knew you'd understand."

"Right," he said, quiet. "Go get some sleep, Red."

Jean left him sitting in the dark parlor before the fireplace, pushing the last glowing coals about with the poker, like peas on a half-empty plate.

Laurie beat Jean down the stairs the next morning and told his mother what the two of them had settled on before Jean got the chance to make her apology. It did not settle Anneke's nerves as hoped: Jean was a fool, courting disaster, and Laurie a traitor for siding with her. Jean half feared Anneke might not ever speak to her again, but when Laurie brought the wagon to the door, his mother came shuffling out of the house in her woolly slippers to hug Jean before she climbed up to sit beside him.

"I'm sorry," Jean finally managed. "I didn't mean—"

"Mind yourself." Anneke cut off her apology, gripping Jean by the chin and gazing at her intently with her sharp raven's eyes, as if to bore the advice straight into her protégé's head. "Stay clear of that house. Don't go acting a damn fool." Anneke's warning was so strained with worry and affection Jean could only squeeze her back with all her might, kiss her mentor's wrinkled cheek, and promise hoarsely that she would do her very best not to.

Laurie was quiet on the trip out along the bay. When he reined in the horse before Jean's gate, he turned to give her a stern look. "Don't go up there, Jeanie. I mean it. It'd be begging for trouble."

She gave his arm a squeeze and nodded before clambering down to fetch Robbie McNair out of the house to ride back into town with Laurie, but she did not promise anything.

15

Jean stood across the track from her gate, watching the sea rolling cold and gray and vast, and wondered what she ought to do. She'd already been standing there long enough that her cheeks stung from the cold wind, and her eyes watered, as the gulls swooped and squalled overhead.

Three weeks had gone by since the day in the mercantile. It felt like three years, and every day Jean found herself more worried.

Tobias had stopped by Jean's house on his way back from town with Muirin and spoken to Robbie McNair about the little vixen, presenting him with a loop of snare wire. Robbie'd told her about it at the end of his report, such as it was, while he was clambering up into the wagon with Laurie.

"I told him you'd not like it, miss. That fox of yours is halfway to tame. I got her to take a boilt egg right from my hand yesterday." The young man had been distressed by the dishonorable idea of laying a trap for someone with whom he'd shared breakfast. "Mr. Silber said I ought to put a snare under the shed anyway, if I was smart. So I told him thank you, but I ain't done it. I made up a little thing for the baby, though? Left it on the table; maybe you can take it over sometime."

Laurie'd raised a significant eyebrow at Jean, though he addressed his comment to Robbie. "Don't worry. I think the *little vixen* knows to steer well clear of Tobias Silber."

Jean had rolled her eyes. She wasn't any more worried for the fox than she was for herself. The creature was clever enough to keep herself out of trouble.

It was Muirin she was worried for. Muirin, who couldn't possibly understand what had happened that afternoon—she'd no idea who Mrs. Keddy was, let alone what the woman would have said to anger her husband. Jean feared what Tobias might have said or done after the two of them left town that day, if he might have decided to vent his ire once they were alone, without an audience. She wanted to know if Muirin was all right . . . Hopefully it was only Jean he suspected.

Every morning after she fed the animals, Jean walked as far as the stream, and looked up into the woodlot, considering. For all his talk of keeping an eye on her, Tobias hadn't darkened Jean's doorway since he'd stopped to talk to Robbie. Perhaps she might slip up through the wood unnoticed to see if all was well? But what if Tobias caught Jean out at it, found her sneaking in the shadows and took it as proof, as good as a sign that read GUILTY hung around her neck?

But by staying away, wasn't Jean practically confirming to Tobias that she was guilty of what Mrs. Keddy's words had most likely led him to suspect? The most she'd ever done was press her nose to Muirin's cheek, even if she'd wished—no. Jean clasped her chilled hands together, rolling the grip of her fingers back and forth. Maybe it was better to act as if she had nothing to hide, as if it were all a misunderstanding. Tobias had made such a point of saying as how they ought to be neighborly; perhaps that was exactly the face Jean should present to him.

She was a respectable woman who had done nothing to be ashamed of.

She was an idiot, maybe. One of Jean's knuckles cracked. Out in the bay, a dark head popped up, a seal slowly spinning and craning its neck as it bobbed in place, as if it were watching Jean just as she watched it. It slipped back under the waves, disappearing as quietly as it had come. There seemed to be more of them in her little cove of late; she wondered what had brought them her way. Jean turned her back on the sea, shaking her hands loose again, and went to pin up her hair, to better look the part of a respectable woman before heading up the hill.

She made no secret of her approach as she came up over the field from the woodlot. Along with the wooden teething ring Robbie McNair had carved for Kiel, a cunning thing with a crescent man in the moon smiling from one smooth curve of it, Jean was also carrying a dozen molasses cookies wrapped up in a tea towel. Each one bore the print of her thumb, a shallow impression filled with jam.

Tobias must have seen her coming out of the bedroom window, for by the time Jean made it up the hill to the house and came around to the door, he was already standing before it with his arms crossed, waiting for her.

"Miss Langille."

Formality had been reinstated. It was not an encouraging thing. "Mr. Silber," she replied, the back of her tongue souring. "I've not been 'round yet since I got back, to look in on Muirin and little Toby, and see how—"

"Aye." His voice was cool, impassive as a stone. "And there ain't no need for you to have come 'round to look now."

"Tobias," she began.

"Nah, my girl. I should have known there was something off about you, right from the first minute you started in with your excuses, keeping Muirin down to yours all that extra time, when there wasn't a single damn thing wrong with her. Teaching her English, just so you could go and put God knows what kind of ideas in her head, and saying as how it's for her good. She's a proper lass, my wife, and I won't have you drawing her into your wickedness, you understand me?"

Jean did, only too well. Still, she tried again.

"Tobias, Mrs. Keddy's hated me for years. Whatever she had to say, I swear—"

Tobias took a single step forward.

Jean stepped back, clutching her bundle of cookies.

"You ain't to be trusted around the ladies, is what she says. And I think she's got the right of it. Any man who trusts you to see to his woman is a fool." His voice dropped, low and threatening. "I ain't about to *share my wife*. Not with anyone, let alone the likes of you." The words hit like a slap of cold seawater.

"Muirin is my *friend*, Tobias! I never so much as—"

"I think I spoke clear enough. Get the hell off my land. I ain't going to tell you twice." He wrenched open the door of the house, stepping back inside. Jean craned her neck, but there was no sign of Muirin in the room beyond him, and Tobias turned on his heel to glare at her once more.

"Go on," he snapped, as if Jean were some wild animal, vermin come nosing about his door. "Git!"

The door swung shut in her face.

She wanted to pound upon it. To yell, to weep, if that would make him understand; that she simply wanted to see her friend, that she missed her, was worried, that it wasn't *like that*.

But it was.

Like that.

Not for Muirin, maybe. But it was for Jean, however much

she wanted to pretend it wasn't, had tried to deny it to Anneke and Laurie. She stood a moment longer, staring dully at the door, before turning and trudging around the corner of the house on leaden feet, back the way she'd come. There was no use staying. Jean's throat burned, and she stumbled blindly over a clump of snow. She should have known better, should never have let herself care—

Tap.

A small, soft sound behind her. Jean froze. Slow and cautious, she turned to look.

Muirin was standing at the bedroom window, watching her go. She pressed her hand flat against the uneven glass, the waver in the pane making it look like she was standing underwater.

Jean raised her own hand, swallowing hard. A mouthful of rough pebbles, hidden shards of glass.

Muirin shook her head and began making a series of quick, furtive gestures that conveyed nothing except urgency. There was a lot of pointing.

Jean raised both hands and shrugged. *What are you trying to say, Muirin?*

Muirin glanced over her shoulder toward the other room. Jean expected her to go; or worse, to hear Tobias suddenly raise his voice within, see him appear behind her. Instead Muirin turned back with round eyes and started frantically flapping her hands at Jean, as if to shoo her off.

The door banged open at the front of the house.

Jean dove forward, scrambling toward the woodpile. She jammed herself into the shadowed nook where it butted up against the house, making herself as small and low to the ground as she could.

There was a heavy crunching of boots, and Tobias came around the corner of the house. He strode past Jean on the far side of the woodpile, storming along the very path she ought to have been walking, not six feet from where she was not so much hidden as caught out in the open, desperately wishing not to be spotted. Jean held her breath, her eyes glued to his back as he passed between the henhouse and the barn and disappeared over the crest of the hill, headed down across the field toward the woodlot. Following *her*, or so he thought. Making certain she'd gone to ground.

Jean hoped that was all he intended. Thank God the snow was so churned up around the house and the barn from his chores, or she'd have left tracks for him to see as soon as he'd come around the corner, leading him right where she'd gone. There was a slide and a thump overhead, as Muirin shoved open the bedroom window, and Jean was back on her feet in an instant.

"Muirin! Are you all right? Has—"

"Jean!" Muirin's voice was a tangle of worry and relief. "Jean, he so angered! Says bad things about you, what he will do. Is not safe here!"

"I know, I know, but is he angry with *you*?" Jean looked over every inch of Muirin she could see, dreading and more than half expecting to see some mark upon her. There was none, aside from the smudge of dark circles beneath her eyes that spoke of restless nights. Jean released a soft breath. "That woman at the mercantile, Muirin, you were right. She doesn't like me. Her daughter, I . . ." She wasn't quite sure how to go on, or how Muirin would react, but Muirin spoke up herself before Jean could choose her next words.

"Know, I. Says much, he, bad things. You and daughter, hers, are . . . friends, before."

Jean laughed once, a bitter thing that stuck in her throat, and she had to cough before she could go on. "Friends, yes. But Muirin, I—"

Muirin let out an irritated huff. "Word is not right! More was like . . . wifes, you, and she." Jean blinked. She supposed that was close enough, and so she nodded.

"I loved her." Jean wasn't sure she'd ever said it so clearly, to anyone. But with Muirin she could only be direct, had no room to call it anything but exactly what it had been. "Her mother found a man to marry her, and they sent her away with him. And now she's gone and told Tobias, to make trouble for me. He thinks that I've . . . done things I shouldn't have, with you."

Muirin was less tactful. "Thinks you want me for wife, will steal. Afraid I will go away with you if he not watch." She made her eyes wide and innocent. " 'Not understand,' I say to him, 'Not know what you mean.' " Her mouth twisted, wry. "Understand, I. But he is angry. Very much, Jean. Calls you bad names, and yells, and Kiel cries. He says, I, in house to stay always now, and not to see you more. Too *much* smile, I."

She wasn't anything like smiling now. Jean could see Muirin's frustration, that her already small world had been made even smaller by her husband's will.

Jean reached a hand up and set it on the windowsill between them. "It's all my fault. I'm so sorry, Muirin. I should go now, before he comes back . . ." Her throat tightened. It wasn't as if she could fight him.

"Jean." Muirin took up her hand, and pressed it, grave. Jean's heart gave a pang—Muirin had accepted this new revelation about her so naturally, and were it not for Tobias, it would have changed nothing between them, except that Jean could have been more open and freer with her than she'd ever dreamed. "Must go careful. Jealous, he is, but is bad man, too. Know this, I. He is good not . . ." She shook her head, pursing her lips. "Not good. I know this for long time now."

Jean had a terrible premonition, suddenly, that Muirin had another story left to tell, something far beyond what Jean had managed to piece together from their conversations. Something

Muirin knew, or had seen, something Tobias had done. Something secret. Something he was desperate to keep hidden. Something very, very wrong.

Jean's heart beat slow and sluggish, her chest filled with cold dread, and her grip tightened on Muirin's hand. "What's he done? What do you—"

Muirin glanced up, over Jean's head, and stiffened, her eye caught by something that Jean couldn't see past the crest of the hill when she turned to follow her gaze.

"Go!" Muirin hissed, low and urgent. "Jean, go now!" Dropping Jean's hand, she pulled her head back inside, shutting the window with a dull thud. Jean ran; around the house, past the front door to the long drive as if a pack of hounds were baying at her heels. She fled down the drive and flung herself face-first in the snow behind a thick patch of juniper bushes alongside the shore road, panting. Her forgotten bundle of cookies was crushed beneath her. Sharp juniper and ginger spice filled her nostrils, and Robbie McNair's teething ring poked into the soft spot under Jean's ribs as she peered out from under the low branches. Tobias came around the corner of the house, knocked his boots against the step, and went back inside.

Jean rolled over onto her back, willing her heart to stop pounding, and stared up at the high, shifting clouds. She needed to find out what Tobias Silber had done and how Muirin was tangled up in it.

But how?

16

Tobias had said he didn't want to see her around the place again, and so he would not. Jean set about making herself every bit as sneaky and stealthy as he might have feared.

She crept through the woodlot, silent as the fox, slipping from the shadow of one tree to the next, walking only in the footprints where she'd walked before, or where Tobias and his horse had come through, pulling logs. She found a path that had been stirred up by some small animal using it over and over, and she used it, too, thanking God that in the deep heart of winter it had gone too cold for snow, even as her toes tingled inside of her boots, and the little hairs inside of her nose crackled with each breath she drew. Jean ventured as far as the tree line at the bottom of Tobias's field, and dared go no farther, for fear of being spotted. For days she shirked her household chores, the whole time knowing full well what Anneke would say, and Laurie, too: that she was out of her mind to be going anywhere near the place at all.

Jean needed to talk to Muirin again, but she couldn't risk

being seen by Tobias. Between his words in the mercantile and the note of terror in Muirin's voice when she'd told Jean to go that last afternoon, she was more than convinced. Tobias was dangerous.

And Muirin was stuck in that house with him. Alone, day in and day out.

Jean had Laurie paying her visits at least, although they did nothing to ease her mind. She couldn't admit to him she'd gone up there, not without first learning something that might justify it to him. He would probably have offered to help her, but she didn't want to face how furious he was liable to be first. On the days between his visits, she watched for her chance, hoping Tobias might go into the woods with his horse for an hour or two, or better yet, into town for an afternoon.

She watched and waited and grew more frustrated with each passing day, for it seemed Tobias had set himself to find each and every task he possibly could to keep busy without ever leaving his own backyard again. She never caught a glimpse of Muirin outside of their house, but *he* was always there: doing some chore or other, forking down hay from out of the loft, feeding the chickens, or chopping wood. After a while, Jean would turn tail and go home, only to return the next day.

One still afternoon, he climbed back up onto the roof of the house, a lean silhouette against the thin, pale February sky. Jean wondered what the problem was with the chimney. Hopefully the man would fix it once and for all, before little Kiel ended up taking a chill. As she watched, Tobias looked up from whatever he was doing to peer off in the direction of her own house. He'd not be able to see anything of it from there, save the smoke from her banked fire above the trees, but Jean was struck with the certainty that he was wondering about her: where she was, what she was doing.

His face turned in her direction.

Jean ducked behind a tree trunk, pressing her back against it with a soft curse, her heart pounding.

What had pulled his eye? She glanced down at her yellow shawl and winced. Stupid. Had he seen her? Or had his attention shifted elsewhere? She didn't dare peek back around the trunk to find out.

After several excruciating minutes spent trying to breathe as little as possible for fear of her steaming breath giving her away, Jean dropped low, praying that she'd be hidden by the scraggy gray underbrush, and crawled away on her belly and elbows until she was sure it was safe to get up and strike out for home.

Most evenings, the two goats waited by the gate to their pen for Jean to come out and shut them away. Two days after she'd spied Tobias on his roof, she went up after closing in the chickens for the night to find Kicker, the wee beast, standing sentry with her front hooves slung up on the third rung of the fence. It could have almost fooled a person into thinking she was more eager dog than milch goat, but the only thing Kicker was ever eager for was a break for freedom the second the gate was open.

Jean wasn't playing *that* game tonight. Catching up the short length of rope she'd left hooked over the gate post, she looped it around the creature's neck before opening the gate.

"Be a good girl, Kick. Come on." Jean tugged on the rope. Kicker flared her nostrils, preparing to dig in with all fours and pull the opposite way. The goat stared at Jean as if it were plotting something . . . and then snorted, shook her flopping red ears, and gave in. Jean blew out an irritable sigh. "Honey—you, too."

She needn't have spoken, for Honey trotted along behind them as meekly as a pet lamb. Jean got the two animals into their shed without any further trouble, although she had to dodge a flying hoof as she filled the rack with fresh hay. She gave the offending party a dirty look—her father would have called it "the hairy eyeball"—and then went to draw a bucket of fresh water from the spring behind the house. By the time she broke the thin slick of ice on the spring and hauled the full pail back down the path to the goat shed—tripping over roots buried in the snow and sloshing her skirts with freezing water on the way—it was edging toward dusk. Jean shut the door of the shed on the goats and hurried back over the yard to the house.

A few feet from her door, she stopped dead.

There were boot prints in the snow heaped under her window. Big ones. Jean's scalp tingled and crept as she slowly turned to look behind her. The yard was empty. Nothing. A lonely gull cried, out over the sea.

She turned back to face her door and hesitated, her tongue gone rough and dry as a cat's inside her mouth. Reaching out a shaking hand, she twisted the knob and pushed the door open, leaping back as it swung away from her into the empty house.

She let out a single shallow laugh—*hah*—then looked back over at the footprints beneath her window and shuddered. Jean went and kicked snow over them before she went inside, so Laurie wouldn't see them when he came to call.

Tobias *had* seen her, and he was making it clear: He was keeping an eye on her, too. Unlike Jean, he had no fear of being caught out—he wanted her to know he was watching, tracking her every move.

Her henhouse unlocked itself not an hour later, and the chickens went clucking across the snowy yard in the gloom. The little red fox ran out to leap on one of them in an explosion of feathers and drag it away into the dry tangle of the marsh grass, but Jean still thought long and hard before going out with her lantern to catch the rest of them back in again.

"I'm telling you, we've both of us been minding our own business."

It wasn't a lie if one ignored that Jean considered it very much her business to mind Tobias's every move at this point, and that her neighbor seemed to be of much the same mind when it came to Jean, of course. She was strung as tight as one of Robbie McNair's fiddles, and Jean was honestly surprised that Laurie couldn't smell the manure she was shoveling from where he sat across the table. He did raise a skeptical eyebrow before setting down his teacup with a click.

"Ma's still huffed, you know. She thinks it's a miracle he ain't been giving you any trouble, and an even bigger one that you haven't been up there yet to stir the pot."

Jean shrugged as if to imply she'd no idea why Anneke would ever suspect such a thing and tried to look innocent.

"And since she's worried about *you,* she won't leave off pecking at *me,*" he went on, irritable. "'Why'd you take Jean back out there, Laurie?' 'You ought to go out and stay with her, Laurie!' 'Why d'you look like someone kicked your dog all the time, Laurie?' She's sending me clear 'round the bend!"

Jean snorted. "You do look like someone kicked your dog since you got back."

"Shut up. So do you."

Jean supposed he was probably right. Whatever was bothering Laurie, it was keeping him from looking too close at what was bothering *her,* even if it did have him twisted up in a knot. She wasn't about to go trying to unravel his trouble for him, not when she already had enough troubles of her own, and she wasn't about to add to his worries by telling him what was really going on, either. Not yet.

Jean could handle it for herself.

After Laurie'd gone, as she was clearing the cups from the table, Jean glanced out her window across the marsh. And then she looked again, out of the corner of her eye, while making an act of fumbling with the teapot so her looking wouldn't be so obvious. Tobias was stood high up on the far bank of the pond, under the birches, just watching. Right out in the open, a warning. How long had he been there? Had he seen Laurie come and go? Jean ducked her head and went on clearing the table as if she hadn't noticed him, a plucked-chicken feeling prickling up her neck and down her back, her arms going gooseflesh. In her mind's eye, there was an explosion of feathers.

Jean double-checked the bolt on her door.

That evening, she set about changing her coat for the winter, more clever and canny now than she'd been before, aiming to become the little vixen Tobias had likened her to. Hanging her yellow shawl behind the door, Jean searched out her father's old brown coat from a trunk in the loft to wear instead. The coat was almost big enough to swallow her; Jean rolled the sleeves so they wouldn't drag down over her hands. She went back up the hill to spy on the Silber house the next morning and found Tobias moving *his* chickens: out of the tidy, whitewashed henhouse he'd built for them and into the barn, two at a time. The birds flapped and squawked and buffeted him with their wings the whole way, treating him as roughly as he did them. Jean grinned a fox's grin, thrilled. If his coop had been paid a not-so-metaphorical visit, it was an irony well and truly deserved.

Two days later, Tobias was back out in the open space before the barn, hitching up his horse with the long lines he used for pulling logs from the woodlot, and Jean's heart leapt up, drumming like a pheasant's wings. Was he going, finally? He finished with the horse, then went 'round and called something into the house as he latched the door. Jean fought the absurd urge to snicker as Tobias circled the henhouse before setting out, looking it over as if worried he might not have found and secured every crack in it yet. At last, he took the horse's lead, giving a low whistle. As the horse started moving, Jean ducked back down the path and off to the left, then darted into a thick stand of spruce trees, crouching low.

The dense, spiking branches blocked Jean's view; her nose filled with the cool sharpness of evergreen. She held her breath as man and horse passed by her hiding place. Jean could make out the creak and jangle of the tack as they went, they were that close. As their heavy footsteps faded deeper into the wood, she let out her breath again, a ghostly puff of white. She crept back out of the spruces, then dashed up the hill toward the house. Her mitten dulled the sound as she rapped on the door.

"Muirin? Muirin, it's me!"

"Jean?" Muirin's voice came through the door, alarmed. "Can not open, is locked! Come to window!" *The man was locking her in the house now?* Things had become just as bad as she'd feared.

Jean went hastily around to the back of the house again, pausing by the woodpile to consider the window. Its sill was level with the top of her head. A sturdy log stood on its end next to the firewood: Tobias's brace for splitting smaller pieces of wood, the deep lines of axe strokes etched into the top of it. Jean pushed it onto its side and rolled it over beside the house. Setting it back up on end under the window, she shifted the log in the snow to stop it wobbling, and then stepped up to stand on it as Muirin shoved open the window.

"Jean!" Muirin leaned out the window, wrapping her arms tightly around Jean, pressing a warm nose to her cold cheek before pulling back, looking deeply concerned. "Should not have come! Tobias, he says bad things . . . goes to your house, watching."

Jean nodded, suddenly breathless. "I know. He's trying to

scare me off. But I was worried about you! Are you well? And Kiel—how's the baby?"

Muirin waved a hand in dismissal. "Fine I am, and Kiel. Can take care myself, and boy." She leaned forward on the sill and caught one of Jean's hands, her dark gaze intense. "But not fine, you, if he catch! He will do bad things, Jean, very bad. I scared for you."

Jean looked down and stroked the back of Muirin's hand before meeting her eyes again. "I'm being very careful, I promise. He won't see me. Muirin, what you said the last time I was here . . . you said that Tobias was a bad man. What's he done?"

Muirin's face darkened. "Thief, he. He says you want to steal, like fox, but is him, a thief."

"A thief?"

She nodded. "Is one who takes what not is theirs, you said. He took a thing, mine." Muirin drew a heavy breath. "I try to get back, he steal me."

A deep uneasiness stirred, roiling in Jean's stomach. She hoped that Muirin had made a mistake, spoken wrongly somehow. "Muirin, what do you mean, he *stole* you?"

"Home, me, with mother, and . . . aunt, was? He came, watching us. Took—" Breaking off, Muirin gave Jean a cautious, measuring look. Jean shook her head, unsure where her friend was going. Muirin curled both her hands to grip the windowsill before she spoke again; a word, two words, in her strange, rolling tongue. Jean did not understand the words, only that they had a *weight* to them. A deep ring of importance. Muirin went on: "Is not word for, in English? But mine is, so I go to him, try to tell him, 'Give me back.' And he took me, too, put in boat and take away. Bring here for wife, his."

For a moment, Jean could not respond. Her jaw worked, and when her voice finally returned it wasn't her own, came out sharp and thin.

"*Took you?* Muirin—he *stole* you?" Jean could hardly make it fit into her head, her thoughts chasing one another's tails in a dizzying whirl. "That's—my God, that's kidnapping! And he *made* you marry him, you didn't—? Muirin, I'm so sorry, I didn't understand before, when you said you had to marry. I thought you meant— Oh." Jean stopped. A dreadful curdling sickness rose up in her; thick, oily bitterness at the back of her throat. "Oh, God. Muirin . . ." Jean spoke carefully, afraid of where her words might land. "The baby?"

Muirin looked at Jean with her big dark eyes. "Am wife," she said, simply, resigned. "Wife does."

A hurricane roared in Jean's ears. She could not think, except that she would kill him. Rip his throat out with her teeth, then lay what was left of him at Muirin's feet.

"Jean," Muirin said, hushed, her brows knitting. "Jean, what thinking, you?"

Murder. I'm thinking about murder. Tobias could wait; he wasn't what mattered. Muirin was what was important. Jean schooled her voice to calmness, tried to keep it from shaking with the force of her anger, and on anger's heels came the nagging stab of her own guilt. "I knew something was wrong. I *knew* it, as soon as you came to my house I *knew,* but I couldn't see what it was. Oh, Muirin, I'm sorry. So sorry. If I'd known, I'd not ever have let him bring you back here. Never."

Muirin gave a small shrug, looking down at the windowsill and her fingers upon it. "How could know, you? Not say, I. Not was safe. And him . . . slippery, is. Like eel."

Jean thought, ridiculously, that Muirin was doing a grave disservice to eels, but she also admired the resolve with which Muirin had faced her situation. Jean didn't know many women who could have carried on as she had, taking care of house and self and baby in such circumstances.

Taking a slow breath, Jean reached out her hand to cup Muirin's soft cheek, so she would look at her again. Jean was as firm and solid as she could make herself, leaning in close to meet Muirin's eyes. "We're not going to let him keep on like this. We're going to get you away from him. I swear it. I have friends who'll help, Anneke and her son, Laurie. I don't know how, exactly, but we'll come up with a plan, sneak you away so Tobias won't know until after you've gone. And then—you can take Kiel and go home again. Even if we have to row you there ourselves!" Jean didn't know why she was making these promises. She had no idea how she would ever deliver on them. Inside, she was quaking, fear and anger and, God help her, love all tumbling together inside her.

Muirin's eyes lit in a new way, glowing from within, and Jean's doubts flew right back out of her head. Raising a hand, Muirin placed it over Jean's and kept it there, pressed against her cheek. "Will you, truly?"

"Truly. Muirin, I promise. Somehow, we'll find a way. We won't let him keep you. We can't."

Without a hint of warning, Muirin surged forward, catching Jean's face between her hands, kissing her full on the mouth. A muffled exclamation of shock escaped Jean, before she pulled away with a gasp.

Pulling away was the very last thing she wanted to do.

"Muirin, I—you don't have to do that. You don't. I want to help you because it's wrong, what he's done, because you shouldn't be here. Because you should be free to make your own choices. I—I don't need anything from you in return. I don't want it." Jean searched Muirin's face, her heart racing. "You understand?"

Muirin's face dropped. "Not like me, you? Not . . . want?"

"No! I mean, yes? I mean—" It was as though someone had spun Jean around too many times and set her to reeling. Everything was turning so quickly, and so surprisingly. "Muirin, you're lovely. And I do like you, very much. But . . . you mustn't think you have to do anything you don't want to, just because I'm helping you. Whatever Tobias might have said to you about me, I wouldn't do that to you, not ever. I couldn't. It's not right. It would be—as bad as what he's done."

Muirin looked at Jean without responding, trying to follow the path of her words before she spoke again. "But think *lovely.*" Muirin's mouth twitched. "Like me, you." She laughed, and Jean stared at her, wondering if Muirin quite understood what she was saying. She broke off again, tilting her head to one side, stroking her throat with her long fingers, her lips curling up at the corners. "Stupid girl. *Do* want, I."

Jean was fairly sure her mouth was hanging open. The cold air was making her teeth hurt. Perhaps she'd fallen off the log and hit her head, and all of this was nothing but a dream.

"Jean . . . ?" Muirin straightened her head again with a slight frown. "What thinking, you?" Jean almost laughed. How could Muirin be asking her that same question again, already, and for such a different reason?

"I—I think I'd like you to do it again? If it's really what you— *mmf.*"

Muirin *did* do it again, diving back in to kiss Jean with more than enough enthusiasm to prove she absolutely meant it, grabbing hold of Jean's coat collar and tugging her closer. Yielding, Jean leaned across the windowsill, closing her eyes and slipping a mittened hand behind Muirin's neck, up under her dark, heavy hair. Jean sank into the kiss as if it were a warm rip current, a deceptive, calm thing that drew her in, then turned desperate and hungry, pulling her deeper and deeper, stealing her breath away. She couldn't escape the siren call of that kiss, and she didn't want to try; she would be content to drown in Muirin's arms, their hot mouths pressed together until there was no saving either of them.

Jean had no idea how long they kept on like that, caught in each other's arms, half in and half out the window. The sound of an axe striking deep into a tree rang up from the woodlot, and they parted with a start, staring at each other, panting. Jean gave a quiet laugh, her knees gone wobbly, and Muirin echoed it. Leaning her high, smooth forehead against Jean's, Muirin closed her eyes, the curling sweep of her long eyelashes breaking against her cheek. Jean could have happily passed a day counting every one of them.

She lifted her head, pulling away. She wished she didn't have to.

"I have to go. Before he comes back." Jean hated saying the words, and worse, leaving Muirin behind. But if they tried to leave now, Tobias would come back and find them gone and they'd be lucky to make it as far as Jean's house, let alone into town. And with little Kiel, in this bitter cold—it was impossible.

Nearly as impossible as leaving them behind.

Muirin nodded. She could see it as clearly as Jean did; she was no fool. Jean kissed her once more and cupped Muirin's cheek in her hand again, leaning close. "Stay strong. I'll be back. I promise. We'll get you free." She stepped down off the log and rolled it back over to its place by the woodpile, setting it up on its end just as she'd found it.

"Careful be," Muirin called quietly, leaning out. "Watch your steps. Waiting, I." She set her hand over her heart, her bright eyes still on Jean, and slid the window shut.

Jean laid her hand over her own heart, and something in her chest rose to meet it as she looked up at Muirin behind the wavering glass, and lifted it in farewell. The chopping in the woodlot ceased, followed by the soft, far-off fall of a tree. Jean turned and set out for home the other way, the long way, over the winding shore road. The cold breeze off the sea whistled down her ears until they ached.

Jean would not risk the chance of meeting Tobias in the wood. Not now. Not when Muirin and Kiel were counting on her.

Now Jean had so much more to lose.

17

Jean spent the next few days buoyed up by those wonderful stolen kisses, but was still at a loss as to how to help Muirin escape.

She kept to her own place and went about her work in plain view: feeding the chickens, hanging her washing to freeze stiff on the line, and putting Honey and Kicker out into their pen in the mornings. Not that there was any grass there for the pair of them, mind, not at this time of year. But it was good for the goats to spend some energy, to get some air outside of their shed and skip about in the snow, and they would still nibble at little dry twigs and bits of the dead marsh grass, even bark if they could strip it off the spindly old tree in the corner of their patch.

Tobias seemed to have stopped watching her so closely. He must have thought she'd finally backed off. He thought she was scared. Not long ago, Jean would have hated that; she'd said as much to Laurie. Now it seemed a blessing, for it meant Muirin's husband no longer saw her as a threat. He'd never expect Jean to make a move against him now, not if she was cowed, keeping to her own home and no longer looking in the direction of his.

She kept her eyes open, of course, and her door bolted, but Jean went about her daily chores, humming with a fresh determination in her step.

Mostly.

Tobias wasn't watching her, and that meant he was keeping to his home as well. The thought of Muirin, trapped there with him . . . that thought hung over Jean's head like a long, dark shadow, even as she pegged her damp shifts and petticoats out in the weak winter sunshine. What he'd done. What he might be doing even now, all the while telling himself how he was such a good husband, it was only his due. That his stolen wife ought to be pleased, to love him back, be happy and contented in the prison he'd made just for her. That Muirin ought to smile. For him.

It twisted Jean's stomach up into snarls. It was a wonder Muirin still knew how to smile, after everything he'd done.

She did, though. Muirin smiled, and it was because of *Jean*.

Perhaps it was madness, but everything seemed possible now, in a way it hadn't since—Jean didn't know when. Since they'd sent Jo away? But now Muirin wanted her, and Jean was filled up with certainty; she would do whatever it took to help Muirin free herself. She had to find a way.

The little vixen came trotting out from the marsh and right under the clothesline, tail flagged high. It was the first time Jean had seen her in well over a week, since the day she'd made off with the escaped chicken. The vixen was bold in her brightness, a splash of red surrounded by the whites and grays of winter, the silver of the dead grasses. Jean smiled, wishing that she could waltz about so boldly in her own dealings.

"You've been scarce."

The fox paused midstride, not ten feet away, and cocked its head at her.

"Lying low? You ought to be, you must be full as a feather bed after the way you've been carrying on."

The vixen twitched her nose, and Jean sniffed herself, amused. "I'm keeping my head down, too. The bastard can think whatever he wants about the both of us, so long as he's off the scent. When Laurie comes next—"

No longer interested, the fox turned and headed toward the house, making for the dark gap she favored, under the woodshed.

Jean sighed at its retreating tail. "Right. Anyway, we'll figure *something* out."

Halfway vanished into the shadows, the fox let out a high, sharp yip, thrashing sideways, and went racing back across the yard as though the very devil himself were behind her. The animal came to a halt just before the marsh, looking back bristled and panting, her red body low, dark paws splayed wide. She pointed her dainty nose toward Jean, golden eyes accusing, as if she had been betrayed. Then she turned tail again and was gone.

Jean stood without moving, staring after the fox long after it had vanished. She turned her head to look at the woodshed, letting the wooden pegs fall from her hand into the woven basket by her feet. Crossing the yard, she got down onto her hands and knees in the crusty, frozen snow to peer into the darkness beneath it. Even then she nearly missed the thing.

A tiny tuft of reddish fur was caught suspended in midair, a few inches above the ground, slowly spinning. As Jean's eyes adjusted to the dim light, it slowed to a halt, then spun back the other way, even slower. She could just make out the dull gleam along the thin copper wire, the noose-like twist that had tightened, snatching the bit of the fox's fur away. It was purest luck the poor creature hadn't been caught by the neck and strangled herself trying to get away.

No. Jean's eyes refocused. That wasn't how it had gone, the fox too clever, too quick, to be caught. She'd not put a whisker back under the woodshed again, ever, probably. Jean tugged off her mitten and put her arm into the gap, feeling carefully around with her shaking fingertips until she found the knot and managed to loosen it enough to draw the thing out.

She sat in the snow, the wicked wire in her trembling red hands, cold and biting. There was only one place it could have come from. Had it been there, waiting, since the day Jean had found Tobias's footprints in the snow under her window, and she'd just not known? Or had he been here again and covered his tracks, grown wary just as she had? She'd been so sure he had given up stalking her now that she was keeping away.

But maybe she was wrong.

The snow and frozen ground were chilling Jean right through the layers of her clothing, hollowing her out. What did she think she was doing? She hadn't dared to do or say anything, or even come up with a way to stand up to Mrs. Keddy, who'd never threatened worse than to ruin Jean's reputation, but somehow she had the spine to take on Tobias Silber?

Why was she so willing to put her own neck in a noose? Jean's breath came short, the snare wire heavy in her hand. She hadn't any real idea of a plan. Maybe she should never have made those promises to Muirin—but how could she possibly have done anything else, when Muirin needed help? It was unimaginable.

Jean squeezed her hand into a fist, and the wire cut into her palm as she shoved herself up off the ground, and her doubts aside. It was Muirin who was caught, trapped as surely as if Tobias had pulled her up from the sea in one of his fishing nets. Jean would come up with something. She had to.

She was boiling potatoes for dinner and had just headed out with the bowl of skins to throw on the heap of things to be forked into the garden come spring when Laurie came around the corner of the house unexpectedly. Jean still had the paring knife in her hand, and it was a damn good thing Laurie was fast on his feet, that sailor's reflex, or she might well have stabbed him with it. She slashed out with a yelp, skittering sideways and dropping the enameled tin bowl on the ground, potato peelings scattering into the dirty, frozen snow. Laurie leapt back, wide-eyed, raising his hands.

"Christ, Red! It's just me."

Jean dropped her hand. She nearly dropped the knife, too, her fingers boneless and clumsy. "God, Laur. You didn't half scare me!" She forced out a shaking laugh.

He raised an eyebrow. "You're jumpy. What's got you spooked?"

"Nothing." Jean knelt to scrape the curls of peel back into the bowl, and Laurie dropped down on his heels alongside her, "helping." He wasn't much help—he plucked up a single long peel between his finger and thumb, dropped it into the bowl, and crossed his arms over his knees, giving her a shrewd look.

"Liar. What's going on?"

Jean shook her head. "You won't like it." It was a gross under-statement. "I know what's really going on up there. With Tobias Silber, and Muirin. It's bad."

He swore. "You *promised* me you wouldn't go up there, Jean!"

"I didn't promise. You just asked me not to."

Sighing deeply, Laurie took the bowl of potato skins from her hand. "Go in and put the kettle on."

Laurie sat back in his chair, staring at her. His teacup sat untouched on the table before him, long since gone completely cold. Jean looked down into her own cup, toying with the handle, waiting.

"I wish to God you'd stayed out of it, Jeanie." His voice was careful and controlled.

"Laurie—"

"It's an awful thing. Sick. Someone has to do something, you're right. But you out here on your own, ghosting around the woods like it's some game of spy you're playing at with him?" He shook his head, taking a deep breath. "No more, Jean. There's got to be a better way. A thing like that—they'd *have* to give her a divorcement, with what he's done. Maybe even a full annulment. Wouldn't they? No one in their right mind would let the marriage stand, I'm sure of it."

Jean couldn't stop her voice from coming out sharp, impatient. "Even if they *would,* you think Muirin would be able to get far enough from that house to report it on her own, or make it to stand up and testify? What, should you and I go down to Lunenburg and try telling it to the law? And those old men probably talking about the scandal of it all over dinner, with their wives repeating it all over town to anyone who'd listen? You know as well as I do how fast rumor flies—it'd be back to him in no time, before a single one of them did anything! And she's a Scot, remember. Her English isn't good. What if he fought her for the baby? What if they didn't even believe her to begin with? Her word against his, a man that's lived here all his life? Laurie, it isn't *safe* to go through those channels!" She found herself half on her feet, leaning on the table, when she paused to draw breath.

"And you out sneaking up and down the hill to talk to her behind his back is safer?" Laurie snapped back. "You *lied* to me! Do you have any idea what a man like Silber might do if he caught you out? The man's kidnapped Muirin and kept her locked in that house for months, and that's just what he does to his *wife*!"

"He won't do anything."

"Jean!"

"He won't!" Jean crossed her arms, shoving herself back in her chair.

Laurie leveled a pointed stare at her, his eyes sharp and hawkish. "What else ain't you saying? You got any other little secrets you've been hiding?" He smirked, a tight, nasty expression that said he maybe had a pretty good idea already. "You really *do* got a torch for her, don't you?"

"Shut up."

He laughed, but bitterly, not amused in the least. "Oh, there it is! I knew it, right from when you first told me about her. Ma's right. No wonder you can't leave it be. It's personal."

"If you'd rather laugh than help me, you can go."

Laurie made an irritable scoff in the back of his throat. It made him sound like his mother.

Jean didn't say so. Dropping the topic of her feelings for Muirin, she lowered her voice and leaned forward over the table again, aiming for a reasonable tone. "Look, Laurie. The best thing to do is slip her away out of there, quiet-like, without stirring things up and everyone in town knowing all about it. I just need a way to keep Tobias away from their place long enough to do it. Your ma said she could hide her, even send her out with your kin on Indian Point if she had to, if I could manage to get Muirin to the house. And then we need to get her on a boat up the coast and back to her people somehow, without him knowing . . . I don't know where they are exactly, but it's on some island, probably within a few days of here. If she could talk to a sailor, a Scotsman, he'd probably know."

"Hmm." Laurie's face went thoughtful, his temper fading.

"Doubt I could draw Silber off without making him wonder. Not when everyone knows you and I are thick as thieves, and not for more than an hour or so, even if I *did* manage it. It wouldn't be near enough time for you to get her to town, especially with a babe. And, much as he deserves it, I ain't about to bash him over the head to buy more time. But if Muirin could hold out another month, month and a half? Well, it'd be spring."

Jean's heart clenched.

"A *month* and a *half*? Laurie, no! How can I leave her up there—"

"Jeanie, I'm sorry. If I could pick her up out of the place for you by magic, I would. But I might have a notion, if you can just be patient—"

"It's not about me being patient! It's about Muirin, trapped in that house, with *him*—"

"Do you want to hear my idea or not?"

Jean clamped her mouth shut, fairly sure she was glaring.

"All right." Laurie raked a hand through his hair and leaned forward. "It's the ass-end of winter now, and spring *is* coming. Not that you'd know to look at it out there yet, but still. As soon as the snow goes and we get a few nice days in a row come the end of March, the fleet'll start clamoring to set a date to get the boats out. You know what they're like, fishermen. And they always go out together those first few days, to bring back a big haul—it's good luck for the rest of the year, one of those superstitious things. Tobias'll have to go. He always does, and it'd look real strange if he didn't show out. That's your chance." He paused, considering.

"I can be your ears in town. It won't be any trouble to let you know ahead, once they set a day. Once he goes off, the same morning, you can fetch Muirin and the babe down here, and we'll sneak you all into town. I can bring a wagon out, after dark, so no one will see and talk later. We could have Muirin on a boat and gone before he's even back if we're lucky; there's never any of them back sooner than two or three days, that first time out to sea." Laurie chewed his bottom lip and shot a glance at her. "Well? You think it'd suit?"

Jean stared down at the table, her neck aching with the need to do something *now*. But she couldn't deny that Laurie's plan made the most sense of any, would keep Muirin and Kiel the safest. Grabbing up her teacup, she downed the last of the tea in it, the tepid bitter dregs, and grimaced.

"It'll have to." It might be the best chance they'd get, maybe even the only chance. But it was so far off. Too far.

Jean hated that it couldn't be tonight.

She also hated that setting Muirin free would mean having to watch her go. Like Jo leaving all over again, except this time Jean would somehow have to send the one she cared for away herself. But what else could she do? Muirin needed to be safe, and happy, back where she belonged.

Jean needed not to think about the part where Muirin would leave her. She set down her cup again, with a dull, hollow *tok*.

"Jean." Laurie spoke less certainly now, softer. "You ought to come back into town. Stay with me and Ma until then, instead of out here. It'd be safer."

Safer for *her*, maybe. Jean's jaw set.

"I'm not doing it, Laurie. If I change anything, he's going to wonder why. I start coming and going to town without a good reason, he'll watch me even closer. And if he thinks he's finally scared me off, he'll think he can do whatever he likes up there, with no one to say boo. No. I'm staying. And, Laur, don't you *dare* say a word to your mother, about any of it. She'll take a fit of apoplexy. She doesn't need to know we're coming until we're there."

Laurie's eyes were dark with worry, but he gave his head a small shake, impressed. "Jeanie," he said, "you're as stubborn as that bloody goat of yours. Your pa would have whupped me for even thinking about letting you stay. I hope to God I don't regret this. That *you* don't."

"I'll regret it more if I don't do anything. What if he hurts her? It'd be my fault for standing by and letting it happen." That sort of regret was a deep, sucking mire.

"You know you won't be able to come back out here once she's gone. He's gonna know it was you that did it."

"She already ran on him once," Jean said with a nonchalant shrug. "She ran again. What's it to do with me?"

"Damn it, Jean!" Laurie slapped his hand flat on the table. "Logic only works if a man's willing to listen! I won't make you come to town now, and I won't tell Ma neither, because you asked and you're right how she'd worry. But after this is over, you're staying with us. I can't hardly believe I'm going along with you as it is! It's a bare half step this side of insane, you doing this."

Jean knew it. If she let herself think about any of it aside from Muirin's well-being, she might end up running straight off to town now, and praying to forget that the woman had ever fetched up at her door.

She couldn't. What sort of coward would it make her? Jean looked around the room, and an odd tightness fluttered in her chest. She'd been here in this same house all her life, aside from the odd trip into town; a night or two at Anneke's, a few weeks helping with this baby or that.

She glanced toward the bare hearth before the fire, where once Muirin had sat laughing at the baby in her lap, warm and rosy in the firelight, while outside rain had pattered on the roof. It suddenly felt like a very long time ago. The anxious fluttering stopped cold. Muirin wasn't like to fill the space on Jean's hearth ever again, whether the plan succeeded or no.

"All right." Jean pushed herself up from her chair. "When it's over, I'll come."

Laurie got up and came around the table to grip her in a tight hug, and Jean appreciated it, though the hug did nothing for the dull, empty ache in her chest. He squeezed so hard it nearly pressed the air clear out of her, before setting her back with his hands on her shoulders and a serious look in his eyes. "Jean," he said, "be careful. Please. Keep to home, and I'll be back again Tuesday next, all right? Don't do anything foolish."

"Don't worry about me, Laurie. I made it this far, didn't I?"

"Is that supposed to be reassuring?" He laughed, more like himself again. "It ain't, Red. I *know* you."

Jean laughed, too, and it felt a little bit like relief. "Go on, then. You'll be walking in the dark if you don't get moving."

Laurie waved as he went out her gate, and Jean stood at her open door until he'd disappeared around the curve of the road. *Anyway, there's one good thing.* Their plotting and scheming had so distracted Laurie from whatever was making him melancholy that he'd been almost his old self while they'd talked.

A few fat flakes of snow floated down from the darkening sky, and she wrapped her arms around herself, lingering at the door a moment longer. The tide was coming in, waves rolling and foaming along the shore. Shivering, Jean scanned the tree line across the frozen marsh, up toward the pale birches on the hill. Hopefully the fox had made it back to her den. There was nothing under the low branches but shadows.

Jean went back inside and bolted her door.

18

It got warmer through the night. It should have been a good thing, the breaking of the winter's back, but with the end of the bitter cold came the return of the snow.

Jean looked out her window at the smooth, unspoiled whiteness and wanted to curse and cry with frustration. Before, she'd been able to secretly follow any one of a hundred paths up through the wood. Now, any step she took would betray her. She might as well write her name in the drifts with a stick as she went.

It snowed off and on for well over a week, while Jean's stomach twisted like a fouled rope. She chafed at being unable to do anything useful and instead stomped paths across her own yard: to the henhouse, to the goat shed and pen. It snowed over them both, and she stomped them out again. And again. After the last squall, there was a single errant trail that ran all over, where Kicker had gotten loose and Jean had chased her down and tackled her. The dying winter was making the goat wild, more contrary and ill-tempered than ever.

Eventually Jean tramped a path out to the road—which sat wide and unspoiled, and utterly useless.

Laurie came to see her twice more, their conversations dreadfully one-sided. Jean was surprised he hadn't yet throttled her, she repeated herself so often: Muirin needed to know Jean had a real plan. That she hadn't just decided it was too hard, too much, and washed her hands of the whole thing, abandoning her. Laurie nodded and hummed in the right places, but otherwise let her talk herself in circles. He was preoccupied anew with his own concerns now they had settled on their course.

Jean ached to see Muirin again. To touch her hand and feel it, solid and warm, see her whole and hale and well, and know that Tobias had not harmed her, at least not any further than he had already done.

The baby was on Jean's mind, too. Kiel was past three months old now, and probably laughing just as she'd once imagined. Even so, he was still small and fragile, and infants took ill in the winter, with coughs and colds and croup. What if something were to happen? She ought to be there, to check on him.

Something had shifted in Jean like a deep crack opening up in sea ice, and she feared it might swallow her whole while she sat doing nothing. She'd somehow grown as protective of Muirin as if she were *her* wife, the child their own. Of course, it wasn't so. Jean knew it perfectly well, even if her gut didn't quite want to hear it.

She wished she had anything else to think about.

If she'd thought it might get them into town faster, Jean might have leapt out of the sledge and tried to carry the horse. She'd just been seeing Laurie off when it had pulled up to her gate, the driver shouting for her to come quick, hurry. Now Laurie was squashed into the tiny box behind the bench seat, holding tight to Jean's basket of tools while Jean perched next to too-young Richie Eisenor with her heart in her throat, clinging to the bench and kicking herself as he frantically laid on the reins, all flapping elbows and terror.

How could Jean not have realized that, by now, she ought to have been back in town, checking on Ida Mae? She'd been certain there was time yet. Was it still too early? What day even *was* it? She couldn't *think*—

"Richie!" She had to yell, the icy wind snatching her words away. "Is anyone there with Ida?" The notion of Ida Mae laboring alone, with no idea what to do and Jean not there to help, was more chilling than the wind could ever have been.

"Couple of her sisters are there, miss, and her ma!" Maybe it would be all right; Ida's mother, Franny Mosher, was a sensible woman, had birthed six children of her own—"It was her sent me for you! She wouldn't let me in to see what was going on, just kept yelling at me, and—" Richie's voice cracked, and Jean's faint hope extinguished. She hardly registered a thing as he went on babbling, all panic, without a single useful word that might tell her what to expect.

Something must have gone horribly wrong for them to have sent Richie off in such haste, for him to be in such a state.

The wind cut at Jean's cheeks, brought tears up in her eyes. They flew over the road, and Jean gripped the bench seat with both her tingling hands to keep from being pitched out as they sailed up and around the last curve of the shore before the village. Stupid, and selfish, so caught up in her own concerns that she'd forgotten her responsibility to anyone else but Muirin . . . Jean could barely get a proper breath, the cold air stabbing little knives into her lungs. If anything happened to the baby, to poor Ida Mae, she would never forgive herself.

She grabbed her basket from Laurie's arms as they pulled up

before the Eisenors' cottage in the dim evening light, throwing herself down off the sledge almost before it had stopped. Her feet landed on a patch of ice, slithering right out from under her, and Jean let out a shriek, her basket flying into the air as she windmilled her arms and made a grab for the low gate of the pigpen, missed, and catapulted straight over it into the icy muck.

Laurie gave a whoop, hurtling down from his perch, vaulting over the gate in a much more controlled fashion to come to her rescue. He levered Jean up from the ground as the bemused pigs snorted and shifted. "Holy mother of pearl—are you all right?"

"I'm fine," Jean huffed, breathless, the wind half knocked out of her. "I'm fine!" Hiking up her stained skirts in one mucky hand, she went scrambling back out of the pigpen over the wooden gate, grabbing up her fallen basket and racing for the house as Laurie took the reins from Richie and sent him along behind her. Jesus, Mary, and Joseph, she couldn't deliver a baby covered in filth! Jean would have to scrub herself raw before doing anything now, but maybe if she stole one of Ida's aprons? There was no *time*—

She burst through the door into the house, nearly running headlong into Ida's mother. "What's happening? Is . . ." Jean's voice trailed off as she looked around the room. Ida's older sisters were sitting calmly at the table, blinking at her, one with a teacup raised halfway to her lips. There was a chill breeze through the open door as Richie came in behind her. Suddenly, Jean could smell herself, and it was not good.

"What on earth did you say to this poor girl, Richard?" Mrs. Mosher snapped, her voice hovering somewhere between amused and vexed. "I said fetch Jean in quick, not frighten her to death! Almighty God, did you throw her in the pigpen?"

"I never did. She went in herself!"

The woman made a sharp *tsk*ing sound. "All this panic for nothing anyhow!"

"What?" said Jean, completely flummoxed.

"What?" said Richie. "But—but—Ida was hollerin' like you was murdering her when I left!"

"Mama?" Ida Mae called from the bedroom. She sounded perfectly fine. "Is that Richie and Jean? Oh, shh, shh, darling—" Her words were interrupted by a baby's thin cry, and Jean took the first full breath she'd managed since leaving her house. Her heart was still racing as if she'd run the whole way into town instead of taking that breakneck sleigh ride, and her backside was starting to ache in a way that implied she might not want to sit down for a while.

"I don't . . . Ida's all right, then?" It was best to regroup before going in to check on the girl herself. That, and wash. "Good lord, I thought she was fixing to die before I got here."

"*Richard!*" Ida's mother was much less amused by this, but one of the two women at the table choked on her tea and started wheezing. The other got up to pound on her back, laughing the entire time.

Richie turned flaming crimson. "You *said* to hurry! I thought it was an *emergency*!" He stopped, blinking. "Wait. Wait. She had it? Is it a boy? Or a girl? Ida!" Everything else forgotten, the young man went tearing through to the bedroom to see for himself, leaving clumps of mucky snow scattered and melting across the floor behind him in his haste.

Franny Mosher shook her head in a way that said that while she might already have thought her son-in-law hopeless, this night had proved it to her beyond all doubt. She didn't waste another word on him. Instead, she took Jean's elbow, drawing her toward the kitchen pump.

"Don't fret yourself, Jean, you look like the wrath of God. It wasn't bad, just a bit early for her time, from what she told me you said, so I thought maybe it was a false alarm—I had some of those with mine? I sent Richie off for you soon as I knew it was the real thing." The older woman dropped her voice confidentially, with a wry lift of her eyebrows. "That boy went so green around the gills when Ida started getting down to business I figured I'd best set him to doing *something,* or he'd end up laid out on the floor for us to trip over the whole time."

Jean had seen it happen before, and more than once, with men a good deal hardier and more worldly-wise than Richie Eisenor. Getting him out into the fresh air had been uncommon good sense, even if he'd scared Jean half to death. She couldn't blame this entirely on Richie, though, even if she wished to. She should never have let herself get so distracted that such a thing could have taken her by surprise.

"I'm sorry I wasn't here. I should have been—"

Franny scoffed at the thought. "Why would you have come unless you've been holding out on us and had the sight all this time? It's not your fault. Babies keep their own schedules, no matter how clever we think we are at guessing their plans. You ought to know that better than anyone." She chuckled as she primed the pump. "I never saw a baby make such a fast entrance in my life, and who expects that with a first? Like a cork from a bottle! I darn near ducked instead of catching."

It painted quite the mental image.

"We did fine; Ima was a big help keeping Ida calm through the whole thing, since she's already had two herself, and Ana's steady as a stone. I'm glad Ada's away up at Western Shore, though; she's about as useful as a sack of hammers when it comes to these things—"

Overwhelmed, Jean nodded as the woman went on with her monologue. All the while, she was fishing to remember which name belonged to who. Jean was pretty sure Mrs. Mosher only had the four daughters. Ana and Ada were twins, she could remember Anneke saying what a shock that had been, there being two of them, and Ima was the oldest, near ten years Ida's senior—

He had his cap set for one of the Mosher girls, whichever, they all have near the same name . . . If she hadn't known Laurie was out unhitching the horse, Jean would have sworn he was right there, whispering out of the past and into her ear. She turned—as Mrs. Mosher kept up her brisk chatter pumping water into the basin—and studied the older of the pair sitting at the table. *She went and married Dan Barry . . . God knows if she's still friendly with Silber . . .* Ima Barry was tall and handsome, but that was as much as she had in common with Muirin. Her hair was darkly blondish, her eyes wide set, a medium bluey-gray.

"Ima," Jean asked, wiping her clammy palms on her skirts again and trying to make it come off casual, "do you still talk to Tobias Silber ever?"

Ana raised her eyebrows at her older sister and leaned on one elbow, pressing her mouth into her hand to stop anything coming out of it. A tiny *pfft* escaped, squeaking between her fingers.

Ima winced. "I don't. Tobias decided I didn't exist anymore the minute I told him I was going to marry Dan." She tilted her head, giving Jean a curious look. "Why?"

Jean shrugged, and looked down for a moment, focusing intently on rolling up her sleeves. "Just curious, mostly. He lives out my way, with that new wife of his."

"Ah," Ima said, her head straightening as she relaxed minutely. "And what's she like? The mysterious Mrs. Silber."

Mysterious. It was the truth. Just not much of it. "Quiet. She's quiet."

Ana tittered. "She'd have to be." Ima kicked her sister beneath the table, and Ana gave her head a pert toss. "What? It's true. With that nitpicking perfectionist? I'm glad you married Dan— you'd never have had a moment's peace if you'd married Tobias like he wanted."

Heaving a gusty sigh, Ima leaned back in her chair. "Dan was just so much more easygoing than Toby was." She fell into the topic like a well-worn path she'd been down too many times, and addressed her next words to Jean, inviting her in for the rehashing of it. "Tobias didn't want a marriage so much as he wanted a fairy tale. It was too much pressure, you know?

"I felt bad about it, really. He was so sure of what our whole life was going to look like, had it all planned out for us. It's funny. Men love to act like it's us women who look at life with blinkers on, expecting everything to be perfect. But Tobias did it more than any woman I've ever met." Ima cleared her throat and glanced down at her fingers, drumming them on the table. Two red spots rose in her cheeks. Jean was struck by a pang of indignation, that Ima should feel guilty for throwing over Tobias. If Ima had any notion what the man had become, the narrow miss she'd had . . .

"It was just . . . it didn't feel like it mattered to him that it was *me,* so much as this image he had in his mind of what a happy family ought to look like, a perfect wife? I'm glad he finally found someone who could be that for him. His folks were always at odds—I think it made it tough for the boys growing up. And he wanted so badly to start a family of his own. To 'do things better,' he always said."

Better. He'd surely missed that mark. Tobias Silber had gotten what he'd wanted: found a way to make himself a family that looked perfect and shiny from the outside, so long as no one looked too close. Jean wondered if perhaps Tobias believed the lie he'd created, too.

No one blamed Jean for not having been there when Ida's baby was born except Jean herself. Perhaps it was fair they didn't, for she hadn't been meant to come by to check on Ida Mae for another week yet, but Jean had a sinking hunch that she still might have forgotten, even if everything had gone exactly as expected. She was too distracted, so single-minded of late that nothing outside her fears for Muirin felt entirely real anymore. What she'd heard from Ima Barry had done nothing to shift her focus.

Fortunately, Laurie didn't try to insist she stay with him and Anneke in the village for the night. Instead, he offered to walk her back home along the bay, in spite of it being near ten by the time they finally set out. It was thoughtful of him, and Jean was grateful for it. Arriving back in town in such a rush had given the evening an unsettling air of unreality, as if she'd been stolen away by the fairies that lived under the hill.

Ida Mae's new baby girl—tiny but perfect, with translucent ears like seashells—didn't need to fear the fairies. The proud grandmother had seen to this with a pair of iron shears laid under the cradle, open like a cross. It would be nice, to believe you could protect the ones you treasured so easily.

"Sometimes I wish I believed in it all still," Jean said to Laurie. "Like when I was little."

They'd been walking along beside each other for some time, in silence aside from the crunch of snow beneath their boots, both lost in their own thoughts. Laurie glanced over at Jean's words, his inquisitive face lit clear and blue by the moonlight reflecting off the snow.

"Believed in what?"

"All those old stories. Maybe not changelings, but selkies and sirens and mermaids and all that. If a fairy stole me away to a ball and the rest of winter just passed overnight, I'd be glad of it. I can't bear this waiting; it's all I can think of, Muirin and Tobias and . . ." She didn't *want* to think about it, what might be going on in that house even now.

"Ah." Laurie tipped his head back, looking up at the stars,

and blew out a long, slow breath, ghostly mist in the dark. "There's more things in the world than you know, Red. Secrets." Jean hummed, wondering what he was thinking of.

"The way you're sticking by Muirin, even with everything? It's mad of you, maybe, but still . . ." He tripped and looked back down at the path beneath his feet. They went on in silence for a long spell before he ventured to speak again, muted and oddly tentative. "Jean? If you found out someone you cared for had kept a secret from you, something important, would you be angry at them?"

Jean looked at him out of the side of her eye. "I guess it would depend," she said. "On what sort of a secret it was, and why they hadn't told me."

Laurie burrowed his hands deeper into his pockets, folding in on himself. Tucking his chin down into his scarf, he spoke into the knit fabric. "Say it was something where you had to . . . really trust whoever you told your secret to, trust them not to tell anyone else, ever. And then they were angry when you got up the guts to tell them . . ."

This was it.

The thing that had been eating at him since he'd first come home. Laurie had finally made a friend on the ship he thought he could trust enough to risk telling about him and Dal. And then they must have turned on him for not saying something sooner. God, a man who took a thing like that amiss might have just as easily gone and told the whole crew! What Jean had put up with in the village after Jo was nothing to the kind of trouble Laurie would find himself in if he put his trust in the wrong man, especially on a boat. A chill rattled down the back of her neck. No wonder he'd been so melancholy and strange; he might have ended up overboard, for God's sake, or *hanged*.

Jean stopped dead in the road, her fists clenched, bristling. "That's not fair! How dare they—it's dangerous to tell someone a thing like that! Anyone who couldn't see that, and understand why you'd . . . What a *bastard*! God, Laurie, that's awful. I wish I could smack them for you!"

Laurie stared at Jean like she'd grown another head, then gave a dry, bitter laugh. "No, Jean. It's me—*I'm* the bastard." He turned and struck out along the path again with quick, unhappy strides.

Jean scrambled after him, her feet slipping in the snow. "What? Laurie, what on earth did you— Oh." The realization finally hit her, drawing her up short in the middle of the road. "Dal?"

Laurie slowed his steps, and she fell back in beside him as he nodded, miserable.

"Three years we were together. Three *years,* and he never told me."

"What could he possibly have been hiding that was so—"

"I'm not going to tell you a thing he couldn't even tell me, Jean. It's a secret, and it ain't mine to tell. But I thought he trusted me, and instead he'd been keeping something from me the whole *time!*"

"So you *ran away*?" Jean was struck with a sudden urge to slap Laurie for the self-pitying whine in his voice, her palms itching on behalf of a man she'd never even met. "Laurie, how could you? Dal *did* trust you if he told you something he thought he had to hide for that long—"

"I *know!*" Laurie wasn't angry about it now. He was anguished—wounded on the blade of his own thoughtlessness. Stopping again, he drew a deep breath and turned away from Jean to look out over the bay as it glittered dark and empty under the moon. "I know. The way I reacted . . . I pretty much proved I ain't the sort of man Dal ought to have trusted. He was right to keep his secret from me. And I hate myself for it."

She didn't want to slap him anymore. "Oh, Laurie."

"I don't know as he'll ever forgive me. Maybe he shouldn't. I don't know that I deserve it. But I have to tell him I'm sorry, at least, don't I? He didn't do anything wrong; it was all me. He wanted to come home with me, you know? Meet Ma, and make a proper go of it, that's why he finally—"

"Laurie."

"Maybe if I sent a letter. Do you think I ought to send a letter?"

Jean snorted. "Yes, Laurence. Send the man a letter. Stop tying yourself in knots. God."

Laurie laughed.

19

There was a solid path going out of Jean's gate now, at least toward the village.

It did her no good. Not when the one place she needed to go was at the top of a snow-covered hill in the entirely opposite direction.

But there was a new track in the snow on the far side of the marsh in the morning. Jean didn't know when it had appeared, only that it hadn't been there before she and Laurie had made their flying trip to town with Richie Eisenor the evening before. It came down in a straight line from underneath the barren birches to the edge of the frozen pond, then ran inland along its shore, toward where the stream flowed into it from out of the woods.

From all the way across the pond, Jean couldn't say for certain that it hadn't been made by an animal, maybe one of the great huge moose that Laurie's cousins said were getting harder and harder to find when they went out hunting. She suspected it was unlikely. There was only one great huge thing she would bet had been skulking over there in the marsh, watching her house while she'd been out of it, and that was Tobias Silber.

She frowned out her window across the pond for a while, then bundled herself into her outdoor things, gray and brown and drab as the winter wood, and trudged her way around to the stream to have a closer look, just to be sure. Up close, separated from them only by the cold black line of the stream cutting through the knee-deep snow, there was no mistaking his footprints. Tobias had come to check up on her, to make sure Jean was keeping to her own land, and well away from his wife.

Jean hoped that was all the man had been doing, unease cramping her gut as she peered at his tracks disappearing upstream, into the thicker forest. What if he'd crossed over somewhere deeper in the wood without her noticing? If he circled around, he might come up on her place one of the ways Laurie used, and she'd not be any the wiser until he was standing in her doorway. Jean shuddered, and looked over her shoulder, back toward the house.

She should check. Laurie wouldn't approve, but Laurie didn't have to find out. Besides, Jean wouldn't cross onto Tobias's land and tempt his ire; she'd just go up the brook a way on her side, and make sure Tobias had stayed to his. For her own peace of mind, little though she had of it of late.

It was harder going the farther into the woods she went. The ground was uneven, and the snow deeper under the trees, hiding fallen branches that caught at her ankles. Jean huffed and puffed and kept her head down, minding her step. The last thing she needed was to break a leg. Now and then she glanced to her left to see if Tobias's trail was still snaking along the far bank of the stream, parallel to her own. His tracks finally peeled away from the water, vanishing through the trees, headed back up the hill toward his house. The woods were still and silent, aside from the creaking of branches as they shifted with the wind, the muted tramping of her feet through the snow. A lone crow let out a stiff croak somewhere overhead. Jean supposed she might as well turn back.

Click.

Clear and unnatural, the sound didn't belong, but Jean couldn't tell where it had come from, and she stopped in her tracks. Turning just her head, her breath held tight, she peered into the trees across the stream.

BANG!

A branch exploded six inches from her nose, bits of bark and lichen and wood spraying into her eyes. Jean threw herself to the ground. Her ears rang as the snowy wood swallowed the reverberating echo of the gunshot, her heart thumping inside the cage of her ribs. Above her, the crow shrieked to the empty sky as it took wing and flapped away. Snow went up Jean's nose and started melting, but she was afraid to move, lest her stirring provoke a second shot.

Crunch. Crunch. Crunch. Footsteps in the snow. They stopped. Then:

"Oops."

Jean lifted her dripping face. On the opposite side of the stream, barely ten feet away, stood Tobias Silber, a long hunting rifle held casually in his gloved hands. He did not look especially contrite as he glanced her once over from his vantage on the far bank, his cheek twitching with amusement.

"Took you for an animal. That fox, maybe." His eyes narrowed. "That's what happens when fools go sneaking around the woods, quiet-like. Be a real shame, an accident like that." Jean managed to nod, her mouth dry and empty. The way Tobias was eyeballing her suggested he didn't think it would be much of a shame at all, except that he'd have nothing to take home for the pot. His face had hollowed out slightly since she'd last caught a glimpse of him up close.

"I best not see sign of you on this side." Tobias glanced down at the stretch of pristine snow that lay between them, broken only by the black burbling ribbon of the stream, and then back to her, his blue eyes glinting hard and sharp as ice. His grip shifted minutely on the rifle, tightening, his finger hooking over the trigger. Jean froze.

"Remember what I said." In one smooth motion, he slung the rifle onto his shoulder. "You ain't wanted here. By *any* of us." Turning, he stalked off, and in a matter of moments, vanished back into the trees.

Jean stayed where she was, not sure her legs would hold her up if she tried to stand.

Maybe Tobias believed what he'd said to her at the end, but she couldn't credit it. There was no way he'd ever have convinced Muirin to turn against her, but Jean was certain Muirin could have *easily* convinced her husband of such a thing. Particularly as it was exactly what he most wanted to think. Muirin knew her own mind. Whatever else might happen, Tobias would never sway her.

What Jean couldn't shake was the gaunt, pinched look about his face, the way it had thinned out since the day he'd threatened her in the mercantile.

"He hasn't been back to town since Christmas. What if he's letting them go hungry just to spite me?" Jean wasn't about to tell Laurie how Tobias had almost blown her head clear off her shoulders when he next came to see her, but she couldn't keep her worries to herself. She simply left out how it was she'd come by them.

Laurie leaned over the table and pressed a finger to Jean's lips. "Stop. Muirin's clever and strong, you said so yourself about a hundred times now. She'll figure out a way to stretch things; they won't starve. And she'll understand why you aren't coming." He was more than a little relieved Jean was being forced to keep to her own side of the marsh pond, a fact that only served to make her irritable and snappish with him.

Jean ducked to the side. "Maybe. But still—"

"She'll know. Honestly, Jean. If Silber caught you out up there—" Laurie shook his head, and then changed the subject entirely, starting in on all the latest village gossip, trying to distract her. Jean let him, keeping her lips shut tight on the fact she'd already had far too close a brush with Tobias for her liking. Richie and Ida Mae couldn't get her mother to go back home again, she was so smitten with her new grandchild, and the young couple were both going spare. Mr. Buchanan's half-wild children had egged one another into taking off their boots and then run a race barefoot through the snow along the main street on another visit to town, and their father had hauled the pair of them back to his boat by their ears. When Laurie mentioned how Josephine Keddy (Gaudry, he said, because that was her name now, though Jean still couldn't call her any other way) was still in the village but had left her mother's house right after New Year's to stay with one of her sisters instead, Jean finally cracked, telling him not to bother coming to see her again unless he had *real* news. Not that Laurie ever listened; besides, he'd written his letter and sent it off to Dal, and as Jean's ear was the only one Laurie had to pour his nervy rambling about how long an answer might take into, she had no doubt he'd be back before the end of the week.

They had a plan. That was what Jean kept telling herself, though the thought was less comforting with every day that passed.

They had a plan, certainly; but Muirin had no idea what it was, or that it even existed. For all Muirin knew, Jean had abandoned her, wasn't coming back at all. For all Jean knew, Muirin was trapped up there starving for the sake of Tobias Silber's stubborn pride, his made-up fairy-tale marriage, and poor little Kiel along with her. Jean couldn't stop imagining his soft, round baby cheeks hollowed and thin, his bright barking laugh exchanged for whimpering. In spite of Laurie's reassurances, it was as if Jean were standing on the ice in the marsh pond, and each day she waited it grew thinner, sagging under the weight of her creeping doubts.

Slowly, too slowly, the weather began shifting again. A breeze came up from the south, and water dripped from the eaves of the house, the snow in the yard growing heavy and wet underneath. Jean wore a pair of gum boots to keep from soaking her feet in the gray layer of slush and went outside one afternoon, unable to stand being trapped within her own four walls anymore, with only the company of her thoughts. She didn't even have the fox to talk to these days. Since its narrow miss with Tobias's hidden snare, the vixen had avoided Jean and her house alike. Maybe it would never come back.

Leaning up against the snowy hump of her father's overturned dory, Jean crossed her arms and gazed out across the half-frozen pond, the black open water where the tide brought the salt in.

Maybe she could get to Muirin along the shore, at low tide? It would be slippery, and dangerous, and Jean hadn't the faintest idea if she'd find a clear track up the long drive to the Silber house even if she did make it around the point, scrambling over the icy rocks. And if she didn't make it all the way back around the point again before the tide turned, she'd be trapped. Stuck at the base of a crumbling forty-foot cliff as the sea came in—

An equine snort echoed from somewhere out of sight along the road, and Jean ducked down behind the boat just as Tobias's big horse and wagon appeared from out of the trees, headed toward town. It was slow going, the wagon wheels sunk deep into the wet snow on the road under a heavy load of logs; the man must not have had a set of sleigh runners to make the task easier. Jean rather pitied the horse. Tobias did not *quite* pull up at Jean's gate, but he slowed the wagon, his head swiveling like an owl's, to glare at her house with narrowed eyes as he passed. In a few moments, the wagon vanished around the bend.

Jean stayed where she was for all of one minute, until the splash and squish of the wheels churning through the slush faded away. Then she was up from her spot behind the boat and running as quick as she could. Even at the snail's pace Tobias had been going, Jean didn't have much time. Maybe an hour, but not more than two. She had to be home again and off the road before he reappeared out of the spruce grove, headed back the way he'd come. If she met with Tobias out in the open road between their houses, face-to-face . . .

It would make their meeting in the woods look like the very model of polite restraint.

Jean focused on keeping her skirts kilted high as she ran, her footsteps within the narrow rut of the wagon wheels, only slowing long enough to catch her breath when she absolutely had to. She almost wept with relief when she reached the top of the long drive—the snow was tossed and muddied all around the woodpile and behind the house from his chopping and hauling. Jean tipped his axe-scarred log onto its side as she had before, rolled it back over beneath the bedroom window again, and climbed up onto it, knocking on the glass.

"Muirin!" she called, breathless. "Muirin!"

There was a faint thump as something dropped to the floor in the other room, and then Muirin appeared in the doorway of the bedroom with Kiel clutched in her arms. Tobias must have been the only one off his feed, for Muirin looked hale as ever, and Kiel had grown so much since the holidays that Jean briefly wondered if she was imagining it. Muirin's mouth fell open when she spotted Jean, and she paused only to settle the baby on the bed, where he waved his hands and babbled to himself, before shoving open the window.

"Jean!" Muirin threw her arms around Jean's neck, pulling her close, bumping her nose against Jean's left cheek, and then her right. Jean got the oddest impression, suddenly, that Muirin might be smelling her, but the ridiculous notion fell away as Muirin pulled back to examine her face. "How? How came, you? Much snow is, to make track, thought I you would not come again! Should not, you! Jean . . ." With a small fretful mew, Muirin broke off her scolding to kiss Jean instead.

Sweetness, and salt, and a sharp pang inside of Jean's chest. Had Muirin been crying? Bringing up a hand, she stroked a thumb over Muirin's cheek before pulling away to look her in the eyes, aching with reluctance. "We haven't much time, I have to get back before he starts home again. I came in the wagon track, so he wouldn't see where I walked."

Muirin gasped. "No other way? Jean, is so dangerous. Go, go back now!" Muirin raised her arm to shut the window on Jean and force her to leave.

"Wait!" Jean caught the frame herself, staying Muirin in midmotion. "I came to tell you we have a plan! We can get you away!"

Muirin froze, her eyes going wide and round.

"It'll take longer than I'd like—but Muirin, in the spring, soon, Tobias'll go out with the fishing fleet. It's a thing they do every year, to start the season. It's unlucky if they don't, they say. He'll be gone at least two days, maybe more. We can get you and Kiel out the window here, and my friend Laurie, he's going to help, come and meet us with a wagon. We'll go away. It won't be more than a month, at most." Muirin shook her head, unshed tears brimming up in her dark eyes.

"Can not, Jean, can not! Must find my *craiceann ròin*—" Jean still did not know the words, and she doubted she could repeat them if she tried, but she recognized them from Muirin's story. The precious thing Tobias had taken from her. "He hid. Not know where it is, I, can not find!"

"Muirin!" Jean was running out of time. "Whatever it is, it's not as important as getting you and Kiel out of here, away from him . . . that's all that matters. Later, after you're both away, there'll be lots to deal with when he comes back—we can try to get whatever it is back from him then."

"No! *Need*, I! Is from mother and father, is—gift, mine!" Muirin was truly rattled, her voice strained as if this would be the thing to finally set her off into a panic, foolish as it seemed. All this time holding on to her composure, captive, stolen— perhaps it was best Jean not push it. Besides, she had no idea what the thing was. Muirin spoke about it like an inheritance, something rare and precious, irreplaceable. It must be, that she would value it above her freedom even for a moment.

"Mine is!" Muirin's words rang with sudden, furious passion. "My *right*! Need for going home, I, can not just *leave*, Jean!"

"All right," Jean said, steady. Gentle, as if she were trying to coax a bird into her hand. "All right. We'll find it before we go, whatever it is. I'll help you. From now until we leave, whenever you can, you keep on looking—just take care he doesn't catch you out at it. Look *everywhere*. Under the apples and things in the baskets in the attic, and up in the rafters, if you can. Check for loose boards in the floor, too. Every drawer and cupboard, inside the mattress, even, with the straw. Just be careful! If we have to, we can turn over the barn or break into anything he's got locked once he's gone.

"But, Muirin, you *have* to get away! I want you and Kiel both on a boat and off to your family before he comes back. This might be our only chance, and I won't leave you here with him again, you understand?" Jean's throat tightened painfully, like a snare closing around her words. "I can't. It's not right, what he's done to you. You don't deserve this."

Muirin regarded her, silent. "Jean," she said, careful. "Coming with me, you, yes?"

Jean's breath caught. She hadn't even considered the possibility. She'd pictured having Muirin and the baby back in her home with her to stay, and in the very same instant dismissed the idea as nothing but a ridiculous dream. Tobias would come after them, and God alone knew what he would do once he realized his wife had betrayed him, fled in earnest, *and* with Jean. It could not be. She'd only ever imagined Muirin leaving, away safe, even if the notion tore at her, a rock covered with barnacles to rasp her heart raw.

It had never occurred to Jean that Muirin might ask such a thing. To want Jean by her side as well, for longer than just the time she was here. They'd not even known each other so long as all that, never had the chance to broach the subject. Jean had skirted clear of hoping, however much she might dream of such a life, but the very possibility that they might be together, that Muirin might wish it . . . it left Jean breathless, her mind gone blank and stupid. A dream she'd never thought possible, at once both more tangible and more intangible than it had ever been before.

"You *want* me to come? With you?"

Muirin caught at Jean's hand, pulling it into both of her own. "Please, Jean. Say you will. With me, with Kiel."

Away from home. The home that Jean had worked so hard to make her own particular place in the world. But maybe she could make a new start: a clean fresh slate, somewhere no one knew her, with Muirin . . .

Muirin's face shone, her eyes pleading.

All memory of doubt disappeared. "Yes. I'll come."

Muirin nearly threw herself out the window, wrapping her arms right around Jean's neck with a happy, wordless cry, and Jean laughed as she pried her off again, coming back to the matter at hand.

"I have to go. I'm taking too long. Muirin—" Jean drew her close once more, her heart fluttering in her chest. "We're doing this. I swear. We'll find your *curr*-whatsis and we'll go, and he'll never find us. But I don't know if I can come back again before then. I'll try, I—"

Muirin shook her head. "Do not, no. No. Later, time will we have. Now, not."

Jean nodded. "Yes. All the time in the world. I promise."

She kissed Muirin, hard and long, pushing her hands deep into Muirin's heavy hair as her heart lifted, beating like the wings of a bird. Jean tried to put everything she couldn't say into the kiss—how she hated to go, how she wanted Muirin, all her hopes and dreams. Tried to make it enough to last until they could leave this place, together. When she pulled back, Jean fancied she'd succeeded, for Muirin's eyes had gone soft and unfocused, dreamy. Jean traced her fingers along the curve of Muirin's cheek, then stepped down off the log into the dirty slush of the yard.

Muirin set her hand over her heart. "Go careful," she said. "Careful, love."

Jean was caught again, her hand stilled over her own heart. It beat heavy in her chest, once, twice. She could not speak but kept her eyes on Muirin as she raised her fingertips to her lips and pressed them with a kiss before lifting her hand in farewell. Setting off down the track to the road, Jean fought a smile that rose steadfastly to her lips over and over again, like a blown-glass buoy bobbing on the waves, and forced herself not to look back.

Love.

Coming with me, you?

For all the wet snow, Jean had never been so warm. She practically flew over the road back to her house. She shut up the animals for the night and was inside with the lamp lit and the door barred before Tobias's wagon rattled past again.

"Anneke," said Jean, "what are we doing?"

She sat in the stern of her father's little wooden dory, exactly where she always used to when she and her father went out in the boat, and absently hoped he would not be too angry that they had taken it without asking his permission. He'd been angry when she'd taken it out with Jo.

Jo had gone away in a wagon, under a bonnet, with a stiff back.

Anneke looked up. Her white hair was caught in two long, thick plaits that hung forward over her shoulders, a style she had not worn in years. A long-handled axe lay across her lap, its blade keen and sharp, silvered by the moonlight.

"Oh, Jean," she said. "You forgot."

The sea around them was as smooth as glass, a dark mirror. Jean couldn't see the land. She wondered if she ought to worry. Anneke was right; there was something important she was meant to be doing, but Jean couldn't recall what it was.

"Anneke," she said again, "I don't understand. What are we doing?"

Anneke lifted up the axe and put it into the water, pulling as if it were a paddle. They went in a circle.

A chill went through Jean, although there was no hint of a breeze. The little boat rocked. She longed for something solid under her feet. "Let's turn back. It's time to go home."

This time, Anneke did not look up. "Never turn your back on the sea."

Something curled deep in the pit of Jean's stomach. "Anneke," she said. "Where are we going?"

Anneke shifted her grip on the axe, tightening her gnarled fingers. "Lost sailors go in circles forever." She raised the axe high into the air, then swung it straight down as if she were splitting a log for the fire. The blade bit into the bottom of the boat with a terrible crack.

Jean opened her mouth, but nothing came out.

Anneke pulled the axe free, raising it again.

A dark gurgling of water.

Jean should be doing something; there was something she'd forgotten. Water was creeping up inside the boat, a tide rose, swirling, around her ankles.

"Jean." She looked up; Anneke was staring at her. "The second wave is always bigger. Never turn your back on the sea."

Moonlight caught the wet blade of the axe, glittering.

Anneke drove it down again, hard, into the bottom of the boat.

Bang.

Jean sat straight up in the darkness, heart pounding.

Bang.

Bang-bang.

A distant, ringing bleat.

It was Kicker. Jean groaned and flopped back down, pulling the pillow over her head. What time was it, anyway?

Another bleat. Another bang, a hard cloven hoof echoing against the inside of the shed, all the way across the yard. Jean sat up again with a curse, pitching her pillow to the foot of the bed and swinging her feet out from under the warm covers.

She was going to kill that bloody goat.

Jean stumbled down the stairs, shivering in the dark, and fumbled to light the lantern before pulling her father's old coat on over her nightgown, and throwing her shawl over that, all to the accompaniment of Kicker's racketing. As Jean slipped her feet into her boots, she tried to remember what dish it was Laurie had once said that Dal made with goat, on that island he lived on. Something spicy, she was pretty certain. Right now, it seemed like an excellent notion.

She paused for a moment, just as she picked up the lamp. What if it was a bear out there that had set the goats off? Jean opened the door cautiously. Fog hung low and thick over the ground, misty in the lamplight. There wasn't a sound in the still, windless night except the slow dripping of meltwater from the eaves. No great, dark, hairy things loomed outside the circle of her light, at least so far as Jean could tell.

Kicker let out another screaming bleat.

Jean had *had* it. She stomped up the yard, splashing slush and freezing water as she went, the lantern flickering wildly as it swung in her hand. She turned over the latch, throwing open the door to the goat shed. "Kicker, you rotten beast, *STOP*—"

Her words died in her mouth.

Kicker let out a single, pathetic, shuddering *meah,* scuttling away into the farthest corner of the shed.

Honey was down. Flat on her side, not moving, and in the swinging light from the lantern a dark, wet shine was spreading in the straw under the goat's body.

Jean sat down hard, just inside the door, her legs gone to jelly. Honey's throat had been cut, neat and clean as if she were to be sent to the butcher. Jean reached out a shaking hand and placed it on the goat's soft, brown-spotted coat. There was steam coming up, and a thick, rank smell like iron or liver that stuck in the back of her throat.

She was going to be sick.

Steam.

Warm.

Still warm.

Jean scrambled back to her feet and whirled about, breathing hard and fast as her eyes darted, scanning for a threat. Beyond the circle of the lamplight, all outside was blackness. Silence.

Tobias. He had to be there. He was watching. Where? God, why now?

Then she saw it. On the ground, not six feet from where she stood in the doorway of the shed. A thick piece of a log sat up on its end. Deep scars of old axe strikes across the top.

Jean stepped down off the log into the dirty slush of the yard. Muirin set her hand over her heart. "Go careful," she said. "Careful, love." Jean set off down the track to the road, and forced herself not to look back.

Jean's vision wavered, went misty and gray-spotted around the edges. She was going to fall; the ground was tilting. *Muirin—*

No. No, by God, she'd never fainted in her life, and she wouldn't start now. Yanking the short lead rope down from the hook on the wall, Jean grabbed hold of Kicker and forced the rope 'round her neck. It was a clear sign of the animal's distress and confusion that she didn't fight, not until Jean had already hauled her the entire way down the yard and was trying to drag her through the door into the house. Kicker dug in all four of her hooves with an unholy goatish shriek. Jean set her teeth, breathing through her nose, and pulled, the rope digging into her stinging palms. Kicker pulled right back. Jean slipped, and almost fell on her ass, her heart skittering wildly in her chest.

Something made a sound, off in the dark; low and rough, almost a laugh.

Her heart stopped. She dropped the lantern in the slush, where it guttered and died as she scooped the squalling goat up into her arms, wrestled her across the threshold, and slammed the door shut, shooting the bolt home with one shaking hand.

Jean put her back to the door and slid down it to sit on the plank floor, her chest heaving. The wood at her back was not nearly solid enough.

Clinging tight to her struggling goat in the faint red glow of the banked fire, Jean waited for the sun to rise.

20

The sky was low and dark, threatening sleet, as Jean dragged poor Honey down to the shore. The ground was frozen solid still, even as the snow was melting, and so it would be a burial at sea. If it had been an animal that had gotten the poor thing, Jean might have tried to save some of the meat, but this was different.

It took three tries for her to float the goat's body out past the breaking waves, and her skirts were sodden and salted, her toes as numb as the empty space between her ears by the time she managed it. She watched Honey drift out with the wind burning her eyes, and stomped her cold, damp feet on the pebbled shore to keep some feeling in them, teeth chattering. The goats were half of Jean's livelihood: the milk and the cheese.

She was lucky he'd not got Kicker, too.

She was lucky he hadn't come for *her*.

A seal popped up out in the cove, drawing Jean's gaze. Her more frequent sightings of them had been a comfort to her of late, but not today. It seemed almost as if the creature could tell. It bobbed there for a moment, studying her with its great, dark eyes, then gave a misty huff and slipped back below the waves. Honey had disappeared, too, lost in the rise and chop of the whitecaps. The only thing floating on the face of the deep was the distant cragged island with the thin white tower on it, the harbor light. It was a shame Muirin's people didn't keep *that* light, so close. It might have made everything different. It certainly might have made getting her away easier.

Jean wondered if the Scots were anything like the German families along the coast, all knowing one another. Maybe Mr. Buchanan knew Muirin's people. If she'd been thinking straight and not distracted by the Keddys, Jean would have asked when she'd seen him in the church at Christmas, with his children. She wondered how far away Muirin's island was, if it was as small and rocky a thing as Buchanan's, with its tiny sweep of beach below the light, and the tall red cliff behind.

She wondered if Muirin's family would accept her, no matter how glad they were to see Muirin safely returned to them.

If they made it there at all.

Anneke's stupid sea adages *were* stupid, but they were right. The second wave *was* bigger; everything in life worse than what had come before, and Jean was going to be swamped if she kept on with this insanity. She ought to have learned, ought never to have let herself care. She couldn't stop Jo's marriage, and that had been nothing compared to this.

There'd never been a hope in hell of saving Muirin, but Jean had been so stupid with wanting her that she'd fooled herself into pretending it was possible; and worse, into letting Muirin believe it, too. Maybe Muirin wasn't happy, maybe it was all horrible and wrong, how she'd been trapped, what Tobias had done—but who knew what *worse* things he might do to his wife if Jean kept on? What would Muirin's second wave be with him? Jean could only hope it hadn't already come because of her carelessness. It would be safer for both of them if Jean gave up, stopped making waves, kept her eyes and her mind on her own business. Vanished, without a ripple. It would be almost like before, like nothing had ever happened, like after Jo had gone away.

Nothing on the surface for anyone to see, just the silent sucking pull of undertow inside her.

Jean could not afford another mistake. Muirin and Kiel could not afford for her to make one, to drag them down with her. Tobias would lose interest in his game of fox and hound once she gave in, stopped tempting fate. She'd made everything worse for all of them, trying to change what was already done. Thinking with her heart instead of her head. A damn fool.

Just as Anneke had said.

It started to rain, steady and chill. Jean stood and let it soak her through to the skin before heading back over the road to her house.

~∞~

"I know," Jean said as soon as she'd unlocked the door. She hadn't dared to open it once in the past two days. "Don't ask, Laurie."

Laurie stood in Jean's doorway for a long moment with a strange expression on his face, his nose wrinkled. He glanced back over his shoulder, squinting into the light before stepping inside and pulling the door closed behind him, taking in Jean's current living situation.

Kicker was tied to one of the table's legs by her short rope lead and hemmed in beneath it with the chairs. There was a thick layer of straw spread on the floor under the lot, and bits of it were strewn all across the room. The milking bucket held water for the goat and was badly dented, having taken a fair bit of abuse. Most of the wooden furniture had been gnawed on, and there was a thick and pervasive goaty funk to the air inside the little house.

From up in the attic, there came a faint sound of clucking.

"Jean, what on earth—"

"What did I say?" Turning on her heel, Jean stomped over to the cupboard, pulling down a pair of cups. She set both of them down just a bit too hard, and hauled out the jar with the tea in it, pointedly keeping her back to him.

Laurie's voice became careful. "What about the other one?"

Jean did not turn around. "Bear," she said. "Honey was too sweet for her own damn good. But Kick's a hard bitch; it couldn't get near her." She very nearly grabbed the hot kettle bare-handed and only just caught herself, picking up the tea towel and wrapping her hands before reaching for it again.

Laurie let out a noncommittal harrumph, eyeing Jean closely. "Didn't realize bears were about already."

Jean focused on keeping her hands steady as she poured the boiling water over the tea. "Early spring, I guess." Putting the kettle back on its hook, Jean turned to face him again. Her voice scraped out of her, brittle and thin. "Laur, we could take Kicker into town today, couldn't we? I know there's room for her in that old shed of Anneke's. I still have to figure out how to pack up the chickens . . ." She didn't *want* to pack up the chickens, or to pack for herself, or worst of all, to have to tell him outright that she was coming, too, or why. She might choke on the words if she tried.

Laurie gave the goat a dubious sideways glance. "Uh." He hesitated, regarding Jean in an appraising way that made her only too aware of the dark circles under her eyes. "Red . . ."

A sea serpent uncoiled within her, steaming hot and hissing.

"*What,* Laurie? Go on, tell me! How you and your ma were right, and I'm a goddamned idiot and I never should have—"

A soft knock came from behind Laurie, and the door swung open. Jean's words caught in her throat.

"I passed her coming up that last rise," Laurie said. "I would have warned you, but . . ."

Jo Keddy looked at Jean with wide blue eyes. "Is it a bad time?"

Kicker rolled her eyes and shat on the floor under the table.

The tea had been abandoned, and Laurie along with it. Jean threw her shawl around her shoulders and hustled Jo out the door again so quickly it was astonishing that her neatly pinned hair wasn't blown back by the breeze of their passing. They stood on the bank of the frozen pond, next to the old fishing boat.

Jean was at a loss.

She'd have given anything to see Jo again, to have the chance to talk to her, from the very moment she'd left. Now that she was here, Jean was so hollowed out she could scarcely function, let alone come up with anything to say. What *was* there to say, after everything that had happened?

Perhaps Jo was having similar thoughts. She gazed off over the salt marsh with a slight pucker between her brows, and a sharp fishhook wedged itself beneath Jean's ribs. Muirin had stood just there, wearing almost that same expression.

Jo couldn't have been less like her otherwise. Muirin was a fairy creature, dark and unfathomable, somehow wild, even in her captivity. Jo was sunshine bright: golden hair, rosy cheeks, forget-me-not eyes, all just as Jean remembered them. Perhaps Jo had lost a trace of girlish softness about her jaw, but that was all that had changed.

"Jo, I—"

"Jean—"

They both spoke at once, and Jo glanced down before meeting Jean's eye again. "You go first."

Jean laughed, but it came out odd and hollow. "What, you don't want to lead anymore?"

Jo gave a tight smile. "We had fun back then." She paused. "I've missed you."

Jean swallowed. "I . . . me, too."

"That's why I finally came home to visit." Jo didn't dance around her words. "I hoped we might be able to talk. I'm so sorry about my mother. I thought maybe by now she'd have let things go, but . . ." A heavy, resigned sigh escaped her. "She's a dreadful woman, and I don't know that she'll ever change. I told her as much, too. I'm staying over with Bess now, while Victor's gone up to see his brother in the city. The whole harbor up at Halifax got blocked tight with sea ice after that last big freeze, but the roads are such a mess he won't be back for a couple weeks still, most like."

Jean drew a trembling breath. "I haven't paid any mind to your mother since you went. Jo—"

"It's not fair you had to swallow her slandering you all over town on top of everything else, and making out like it was all you, and nothing to do with me at all!" Jo stopped short again and squared her shoulders. "I hear you're doing well for yourself, in spite of her. Everyone says you're a wonder; Evie Hiltz talks like you hung the moon. I was so happy when I heard. I'd worried for you—"

She reached out for Jean's hand; Jean flinched back, and the words she'd not been able to find came spilling out.

"Jo, I'm sorry, so sorry. It was all my fault, what happened to you, and I never did anything to stop it—"

Jo stepped forward, and now she did catch Jean's freezing hand, pressed it tightly between both of her own.

"Jean. Jean, it wasn't. It wasn't up to you to stop anything."

"But that night, your sister, she heard us and—"

Jo snorted, indelicate and equine. "Margie hadn't a single damn clue. She was mad we kept her up all night 'making noise and acting like idiots,' and she told me I ought to grow up! It wasn't her." She paused and wetted her lips with her tongue before continuing.

"I think Ma'd maybe suspected something for a while, if I'm honest. You and I were always close, but we were together near every minute that last summer, and she wasn't ever happy about it. She was always saying I ought to act more proper, you remember. I just wanted to have fun, but she thought I was too bold and loud, unladylike. Anyway, Vic came by to talk to Papa about me a couple days after you were over; you know how he was always hanging around back then. Ma asked what I thought about him for a husband, and I said I didn't know if I wanted to marry or not. That you and I were talking about maybe sharing a place together. 'If we didn't find the right fellows,' I said; I figured it sounded innocent enough that she wouldn't be upset about it, but she got just wild. Like I never saw before, and you know how she could be touchy . . ."

Touchy was mild compared to some of the choice words Jean had assigned to Mrs. Keddy over the past few years, and Jo's story was not improving her opinion of the woman in the slightest.

"She started in on a tear: about you being a bad influence, and how she should have put a stop to us palling around together ages ago, and how she'd not see me end up a strange old spinster aunt—that's what she called it! I about laughed at her, except she was so furious I knew she'd slap me if I dared, and even if the *way* she said it was ridiculous, she made it sound terrible and filthy, like we were doing something awful! Ma said she'd be damned if we were friends anymore, that it wasn't natural for girls to be so close, and if I didn't marry Victor, she'd pick someone else for me." Jo looked down and drew a shaky breath, finally dropping Jean's hand to twist her plain marriage band around her finger. "I was afraid you'd blame me for saying yes."

"You? Never!" Maybe at the very first, before the shock of it had worn off. Jean couldn't have held on to her anger if she'd tried. "You hadn't any choice!"

"I suppose. But, well, I agreed to it—and you knew it was never that I *didn't* like the boys, I just liked you best of anybody. But I'd danced with Victor at the hall that summer, and said I thought he was nice, even, so I was afraid you might have thought . . ." She trailed off.

"Jo, you were always the truest—even when we were little and the other girls got mad at me, you'd stay friends with me over the lot of them. I know better than to think that of you. You aren't a cheat. And even if you didn't mind *him,* you still didn't have any say . . ." Jean stopped, sickness churning in her belly, reminded once again of Muirin, her grim resignation, the marriage she'd been forced into. Jean wasn't sure she wanted to ask the question, or hear Jo's answer, but she had to know.

"Is he good to you? It's not . . . terrible?" Jean had a fair idea now just how terrible such a thing could be, and it was so much worse than she'd even considered back then.

Jo shook her head. "It's not. Victor's the kindest man, truly! He knew I wasn't happy, even though I tried not to let on to him about it. It was all Ma's doing, the wedding happening so fast. Vic got caught up in it as much as me, really. He wasn't easy about the speed of everything, he'd only been looking to court me, and he felt just awful when I told him what had really happened, about you. He cussed my parents for forcing me into it, even said he'd move into the barn with the cows instead of staying in the house, if I wanted. I said he shouldn't. That we ought to make the most of it, even if it was a bad start." She flushed. "It took work, us getting to know each other after all that. But he was patient, and sweet and . . . I really do love him now." Jo cast Jean a sidelong glance. "Do . . . do you mind?"

It was so very far from what she'd expected. Jean didn't mind, but she was stunned, unsure if it was shock or relief flooding through her. Maybe it was both. "No, it's . . . I'm glad. I wanted so badly for you to be happy somehow, and I'm glad you ended up liking him. All this time, I was just so afraid you were miserable. I watched when you were driving out of town."

"I know." Jo turned to face her. "I never thought I'd be happy again, that day. But it turns out I am. The awful thing was wondering if *you* were all right." She hesitated. "That woman, from the mercantile, the dark handsome one. I know what Ma thought, but . . . are you two . . . ?"

"Not then." Jean took a deep breath, held it, let it go again. "Now? It's complicated. Her husband . . . It's a long story."

"You'll tell me about her, won't you? I hope you will. You can come see me if you want, now I'm with Bess and not at Ma's. We can catch up proper." Jo tilted her head to the side, considering her words before she spoke them into the air between them. "You could . . . give me some advice, maybe . . . ? You'll have to tell me everything." Jo set a hand over her belly with a shy smile Jean recognized. She was the first one being let in on a secret, the sort you told your dearest friend before any other.

Jean smiled back. "You have to tell me everything, too."

21

Jean wasn't sure how long they leaned against the side of her father's boat, just talking, before Laurie came out of the house. He had Kicker on her short rope, and he led the goat down to the gate to attach her to the back of the wagon he'd come in. *Led* was perhaps not entirely accurate; it was more like he and the goat were having a tug-of-war, and Laurie only just happened to be the winner. He looked over at them once he was done and waved.

Jean waved back, then turned to Jo. "I guess that's you, then, if you're going to ride back together."

Jo glanced back at the old dory as they started toward the wagon. "Oh. I never said: I was so sorry when I heard about your father. Remember the day we took the boat?"

Jean nodded. "Da was so angry. But he was always afraid I was going to end up drowning myself, pulling stunts like that. He washed all that mud out of your hair, though, before we took you home. As if it'd make your folks less upset about the mess you were in!"

"There wasn't much he could do about the dress. Ma was *livid*." Jo grinned ruefully, then grew more serious. "Your da was always so kind to me. Did he ever guess about you and me, do you think?"

"We never talked about it." Jean scuffed the heel of her boot in the lumpy slush. "I think he had to have known, though. People talked about me in the village after you left, and I was . . ." She paused. "I wasn't myself. Da was really good about it, though. He even talked about Mama some, more than he used to. He wasn't ever easy saying how he felt about things, but he tried, you know? After everything that happened, he regretted that he didn't talk with her more, and I think he could tell . . ."

Jean's throat tightened, choking off her words. She swallowed, hard. "Josie," she got out, "even if things did come out all right for you and Victor . . . I'm still sorry. I should have done something. Said something, instead of just letting them force you into a thing you didn't want without a fight."

Jo regarded her with a tender, lopsided smile. "What would you have done, Jean? It wasn't your responsibility, no matter how much you like to think everything is. I know if there was something you could have done, anything, no matter how ridiculous, you would have tried. I *know* you would. I'm bolder maybe, but you're the brave one; you've always been stupid reckless if you thought it'd save somebody you cared about any pain. I didn't fight Ma, and maybe I should have. But it wasn't your job, or your fault, and I never blamed you for any of it. Not for a minute."

Jean wasn't sure what to say, but something old and tight and aching eased in her chest. She was so used to feeling like she had to fix everything for everyone. But maybe Jo had a point, maybe it wasn't Jean's job to fix everything, even if she was doing it out of caring. Maybe she needed to trust people to ask for help when they needed it, and let them decide for themselves when that was. Jean hooked her elbow into Jo's, and her steps were lighter than they'd been in forever as they continued down to the road arm in arm.

Laurie gave an amused sniff as they approached. "Christ. Just like old times, this is. I feel like I should watch my back, in case one of you has a snowball to drop down it." Jean laughed, and Jo held up both her hands, putting on an injured air.

"I'm innocent, I swear it! Grown ladies like us don't carry on so, do we, Jean?"

"Speak for yourself. I'd just rather a frog than a snowball, but it's not the season."

Giggling, Jo turned and pulled Jean into a tight hug. "I missed you so much." She pressed a short kiss to Jean's cheek before pulling away. "You'd better come visit me at Bess's place! And, once I go home again, we can write. I'll send you the address—you'll think it's all backward. Vic and I use English at home, but in the village everything's *en français*! I'm still dreadful, of course, but Vic says I'll get the verbs straight eventually."

It was a reassurance Jean hadn't realized she needed. She nodded, a last knot inside of her loosening. Accepting a hand up from Laurie, Jo climbed into the wagon. Once she was situated, he turned back to Jean.

"You're sure you won't come in with us? The offer still stands. I don't like it, you alone out here with . . . *bears* and all."

It was strange. Jean had been so ready to go with Laurie when he came today, to give in and give up, run away to town even though the thought of it made her heartsick and hollow. She looked up at Jo, where her friend sat in the wagon.

I know if there was something you could have done, anything, no matter how ridiculous, you would have tried.

When Jo'd gone away, Jean hadn't had any hope of changing things, and as Jo had said, maybe it had never been Jean's burden to take on. This time was different. Muirin really did need help.

Perhaps if Jean hadn't been so anxious to involve herself at the beginning, so sure she had to try to solve everything on her own . . . maybe things wouldn't be such a mess as they'd become. But she had her own help now, from Laurie, and Anneke, and she had a plan, a real plan that would *work,* so long as she could keep her nerve and see it through. A plan that Muirin was making ready for, even now, because Jean had told her to.

Jo hadn't expected Jean to do anything, had never blamed her at all. Muirin was counting on her. Loved her. Jean couldn't abandon her; she had to try. *Anything, no matter how ridiculous.*

Even if it was, as Jo said, *stupid reckless.*

Jean lifted her chin, a new lightness swelling in her chest. "I told you before, Laurie. I'm not going anywhere. Muirin needs me here, and this place is mine. For now, anyway. I'm not leaving it. Not until I have to."

As they drove away, Jo turned back to wave at her, smiling.

Over the course of the next week Jean cleared up the mess Kicker had made of the house, although there wasn't much to be done for the chewed-up legs of the table. The next time Laurie came out to check on Jean, she sent him off again with the chickens in tow, packed into a pair of deep baskets and clucking furiously at the indignity of it all. It had been raining on and off for days, and the last of the snow had finally gone, although the ice still hung on stubbornly in the marsh. Everything was muddy and gray, and as the days dragged by, that included Jean's mood.

Laurie's mood wasn't much better than her own. He'd had no response to his letter to Dalian, and perhaps it was too early yet for him to expect one, but that didn't stop Laurie fretting over it like a man obsessed.

Jean hoped he'd hear something soon; he kept dragging her

out of the house in the damp to walk the beach with him while he fussed, and pined, and threw rocks at the waves, scanning the water to the horizon like it might somehow throw him back a reassurance, a message tight-rolled inside a bottle: *All forgiven.* She had a vague sense of uneasiness about the whole business, wondering what secret Dal could possibly have told Laurie to send him reeling so to start with, and what it might do to him if the word he got back was no word at all.

The first week bled into a second, and Jean sent Laurie into town with a long note for Jo because she couldn't bring herself to make the trip, plagued by the fear that some awful unknown thing might happen to Muirin while she was away. Although Jean wasn't entirely sure what it was she thought she'd be able to *do* if anything happened up there, or how she'd even know if it did. She hadn't seen hide nor hair of Tobias since Honey's murder, and his conspicuous absence only served to make her even more worried about what he might be up to, but she dared not risk creeping back up the hill to check on Muirin and little Kiel. Instead, Jean spent hours gazing out her window across the marsh without truly seeing anything, massaging her palms with her thumbs as she rehearsed the plan in her head, hoping desperately that Tobias had not felt his wife in need of a lesson like the one he had tried to teach her. It scared her that he had no qualms in slaughtering an innocent animal, a vital part of someone's ability to survive, just to make a point.

He'd very nearly succeeded in scaring her away, just as he had the little vixen with his snare. But, like Kicker, she had dug in her stubborn heels. Jean was not going to be moved; she had found her resolve, and it was to be as hard as was necessary. She had seen how Tobias Silber dealt with soft, sweet things.

A third week, and a storm blew down from the north with teeth of sleet, laying ice half an inch thick over the whole South Shore, turning the trees to a blinding bright lacework that glittered against the sky. The ground became a sheet of slippery, uneven glass. Jean had to fight to keep her feet under her, clinging to the tree trunks as she went up to break the thin crust of ice on the spring for water.

In a matter of days, the temperature rose again.

The last of the yellowed ice at the edges of the marsh pond went soft and rotten. It would likely vanish within another week.

Jean grew more restless by the day. Once the last traces of the ice storm had melted away and she could walk outdoors again without her feet striking out in two separate directions, she took to crossing over the road by herself as she'd been doing with Laurie, to walk up and down the shore for as long as she could stand the damp chill. The days had warmed enough that she abandoned her father's coat, and went about bundled in her shawl again, the goldenrod color of it a defiance of the gloom of winter's end.

A seal surfaced to swim abreast of her as she paced, then disappeared again. Gulls swooped and kited against the low gray sky, screeling. Jean kicked at the loose pebbles, making them scatter, and stepped over the green and brown piles of bladder wrack that the tides brought in as the sea heaved beneath a thick bank of fog.

Mostly, she thought about Muirin and her mysterious family. A mother, an uncle, an aunt. Some small cousins. Jean knew nothing about them, really, for Muirin had had so few chances to say anything of them, or of her past. Tobias had taught his stolen wife to hide behind silence like a shield. Would it be a problem, how little Jean knew of Muirin's life before? So many secrets. Once Muirin was free of her husband, Jean hoped that secrets between them would only be a matter of language.

That was another question. The language.

Muirin had no hesitation about Jean finding a welcome with her people, but Jean was desperately afraid she was unlikely to be as good a student of Gaelic as Muirin had been of English. Soon, Jean would be the one unable to speak a word to the people around her, or even to understand them. The few things that Muirin had tried to teach her had tied her poor tongue up in knots, and contemplating the situation did the same thing to her stomach. Still, Jean would have to muddle through and learn somehow if she were to keep up her work, to make herself useful, if they were to live there.

Wherever *there* was.

Jean wondered, grimly, if Tobias might try to follow them. It didn't seem outside of the realm of possibility, but she pushed the horrifying notion out of her mind before it could start her insides quivering yet again. They had more than enough bridges to cross before it would matter what he did. Jean rubbed her mitten against the tip of her nose, which was growing chilly.

"Jean!"

She turned. Laurie was waving from the road, and he came down across the beach toward her wearing a grin that set her tingling from top to toe. He was pleased. He hadn't been pleased for a solid month. It had to be news.

"What?" she said, breathlessly coming up the beach to meet him halfway. "Laurie, what is it?"

He laughed. "Don't care about me visiting; it's just the news you want! Maybe I shan't tell you anything!"

"Don't tease, Laur. I can't stand it."

"I know, Red, I'm sorry." Laurie took a breath, setting a hand on her shoulder. "I have your day."

Jean almost let out a squeal, but managed to keep it back, although she was sure she was about to vibrate clear out of her own skin. "Well? When, Laurie? What are they saying?"

"A week Tuesday, if it doesn't come on stormy again. Everyone's got this notion it'll turn fine in the next couple days."

Jean couldn't sort out how to respond, caught out flat-footed and staring. Barely more than a week. A week, and Muirin and the baby would be out of that awful house. A week and they would be away, safe. Together. It was all that mattered.

Laurie gave her a comforting smile, understanding her sudden stillness. "We'll get her, Jeanie. It'll be fine."

The tense bubble around Jean suddenly popped. Throwing her arms around Laurie's middle, Jean buried her face in his jacket and laughed. Laurie squeezed her, then stepped back. Good news delivered, his happiness drained away like well water slipping through the fingers of a cupped hand.

"Any other news?" Jean asked. "Word from Dal?"

Laurie looked down at his feet, shuffling the toe of his boot into the loose pebbles. "I think . . . maybe I left it too long. And it'd be his right to not want to see me again."

"Laurie . . ."

"No, it's the truth. He trusted me, and I failed him. And now I have to figure out how to carry it, because no one can do it for me. Please, let's not . . ." He met her eye again, all trace of his earlier spark fled. "Just let me be glad I can help make things right for you, even if I can't for myself."

Jean nodded, and smiled. Her heart ached for him. "So, you'll come out after dark, a week Tuesday, then. You're sure you can get the wagon from Noble?"

The wind continued blowing chill over the sea, but the sun came, and held, and each day burned off the previous night's thick cover of frost. The last of the ice went from off the marsh and left the open water black and cold.

Tobias drove past Jean's house on Friday afternoon, headed toward town with his horse and wagon. Jean stood at her window, fidgeting with her fingers as he passed. She wasn't foolhardy enough to try to visit Muirin while he was gone this time; not when they were so close. He returned much later, on foot. Of course, his wife couldn't tend animals while he was gone at sea for two or three days if she was locked up inside their house, a prisoner. He'd found someone to board the horse for him.

Jean knew for certain now—Tobias Silber would sail with the fleet, just as Laurie had guessed.

Tobias paused in his walk home to linger at Jean's gate for an uncomfortably long time before he continued along the road, giving her house a hard look that slowly raised her hackles. It was the most she'd seen of him since the night of Honey's murder. Perhaps he was convinced that Jean had, at last, gotten the message.

He was in for a surprise.

Jean went through her whole house the last Sunday, picking things up and putting them down again. She could not carry her whole life along with her when they went. By Monday evening, she had it pared down to a single large carpetbag and her basket. It held all the tools of her trade, plus the one book she'd come by on the art of midwifery that she sometimes checked as reference. Her father's old pocket watch was safely stowed among her tools, wrapped up in a length of soft cotton bandage. The carpetbag would carry her few clothes, including—possibly ridiculously—Jean's Sunday best dress, which she hadn't worn once since she'd finished stitching it.

She'd laid it out on the bed for a while, run a hand over the cream-colored poplin with its thin brown stripes and rambling print of yellow flowers. The dress was fashionable, with impractical fat sleeves. It was nice enough to be a wedding dress, and Jean had never thought to see herself wed, but when she pictured herself stepping onto a boat next to Muirin, headed for a new life? It seemed the closest thing to a wedding she'd ever have, an occasion worth marking. Jean decided she might wear it, finally, in place of her normal day dress when they left to go to Muirin's family.

As evening came on, Jean opened her door and went out to stand on her stone step. She tried to commit her small world to memory: the silver hump of her father's old upturned boat and the marsh pond with its dead winter grasses, the little vixen's birch grove up high on the far shore. Jean was struck by a sudden pang—her last glimpse of the fox would remain it fleeing, terrified, from beneath her woodshed. It was no fit way to say goodbye to a steadfast friend.

The big waves of a spring tide rumbled upon the pebble beach on the far side of the shore road, echoing in her ears. Jean took a deep, steadying breath of the familiar salt air, and then she blew it out again, the ghost of her breath slowly fading away into nothing. Wrapping her arms around herself, she tightened her shawl against the creeping chill of evening, the shaking feeling in her belly.

If all went to plan, this was the last night Jean would see the sun set from this doorway. She stayed on her step and shivered with cold as the light went pink, and orange, and red as a sailor's delight.

22

The hours between the gray light of false dawn and midmorning were longer than the entire week that had come before them, every minute stretched thin by Jean's desire to be off. Still, she waited until the sun was well up before starting out, even though she'd been awake, dressed, and pacing the floor long before it had risen. Tobias would have put out with his boat in the early gloom to join the other men for a sunrise start, but Jean wasn't taking any risk of arriving too soon and catching him still at home if he were to have been held up for some reason. She and Muirin would have the entire day once he was gone.

Jean left the fire banked when she let herself out of the little house. They would likely want the heat when they got back, especially with the baby. Laurie wasn't coming for them until evening, and their plan was not to set off for the village until after dark, so it would be foolish to douse the flames before they were leaving the place for good.

The morning was bright, with high, thin clouds rippling like a sandbar overhead, and a brisk breeze pulled her along as she

went around the pond, tugging at her skirts and errant strands of
her hair. It was hard not to be buoyed up by hope on such a
morning. Jean lifted her skirts high to skip across the stream,
which rushed around the stone swift and cold, foaming with
meltwater from out of the deeper woods inland, where late
snow still hid in the dark shade of the pines.

Even just in the woodlot, it was cool, compared to the low,
open space of the marsh. As soon as Jean passed under the trees
and into the shade of the evergreens, she found herself pulling
her shawl tighter to keep the chill from her spine, quickening
her steps as she pressed on up the hill.

The world was strange. Had it only been four months since
she'd first come this way looking for Tobias, with Kiel just a few
hours born? Only four months since Muirin had been no more
to her than a stranger and a mystery, the fisherman's wife?

Now every step that brought her nearer to Muirin felt more
urgent than the last.

Jean paused at the top of the woodlot before edging out into
the muddy field. She would be exposed there, and she'd grown
used to watching her steps. Something flashed orange-red in the
corner of her eye, and she froze, then turned just her head. The
little vixen, hovering just as motionless along the tree line, one
paw stilled in midair, gazed back. Dropping her foot, the fox
made a graceful leap up onto a fallen log, picked her weaving
way along the length of it, and hopped down again, ghosting off
into the wood.

Jean smiled and struck off up the hill.

There was no smoke coming from the chimney. Muirin had
already let the fire die. Jean recalled the first time she'd come to
visit after Tobias had taken Muirin away again, when he'd waved
to her from the roof like they were friends—

She nearly tripped over her own feet.

The roof. Tobias had been up there twice, mucking about with the fieldstone chimney. Would a man go to such trouble to hide something from his wife? He might, if he wanted to keep it from her badly enough.

The only way to know was to check.

Jean continued up to the house, but instead of going straight to the window, went around the side. There was a wooden ladder fixed to the wall of the house, and above it a set of bracings leading up the steep-pitched roof. Jean considered the ladder, and she steeled herself; she did not climb a great many roofs. Bending, she reached back to grab the bottom of her skirts, and pulling them up between her legs, tucked them at her waist to keep them getting fouled beneath her feet as she went.

The climbing was awkward, the low heels of her boots catching on the rungs of the ladder, but it went well enough. Jean chanced a look down once she arrived at the very top, and wished very much that she had not, the inside of her mouth gone dry as if she'd bitten into a chokecherry. She had to hug tight to the chimney with her eyes pressed shut for a few breaths before she could gather up the nerve to open them again.

Peering down into the chimney she saw nothing but blackness, a pale square of light at the bottom illuminating the cold ashes and the stones of the hearth where the fireplace opened to the room. Muirin was speaking faintly, some nonsense babbled to the baby. Her voice echoed up the chimney as if from the bottom of an old well, the stones playing a hollow game of catch with her words.

Jean blew a loose wisp of hair out of her eyes and stuck her arm down into the chimney, feeling around. Nothing there but stones, sooty stones, and the small cracks between them, as far down as she could reach—and then an unexpected empty space under her wriggling fingers that should have been a stone but was not. Open air. She twisted her wrist and elbow around, fingers questing. The gap wasn't huge, but it was far too big to be an accident. Some sort of a box could have easily fit into that hole.

It had been here, whatever it was. Had been, and was no longer.

Jean would have kicked herself except that it might have sent her tumbling. Of course it was gone, and it was Jean's own fault. Tobias must've been checking on his treasure the last time she'd spotted him up here. He'd seen her spying and moved it somewhere else.

She carefully made her way back down from the roof, dropping to the ground from the lowest rungs of the ladder. Untucking her skirts, Jean brushed her sooty hands on them.

When she came around the corner of the house, the window was already open. Muirin had her head stuck out and was craning her neck to peer up at the roof with a concerned look on her face. Jean must not have been as light-footed coming back down as she'd thought. When Muirin spotted her, she let out a gasp.

"Jean!" Her voice shook. "Was you, up on top?"

Jean nodded. "I had an idea, but no luck."

Muirin was pallid and careworn, thinner than she'd been a month before. Her eyes were dark-shadowed and rimmed with red, as if she hadn't been sleeping. Jean's stomach lurched. "Muirin—" she began, setting a hand up on the windowsill.

"Afraid, I!" Muirin blurted, grabbing Jean's hand and clutching it to her chest. "Was so afraid! After you were here, last day, he come back and—quiet he got. So quiet. Strange, was. Out goes he, in the night, late, and comes back— Oh, Jean! Thought I—thought he—" Muirin's normally rich voice wavered and cracked, reed-thin.

Jean could imagine only too well what Muirin must have thought; Tobias returning home in the dead of night from some mystery errand, probably grinning and gore to the elbows, if not worse. Of course, he'd never have told her what it was he'd really done, only too happy to let her assume the very worst.

Jean squeezed Muirin's hand as well as she could with her arm so stretched. "It's all right, Muirin. I'm all right. Here—"

She took her hand back, jumping up to hook her elbows over the windowsill. It took a fair bit of scrabbling and kicking her feet against the wooden shingles, and Muirin catching hold of her arms and tugging as well, but Jean somehow made it up and in the window.

For a long moment, they just stood there, silent and staring at each other. Then Muirin latched onto Jean, throwing her arms around her as if she did not ever mean to let go, and shaking as she repeated something over and over in her own tongue. Her words were so broken with hiccuping that Jean couldn't have understood them, even *if* she'd known the language. She awkwardly stroked Muirin's back while being slowly crushed, and spoke calm and soothing words into her thick black hair. "Shh. It's all right. He didn't get me; it was one of the goats. Only one of the goats. I'm so sorry he frightened you. It's all right; really, it is. Come on, Muirin, we can't stay like this all day."

Muirin took a deep, shuddering breath and stepped back, her dark eyes roving over Jean's face, inspecting her as if to be sure she was, indeed, whole and well. Muirin's intense regard kept Jean fixed to the spot, holding her breath. Her shawl slipped down off her shoulder. Muirin's eyes darted to the yellow wool. Reaching out, she caught the trailing end, giving it a gentle tug. Jean released the other end, allowing Muirin to draw it away as her heart skipped and stuttered.

Muirin let the shawl drop on the floor without taking her eyes from Jean's.

Something tightened deep in Jean's belly. She had to put out her tongue and wet her dry lips before she could speak, with no idea what would come out of her mouth. "Muirin—"

She didn't manage to find any other words. Muirin began kissing them all from her mouth, greedy, her hands stroking Jean's face and hair. Her arms looped around Jean's neck again, as if she feared Jean might vanish into thin air were she not held in place and proven beyond a doubt to be real.

Jean did not see any reason to go against Muirin's wishes, not when all she had wanted for weeks was to be able to touch those hands, that hair, those lips, and know they would not be wrenched away from her again. A surge of warmth went through her, and one of her arms tightened around Muirin's waist as she buried the fingers of her other hand deep in the heavy hair at the back of Muirin's neck. Jean's feet shifted; Muirin was turning her, walking her backward, and Jean's heart stuttered and skipped like a flat rock skimmed over the top of a pond. Their teeth knocked together as Jean tripped, a foot catching on her abandoned shawl. Impatient, she shoved it out of the way with her heel.

The back of her knees hit the edge of the bed with a thud, and Jean fell backward onto it with a gasp, pulling Muirin down on top of her. They paused, their faces an inch apart, staring at each other, panting. Jean's eyes were drawn to the pale, irregular freckles across Muirin's nose, and she was struck by an impulse to kiss every one of them she could find, and then go hunting for more of them, the ones she had only ever glimpsed, scattered over Muirin's shoulders like a constellation of stars.

It flashed through the back of Jean's mind that maybe she ought to try to stop this, that they *couldn't,* not now, not here, in this bed—

Muirin murmured something in her own tongue and kissed Jean again, hungrily, pressing close against her, with soft lips gone demanding. Her hand clutched at Jean's leg, tugging at her skirts, and she made a sharp moue of frustration against Jean's mouth. A keen pang of desire hit the base of Jean's spine, blurring her vision and reverberating up to her brain, ceasing its weak objections entirely. Her pulse beat thick and heavy in her ears as she lost herself in the salt-toffee sweetness of kissing Muirin back, their hot hands tangling together as they ruffled up sea-foam layers of petticoats between them, desperate to find each other.

Where they were didn't matter, nor when. Jean couldn't care less about the bed, wouldn't have argued if they'd ended up on the floor. If Muirin wanted this, or anything, here and now, anywhere, ever, Jean's heart pounded out the message that they most certainly could, and would, for she wanted it just as badly.

23

Muirin groaned, burying her face in the crook of Jean's neck. Kiel had begun kicking up a fuss from the other room.

Jean laughed softly and brushed her lips across Muirin's forehead before slipping from her arms to go and fetch him from the cradle. The baby was never going to nap forever, no matter how little Jean or his mother wished him to stir. It was a reminder: They could not ignore reality, the world existed outside of just the two of them, and they ought to be up and moving again.

Still, it was so easy to snatch at happiness, to let the peaceful moment stretch out. Jean came back to sit on the edge of the bed in just her chemise, bouncing the babe on her lap, and watched as Muirin began to slip her clothes back on, admiring how she made even this graceful. The baby squirmed in Jean's arms, and as she adjusted her hold on him, she marveled at how much Kiel had grown since last she'd seen him. She would have sworn he was closer to six or seven months than four if she'd not known better, but then his father was no small man. Perhaps it only made sense he was such a big baby. Jean frowned and pushed the thought of Tobias away again as Kiel gave a bright, chuckling laugh and caught at her wild hair for the fifth time in as many minutes. She pried his little fingers loose.

"Ah-ah. No, Kielie, sweetheart, that hurts."

A different, long-fingered hand caught at the same lock. Jean looked up, and Muirin grinned at her, eyes sparkling as she slowly wound the single long curl around her hand, giving it a light tug. "Both like red, we."

Jean gave a huff of amusement. "Too bad. It's mine, and you two can't have it."

Muirin's lips twitched up at the corners. "Mine, is, now. Mine, you." Bending, she pressed her lips to Jean's again, fingers still twisted into her hair. They might very well have gotten themselves sidetracked for a second time—and quite badly—except that Kiel glommed on to the other side of Jean's frizzing hair with a gleeful squeal and a sharp yank, trying to stuff a handful of curls into his gummy mouth. Muirin and Jean broke apart, laughing, and Jean carefully untangled the babe's wee webbed fingers from her hair yet again, her cheeks flaring with heat.

She was fairly sure she'd gone as red as a fresh-boiled lobster, although she wasn't certain why. Muirin ducked her head, giving Jean a little sideways look that made her heart flutter before turning away to look in the mirror atop the chest of drawers. The warm glance, short as it was, left Jean more optimistic than she'd been before about going away with Muirin to a strange new place. If they had managed to win this much happiness already, surely they would do just fine wherever they finally landed, so long as they were together.

As Muirin bent her elbow up to fasten the small buttons at her wrist, she began to talk again. Even fearing that something terrible had happened, she'd tried to keep faith that Jean would still come as she'd promised. Muirin had searched through the entire house in the moments when Tobias was out of doors but had found no sign of the thing she was looking for, not in any of the cupboards or drawers, nor upstairs in the bins of apples and winter squash. Nothing had been tucked into the rafters of the house, nor were there hollow spots hidden beneath its floorboards, and the despair that crept into Muirin's voice—combined with the detail of her accounting—spoke volumes about how very much it meant to her that she find whatever it was before they left.

Jean could not bring herself to admit to Muirin that she knew where the treasure *had* been, once, but that it was gone now, moved, and she had no clue as to where. It wouldn't help matters, so Jean determined to move forward. They had hours yet to search, could turn the entire place upside down if need be. Laurie wasn't coming for them until after nightfall.

She should make a start by searching the outbuildings: Perhaps the thing might be up in the barn's loft somewhere, under the hay? Or maybe there would be another missing stone like the one she'd found in the chimney inside the top of the well. Jean just hoped Tobias hadn't buried the blasted thing somewhere, like Captain Kidd's treasure up on Oak Island, or they'd never find it. It had been the dead of winter when he'd moved it, though, so he couldn't possibly have done that. The ground was still frozen near to solid even now.

There was a worse option: He might have taken the treasure along with him when he went off to sea. Jean didn't want to even consider it; Muirin would be crushed.

Muirin smoothed down her skirts, and Jean stood to pass Kiel back into her arms before beginning to gather her own clothes together.

"Muirin," she said as she untangled her petticoat from the rumpled bedding, "would you light a lantern for me? I'm going to go out and look in the barn, and I'll need a light." Jean paused and looked up at Muirin again. "I really do want to find it for you if I can, whatever it is. I can see how much it means to you."

Muirin smiled and caught Jean's hand briefly, squeezing her fingers. "Somewhere it must be, here. Would know, I, if not." Muirin's simple faith was touching. Turning, Muirin headed through to the front room to get the lantern from its hook over the table, carrying Kiel along with her as she went.

Just outside the bedroom door, she stopped abruptly with a sharp indrawn breath.

Jean glanced up from shaking out her petticoat. "Muirin . . . ?"

Muirin didn't look back. Reaching behind herself with one hand, she pulled the door between them shut without a single word.

Jean was about to move forward when a low thumping arose at the front of the house, the dull, heavy knock of muddy boots upon the doorjamb. She froze, her throat closing up tight as a pinhole, her mouth going dry. *No.* No, it couldn't be. He was *gone,* gone for three days with the fleet; at least three days, that was what Laurie had told her. Jean began whisking the rest of her clothing into her arms, silent and frantic.

The front door opened. "Why've you let the fire go out?" Tobias's irritated voice came to her right through the bedroom door, which suddenly seemed all too thin. "Fine thing, a man coming home to a cold house." He paused. "What, nobody here but us chickens?"

He was . . . disappointed.

Tobias hadn't expected to find Muirin alone.

Muirin's answer—and whatever Tobias had to say in reply— were swallowed by the wild drumming of Jean's heart in her ears. Her mind whirled, quick and rabbity. No wonder he'd paused at her gate for so long after leaving his horse in town. Tobias had *wanted* Jean to see him there, to think that he was making ready for going away to sea, so she would make another move against him. He'd never been going off with the fleet. Instead, he'd set a snare for her, and she'd gone and put her fool neck right into it.

Trapped. She was trapped. Jean's eyes darted about the room.

No, there was the window. She'd leave as she'd come, and maybe, somehow, Tobias wouldn't know.

Carefully, quietly, Jean slipped her feet into her boots, not bothering with the buttons. Setting the small pile of her clothes down on the bed, she turned to the window and hooked her fingertips under the wooden frame. She slid it open as slowly and smoothly as she could, just wide enough to allow her to squeeze through the opening. There was a faint creak, and she froze again, breath stilled, ears straining.

Muirin's voice drifted through the door. "No, not can light," she was saying. Her words were strained, just a bit too loud. "Tobias, no. Smoke was, before." Bless her, she was trying to distract him, trying to buy time for Jean to make an escape.

There was a deep sigh from Tobias, followed by some shuffling sounds, and the squeal of a piece of wooden furniture being shifted along the floor. His voice echoed strange and hollow when he spoke again, as if it were coming up from the bottom of a well. "It ain't blocked. I can see the sky clear enough—"

Jean picked up her bundle of clothes and dropped them out the window, then wriggled out herself, landing in a heap beside them in the muddy yard. She didn't waste any time in getting her legs back beneath her, scooping up the lot, and racing for the nearest shelter to hand before Tobias could have time to get his head back out of the fireplace and come to open the bedroom door, to look out the window. Jean turned the little block of wood that served as a latch for the door of the whitewashed henhouse on its nail and scrambled inside. Then she pulled the door shut behind her, careful not to let it thump as it closed.

The door was well constructed and sealed tightly. The hinges didn't squeal, and it didn't swing open again when she cautiously let it go. The turned latch might escape notice for a while, if she was lucky.

Jean blinked against the gloom of the cramped building as she fought to steady her breath. Strange that there was so much straw spread deep across the floor; it was a complete waste; if there had been any birds, they would have made an ungodly mess of it and laid eggs everywhere but where they were meant to. There was a faint hint of light coming in through a little window high up opposite the door, and she could make out a long perch to her left and a row of empty nest boxes along the wall to her right. No straw in those at all, they were empty of everything but dust. Jean shook her head. Why did she care about any of that right now? She began to struggle back into her damp, mud-splotched clothing, shivering, and only partly from reaction. It was freezing in here half dressed, without even the heat of the chickens. Although at least Jean was spared them giving her away with clucking and cackling, and there wasn't much smell.

Head bent in the half-light, her shaking hands fumbling with the tiny buttons on her dress, Jean took a step toward the one high, narrow window. Her toe cracked against something hard buried under the straw, and she only just kept herself from letting out a yelp, mutely hopping about on one foot and trying to make out what she'd connected with.

Jean stopped hopping, set her foot down, and stared.

It was a box.

It couldn't be. Could it? There hadn't even been a lock on the door, but then a lock would have looked out of place on a henhouse, might have drawn notice . . .

The box was wedged in under the nest boxes, and if Jean had not caught the protruding corner of it with her foot, she'd never have spotted it. She pushed the straw away from it with her still-throbbing toe, then knelt and pulled it out from the shadows to examine it more closely. Medium-small, and made of hammered tin, the unassuming box was fixed shut with a solid and outsized iron lock.

Jean ran a hand over the lid, and her fingers came away smeared with thick black soot.

This was it. The thing that had been in the space between the stones of the chimney, Muirin's mysterious treasure. It had to be. Tobias had spotted Jean watching him on the roof, and then he'd moved all the chickens out from the coop and sealed tight its cracks. She'd watched him doing it, and thought he'd had a fox in the henhouse, had even taken pleasure from how richly he deserved it. It had never been anything of the sort. He'd been hiding his stolen treasure in the chickens' place, sure it was the last spot anyone would look. No one in their right mind would search for something of value where they expected to find a heap of stinking chicken shit.

Jean had to admit it was clever. She'd not have thought to come sniffing around the henhouse, but she still wasn't quite sure if she ought to reckon it good luck or ill that she was holed up in here now. So long as she wasn't caught out, though, she might be able to steal away with the box once night fell and keep it safe for Muirin somehow. If she could make it back down the hill, and meet Laurie—

God, that was still hours off. Jean's heart sank. She didn't even know what time it *was,* how much time she and Muirin had wasted, thinking they had the whole day before them. Wrapping her arms around herself, Jean tucked her chilled fingers under her armpits. It was best to accept that she was in for a long, cold afternoon. She didn't even have her shawl.

Jean's stomach turned over.

Muirin had taken the yellow shawl off her and dropped it on

the floor, and then their mouths had been pressed together, and Jean had been tripping over it, impatient, kicking the shawl away—probably it was still under the corner of the bed, buried beneath the tumbled sheets and blankets. It would not stay hidden for long.

How long could Jean stay hidden? She crouched into a low ball, pressing her hands tight over her face as if somehow that might help. Would Tobias go to her house first when he realized what she'd done, or would he come to check on his treasure?

"Damn it, Muirin!"

Jean nearly toppled over as Tobias's voice rang out, sharp and harsh. Fear stretched her ears, rendering his every word clear and distinct, even across the yard and through the thin walls of the chicken coop.

"Smoke or no, you can't just go leaving the bloody windows open! You want to freeze us out of the place and sicken the baby? And why the hell isn't the bed made up yet, it's gone past noon! I think I've been plenty patient up 'til now, but—" The bedroom window slammed shut with a solid bang, silencing the rest.

Jean pulled the box toward her through the straw and picked it up. It wasn't heavy. Nothing clunked or rattled, although she could tell there was *something* inside, a weight that slid smoothly from one end to the other when she tilted the box in her trembling hands. She couldn't stay here. She would give Tobias one minute to walk away from the window, and then she'd bolt for the woodlot. It was a terrible idea, but it was better than sitting there waiting to be caught. She rose and moved over to the door, taking a deep breath to steady herself.

A muffled roar went up from inside the house, echoing through the walls loud enough to make her jump, and a thin wailing rose behind it—the baby, frightened. Jean wasn't waiting to see what would come next. Heart hammering, she shoved open the henhouse door with her hip and lit out for the woods at a dead run, clutching the soot-smeared box in her arms.

She hadn't gone more than three steps before Muirin let out a terrible shriek.

Jean slipped attempting to change direction and nearly fell facedown in the mud. Somehow she managed to keep her feet, and went sprinting back toward the house. "Muirin! *Muirin!*"

Inside, Muirin was screaming, babbling something in her language, and Tobias was howling right back at her: "Unfaithful, ungrateful *bitch*! Just you wait! I don't have to be so—"

Jean shouldered the door open just as Muirin hurled the burning oil lantern across the room at Tobias, who was advancing on her. It missed him and shattered, exploding in a great gout of flames across the floor between them. He leapt back, toward the bedroom. Muirin froze in place, shocked, as if she couldn't believe what she'd done, hadn't expected to be able to defend herself.

"The baby!" Jean yelled from the doorway. "Muirin, the baby!"

Muirin jerked like she'd been stung and grabbed Kiel up from his cradle, along with all the blankets, bolting out the door past Jean as hot, orange flames began crackling up the front of the cupboards. The baby had stopped crying, terrified into silence. Tobias's gaze fixed on Jean across the growing wall of fire roaring between them, and then on the box she held in her arms. Jean stared back, struck by the feral glint in his eyes. They narrowed, and his teeth showed as he growled and made a move to come for her.

The whole floor was blazing, and a bright burst of flame shot up right in his face, forcing Tobias back with an arm flung over his eyes.

Jean turned and raced after Muirin, her heart pounding. As they tore down the field toward the wood, Kiel's small face bounced above Muirin's shoulder, looking back behind them, his dark eyes huge and round. Jean slowed, glancing back as well. A thin line of white smoke rose into the clear sky above the house.

For a single instant, Jean was four years old. A ship was burning, far across the bay. A seal, just out of her reach—

She shook herself.

The white line darkened and widened, billowing. A red tongue of flame licked hungrily over the ridge of the roof, and there was the faint, distant crash of shattering glass, as the windows began exploding with the heat. Tobias was nowhere to be seen.

Jean looked back around; Muirin was already disappearing into the trees.

24

Jean caught up to Muirin at the swollen stream. She had stopped dead in her tracks, surveying the high, rushing spring runoff in dismay, and Jean nearly ran headlong into the back of her. Muirin's eyes were wild, her chest heaving. The distance from this side of the bank to the rock was too great to be spanned in a single step, even with Muirin's long legs, the reason for her hesitation clear. She did not want to risk a misstep with Kiel in her arms.

They couldn't afford to waste time picking their way along the shore of the marsh out to the road, and Jean was certain they dared not backtrack. Perhaps Tobias was not following them, was burning along with his house, but Jean couldn't bring herself to trust fate that far. If she had managed to escape the house earlier, so might he.

Setting the box down in the path, Jean breathlessly held out her arms. "Give him to me," she said. "You go, and I'll pass him over to you."

Muirin tightened her arms around Kiel for a moment, gazing

down at him, then thrust the babe into Jean's arms as if she feared changing her mind. Hitching up her skirts, Muirin made the short jump to the stone, and then turned back, reaching out her arms. Jean got as close to the soft edge of the stream as she dared, and stretched to pass Kiel over the rushing water to his mother. It wasn't a long reach, but her insides still quaked at the danger of it, and Jean breathed a massive sigh of relief when Muirin caught the baby from her hands, blankets trailing, and bundled him securely back into her arms. Muirin continued the rest of the way over the stream without difficulty, then turned back on the far bank, waiting for Jean to follow.

"Hurry!" she urged. "Must go!"

Jean shook her head, calling across to Muirin: "You go ahead. Get inside and bolt the door. I'm going to hide this, I'll come after!" She bent, taking up the sooty tin box once more. Muirin opened her mouth as if she might argue, then shut it again. She had to see the sense in it, when they'd gone to such trouble to find the thing. Whatever else happened, Jean wasn't about to let Tobias get it back again.

"Muirin!" She had to say it. "Don't open the door unless you know for certain it's me. Hide." A breath. "I love you."

Muirin's eyes were huge and round, shining black with fear. "Careful, Jean. Go fast."

Jean nodded, and then veered off the path, skirting as swiftly as she could along the edge of the stream and around the tangled grasses of the marsh, angling back up the hill again, toward the birch grove. She paused before entering the trees. Across the marsh, Muirin hurried over the yard to the house and went inside. Jean took a deep, shuddering breath and darted in among the trees, striking out up the ridge that she'd so often spied the little red vixen trotting along.

As she crested the ridge, the maples and pines gave way to birch. The tall trees were still bare this early in the year, their skeleton trunks around her spindle-slender and pale, peeling with silvery-white bark. Jean looked around, low amid the scraggy bushes and the heaps of last year's rotting leaves.

It was here, somewhere. She'd found it once before, while picking blueberries, but Jean had always skirted around after that, out of neighborly politeness—there! A dark place, under a twisted root. The fox's den.

Jean hurried over, dropping down on her knees. Her nostrils filled with musk and the scent of old loamy leaves as she pressed her cheek to the forest's damp floor, peering into the hole. It would fit. The poor fox was going to be so confused when she came home. Jean shoved the box into the opening as far as she could reach. There was a sudden subterranean scuffling, and she yanked her fingers back out in a hurry. Leaning to peer down the tunnel again, she spotted a gleam in the darkness beyond the tin box, daylight reflecting from two bright eyes deep within the little den.

"Sorry." Jean breathed. "I won't leave it long, I swear." Scrambling to her feet once more, Jean went dashing back the way she'd come.

Halfway down the ridge she caught sight of a red flash, ghosting alongside her through the underbrush. The fox was following her like a guilty conscience. She paused, and the vixen stopped as well, fixing Jean with a golden stare before pointing its sharp, black nose back up the ridge toward its den. It looked at her again, came a step closer. Jean flapped her hands at the fox in a shooing motion, widening her eyes significantly as if it might somehow make the creature understand her, and then kept going. She'd already taken too long.

The fox continued trailing Jean back down the hill, stepping out onto the path several paces behind her.

She'd barely registered the sound of something large crashing down through the trees of the woodlot before the fox let out a shocked yelp. Jean whipped about as the animal snapped her wicked little teeth at Tobias, who aimed a kick at her with a curse. He'd nearly stepped right on the little vixen as he barreled headlong down the path. Smoke-stained but unharmed, he looked up as the fox went bounding off into the trees and realized Jean stood in the path ahead of him.

For a moment, they both froze, neither of them even breathing.

Tobias grinned.

Jean broke toward the stream, her heart pounding as hard in her throat as her feet did on the path. She made a leap like a deer well before she reached the bank, and was hit hard from behind in midair, strong arms pulling at her waist. Swirling water came rushing up at her, the rippling reflection of her face and rusty hair, and the air knocked out of her lungs as she landed; sprawled midstream on her stomach, flat across the rock with Tobias on top of her. She gasped painfully to draw a real breath. Jean's feet and legs were trailing in the water, a cold shock, and she scrabbled, kicking and splashing as she tried to get over onto her back, flailing to land a blow on him.

Tobias grabbed a handful of her hair, and Jean's ragged breath caught again as he jerked her head back. His smoke-roughened voice rasped low and intimate beside her ear, his breath hot on her cheek. "You thieving little redheaded *bitch*. A cunning little vixen, aren't you, stealing into a man's house, into his *bed*—" His hand tightened painfully in Jean's hair. "What's mine is *mine!*"

"You *stole* her!" Jean gasped out. "She doesn't belong to you!"

"She's my *wife!*" His voice rose, and Tobias yanked Jean's head back even harder, straining her neck, forcing her to look at him, his weight holding her in place. "I was a good husband. I did *everything* for her, and it was perfect, just like in the tales—" Bile rose in Jean's throat. "And she never argued, not once. I never had to raise my voice and she would have never left me, she never *could,* not before—" Tobias stopped abruptly, and Jean was almost grateful. Then he wrenched her head sideways again. "Tell me where it is! You hid it someplace, or she'd be gone already! What did you do with it?"

Jean would be damned before she told him. It wouldn't change what happened, only give him one more thing to hold over Muirin.

"But then"—he hummed, considering—"if I don't find it . . . neither will she. And you'll not set your filthy paws on her ever again."

Tobias smiled, and Jean saw her future in it, short and brutal.

"I'll tell them you fell," he said, "helping Muirin. You were always *so* good to us, Jean. I got here too late. They'll believe it." His hand tensed at the back of her head.

Jean squeezed her eyes shut.

Her mother, Janet, had drowned in this stream, somewhere back in the woods. Jean's father's voice echoed out of her memory, clear as if he were beside her. *Jeanie, you be careful! Split your head on that old rock, and you'll be gone without a ripple to tell the tale!*

Anneke had warned her: *It's not your business. Don't go making things worse for the girl, even by accident.*

Even Muirin had known. *No other way? Jean, is so dangerous. Go careful. Careful, love.*

Tobias would take Muirin back again, and it would be worse than ever for her because he knew now—absolutely—that she did not love him, and never would.

Everything Jean had done was for naught; she'd let them all down—

"*No! Mine!*"

There was an earsplitting *crack* close over her head.

Tobias jerked, letting out a soft grunt. His hand went slack and loose in Jean's hair, and he toppled sideways off her, rolling into the stream with a splash.

Jean opened her eyes. Muirin stood on the bank of the stream, panting like she'd just outrun Satan and all the hounds in hell, one of the old gray oars from Jean's father's boat clutched in her white-knuckled hands. The oar was snapped nearly in half, its broken blade dangling by a fraying bit of wood fiber. Her eyes were fixed, staring.

Jean followed Muirin's gaze.

Tobias did not try to move, to turn over, to swim. He floated, facedown and limp, a red stain spreading in his wet blond hair as the stream's current pushed him away from them into the marsh. Muirin didn't move.

Slowly, carefully, Jean gathered her legs under herself on the rock, though they were so jellified she feared they might crumple. Her entire scalp ached. Pushing herself upright, she took a wobbling step across the stream to join Muirin on the bank.

"Muirin," Jean said, hoarse but gentle. "Muirin." She took the oar from Muirin's unresisting hands and dropped it on the ground. Then Jean lifted her own hands and caught Muirin's face between them, made her look away from the thing in the pond. She was trembling.

"Muirin," Jean said again, more firmly, trying to meet her eye. "Go back to the house. Take care of Kiel. I have to try and get him out of the pond. If anyone asks"—she paused and swallowed hard—"he fell."

Muirin stared at her a moment longer, then nodded mutely and turned away, drifting back toward the house like a sleepwalker. Once she'd reached the door, Jean bent and picked up the broken oar. She carried it along with her as she circled around the marsh to where her father's old dory lay, then paused to look it over.

There was a red smear on the dangling blade. Jean heaved the oar out into the pond with a splash. She'd broken it herself, getting the boat in.

Her strained neck twinged at the effort required to turn the boat over and drag it into the water. Then she almost tipped it over climbing in. Jean couldn't steady herself any more than the boat; it kept trying to turn, tilting first one way and then the other as she rowed out into the pond with the one remaining oar. When she finally reached Tobias, she realized she had a bigger problem: There was no way she could get his body into the boat on her own. He was too heavy for her to lift to begin with, and his waterlogged clothes were starting to drag him down.

She had to make it look like she and Muirin had tried to help him, or people would ask questions, wouldn't they? It would look wrong if Jean didn't get him out. She managed to hook Tobias's arms over the side, one at a time, although they kept slipping, and Jean's fingers and soaked feet were starting to go numb.

Jean let the boat drift. The current would take her under the road and then she could maneuver them into the shallows, where the stream curved 'round before opening out into the waves. Instead, she found herself trapped in an eddy just past the bridge. Every time she pointed the boat toward the pebbly shallow, it caught in the current and turned, making slow circles in the deep curve of the stream, under the steep bank on the wrong side. Tobias's arm fell again, and Jean grabbed at it, almost dropping the oar. He was sinking, and she couldn't hold on to him and paddle at the same time, and she was done with caring what everyone *thought*. He deserved for her to let him go, to disappear forever in the sea, he did; he deserved it all, and more besides—

There was a thunder of pounding hooves as a wagon came around the curve of the road at speed. Someone let out a yell, and it came to an abrupt halt, the horse protesting loudly.

"Jean! Jean! Jesus Christ!"

It was Laurie, and Noble Burgoyne with him, and another man, solid and dark-skinned, who she'd never seen before in her life. The stranger slid down and went dashing toward Jean's house as Laurie leapt from the back of the wagon, calling out to her.

"Hang on, Jean! I got you!" He crossed the thin strip of beach at a dead run, splashing into the stream clear up to his shoulders as if it were nothing, although he gasped at the cold. Swimming the last few feet, Laurie caught the pointed bow of the boat and pulled it free of the circling current, dragging it toward the shore.

Noble Burgoyne came wading out to meet them and took Tobias from her, dragging him up onto the beach. As Laurie got the boat landed and lifted Jean out of it, setting her on her shaking legs again, Noble laid the dead man out on his back, and then tipped his head to the side, examining the wound above his ear. He glanced over his shoulder at Laurie.

Laurie looked at Jean.

Jean shuddered and buried her face in Laurie's wet shirt as if she could somehow hide there. "He fell," she said, her words muffled against his shoulder. "The house caught fire. The rock . . . he fell."

"All right," Laurie said, wrapping his dripping arms around her. "All right, Red. He fell."

25

"Muirin?" Laurie asked, wary of Jean's response. He began steering her up from the beach toward the house. It was as if Jean had left her brain behind at some earlier point in the day; it was easiest to just go where Laurie pointed her. "And the baby?"

"In the house. They're safe."

Laurie let out a heavy breath. "Thank God. I was scared by the time we got here—"

The millrace in Jean's head started running again, if only by a trickle. "How did you know to come? You weren't supposed to be here for hours yet."

Laurie hesitated.

Something else occurred to her. "Laurie . . . that other man, who—"

"Dal." Laurie broke into a broad grin. "He made town this morning, early, and got caught up in the excitement on the docks, with all the fishermen setting to head out. He overheard one of them spinning the others a line about how his wife was taken sick, that he wasn't going to sail out with them after all.

"Anyway, I was up to Noble's, off-loading wood so the wagon'd be empty before I was supposed to come get you, when here comes Dal, busting up the hill from the harbor looking for me!" Laurie was gesturing so vigorously that the dripping ends of his hair fell forward into his sparkling eyes. "I couldn't believe it when I saw him, nearly broke my neck getting off the wagon, too, except Noble caught me by the belt before I took myself down!" Laughing, Laurie shoved his hair back, tucking it behind his ears.

"But then, of course, Dal said straight off how he'd seen this fellow—"

Laurie's words stopped short, as if someone had clamped a lid on the bubbling pot of his excitement. Jean could practically see the wheels spinning behind his eyes as his mind scrambled to catch up with his tongue.

"Dal thought he seemed . . . off," Laurie went on, more cautious, then pushed forward with his tale again before Jean could get in a word. "And as soon as he said about the 'sick wife,' and described the man, well! I realized who it had to be, that it must have been on purpose, Tobias Silber trying to catch the two of you out. He spotted the opportunity to slip Muirin away as clear as we did, the bastard."

Turning his head, Laurie spat on the ground beside the road. "We saw the smoke rising halfway out the harbor, and I knew it'd all gone wrong. And when we came 'round the bend and I saw you down there in that boat, and him—"

Jean frowned at the path before her feet, the rest of Laurie's words drifting over her head. It didn't make sense. Dal was a stranger, fresh arrived. A stranger, to somehow notice a thing like that, mark the odd behavior of a man he'd never even met? The man would have to have the sight to know something was wrong from nothing more than a passing word.

A stranger, bursting into the house on Muirin after everything that had just happened.

Jean's head jerked up, her breath catching. What was she *thinking,* out here jawing like it was company come calling and nothing amiss? "Oh, *hell!* Muirin—"

She dashed up the path to the house and shoved the door open, more than half expecting to discover Muirin had brained Laurie's love with the copper teakettle, or something more like to do the man permanent damage—

Instead, Jean burst in to find Muirin weeping in Dalian's arms like he was her long-lost brother. He stroked her hair, speaking to her gently in a low, soothing voice. Jean couldn't understand a word the man was saying, but already Muirin was beginning to calm, although she clutched Kiel to her chest like she intended to never set him down. Dal glanced up at Jean, then spoke into Muirin's ear: quiet, but a clear question.

Muirin shook her head and asked a question herself.

Dal nodded and then said something else in reply, his face becoming serious, almost stern. Muirin darted a glance at Jean before nodding as well. She murmured a short, seemingly affirmative response before burying her face in Dal's shoulder again.

"See? It's all right." Laurie came up behind Jean in the doorway. "Dal's good with people."

Jean turned to him, completely adrift. "I thought you said he spoke Spanish. Where on God's green earth did he pick up *Gaelic?*"

"Uh, well, I don't know, maybe there's—Scots among his da's people, somewhere along the line or something? I guess that's where he picked it up. Some people are good with languages. That's why he took off up here straightaway; when I explained about Muirin he said he could talk to her." A sappy smile was spreading across Laurie's face again, but he caught himself and started taking things back in hand. "Look, you go upstairs and get changed, and see if you can't find something for Muirin, too. You're both a mess. I'll put on the kettle and then go back out and help Noble with . . . you know."

Jean did as Laurie suggested, then went digging into a trunk of her father's old things to find a change of clothes for him, too, before he took a chill, and perhaps a dry pair of trousers for Noble. When she came back down, he was standing before the fire with a threadbare towel draped over his shoulders, talking in hushed tones with Dal, their heads leaned close together. She caught the edge of their conversation and stopped on the stairs, not wanting to intrude.

". . . probably take it more sensible than I did, at least I think so?" Laurie ducked his head. "I was a fool. I'll never take off on you like that again, I swear." His voice dropped, softer and more earnest than Jean could ever recall hearing in all the time she'd known him. "I'm sorry, Dal. Truly." He laid a hand on Dal's chest as he raised his eyes again.

"I might've tried to explain before I went and sprung it on you like I did." Dal's voice was as kind and soothing in English as it had been in Gaelic and gave an impression of great patience. "There are things you ought to hear of before you see them. Wasn't only your mistake, Laur." He set his hand over Laurie's, held it there. "I shouldn't have left it as long as I did."

"You had damn good reasons, and I was wrong to react like I did, however you told me. I'm just glad you came. I was afraid you'd burn those letters, not want to hear hide nor hair of me . . . and God, you couldn't have picked a better time! But look, once the girls get their chance to talk, and Jean—" Laurie looked up, spotted her hovering halfway down the stairs, and stopped. Dal followed his gaze and hummed, giving Laurie's hand a subtle squeeze.

Jean met Laurie's eye and raised her eyebrows. Laurie's mouth twitched in a vain effort not to break out into a grin again. It failed, and he beamed at her from across the room. Jean smiled back, pleased that Laurie and Dal had begun to sort things between them after so long apart.

The sun was sinking by the time the men were ready to leave with Tobias laid out in the back of the wagon. He'd be put into the dead house in the village cemetery, to wait on a burial once the frozen ground thawed enough for digging. Muirin and the baby would, of course, stay with Jean. Everyone agreed, even Noble Burgoyne; it was a terrible tragedy. The family fleeing the burning house, a slip crossing the stream. There was nothing Jean could have done by the time she'd gotten her father's boat out.

Laurie came to get in a last quiet word with her after the wagon had been loaded up with its unfortunate cargo, the pair of them standing at the gate. The dry clothes Jean had found for him fit badly in both directions: big in the body, but too short in the arms and legs. Nonetheless, there was something comforting about Laurie standing there in her father's old oatmeal-colored sweater. Dal was still in the house, trying to suss out exactly where Muirin's family was, so they could be sent word.

"Noble doesn't know anything about what's been going on. Far as he knows, I came over with a bad feeling something was wrong out here. He'll be telling folks I have the sight." Laurie rubbed the back of his neck with one hand, then raked it forward through his hair. His voice dropped as he met Jean's eye. "Jeanie," he said, "whatever happened with Silber, you know you can tell me. I ain't gonna say a word."

Jean just looked at him. "He fell." She'd repeated the words a thousand times already.

Laurie set a reassuring hand on her shoulder. "Won't anyone hear any different from me. Now, you and Muirin both try and get some rest, will you? Toast the siege of Gibraltar while you're at it. You girls look like you've been through a war, and I doubt it'd do either of you any harm. I know for a fact you've a bottle hid up in the back of the cupboard—"

"I still don't see why Dal thought twice about Tobias." Jean cut off the flow of Laurie's advice. She'd gotten sidetracked before, but she had the distinct impression that he knew something she didn't and was trying to avoid explaining it to her. "He was just in, dead set on finding you. I mean, thank God he said something, but why on earth did he think to mention the man?"

Laurie kicked his foot against the gatepost. "Well. I mean, Dal's got a bit of a sense for people." Jean narrowed her eyes at him.

"Laurie Ernst. Are you seriously going to tell me he *has* got the sight? Because if *that's* why you were such an ass—"

"Course not, don't be stupid."

"Well, then, what—"

A deep chuckle came from behind her, and Jean jumped.

Dal smiled at her as he joined them, all gentle good humor. Jean instinctively liked him. The easy warmth she sensed in his wide, toothy smile was surely half of how Laurie'd found himself hooked. Dal's dark good looks probably hadn't hurt matters, either.

"Maybe I got a touch of the scent?" His deep brown eyes crinkled with amusement, but then his tone grew serious again. "Bad intent leaves stink on a man, and I could smell lies on that one before he even opened up his mouth to tell them. When I hear a man tell what smells like lies, I ask on him soon as I get the chance."

From the corner of her eye, Jean caught Laurie widening his eyes at Dal and shooting a pointed glance her way.

Dal just laughed, leaving Jean unsure if there was truth buried somewhere in his words, or if he was putting her on, trying to take her mind off the day's events.

"You want to see a man turn a sick color?" Grinning, Dal propped one of his elbows on Laurie's shoulder, leaning on him as casually as if he were a particularly tall fence post. "Our Laurie, he come over the shade of pease porridge when he put things together. I thought he might get out and push the horse to speed us up coming here."

Laurie scoffed. "And who said they'd swim it faster, hmm? Don't you even."

"Oh, lord." Jean rolled her eyes. "Forget I asked. Dal, it's nice to meet you, finally, even if . . . well. And thank you. It's a miracle, you showing up when you did, and I shouldn't go questioning that sort of luck." *Even if it* does *sound like there's more to it.* There was *something* going on neither man wanted to get into with her, no matter how it strained the credibility of their tale. Not right now, at any rate, and all considered, whatever it was could probably wait. "You being able to talk to Muirin was good luck, too. I'm sure it helped, even if she's not much like herself."

"Pff." Dal waved a hand. "Ain't no thing. Anyhow, I said I'd get word off to her people tonight. Laurie?"

Laurie blinked as if this were news to him, darting another glance at Jean. Dal shrugged, flashing an impish grin, and Laurie snorted, shaking his head with amusement. "I suppose we'd best be off, then," he said, though his voice still held a faint air of reluctance, "before it gets any later."

Dal favored Jean with another of his warm smiles, then caught up her hand and pressed it between both of his, giving her a deep, searching look. She was sure he was about to say something further, but instead he bestowed on her a nod and a slow wink, then went to climb up into the wagon with Noble.

Laurie stepped closer to Jean. He opened his mouth, then shut it, shooting a quick look back over his shoulder at Dal. "You and Muirin have a lot to talk about now everything's done with. Just . . . be calm about it. No need for hasty decisions, all right? Tomorrow, Dal and I'll come back and we'll sort things out together. Ma'd been looking forward to seeing you two, you know, and meeting Muirin finally. Maybe you both could come stay with us, until her folks send word."

He seemed uneasy, leaving her and Muirin alone. "Don't worry, Laurie," Jean said. "We'll be fine until tomorrow. No more surprises."

Laurie hummed, one eyebrow quirking, then caught her up in a sudden, crushing hug before he turned to go.

Jean stood sentry at the gate until the wagon had disappeared around the point before she walked back up to the house. Muirin sat before the fire, wearing one of Jean's long nightgowns, with a woolen blanket draped over her shoulders like a shawl. She hardly blinked, staring into the flames as they danced. Jean's nightgown was far too short for her, and there was something achingly vulnerable about Muirin's bare knees showing below the hem.

Kiel snored softly in a bundle on the bed, where Dal had convinced Muirin to set the baby down after the better part of an hour. Except for the moments spent crying and speaking with Dal in her own tongue, she'd stayed silent. Jean wasn't sure what she ought to say to her, now they were alone again. Muirin's whole manner put Jean in mind of a blown-glass bottle, only too easy to topple and shatter.

Finally, she knelt on the floor at Muirin's feet. Looking up into her face, Jean set a hand on her knee, careful, as if she were a barely tamed thing, likely to bolt. "Muirin? They've gone. It's all right." Jean gave her leg the softest of squeezes. "Please say something?"

Muirin did not say something. She slid out of the chair and onto the floor with Jean, pulling her into the circle of her arms. She buried her face in the curve of Jean's neck. Jean was certain Muirin was going to start weeping again, but instead she took several long, deep, trembling breaths. Then she lifted her head and bumped her nose against Jean's jaw, pressed it into her cheek. Jean rubbed her cheek up and down, then tucked her own face into Muirin's neck. There was a faint hint of smoke in her hair, but otherwise she was her same self.

Cracked or no, Muirin would mend. Jean let her forehead drop onto Muirin's shoulder. She wasn't sure she wouldn't have cracked herself if Muirin hadn't responded.

"Is over." Muirin spoke into Jean's ear. "Gone, he is." She pulled back and looked at Jean, clutching her by the arms. Muirin's dark eyes glowed, reflecting the firelight. "He would have killed you. Jean—" Muirin pressed her lips to Jean's, kissing her so fiercely it made her dizzy, before breaking off to look at her again. "*Mine,* you."

Jean couldn't help it. She burst out laughing, wild and inappropriate. Muirin tilted her head, her eyes concerned. She kept hold of Jean's arms, but carefully, as if Jean were the fluffy head of a dandelion and might blow apart in a stiff breeze. Jean pressed her face into her hands for a moment, trying to collect herself. She'd become oddly giddy.

"I'm sorry," she managed. "I don't know why I'm laughing! It's only . . . everything he did, and you turn on him because you're *possessive*?" Jean dissolved into another fit of giggling. Muirin didn't quite seem to follow, but she caught Jean's hands between her own.

"Still coming with me, to see family mine? Not . . . make me stay, you?"

Jean stopped laughing, her outburst extinguished like a snuffed candle. Muirin still wanted her, now that the danger had passed, and the threat of Tobias's retaliation with it. It made everything between them more solid and real than it had ever been. No danger to press them, no dark secrets left to uncover, and Muirin still wanted Jean to be part of her life. Jean smiled, her cheeks heating for no clear reason.

"If you want me, of course I— Oh! Your box. You wanted it so badly, to take back home, and I almost forgot all about it!" Muirin sat up very straight, clutching Jean's hands even tighter.

"Where?" she demanded. "Jean, is where? Must show you, I, need to see!"

Jean laughed again. "Impatient! I hid it down the fox's hole. It's safe, I promise. You're going to make me go get it *now*?"

Muirin gave her an imploring look. "Please, Jean." A sorrowful depth underpinned her words. "Not laugh. So long was, and is mine. Want, I." Jean was instantly ashamed. How could she deny Muirin anything, especially now? Lifting Muirin's hand, Jean held her gaze as she pressed a kiss to her knuckles, solemn and sincere.

"I'm sorry. I wasn't thinking. I'll go, right now. Forgive me?"

Muirin gave a jubilant squeak and dropped Jean's hands, lunging forward to kiss her again.

Jean didn't cross the stream to return to the vixen's den. She wasn't sure she'd go that way for quite a while, for the very notion made her stomach quake. She went the long way around, over the bridge, following the road halfway up the rise before turning off into the wood. The sun hung low and heavy behind the trees, casting long, blue shadows. The air in the woods had turned thick and chill, and Jean was sure there would be another hard frost overnight.

The little tin box was right where she'd left it, but the fox was nowhere to be seen. There were marks, though, of the vixen's clawing in the dark earth around the box, an exploration. Jean had made quite a stir with her uninvited visit to the fox's den, imposing on the poor thing's hospitality. She hoped the fox would return home once she realized she had her bolt-hole to herself once more. Maybe she'd resume her habit of visiting Jean's side of the pond one day, if she was given enough time.

Jean and Muirin knelt before the fire, the box on the floor between them. Muirin reached toward the lock but pulled her hand back at the last moment, as if having come this far she feared the treasure might vanish into thin air if she dared touch it. Jean gave her a reassuring smile and turned the box up onto its end, bracing it between her knees.

"We won't break a solid iron lock like that," she said. "But this hinge, I bet it'll give." Tin wasn't terribly strong, and the heat of being kept up the chimney all that time would have further weakened it. Jean took the fireplace poker and wedged the point of it into the seam where the lid and the base came together, prizing it back and forth. There was a creak of metal, a dull cracking.

Kiel woke at the strange noise, setting up a wail. Jean winced. "Sorry. I didn't think. Muirin—"

Muirin shook her head, her wide eyes still fixed on the box. "All right is. Open."

Jean bore down on the poker, twisting, and the hinge snapped. Setting the box upright again, she lifted the lid backward over the lock.

A rank smell hit Jean, making her nose wrinkle. A hot, damp, fishy thing, like the seaweed and crab shells that rotted along the high-tide line on a summer's day. A stinging note of salt and

acrid woodsmoke, a pungent, wet animal scent. It reminded her
of smoked herrings, and made her breath catch in her throat.

"Oh, God. Muirin, I think it might be ruined." Jean reached
into the box and lifted out the thick fabric piled within it.

Not fabric. Soft and smooth and spotted, mottled dark and
silvery gray, it was a fine short velvety fur. Jean looked for a
shape to the garment and found none. A sealskin. There was
nothing else under it or folded up inside. She looked at Muirin,
and her throat convulsed in an attempt at swallowing.

Jean's voice came out brittle and dry as driftwood.

"Muirin," she said slowly, "what is this." It was less a question
than a demand. Had this really been what Jean had nearly gotten
herself killed over?

"*Craiceann ròin.*" Muirin breathed out the strange words as if
they meant something, as if the reeking pelt Jean held was a
marvel. Muirin reached out, stopping her fingers just short of
stroking the thing. "Mine. Give me, Jean. Please."

Jean's fingers tightened on the soft skin as a smothering hot-
ness welled up within her, pounding in her ears as she stared at
Muirin. A sealskin. The thing Muirin hadn't been willing to
leave without was a stinking old sealskin.

They'd killed a man for a sealskin.

Tobias had done a thousand things to deserve it. He'd have
done the same to her. But still.

A bright flash of anger exploded in Jean, and she flung the
skin at Muirin.

Muirin caught it, cradling it in her arms like a child, and she
stared at Jean with wide, surprised eyes.

"All of this, for *that*? *That's* what meant so much to you that
you'd risk your life?" Jean's voice kept going up, loud and sharp,
her jaw pulsing in time with her ears. "We could have been
away the minute he left! But you needed *that* stinking thing? Are
you *mad*? Kiel could have been *killed*! You could have been

killed! I could have been killed! Do you have any ide—" She broke off, afraid if she didn't clench her teeth closed she might be ill.

"Jean—" Muirin stretched a hand toward her. Jean batted it away.

"Don't. Don't you dare." Her eyes prickled, heat rising from her cheeks, and she looked toward the ceiling, blinking hard, her eyes smarting.

"Can not tell you, Jean, only can see—"

"What is there to see, Muirin? What? I'm meant to give up the whole life I made here, spent years building, throw it all away for you, and you thought it was worth risking all of our lives to have *that*?" Kiel was still crying. Jean scrambled blindly to her feet. "I can't believe you'd do that."

"Jean!" Muirin put her hand out again.

"No." Jean fled.

She tripped over every root on the path to the spring, her hot eyes full of mist. She'd be damned if she was going to cry. All this time, everything Jean had done, and Muirin was still keeping secrets, secrets that didn't even make *sense*! It was more than just the language. What else didn't Jean know? What else did Muirin think was more important than anything, than all of their lives?

Jean aimed a kick at a bush, and her heel slipped out from under her. She landed flat on her ass next to the spring.

For a second, she just sat there, gulping air.

"Damn, damn, *damn it*!" Jean pressed her skirts over her face, squeezing her eyes shut.

It had been a long, trying, terrifying day, for both of them, and perhaps she was wrong to be so angry, but she could see no good reason why Muirin had put them all at risk for such a ridiculous thing. There was no excuse for it.

She and Jo had never kept secrets, not from each other. Although Jean supposed their whole life had been a secret that last summer, and that had blown up in her face, too. But even with all the regrets she'd had after, at least she'd known where she and Jo had stood, that they'd told each other everything in the time they'd had. But Muirin . . .

Muirin.

Muirin had been forced to keep so many secrets. First by Tobias, and then from him. She had so much reason not to trust at all, but she'd let Jean in as if it were easy, and little by little she'd made Jean want to do the same, when she hadn't dared do that with anyone since Jo. They'd had so little time to talk, or even get to know each other. It had been nothing but running and hiding and stolen conversations from the moment Muirin had gone back to her husband's house.

It was only now that they had time.

Jean hadn't let Muirin even try to explain, and a wave of shame washed over her, her stomach sinking. *She* was the one who had done the inexcusable, had botched this as badly as Laurie had his own situation after learning whatever'd set him running from Dal, and what had Jean said about that? *Laurie, how could you? Dal* did *trust you if he told you something he thought he had to hide for that long—*

Muirin had been through so much. How many times might she have been able to explain the situation with Tobias right from the very beginning if Jean had taken the time to listen before rushing to draw her own conclusions, acting on what she only thought was the whole story? It was dreadful that Jean had yelled at her, unthinkable after everything that had happened. She needed to go back and apologize, find out what Muirin had been thinking with that sealskin. Try to understand.

Jean opened her sore eyes, lifting her head from her arms. It was nearly dark, her breath a faint ghost in the purple dusk. She broke out in a fit of shivering that came right from her spine. How long had she been sitting there? Climbing to her feet, Jean started back down the path to the house, this time picking her way more carefully over the shadowy bumps of roots. Everything would be all right; she would make things right with Muirin, just as Laurie had with Dal. They had time.

Jean pushed the door to the house open. It was cozily warm after the outdoors, the fire still crackling merrily in the hearth, incongruous with Jean's creeping shame over her behavior. Kiel had stopped crying, tucked into his old basket next to the chair. It was almost too small for him already. Muirin must have gone upstairs to lie down in the big bed. Jean couldn't say she blamed her.

When Jean peeped at Kiel on her way past, he gazed back at her with his round, serious black eyes, alert as ever. Jean put a finger to her lips. "Shh," she said. The baby stayed silent, though his eyes followed her as she went to the stairs. "Muirin?" she called softly.

No answer. Jean went up the steps. As soon as she was high enough to see into the loft, she realized the bed was empty.

"Muirin?" Jean said again, louder. Silence. Muirin wasn't in the loft. Something dark and heavy curled under Jean's breastbone. She turned and looked back down the stairs, but Muirin didn't magically appear in the room below. Jean's heart started beating as hard and quick as the wings of a bird closed up in a box.

Kiel began to cry again, alone in his basket before the hearth. Where was Muirin?

Jean remembered the story about her mother; her father, returning to an empty house.

Oh, God.

26

Oh, God.

Jean's breath caught in her throat.

Where was Muirin?

How long had she been gone?

Jean stumbled out the door of the little house, leaving Kiel to cry in his basket. "Muirin!" Turning about, she took in the empty yard, the still marsh, the darkening wood. The sky was indigo, the light nearly gone. There was no one.

Running down the yard and through the gate, Jean looked both ways along the road, a terrible tightness in her chest. She shouldn't have forgotten her first fears for Muirin, even with everything that had come after. She should have been kinder; she *knew* how far Muirin had been pushed off-balance, how much had happened . . . Jean tried to take a deep breath, but her lungs refused to fill, a ragged white puff choking out of her mouth.

Then Jean spotted her, down at the shore. Muirin was in the freezing water clear up to her waist, trying to pull the little dory that had been left behind on the beach out through the breaking waves. All she had on was Jean's thin, white nightgown, and something dark draped over her shoulders. The sealskin.

The boat pitched up under Muirin's hands, hit a wave of rolling foam, and dropped back down again with a splash. Jean raced down the beach, trying not to trip as pebbles turned beneath her feet, her ankles rolling.

"Muirin! Muirin, *stop!*" Muirin kept trying to point the boat out into the open sea, fighting against the surf, and didn't look up at Jean's call. Jean went splashing into the water still at a run, gasping at the freezing shock of it, her skin tingling. "Muirin!" she yelled again, grabbing the opposite side of the boat, yanking it back toward the shore. *"Muirin!"*

Muirin gave the dory a hard tug, the wind whipping her hair around her face. "Must go, I!" she insisted over the crashing of the waves. Her voice was set and rang with determination. "Have to see!"

"Muirin, no!" It was madness; she would drown. What on earth was Muirin thinking? Jean struggled forward, ducking around the front of the boat, trying to put herself between Muirin and the sea. A wall of water hit Jean in the middle of her back as she faced Muirin again, a numbing shock of spray, and one of Anneke's old warnings echoed in her head.

Never turn your back on the sea.

Jean grabbed hold of the side of the old dory, shoving it back toward the shore again. Her fingers, already burning with cold, protested at closing on it, and her teeth clattered together as she cursed the extra time it took to spit out her words. "Please, Muirin, I'm sorry! Come back! I didn't mean it! The baby, Muirin!"

Muirin shook her head. "Can't tell, Jean! Only can see." She kept her head down and shoved the boat forward. Jean's feet slid in the loose pebbles under the water, and she fought to keep her balance.

"Muirin!"

Muirin stilled, gazing down at their hands clinging to the side of the dory. Relief washed over Jean: Muirin was afraid to let go, wouldn't do this thing.

Finally, she looked up at Jean. Dark-eyed and silent, Muirin drew a deep breath, setting her shoulders.

Releasing the side of the dory, she plunged past Jean into the sea.

For a single second, Jean stood clutching the side of the boat in complete shock. Good lord, Muirin could *swim,* was swiftly putting distance between herself and the shore. Jean knew the draw of the beach; already Muirin was in deeper than she could have hoped to stand, and in this cold, she wouldn't last more than a few minutes—

Jean planted her feet and shoved the little boat forward, hard, driving the nose of it past the foaming break, heaving herself up and over the side. The boat rocked wildly, taking on water, but it didn't tip, and Jean scrambled for the single oar, tugging it from under the plank seat. "Muirin!" she screamed. "Come back!" Jean drove the oar down into the water on the left side of the boat, lifted it and plunged it in again to pull on the right. A single hard stroke on each side, over and over. Her palms were smarting from the friction of the wood, but she was going forward, faster, and straight as an arrow. Muirin wasn't so far away, only a few strokes more . . .

The sleek, dark head in the water vanished.

Jean was on her feet, throwing the oar aside, heart thumping. She launched herself into a dive, straight forward over the bow of the boat, aiming for where Muirin had been.

The water closed on Jean like a fist of ice, so crushing cold that she nearly swallowed a lungful of sea from the shock of it. She broke the surface with a gasp, then sucked in a breath and dove back down, deeper, kicking hard. She had to find Muirin.

It was impossible to make out anything under the dark, heaving sea. Then, suddenly, a pale thing wavered in the water ahead of her. Muirin's shift! Jean kicked again, reaching toward it, her lungs burning. A solid shadow rolled up over the light shape, streaming a trail of bubbles. Whatever she had seen was lost.

Fighting her way back to the surface against the pulling weight of her skirts, Jean's head came up just in time for a cresting wave to slap her across the face. She spluttered, twisting about in the black water, paddling in circles like a dog as she desperately tried to shake the salt from her eyes.

"Muirin! *Muirin!*"

The second wave caught Jean from behind. It lifted her like a bit of driftwood as it crested and broke, crashing back down, tumbling her forward, rolling her over herself like a ball.

Jean could not tell up from down, and her skirts ensnarled her kicking legs, her hair whipping like a tangle of seaweed across her eyes. Everything was ice water and foam, swirling dark green and bubbling white. Stone grated under Jean's back, and then sharp against her cheek, and she tried to put a hand down, but the bottom was whirled away again. Water burned in her nose, salt stinging in her mouth, and the sea roared in her ears.

Something caught hard at the back of her dress, jerking her upward, and suddenly there was air again, a knife of cold wind cutting across Jean's face as she coughed and choked, still fighting and twisting to try to see where Muirin was.

Muirin—

She had to find Muirin, had to save her, Kiel needed his mother—

Kiel. The realization came to Jean late, and sluggish. She'd left him alone. Someone had to go back to the baby. Jean tried to make a grab for the hand pulling her through the water by her collar, but her numb fingers wouldn't work, had gone stiff and strange. Her heels dragged against the bottom. Pushing at water as heavy as blackstrap molasses, Jean tried to get her feet beneath her. They were two dull, far-off blocks of wood, not hers to command.

The grip on her collar dropped, and there was a great splash beside her. Staggering forward, Jean fell face-first onto the shore. She turned her head against the stones. A boat was being shoved up onto the beach not ten feet from where she lay, half in and half out of the water. The sea dragged at her listless legs.

It was not her father's boat; there was an old man pulling it from the black water, an old man with a gray beard.

Muirin—

Jean tried to push herself up, but she couldn't make her arms obey. Leaden and heavy and unaccountably warm, they wouldn't do as she asked; they barely moved. There was a high, quick chittering nearby, and a loud, anxious bark, and then something large and silvery dark slid up from the water, onto the shore beside her. A seal. It stuck its soft, whiskered nose against Jean's face, snuffling wetly at her cheek, studying her with dark, concerned eyes.

Woo?

It was a question, soft and breathless.

Jean wondered vaguely if she was asleep, dreaming. She was tired enough to be asleep, the cold sea wrapping her up tight in a thick, mercifully warm blanket.

The seal rippled like a sparkling sandbar before Jean's eyes, blurred and smudged like a watercolor, a mackerel sky. It threw off its shifting, changeling skin, and somehow . . . it was Muirin.

Jean blinked, slowly.

"Jean!" Muirin was pulling at her shoulder, rolling her over onto her back. "Jean!"

Muirin is scared. I ought to say something to her.

Muirin leaned over Jean, pressing hot hands to her stiff cheeks and tugging at her heavy arms, pleading with her to get up.

"You were right," Jean managed, slurring. "I had to see."

Voices were speaking over her head in a language she didn't understand, low and growling and urgent. A sharp bark was followed by an animal whine, and someone's arms were lifting her, carrying her up the beach. Tiny stones crunched and rolled. Jean leaned her head against a shoulder . . . and drifted.

27

*M*uirin . . .

The sea was roaring in her ears, and Jean could not move.

Kiel, oh, God . . .

She'd left the baby alone in the house.

Her eyes flew open. A fire roared in the hearth, built up to a ridiculous height, heat rolling off it in waves. Jean tried to move her arm and met resistance. It seemed as if every blanket in the house had been piled on top of her.

Half a dozen voices all began speaking at once, rapid and excited. Jean understood only one of them, but hearing it made her dizzy with relief, even lying down.

"Jean?" Muirin leaned over her, her face and voice both tight with worry. The other voices fell silent.

"Urgh," Jean replied, and began fighting the heap of blankets to sit up. Then she froze. Five pairs of dark, round eyes stared at her. The room was crowded with unfamiliar faces. "Oh," Jean said then, and clutched the heavy blankets closer to her bare chest. Someone had stripped her out of her wet clothes before putting her into the bed. Jean's face burned. She was surrounded by strangers, and she was stark naked.

Not that she was terribly out of place.

Muirin perched on the side of the bed, clad in nothing but long dark hair and artfully draped sealskin. Two older women Jean guessed to be somewhere in their late forties sat in the chairs before the fire, similarly underdressed. One had very long, very thick salt-and-pepper hair, and a dark sealskin much like Muirin's wrapped around her shoulders. She had an oval-shaped face like Muirin's, too, and even sitting down Jean could tell the woman was as tall as most men. The other woman was shorter and softer, rounder in her cheeks. She had a smooth grayish pelt laid over her lap like a blanket and a wide streak of white in her dark waving hair. The taller woman held Kiel, and the baby babbled cheerfully in her arms as if the rest of the room had not suddenly left off talking, waving his webbed fists under his care-taker's nose.

"All right, you?"

Jean looked back to Muirin again and nodded, although she wasn't entirely certain she hadn't lost her mind.

Muirin dropped her gaze to her hands, which twisted around each other like a pair of otters in her lap. Then she raised her eyes again, her expression pained. "Sorry, Jean, I am so sorry. Thought I, you—" She broke off for a moment, her voice gone rough. "My fault, was. So angry, you, and I thought better to go, and—"

"No!" Jean grasped one of Muirin's hands. "No, Muirin, no, it was me, my fault! I got upset, when I ought to have let you explain, and after everything that already happened? I shouldn't have yelled like that, I don't want you to go, and Kiel—" Jean caught herself, afraid she was about to start babbling. Or bawling like a child, and she wasn't sure which would be worse.

Muirin squeezed both her hands tight around Jean's. "Fool, I! Coming back was I, once I knew—" She stopped, shaking her head. "Should have tried to tell you before. Thought I, you would understand it not."

"I'm not sure I understand it *now*. Muirin—" Two children of about twelve or thirteen stood at the foot of the bed, regarding Jean as if she were a great curiosity. Something about them was familiar, but she couldn't have said what, for they seemed like children she wouldn't forget. They were nearly identical, with long dark hair hanging over their shoulders and shining black eyes much like Muirin's. One was a boy, with a sealskin—gray and spotted—thrown over one shoulder, hanging down his back. He had it hooked on a single webbed finger, like an insouciant schoolboy might hold on to his jacket, his other hand resting on his hip. His nose was sprinkled with freckles.

The other child Jean wasn't sure of because they wore her bib apron as if about to go make up a loaf of bread, and it came down past their knees. They had freckles as well, lighter ones, and they, too, had a sealskin, knotted over their shoulder like a sash. It was a pale, silvery thing, with a great many white speckles on it. The child in the apron turned and said something to the boy, flashing Jean with a glimpse of bare bottom. The boy laughed and said something back, poking Apron hard in the ribs. Apron growled, baring their teeth, and then tackled him to the floor. The two disappeared behind the foot of the bed in a tangle of limbs, squealing and thumping and thrashing about. Jean wasn't sure if what she was seeing was some sort of game, or if they were trying to kill each other.

White Streak Woman turned around in her chair and said a few sharp words. At least, Jean thought they were words. One of them sounded suspiciously like a snarl. The two children leapt back up and started speaking rapidly at the same time. While Jean couldn't follow a single word, she was absolutely sure it was an elaboration on the theme of *They started it!*

Muirin whipped her head toward them and—there was no

other word for it—*barked,* loud and sharp enough that Jean flinched, staring at her. Both children stopped talking immediately, the boy peering down at his toes and squirming. The woman holding Kiel looked over at Muirin and spoke briefly into the reestablished quiet, her voice lower, soft. Muirin sighed and gave her a small nod before turning back to Jean.

Jean was not sure what to ask her first, and finally chose what seemed most pressing, although she dropped her voice when she spoke. "Who are *they*?"

"We're her family, lass."

Jean nearly dropped her blankets at the sudden voice so near to hand, clutching at them as she turned her head. There was a man in the corner, leaning against the handrail that went upstairs to the loft. Not as old as she'd thought when she'd glimpsed him on the beach, although he did have a neatly kept gray beard, but she'd not been taking in much then, had she? He was younger than Anneke, maybe somewhere in his fifties. He smiled at Jean, and the corners of his blue eyes crinkled with it.

"Mr. . . . Buchanan?" Jean asked. "From out at the light—?" *The Scots* are *all related,* she thought, stupidly, wildly, trying to make his presence, so normal and solid among all the strangeness, fit into her spinning head.

"Aye." He nodded. "Muirin's my niece."

Maybe Jean's brain had not completely thawed out yet, after all.

"Wait. *You're* the uncle with the lighthouse? But that's so *close*! I thought—" She stopped. Jean wasn't quite sure what she'd thought, or even what she was thinking now. If only she'd spoken to him in the church, at Christmas, instead of running away from the Keddys. And the children . . . that's why their bright, curious eyes were so familiar! They'd gawped at her so . . .

"Aye, and a good thing we are. That new fellow bringing the news out to us fast as he did, we were already—"

A part of Jean became rather distracted with being incredibly grateful that Buchanan was not as naked as the rest of them. He had on a thick woolen sweater and a plaid kilt, and Jean was absolutely certain: An old man in a skirt was a marked improvement over an old man in nothing. Hairy knees were definitely better than the alternative.

She shook her buzzing head. Buchanan was still talking.

". . . her mother, Muireall, with the bairn, and then that's my wife next to her, Iseabail, what came over with me from Scotland. The twins are ours: Cowan and Coira. They're only but eight, and *she* likes to get *him* wound up, so don't mind about them carrying on."

Jean gaped. *"Eight?"*

He nodded sagely. "Oh, aye. Surprised me, too, at first, how they grow? They come up a bit fast, ye see, like seal pups do. Slows down again once their skins grow out, or so my Issy says. They'll stay about as they are for a few years now, 'til they catch themselves up, then go on more how ye'd expect."

Baby Kiel, laughing within a week, and the size of a six-month-old at three.

Jean realized her mouth was hanging open.

Muirin said something to her uncle. Her words still rolled, but when she spoke to Buchanan there was less of the growl that Jean was used to hearing in her voice. *This* must be what real Gaelic sounded like. Muirin's usual language was its near cousin, perhaps, but not the same thing at all. Jean felt like a bit of a fool that she'd thought Muirin had been speaking Gaelic all this time, harping on about it to Laurie and Anneke as though she knew what she was about.

"Wait," Jean said yet again, her mind whirling. "Are you all—" She broke off. "What *are* you? Seal people? That's mad, it can't be, but I saw—!"

Laurie had told her all those wild old sailors' tales, but Jean had never once assumed they were anything more than what they seemed. Stories.

There's more things in the world than you know. All winter, Laurie'd been heartsick, ever since he'd come home, over his lover's long-kept secret that he didn't know how to deal with. *It ain't mine to tell.*

Dalian could speak Muirin's language, one he knew from his father's people. Had already made a trip out to Buchanan's island, bearing news to her family faster than any sailor possibly could have. Could *smell lies* on a dishonest, thieving fisherman . . .

Or, maybe, what Dal had smelled on Tobias was *kin*.

Dal was one of them, too. He had to be.

"*Selkies,*" Jean breathed. She stared at Muirin, with her dark, deep eyes and long lashes, her high, smooth brow. A selkie. Jean almost reached to touch Muirin's cheek, then stopped herself, aching, unsure if it would still be allowed. "I thought it was a fairy story. Not real. But you are. Real. Muirin—"

Jean looked around the room again, taking in all of them, their black, sparkling eyes, all fixed on her. The spotted sealskins that they could put on and take off as they wished. They were people, all of them, but they were seals, too. Wild things, and free. By morning they would all disappear into the sea again, and they would take little Kiel and Muirin along with them.

It was what Muirin must have wanted all along, from the very first night when Jean found her in the marsh. *Water.* She'd been trying to go back to the sea. Right now, she was regarding Jean with her expressive brows drawn together, the tips of her fingers worrying unconsciously at the flat spot over her breastbone. Jean swallowed around a hard and painful lump in her throat.

The tall woman—Muirin's mother—started speaking. "Muirin . . ."

Jean didn't understand anything the woman said after Muirin's name, but her tone was kind, and the words rolled from her tongue mellow and soft, rising at the end like a gentle wave that did not break: a question.

When Muirin replied, her words circled around themselves with an air of uncertainty—what if, what if—a current looping back on itself.

Buchanan put a hand on Muirin's shoulder. He spoke in English, for Jean's benefit, and it landed strange and clumsy upon her ears after that musical selkie language, like a stone dropped into a stream. "Ye should tell her, then, all of it, and see what she says."

"Have not all the words, I," Muirin said in English. "Explain, I must. Can help, you?"

Her uncle nodded and said something in Gaelic to one of the children, made a gesture. The one with Jean's apron—*Coira, Jean reminded herself, a girl, but a seal girl*—went to the door and fetched him over the three-legged milking stool from beside it. Then she hopped up to perch cross-legged on the bed by Jean's feet, leaning forward on her elbows, waiting for a tale.

Muirin shifted a little on the edge of the bed, taking Jean's nerveless hand up into her own once more. Jean's heart twinged painfully, but she couldn't bear to let go, not until she had to. Buchanan set the stool down at Muirin's knee, and himself upon it. Then he began to help her find the words.

28

My uncle is not one of us. He's like you.

He slipped and fell off a rock near the light at Islay many years ago, but my aunt Iseabail had been watching and she fished him out of the sea so that he wasn't drowned. They fell in love. But he knew that there would be too many questions for them in the place where he'd lived his whole life, and so they crossed the sea together on a great ship, like so many other people were doing just then. They were married in the village, and then took up the lighthouse in the bay, for there it was easy to keep the great secret: My aunt is not like other women. She is selkie, can take off and put on her skin as she chooses and disappear into the sea.

My parents followed them here a few years later, but they came another way. My father, Kiel, was an adventurer, bold. It was what my mother always liked best about him. She wanted to come and be near her sister when she realized that there was to be a me, for Iseabail was all the other family she had. To my father, their journey was simply another adventure: a long swim from island to island together, clear across the northern sea, and then down this wild coast, where everything was different and new.

So they also came to live on the little island with the light, and soon after, I arrived into the world. Mama and Da both were selkie, so I had my craiceann ròin *from the very first and was born in the sea, as they had been. My name means that: Muirin, Born of the Sea.*

I was never much on the land. Adventurous, you know? Curious. Always swimming after something new. Like my father. Maybe too much like him.

He decided one day to make himself a new adventure, to go up onto a boat with men. I was still very small then. "Privateering," they called it, and it was all hiding and racing, and taking things from other, richer men, something to do with one of their wars. Da thought it was exciting. Then one day their ship was caught, cornered in the bay by a bigger boat, one with soldiers on it, and many, many guns.

The things they had been doing were outside the law.

One of the men on my father's ship was certain they all would be hanged. He lit a fire, and it blew them up before they could be taken. Da was lost along with nearly all the rest of them.

You told me the very same story once, not knowing it was mine. That I'd been there that day, and seen it, too.

Mama didn't want to leave here, after the Teazer *burned, wanted to stay close, live where she and Da had been happy together. I grew up out in the bay with our family.*

We kept away from the townspeople. Mostly.

Sometimes I was bad, as I grew older. I would go in near to the shore, where I was not supposed to be, and there I played at siren, trying to lure the pretty fishers' and farmers' daughters to the water's edge. Not to hurt them; I was hoping to steal kisses. It even worked, once or twice.

Sometimes, I went swimming close to the village. There was so much to see there, and to smell. I'd spied a girl there sometimes who I thought was interesting, because her hair was red as a sunset and I liked her pointed chin, how she lifted it when she walked over the bridge. Sometimes she walked together with another girl, link-armed and laughing, but when she was alone she was quiet, and watched the water in the

*place where the rivers make the current circle. I imagined maybe it was
me she was looking for.*

Don't laugh. All right, I guess you can. It is funny, isn't it?

*Time passed. I swam in the harbor, and out of it, and in almost all
weathers. That's a thing we share with the seals; the cold doesn't bother
us. You had no way to know, before, and I forgot it wasn't the same for
you. And you tried to come for me anyway, to save me, when there was
no need. I am so sorry. No, I mean it, Jean, you might have——*

Fine. I'll keep going. But it does matter.

*I followed the lobstermen, and stole from their traps, as bold and
foolhardy, perhaps, as my father had been. I wasn't scared of them, for if
I was seen it was easy for me to disappear in the waves like I had never
been. I learned the best places to find scallops and oysters, and where to
dig for the fattest clams. I knew the sharp winds and the swift currents,
when the tides would run high or low, which beaches had the most sea
glass.*

*When my aunt and uncle had twins, a boy and a girl, long after
they'd thought they would have any child at all, I was fascinated with
them. They seemed so fragile at first because they were only half selkie
and born without their skins to keep them safe, but they were also
charming wee things, with the sweetest little hands, webbed like a duck's
feet. They grew quickly, and I stayed home more after they came because
I wanted to play with them, to show them things and teach them as if I
were their bigger sister.*

I didn't go near the village as much as before.

*They were making more boats, and the trees were disappearing from
along the shore. The water wasn't clear like it had been when I was a
child, and it had grown crowded in the harbor, exposed. I wasn't the
only one who avoided the village; the girl I'd liked to see when I went
there had stopped coming as often as she used to. When she did come,
she kept her back very straight. Her steps were fast, and she only ever
looked ahead of her. I didn't know why. It seemed like something had
happened.*

I wondered about it, even worried, for she seemed so very changed. Now I think I understand.

Maybe I was a bit lonely sometimes. I had only my family, and they were all either older or younger than me, but I was still happy. I did silly things to keep myself occupied: floated on my back at night to watch the moon, or sat on the shore popping the green bubbles of the wrack between my thumb and fingers. I fished a lot, and fed us all well, on all my favorite things, of course. I did riskier things, too: I took up dancing on the shore, and that was fun, trying to make my body move and twirl as gracefully out of the water as I could in it.

It was spring when it happened, early, the tides running high, and the water still cold. Just after the little ones' skins had grown out. Coira managed to take hers on and off first, but Cowan did it more smoothly, and I would tease them both and have them chase me out around the rocks, for I was quicker than either of them.

I suppose it couldn't be much more than a year ago.

Strange. It feels longer.

The fishermen weren't yet out together, so it felt like it always does in winter on the sea. Like you are completely alone.

There's a sandy strip at the back of our island where I'd go to dance, and sometimes I could convince Mama and Aunt to come with me because there it seemed safe and sheltered, and so we would stretch our legs and shake our hair together, and race against the wind. One day in the fall, we saw a boat in the water there, when we hadn't expected to, and nearer than we liked. We hid until it was gone, and after that stayed away from the beach. But winter had been long, and I was bored because we stay closer to home in the winter, the same as you, Jean. I looked from behind the rocks and didn't see any boats, so I told myself it would be all right.

I should have known better.

I took off my skin, hung it on one of the bay bushes to let it get the good salt-air smell in it, and went for a run up the beach. I spun in circles, and jumped the restlessness out of myself, and when I felt nice and warm, and tired, ready to be finished, I went back.

My sealskin was gone.

I didn't know what to do. None of us had ever lost our craiceann ròin; I had not thought it possible. I should have gone back up to the lighthouse and asked for help looking, but I could feel my skin calling out to me, like a tugging under my ribs, in the back of my mind. The call led me over the tumbled rocks at the bottom of the cliff, and around the twisted trees of the point.

There was a wooden boat hidden there.

And a man.

He held my skin in his hands. He took it onto the boat, and I could not do anything but follow him, for as soon as my sealskin was on the water and I was not, something in me stretched as if it might tear.

I went.

I wanted to hit the man and take my skin back but found I couldn't raise a hand against him while he had it. Then he started talking. I didn't understand the things he said to me, not to start. He didn't seem unkind, exactly, but I didn't know what it was he wanted me to do, only that I had to do it. I needed him to give me back my skin, or I couldn't go home. We sailed far down the shore in his boat, to a proper town, with houses in every color that ever was. The whole place smelled of fish, and he made me hide in a wooden shed on the dock while he went away. He took my skin with him, in a net sack, but he must have stayed on the land, and close, for nothing happened. He came back with clothes for me, fine clothes fit for a lady, and a little box with a lock on it.

He put my skin inside the box, and me into the clothes. He was gentle about it, but the clothes were strange, and tight, and made my neck itch. The bonnet was pretty, but I couldn't see around it. I saw only what was before me, and he made sure that it was him.

We went back in the boat, and I almost thought he was taking me home, but we passed wide of the island, and he took me into the village, to the church, and an old man there asked me questions I didn't understand. But Tobias—I knew his name now—looked at me, and smiled, and nodded, and so I nodded and smiled, too, because it seemed like that was what he wanted.

So we were wed. And we went in the boat again, and then to his house, up on the hill. He put me in the room with the bed and closed the door on me, and when he let me out again, he had hidden the little box away. I looked every time he went out of doors, but I could never find it.

I learned quickly how to be his wife. What I was to do and be. I did not think I had any choice. All I could do was try to please him and hope he would decide to set me free.

I hoped my family would come for me, but of course they did not. They had no way of knowing what had happened to me, although I know they searched. Uncle heard a rumor of me, finally, in the village, but what could he do? It was secret, what we were, and he couldn't risk trying to take me back if it would put everyone else in danger, his little ones and wife. I would not have wanted him to. And, without my sealskin, I could not have gone with him. But my mother and aunt often came into your cove here after that, and watched, in case they might see me on the road.

I started to understand the things that Tobias said. He was not cruel to start, not completely. I think he was trying to be good to me. He said he loved me, and believed I ought to be happy, and grateful. But I was captive, and that was the cruelty. He did not see it. He had heard a tale of us, you see, but to him it was a love story. A fisherman, with a perfect wife. A selkie wife, who would love him for taking her from the sea.

For giving her children.

I realized there was going to be one, and I despaired. I did not know what would happen, or how, but when the time came, I knew, for I felt a terrible thing, worse than pain. Instinct. I wanted to be in the water. I had to be.

I ran.

I found I was not held by my skin so tightly as I had thought, for I made it down the field and through the trees, over a stream . . . but then I tried to go into the water. I knew better than to try to set foot in the sea, but convinced myself the marsh would be safe, fresh water mixing with the salt. It was not the baby that made me stop where I did, or cry out as you heard. I tried to step into the water, and the thing that holds me to my craiceann ròin *strained so tight and thin I feared it might snap. I drew back from the shore, and it eased. I wanted to weep. The child was coming, and I could not go any farther. I would die if I tried.*

And then . . . you found me.

I could barely believe that it was the same red-fox girl I'd seen in the village all those times before. And somehow she knew what to do, took me in, and saw me through it all, held my hand. I bore a son and named him for my father. I looked, and I saw he had a web in his fingers, and I knew he would be one of us. And then I looked at you, and you smiled and said that it was perfect.

For that night, it was.

You faced down Tobias, and you kept me with you, and for that whole week it was more perfect than I could have imagined. I should have told you everything then, but I hadn't the words. Even when I began to have them, they were not near enough, and I was scared. It was secret, a secret meant to keep my family safe. A secret I thought you would never believe, Jean, even once I trusted you to keep it. Not if I couldn't show you. That's why I went tonight, and why I took the boat. I did not know if my old skin would fit who I was now, if I was still myself after everything that had happened to me. But I am.

What Tobias had done was a secret, too. A terrible one, held between the two of us, and I feared what might happen if he thought I had not kept it, for it was no longer only me that was caught in his trap but my son, too, and you. You kept trying to help us, getting closer and closer, first not seeing how dangerous it was, then not caring once you did. He could see that there was something between us, you and I, even before he knew what it was that he saw.

He began, finally, to realize I could never love a man who held me in a cage. A better man might have let me go then, but he had decided I was his, and instead chose to bind me closer, and tighter, whatever it might cost him. It made him furious, that you could make me smile when he could not.

Everything else, I guess you know, Jean.

You were there, after all.

Everyone had drawn in close around them as Muirin told her story. Her mother stood behind her with Kiel in her arms, a warm, solid presence. One of Muirin's aunt's hands rested on Buchanan's shoulder, where he sat on the stool. Cowan had draped himself over the foot of the bed with his chin in his hands, and his sister, Coira, sat propped against him, with an arm flung over his back, and one foot dangling off the side of the mattress.

They all turned their dark eyes away from Muirin. They stared at Jean, waiting.

Jean looked around at them all, and then at Muirin again.

"No wonder you wanted to go home so badly." There weren't any right words. Jean swallowed, her mouth gone as dry as if she'd been the one doing all the talking. "I'm so sorry, for all of it, for everything that happened. That I never figured it out sooner, what he was, what he'd done. But this—Muirin, I couldn't ever have guessed it. Your family is something from out of a story to me, like magic. I didn't know it was real. That *you* were real. You came to me right out of one of Laurie's tales, and now—" She pressed Muirin's hand, trying very hard to keep her voice from trembling as it strained in her aching throat. "I'll miss you when you go. So much, Muirin, I—"

Jean stopped again. She wasn't sure she could bear to say it, not when Muirin was going to leave her.

Buchanan said something, softly, in Gaelic. Jean had the impression he was trying to explain what she'd said to everyone else. Muirin's aunt gave Jean a pitying sort of look before saying something back to him. The little boy laughed, and the girl turned and swatted him, then leaned forward again on her elbows, waiting on Muirin, entranced.

Muirin's mother bent and spoke into her daughter's ear. Muirin glanced up at her and shook her head, then turned back to face Jean. Pulling the sealskin from around her shoulders, Muirin laid it over the blankets of the bed, across Jean's lap. The smoke smell had gone from it, leaving behind only the freshness of a salty breeze. Muirin carefully smoothed the skin with her hands before meeting Jean's eyes again.

"Would stay, I, if you ask, Jean."

Jean stared, her vision blurring with stinging mist.

"No," she said, and the word split her heart in two. "No, Muirin, I couldn't. I would *never*—" Jean pushed the heavy velvet skin back across her lap toward Muirin. "It's yours. Your magic, not mine. I wish you would stay; I *want* you to, but—" Her voice betrayed her, cracking along with her heart, her eyes welling over with hot tears. "I love you, but I can't hold you here. I won't. You're free, and you don't belong to me, or to anyone. If you stay, stay because *you* want to. It's not love if you aren't free to choose it."

Muirin smiled, blinding bright, and her eyes were shining, too.

"Knew you would say so, I."

She drew Jean into her arms and kissed her.

EPILOGUE

"Ma! Ma!"

Jean turned away from the sea, bracing herself before the little boy leapt. Kiel fully expected that she would catch him, of course, though she almost went down with him in a tangle of warm wiry limbs when she did. She turned half a circle, Kiel's legs swinging out wide and kicking before she set him back down on his feet.

Kiel could not sit comfortably on Jean's hip anymore, even if she would have liked to put him there still. He was a lad of nearly six, and well-grown in the way of his mother's people—anyone would have thought him a great boy of eight or nine. He would be taller than Jean in a few more years, and then he'd have to be the one to carry her instead.

"Ma," he said again, shaking his dark hair out of his eyes, "you ain't worried? They're only fishing; no one'll catch them. Mama's going to laugh at you!"

"Not as much as she'll laugh at you, half dressed. Where on earth did you leave your shirt?"

Kiel shrugged, more than happy to be in nothing but his trousers, and those rolled up almost to the knee, salt-stained and splashed with mud. His feet and ankles were bare and mucky—he'd been wading through the marsh again, probably chasing the fox cubs. Jo and Victor had come to visit right around the time the cubs first ventured out of their den that spring, and their little daughter had been so taken with them that Kiel had decided he might impress her by making one a pet by the time they came next.

Jean shouldn't have been surprised that he was shirtless, given the rest of the family. At least it was midsummer, and not February. It had been next to impossible to keep a stitch of clothing on the boy from the moment he realized how to wiggle back out of them again. Once, when he'd only just been walking, Jean and Muirin had taken him into the village to pay a call on Anneke, and there'd been a right scene when Kiel and one of Anneke's cousins' wee lads both got stripped down and made it out the back door. They'd gone on a mad dash down the middle of the main street, squealing and naked as a pair of little piglets. Laurie'd finally caught up to them, and he'd come back with a squirming, shrieking toddler tucked under each arm, face red as a beetroot and trailing laughter behind him.

Anneke had been thrilled, of course. She loved Kiel to bits, the two of them fast friends from the first time they'd met. He called her Nana, the same as Mary Beth's little ones did. Anneke pronounced Kiel to be "some bad" that afternoon, in a tone that made the words into a badge of honor.

She'd also slipped him an extra cookie as they were leaving, which was never eaten, but did leave a crummy glob of raspberry jam in Jean's hair along the way home. Muirin had found the whole thing hilarious.

If Anneke ever wondered at how fast the child grew, she

never said a word of it, which was a surprise, knowing her, but Jean was grateful. She did not want to have to lie. It was better to only mildly sin, through omission. Anneke might even suspect, for all Jean knew. Not just about Kiel but about a great many things.

If she did, it was Jean's own fault, for she talked a bit too freely with her old mentor sometimes. Anneke might have believed it all if Jean had told her, but the woman never pushed, content to let them keep their secrets. When Muirin and the baby had stayed on with Jean, Anneke immediately took to treating Muirin as if she were one of the family. The two of them shared a keen sense of the absurdity of human behavior, even if they'd arrived at it in different ways, and they found similar things amusing. Anneke had said more than once how pleased she was to see Jean so settled.

She said the same thing about Laurie and Dal. Laurie still went out with the ships, of course. Nothing could keep him from the sea, but he never stayed away for long, and was always home in winter. He joked that it was because if he didn't return, Dal might freeze to death without someone to share the bed. Dal might have been excited to see snow his first winter, but he'd not been prepared to face near six straight months of it in a year. Just because the cold wouldn't hurt him, he said, didn't mean he had to like it.

Dal and Laurie were their neighbors now. Muirin hadn't wanted another thing to do with Tobias's land, and she'd gifted the whole lot over to the boys. Together they'd built a new house on top of the hill, with a steep peak and a window of colored glass at the front, above the door. They'd gone out of their way to make it as little like the old house as possible, Laurie asking Jean for every detail of the one that had stood there before. The new house was white, with a door and shutters painted the kind of red that would give even the boldest fairy pause, and Dal hung their home all over with witches' ladders of driftwood and shell.

Even so, Muirin had only ever ventured up the hill to see it once, to know that the old house was truly gone. She never went back again after; they all understood.

More often than not, Dal was away from the new house as much as Laurie was. He followed in his other skin as Laurie sailed from port to port on his ship, greeting him anew on every shore. Laurie suspected this wasn't as recent a habit as Dal tried to pretend it was. It had come out that their first meeting had involved Laurie going overboard with some poorly stowed cargo, and Dal having been at an awfully convenient distance to fish him out again. Dal grinned whenever the topic came up, and sweetly said that, another time, he'd throw him back. Too mouthy. Dal was the only man Jean had ever known to leave Laurie at a loss for words, and what was even more astonishing, Laurie seemed to *like* it.

Jean was happy for him.

Between them, Muirin and Dal had charmed near the entire village. Not old Mrs. Keddy, of course, but her tongue had moved on to flapping about other people, and no one paid her as much mind these days as they once had. Mrs. Keddy's free-flowing vitriol had made her widely disliked, in fact, and her viciousness toward Jean played no small part in her lack of popularity: As Muirin began to make friends in the village, Jean had come to learn that she truly *was* respected there, and what was more, she was liked. Not as much as Laurie, of course, but who else could be a Laurie? Jean would never be that gregarious or outgoing, but she didn't need to be. People hadn't just put up with her for what she could do for them, it turned out. With Muirin beside her, Jean had found herself being drawn into village life again, lingering for tea with her new mothers, making friends.

Kiel broke back into her thoughts. "Auntie says your pies are done." He gave her a big-eyed, starveling look. "Can I have pie now? I'm hungry." Jean managed not to laugh.

"You had bread and jam not an hour ago, and I don't want you spoiling your dinner, not when we're all eating together tonight. Besides, I bet there'll be oysters. Your favorite. You have to save room!"

It was to be a bit of a family party. Muirin had taken Cowan and Coira out on their first long fishing trip of several days, and they were due back on the evening tide. No doubt they would not only have the oysters Jean was trying to bribe Kiel with but a great many other things as well. Purple-shelled mussels to steam and swim in butter, clams for milky chowder, and her own favorite, the tiny smelts that crunched when you ate them, fried crispy.

Jean didn't quite get the allure of oysters, although she'd tried. Muirin and Kiel ate them raw, right out of the shell, drinking down their briny juice, so many that the vegetable garden had long since grown a border of oyster shells. Sometimes, though, Muirin would make up an oyster pie, creamy and rich. She'd embraced her early joy in baking and learned the knack of an impossibly flaky crust, and Jean always ate too much whenever one of those pies appeared on the table, for they made oysters much more to her liking. If they were to start selling Muirin's pies they might just make a fortune.

But then . . . they were rich already.

They had the goats for milk and cheese—Kicker had retired and was something like a guard dog for two new goats: Spot, who had one in the middle of her chest, and black-footed Carp. Kiel had been learning the names of fishes at the time.

They had chickens for eggs, and sometimes one to roast on a Sunday. There were vegetables from the garden, too, and wild blueberries from the woods, and they had the whole wide sea for fish, for that was what Muirin loved best to do: to go off into the sea and return with her small net full to bursting.

It hadn't been easy at first, when Jean's heart still took to pounding in her chest whenever Muirin was gone for more than an hour, but over and over again she returned whole and happy, and so Jean learned what the fishermen's wives knew: How to look to the horizon and wish for fine weather, a calm and gentle sea. To let Muirin go and hope she would be held safe by the waves, and wonder how soon she would return.

Jean couldn't have asked her to do anything else.

She held her love in an open hand.

Jean had already put on her Sunday best dress, the one she hardly wore. There was more room for all the family if they ate out of doors, so she and Kiel had piled up driftwood to build a fire on the beach once it was dark, and the table had been pulled outside into the yard, the extra leaf for it brought down from under the bed in the attic where Jean and Muirin slept. Jean tried to explain that they should tip the table to the right as she and Muirin's mother wrestled it through the door together, but Jean's Gaelic was still dreadful and Muireall's English even worse, so they accomplished the task with more laughter and guess-work than anything else.

Aunt Iseabail had shooed Jean out of her own kitchen after catching her gazing out the window for the tenth time in as many minutes, old Buchanan laughing at the look on her face as she went. "Well," he'd said, "I can't argue with her, lass. If ye got a mind to be watchful, you might as well go and watch." So Jean had left her apron and made her way over the road to stand in the tall, waving grass above the beach and wait. Muirin waited for Jean sometimes, too, when she went into the village to attend a birth. Sometimes she was gone for almost as long as one of Muirin's fishing trips, but it was different. In the village, Jean was only ever a walk—or a swim—away, but Jean could not hope to follow to the places Muirin went.

Pulling Kiel into her side, Jean wrapped her arm around his sun-warmed shoulders. They were growing dark and freckled this summer, and not just from the sun. Jean fancied there was the barest hint of soft fuzz starting there, when she set her hand on his back. "You have sharp eyes. Do you see them yet?"

He squinted at the sunlight sparkling off the waves, shielding his eyes with his web-fingered hand, and Jean smiled. Kiel was more precious than anything they owned, as much her child as if she and Muirin had borne him together. In a way, Jean supposed, they almost had. She remembered holding him, wailing in her hands, when he had not yet been a minute in the world.

"Oh!" he exclaimed, and broke from under Jean's arm, racing down the beach in a headlong run. "Mama! Mama!"

After a moment, Jean could make them out, too, three dark heads in the bay, coming toward the shore. She ran after Kiel, down through the stinging beachgrass, and over the pebble beach. Maybe it was ridiculous, with Jean supposedly a woman grown. A wife, or near enough. She even had a ring with a small, shining pearl Muirin had found inside one of her oysters.

Muirin stood up from the waves, throwing her sealskin over her shoulder, and she caught Kiel as he launched himself at her, swinging him high up into the air. Jean was only a few steps behind.

They all three came together where the land met the sea.

AUTHOR'S NOTE

First and foremost, this is a work of historical fiction. Emphasis on *fiction;* I'm more interested in the day-to-day lives of people in the past than in major historical events, and *A Sweet Sting of Salt* is a prime example of that. There's exactly one true, historical event in this book: The privateer schooner *Young Teazer* really did burn in the waters of Mahone Bay, Nova Scotia, on the twenty-seventh of June, 1813, near the end of the War of 1812. I put almost as much detail into explaining the making of cheese as into explaining the *Teazer,* which should tell you something.

I started writing this book during a cold, damp winter in a six-square-meter room in Paris. Unable to find work as a pastry chef, and busy planning a move home to Nova Scotia, I dreamed up the village and the pebble beach, Jean's little house by the pond, and Tobias's atop the hill, influenced by memories of the places I'd known as a child.

On arriving in my new town, I was stunned to discover nearly everything I'd invented had some unexpected local equivalent, right down to the legend of a flaming ghost ship. The fictional town of Barquer's Bay ended up being drawn in large part from the flavor, geography, and historical shipbuilding past of the town of Mahone Bay, where I lived and worked while finishing that first draft. Nearby Mader's Cove, located approximately an hour's brisk walk along the shore, is so close a match for the imaginary place I created for Jean's home that I almost drove off the road into the pond the first time I saw it.

Character names are a mix of surnames common to the area and first names I guessed might be culturally appropriate—except where I've stolen them directly from my own family tree, which has a high degree of overlap. Poor put-upon pig farmer Richie, for example, is named after my father, who I hope finds that funny. I may have done *too* well making up names: I've met three Tobiases at this point, all three tall, blond . . . and really very nice. Characters themselves are imagined entirely, although Robbie McNair, the young wood-carving prodigy who teaches himself to build and play instruments, was very loosely inspired by a shipbuilder whose name I managed to forget within five minutes of reading about him.

While I hope I've given a general sense of the South Shore's historical way of life, and the sort of people who might have lived it, my main aim with *Salty* was to tell a story centering queer characters in the past, within the context of a reimagined folktale—one I've had mixed feelings about from the first time I heard it. Ostensibly, the story of the selkie wife (story type ML4080 under Norwegian archivist Reidar Thoralf Christiansen's classification of migratory folktales) is romantic and melancholy. I always got the sense I was meant to feel sorry for the fisherman at the end, when his wife reclaims her sealskin and returns to the sea, but I was never able to get over my horror that he'd kidnapped her, forcing her to stay with him through supernatural means. He never sees the error of his ways: In many versions of the tale, it's one of their children who finds the seal-skin and sets her free. It was this idea of a young woman stolen away from everyone and everything she knows, forced into a marriage and realizing she's going to have a baby, that led me to the invention of Jean Langille, the lonely, prickly midwife who can't turn a blind eye once she realizes something is wrong next door.

Jean's mentor, Anneke, and her family were written as being of Mi'kmaq descent from the very start, with a background similar to that of some of my friends and extended family members. It was important to me that if I set a book in Nova Scotia's past, it would include the original inhabitants of Mi'kma'ki in some way, to make certain no one could overlook their existence and importance, both past and present, within the communities where I grew up.

Like most storytellers, I've been known to take liberties with facts for the sake of a good yarn. Sometimes, I just plain get things wrong. Do remember, this is also a book where a woman turns into a seal. I can neither confirm nor deny the existence of selkies, but for anyone interested in learning about the real town of Mahone Bay and the history of the South Shore, I recommend checking out the Mahone Bay Museum (www.mahone baymuseum.com).

ACKNOWLEDGMENTS

Before anything else, I probably ought to acknowledge that if I'd had any idea when I first started writing this novel "for myself, to see if I can do it" that I'd one day be staring into a blank page trying to recall everyone who helped me in this journey, in ways big and small, I might have made a point of writing all their names down as I went along. I'm probably going to leave someone out no matter how hard I try, but please know if you talked to me about this book at any point in its creation, for even just a moment, I remember, and I'm grateful.

I'll start with the people who worked along with me on "Team *Salty*" to make this book all it could be, and more than I ever dreamed of, and go from there: To my amazing agent, Jill Marr, thank you, thank you, thank you for your incredible faith and belief in *Salty,* and me. I knew you would have my back and push me toward bigger and better things than I'd dared to imagine from our very first chat. You're a total powerhouse, but more important, you're genuinely kind and you genuinely *care,* and

I'm so grateful to have you in my corner. Hopefully this is just the beginning!

To my two marvelous tag-team editors, Caroline Weishuhn at Dell and Amanda Ferreira at Random House Canada, I am grateful not only for your taking a chance on *Salty* and me, but for your incredible insight and sensitivity in helping me find things in Jean and Muirin and their relationship that I always knew were there but couldn't quite figure out how to put into words, and for teaching Jean and me the importance of "we." I'm so glad we found the best way to untangle a good knot. Thanks as well to everyone else behind the scenes at PRH for working to make this dream a reality.

Production editor Cara DuBois and copy editor Michelle Daniel, I appreciate, more than I can say, your incredibly keen eyes and your excising all my many, many superfluous commas without complaint.

Thanks to Derek McFadden for very helpful revision notes before *Salty* went out on submission, and in particular for calling me out on my addiction to the word *that*.

Ella Stainton, my wonderful Author Mentor Match mentor: You were the first person to pull *Salty* from a slush pile and see something special in it. You've been unfailingly kind and generous and caring, and taught me so, so much. I'll carry your craft lessons wherever I go for the rest of my life, but more than anything, I'm glad you're my friend. Thanks for making me feel like a real unicorn.

Janna G. Noelle, thank you for insisting I had to keep going after you saw the first draft, and then giving me the tough love and tools to transform it into what it's become. You're my dearest and longest-standing critique partner, and this book literally would not exist without your generous advice, support, and guidance, particularly in showing me the parts of the process that I didn't know I didn't know. You've been making me a better writer and a better *human* since we were sixteen, and I'm lucky to call you my friend. Thanks for putting me on your vision board; I'm glad it worked!

To Isa Arsén and Katie Crabb, it's been a joy having you both to scream and cry and share words and talk smack with in the DMs (may they never be subpoenaed) every step of the way. I appreciate how kind and generous you always are, both with critique and with talking me down when I get anxious about it all—this goes for Janna as well. I'm so grateful to be along for your journeys, and happy you're part of mine, too. Oh, and Isa, thanks for explaining so much to me from approximately six to eight weeks in the future—very on brand for you! Katie, thanks especially for your lessons in the fine art of crafting a query letter.

Merci beaucoup to Dorian Ravenscroft for sharing so much of your own process and work with me and beta reading right from the earliest chapters of the first draft, for patiently explaining childbirth and pointing out what turned into a happy accident in early childhood development—but most especially for insisting, quite rightly, that I was a coward and the goat had to die.

Thanks to Felicia Grossman for coming in clutch with a last-minute read of my pre-query manuscript in record time, and for your helpful pacing advice for the first chapter.

To my parents, thank you for sharing your love of books with me: for reading to me early and often, for handing me my first library card, and for giving me a world of words to escape into, but also for being people who tell the family stories over and over again, laughing. Some of our oral history has been gifted to Anneke's family—I hope you don't mind. To my brothers: The best of both of you crept into Laurie. Thanks for always having my back.

To my wonderful and supportive friend-family, Robin North,

Nathan Phillips, and Maryanne Macdonald, thank you for sharing in my celebrations and my sorrows, for always being up for a libation or six when needed, and for always supporting me and making me feel incredibly loved and seen. I love you, too. I also owe Robin big-time for pointing out that I'd made Jean do something unforgivably thoughtless in an early draft, and saving me from it.

To Kate Arms, for long walks and long talks, for delighting in my wins and holding space for my losses, and for always somehow knowing what questions to ask, thank you. Thank you for being my friend, the magician on my island who reminded me that your people are often hiding where you least expect them.

To my oldest, dearest online friends, Maria Reme, Jess Jones, and Krista Lindemann, thank you for including me in your lives no matter how far apart we are. You've taught me a whole lot about *everything* . . . but not least about how to build a compelling character and improvise like your life depends on it.

Paige Ferguson and Tobias Lange, I can never thank you enough for allowing me to house-sit for you after my theater job disappeared in 2020. You put a roof over my head during the longest, hardest days of the pandemic, giving me precious time and space to complete revisions while I flailed trying to find another day job, and I am grateful. Also, Tobias . . . I swear to God it's a coincidence! I finished my first draft before you two started dating, and even though I tried to change it later, I could never make another name stick to the guy.

Special thanks to my long-suffering bakery coworker Marisa Peterson, who had to hear far too much about this book as I was writing it, usually at ungodly hours of the morning, but who always managed to seem like she was genuinely interested. The same goes for my wonderful roommate, Lindsay Langdon, for putting up with my ranting and ridiculousness.

Extra-special thanks to the *Les Mis* fandom on Tumblr. Y'all are something special. Some of you were my very first beta readers, and I've been touched by your kindness over and over: Pilf, thank you for encouraging me to write my first fan fiction in twenty years. The response I got to that fic convinced me I might actually be able to write an entire novel. Wild-oats-and-cornflowers, I appreciate every comment you've ever left me. Bernard-the-rabbit, thank you for bringing Jean and Muirin (and Kiel!) to colorful life in your art. Alice, thanks for popping up under all my most random "What am I *doing*?" posts to offer helpful advice, and a special shout-out to Rae, whose intense hatred for Tobias burns with the heat of a thousand suns and never fails to make me howl with laughter. The original idea-spark for *Salty* came after reading one of Laura mysunfreckle's modern fairy-tale posts, and I am grateful. Without your snippet about selkie trafficking victims testifying before the United Nations, this might never have happened.

Last, but absolutely not least, thank you from the bottom of my heart to Dawn Currie-Adams, my childhood "babysitter," for handing me my first book with a queer protagonist, and reading my earliest fumbling writings; for opening up your bookshelf to me and introducing me to the internet; but most of all, for befriending a lonely little girl who desperately needed someone to look up to, and telling her there was a bigger, wider world than the one she knew. You saved my life.

A
SWEET
STING
OF
SALT

Rose Sutherland

A BOOK CLUB GUIDE

AN INTERVIEW WITH ROSE SUTHERLAND
Warning: Spoilers ahead!

Q: What inspired you to write *A Sweet Sting of Salt,* and why did you choose to reimagine "The Selkie Wife" as you did?

A: Bless the internet; it was a post on Tumblr! About selkies and human trafficking, an urban folklore riff. Which got me thinking about selkies, and how I've always found the original folktale really disturbing. I keep a journal, and my entry from that morning says, "I want to try to write a novel, just for myself, to see if I can do it. Something about selkies, and the sea. A young woman . . . a midwife. On a stormy night, finds a pregnant woman in her backyard, about to pop. Oh, I guess we're at ideas . . ." And then, three solid pages of utterly unhinged notes. The character stuff holds up, the plot . . . not so much. I knew I wanted to emphasize in that story how awful the situation is that the selkie finds herself in, and that I wanted to help her escape . . . and I wanted it to be a romance somehow, between these two interesting, intelligent women. Oh, and I wanted to take the toxic "nice guy" trope to a horrifying extreme with the fisherman.

Q: You chose to set the novel in Nova Scotia in the 1830s— what made you choose that particular time and place? Was there something special that drew you to it, or something you thought would lend itself particularly well to the story you wanted to tell?

A: Nova Scotia is where I grew up. I love the North Atlantic, and I am always pulled back to her eventually, no matter how far I go. In many ways this book is a love letter to all the things I like best about home, and the people there. It's a place with a lot of ghost stories and superstitions, beautiful but sometimes harsh and dangerous surroundings, and a very romantic atmosphere. It struck me as the perfect place for a person like Jean—practical, smart, no-nonsense—to be broadsided by a folktale turning out to be true.

The 1830s bit is kind of silly: I'm a huge *Les Misérables* nerd, and when I was trying to decide on a year for the story, I said, okay, fine, 1832, same as the student uprising. When I learned about the wreck of the *Young Teazer*, I was thrilled to discover the dates lined up properly for my previously un-named ghost ship to have a real-life backstory!

Q: What kind of research did you do as you set out to write *A Sweet Sting of Salt*? Did you look for commonalities in selkie stories to determine which features to include in your own retelling? Did you invent any new selkie characteristics?

A: I read a few versions of the folktale at the start, to make sure I wasn't misremembering the basic details, but otherwise avoided reading (or watching) anything to do with selkies while I was writing. I wanted to see what my subconscious and imagination would pull up from the depths if I gave them room.

I hit on Muirin speaking another language almost right away, because it made an interesting challenge to throw at Jean, but I also wanted to give her some seallike traits. Watching nature documentaries influenced the scene where Kiel is born, and Muirin smelling Jean in a nod to the way animals greet each other struck me as hilarious—and turns useful later, when Dal runs into Tobias and smells selkie on him.

Kiel's webbed fingers just seemed logical, but the acceler-ated growth of half-selkie children arose from a happy acci-dent: Apparently, babies don't laugh for quite a while after they're born, but I had Kiel doing it after less than a week! It became one of the first things to make Jean wonder if something odd is afoot, and only got bigger from there.

Q: By the end of the novel, Jean and Muirin have developed a beautiful relationship—did you always plan for them to end up together, or is that something that happened as you were writing?

A: I always intended them to end up together. Muirin appearing in the marsh behind Jean's house was the leaping-off point from the very start, and the moment when Jean refuses the sealskin, insisting Muirin is free to choose for herself if she wants to stay or go, was always the destination. Everything in between ended up surprising me quite a bit.

Q: On writing—what does your writing process look like? Do you have a dedicated time and space, or do you write when inspiration strikes? Do you have any advice for other writers out there?

A: My process is still evolving. This was my first novel, so I made a lot of discoveries about how I work best as I was working on it, and I'm still trying things out as I'm drafting my next book. I find as long as I can sit down and *start* (sometimes a challenge, my executives are highly dysfunctional), inspiration usually finds me, eventually. I do prefer writing earlier in the day—my best work often happens right after breakfast and results in me never finishing my coffee. I also enjoy taking my laptop outdoors when I can.

It feels odd, being asked for advice when I feel like I still have so much to learn. But here are a few things I've picked up so far: If you want to be a writer, write. Write what excites you, what you most want to read, what you love, because you're going to have to read it a lot. Get good people in your corner, people you trust to tell you the truth and not just blow smoke up your wazoo. Show them the same respect. Trust your instincts, but don't listen to your brain goblins. Cultivate at least one hobby that has nothing to do with writing.

Q: And last but certainly not least—what was your favorite part of writing *A Sweet Sting of Salt*? And do you have a favorite scene or character in the novel?

A: My favorite part was how my creativity exploded once I started revising the first draft with input from beta readers and critique partners. Hearing their thoughts on the story was such a joy and made me feel much less like I was writing in a bubble. This was my first time revising so intensively, and I was thrilled by how their questions and comments pushed me toward finding new answers and making choices I'd never have conceived of otherwise.

I can't pick a favorite scene because I love too many of them for entirely different reasons, but my favorite one-liner is Jean's aside about Buchanan's hairy kneecaps.

Laurie is my *second* favorite character. My *actual* favorite is Kicker.

QUESTIONS AND TOPICS FOR DISCUSSION

1. *A Sweet Sting of Salt* is a retelling of an old Scottish folktale, "The Selkie Wife." Had you heard the tale before? If so, did you like how the author reframed it using a woman's point of view? Are there any other folktales or fairy tales that you think could also benefit from a new lens?

2. What did you think of the setting? Did you like the atmosphere it lent to the story? What elements did it bring to the story that other settings may not have been able to?

3. A key theme of *A Sweet Sting of Salt* is longing—longing for the sea, longing for home, longing for a family, longing for a place to belong. How did you see this theme take shape throughout the novel? How did this theme shape each of the characters and influence their actions?

4. Water is an element that is present throughout the novel. The village is populated by men and women dependent on the bay, whether as fishermen or sailors; the pond behind Jean's house is where she lost her mother, where she found Muirin, and later where she found freedom from their situation; and the sea is what allows several of the characters to reunite at the end of the book. What do you think of the role water plays, and why do you think the author chose to give it such prominence?

5. Shortly after we meet Jean, we learn that she is a vital and necessary part of the community because of her role as midwife, and yet she has felt it necessary to live a solitary life away from the village because of certain attitudes. What did you think of that dichotomy, that people she'd known her whole life would ostracize her and yet come calling the moment they needed her help? Do you see that dichotomy anywhere in the world today?

6. Tobias has a very particular perspective in his views toward women, which we see in more detail through Jean's conversation with Ima Barry. How do you think that perspective influenced the way he viewed his relationship with Muirin?

7. Speaking of relationships, what did you think of Jean and Muirin's relationship? What was your favorite part of their relationship? How did it contrast with Muirin's relationship with Tobias?

8. Both Jean and Muirin are women living in a world that disadvantages them in many unfair ways, and yet they were able to find strength and power in each other and take control of their own lives. Did you admire them for what they were able to do? Can you think of any real-life situations in which women have been able to do something similar?

9. The novel is written with a dusting of magic throughout— did you pick up on the clues the author gave about Muirin and Kiel, or was the ending a surprise to you?

Born and raised a voracious reader of anything she could get her hands on in rural Nova Scotia, ROSE SUTHERLAND has an overactive imagination and once fell off the roof of her house pretending to be Anne of Green Gables. She's continued to be entertainingly foolhardy since, graduating from theater school in New York City, apprenticing at a pâtisserie in France, and, most recently, moonlighting as an usher and bartender in Toronto, where she is currently based. Her hobbies include yoga, dancing, singing, hurling herself into large bodies of salt water, searching out amazing coffee and croissants, and making niche jokes about Victor Hugo on the internet. She's mildly obsessed with the idea of one day owning a large dog, several chickens . . . and maybe a goat. *A Sweet Sting of Salt* is her first novel.

rosesutherland.com
Twitter: @suther_rose
Instagram: @suther_rose

RANDOM HOUSE BOOK CLUB

Because Stories Are Better Shared

Discover

Exciting new books that spark conversation every week.

Connect

With authors on tour—or in your living room. (Request an Author Chat for your book club!)

Discuss

Stories that move you with fellow book lovers on Facebook, on Goodreads, or at in-person meet-ups.

Enhance

Your reading experience with discussion prompts, digital book club kits, and more, available on our website.

Join our online book club community!

📘 ⒢ randomhousebookclub.com

Random House Book Club ™

Because Stories Are Better Shared

RANDOM HOUSE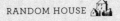